MW00326052

THE CIPHERS OF
MUIRWOOD

Books by Jeff Wheeler

The Covenant of Muirwood Trilogy
The Banished of Muirwood
The Ciphers of Muirwood
The Void of Muirwood

The Legends of Muirwood Trilogy
The Wretched of Muirwood
The Blight of Muirwood
The Scourge of Muirwood

Whispers from Mirrowen Trilogy
Fireblood
Dryad-Born
Poisonwell

Landmoor Series
Landmoor
Silverkin

THE CIPHERS OF
MUIRWOOD

The Covenant of Muirwood
Book Two

JEFF WHEELER

47N⬤RTH

This is a work of fiction. Names, characters, organizations, places, events, and incidents are either products of the author's imagination or are used fictitiously.

Text copyright © 2015 Jeff Wheeler
All rights reserved.

No part of this book may be reproduced, or stored in a retrieval system, or transmitted in any form or by any means, electronic, mechanical, photocopying, recording, or otherwise, without express written permission of the publisher.

Published by 47North, Seattle

www.apub.com

Amazon, the Amazon logo, and 47North are trademarks of Amazon.com, Inc., or its affiliates.

ISBN-13: 9781503947115
ISBN-10: 1503947114

Cover design by Ray Lundgren
Illustrated by Magali Villeneuve

Printed in the United States of America

To Gina

TABLE OF CONTENTS

Chapter One | *Execution*. 1

Chapter Two | *Binding Sigil* 10

Chapter Three | *Suzenne*. 25

Chapter Four | The *Queen's Garden*. 36

Chapter Five | *The Aldermaston's Kitchen* 46

Chapter Six | *Celia Lavender* 56

Chapter Seven | *Forshee* 68

Chapter Eight | *Alone* 78

Chapter Nine | *Guilt* 89

Chapter Ten | *Resentment* 98

Chapter Eleven | *Gallows* 109

Chapter Twelve | *Kishion's Threat*. 119

Chapter Thirteen | *Winterrowd* 128

Chapter Fourteen | *Chancellor Crabwell* 138

Chapter Fifteen | *Alliance* 148

Chapter Sixteen | *Counsel* 157

Chapter Seventeen | *The King's Captain* 169

Chapter Eighteen | *Confessions* 179

Chapter Nineteen | *The* Holk 190

Chapter Twenty | *Simon Fox* 199

Chapter Twenty-One | *Forbidden.* 209

Chapter Twenty-Two | *Princess of Comoros* 220

Chapter Twenty-Three | *Forsaken* 232

Chapter Twenty-Four | *Kranmir* 243

Chapter Twenty-Five | *Apples.* 256

Chapter Twenty-Six | *The King's Will.* 269

Chapter Twenty-Seven | *Fog of the Myriad Ones* . . . 279

Chapter Twenty-Eight | *Kishion* 290

Chapter Twenty-Nine | *Victus.* 301

Chapter Thirty | *Covenant Fulfilled.* 313

Chapter Thirty-One | *The Battle of Muirwood.* 323

Chapter Thirty-Two | *Irrevocare Sigil.* 334

Chapter Thirty-Three | *Whitsunday* 346

Chapter Thirty-Four | *Assinica* 356

Chapter Thirty-Five | *Pent Tower.* 366

Chapter Thirty-Six | *Deorwynn's Fall.* 375

Epilogue 383

Author's Note 385

Acknowledgments 387

"There was never an angry man who thought his anger was unjust."

—Richard Syon, Aldermaston of Muirwood Abbey

CHAPTER ONE

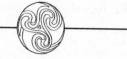

Execution

Sanford Price was a bull of a man even in his sixtieth year, and his time as a prisoner in Pent Tower had not broken him. He was tall, fit, and had a restless energy that drove him to pace and mutter to himself—habits that annoyed the sons who shared his prison. He had been the Earl of Forshee and a member of the Privy Council until his title and lands had been stripped away for his outspoken denunciation of the King of Comoros's bad example to the realm. As if being stripped of his birthright were not punishment enough, the king's guard had arrested and imprisoned him.

He did not regret his words, which were true.

What he did regret was that he had not realized how vengeful the king was or how far he had fallen from his maston oaths. And he regretted that his words had not only impacted himself, but also his sons. They had been one of the premier Families in power, reputation, and wealth. While the earldom had been stripped from him, Sanford knew that the people in his Hundred were loyal to the man, not the rank. Yes, another might be parading the title in his place, but if Sanford Price were to escape Pent Tower and ride north, all would see the meaning of true loyalty.

The prison that held him and his sons had once been furnished to house nobility. Traditionally, the highborn who were punished were still allowed splendid food, comfortable clothes, and occasional privileges like hawking or hunting. That had changed under the rule of King Brannon. The chambers had been converted into dungeons more terrible than a bleak underground cavern would be. From the towers one could see the parks, the river, the bustle and jostle of the markets beyond the palace walls. To view the frenzy of life but not be able to participate in it—that was a mental torture, to be sure. Pent Tower had been transformed into such a miserable place that the curtains had been removed for fear of fabric being used as ropes to escape through the windows. They were high enough up from the greenyard below that any attempt to descend would be fatal.

Sanford's anger and brooding temperament were legendary, inherited from his forefather Colvin Price. His Family had a long history of valuing respect and duty, a legacy in which he took pride. As he had watched King Brannon flout the maston beliefs and customs at every turn, he had grown increasingly angry and restless. Someone needed to stand up to the man, and so Sanford had chosen himself to play that role, believing that if he did, others would follow his example.

It was shameful, truly, that a king would seek to disavow his lawful wife, bound to him by irrevocare sigil, for a strumpet. He ground his teeth in anger and frustration. When sacred things were mocked, it would bring disaster upon the realm.

And it had.

It reminded Sanford, darkly, of the days of his ancestor. Colvin had lived under the reign of a brutal king as well. The one man who had dared to stand up to him, Sevrin Demont, had been killed in battle. His son, Garen Demont, had continued the rebellion and eventually defeated the cruel king at a field called Winterrowd.

He stopped by the window, brooding, rubbing strands of his growing gray beard. Did there come a time when rebellion was the only course of action left to men of honor? Colvin had felt that emotion. He had joined Garen Demont's rebellion against the king after learning that mastons were being secretly murdered throughout the realm. The king and his hetaera wife had sought to destroy the maston order subtly. Even though joining the rebellion had meant risking his own life and the future of his sister, Colvin had not hesitated.

Had such a time come to Comoros? An evil king could cause much suffering. If Sanford managed to escape Pent Tower, or—if the Medium willed it—he was set free, was this the moment to start a civil war? War always brought death, disease, and suffering for the people. Though the loss of his rank, wealth, and position was felt grievously, this was not about regaining what he had personally lost. It was about justice. It was about fairness. It was about the rule of law.

The rage smoldered inside of him. Four of his sons were trapped in the tower with him. Two of them—Tobias and Mennion—had been forced to part with their wives. Tobias had a baby who did not know his father's face. He had heard they were all living in a cottage deep in Forshee, where they endured the persecution of the new earl. A sympathetic guard brought occasional reports, so at least they knew their Family was not going hungry. Many of the villagers throughout the Hundred regularly brought them cheese, sheep, and cows. Sanford himself had been known as a stern but compassionate earl; he had always erred on the side of giving too much instead of too little.

"You look angry, Father," said his firstborn, Tobias. He joined him at the window and put a hand on his shoulder.

"I was thinking about our womenfolk," he replied. "It is unjust that they suffer for my words."

"When I think on how the king treats his own daughter," Tobias said, "I can hardly be surprised that he treats us so ill."

"Yes, he treats his daughter shamefully, but this is not how you reward loyal service. His actions encourage sycophants," said Mennion from the trestle table where he was scooping up the remains of their breakfast. He was always hungry.

"Anyone who served him honestly was put to shame," Tobias said. "Look no further than the Privy Council. None of the older advisors are left."

"Like Morton," said Sanford. "He is here in Pent Tower with us."

"I wonder what Dodd is doing?" said Elder, who was sitting at the table too, leafing through a book with obvious boredom.

Sanford felt a stab of pain and pride at the thought of his youngest boy, Dodd. He shook his head and sighed gruffly. "He is every bit a prisoner as we are."

"I would gladly exchange cells with the lad," Mennion said, tapping his spoon on the table. "The best pastries in the *world* are at Muirwood Abbey."

"Only on Whitsunday," Elder said, grabbing his brother by the neck and throttling him gently. "Whitsunday," he sighed after the mock abuse. "Do you think we will be out of here by then? Missing it last year made me dreadfully melancholy."

"You truly miss the maypole dance?" said Gates, Sanford's fourth son. He had been quiet up to that point, leaning against the wall and watching them, but he could not pass up the opportunity to tease.

"And you do not, Gates?" said Elder.

"No! I hate dancing."

"Then how will you pick a wife?" put in Mennion, grinning.

"You are all fools," Gates said. "I want to fight in at least two wars before I even think about choosing a wife. I swear, I hope Dahomey invades and we are released to draw arms. When it is time for a wife, I will let Father and Mother choose for me. Any girl will do, even a wretched lass. If she cooks anything like our ancestor Lia . . . I could not be happier! Now save some of that pie for later, Mennion. You will eat yourself sick."

That earned a chorus of laughter from the brothers. It was a good sound to hear, and it soothed the worst of Sanford's blistering anger. There were moments when the ribbing was not so good-natured. Five men cramped together in a single cell was enough to drive any one of them mad. Sanford had always detested cramped spaces.

"Do you think Dodd is well?" Tobias asked at his shoulder, pitching his voice lower. "I worry we have heard nothing from him of late."

Sanford folded his arms, leaning back against the wall next to the window. Dodd was clever and loyal to his Family. He was a learner at Muirwood, and after Sanford and his other boys were arrested, riders from Comoros had gone to fetch him to the dungeon, little expecting the truth. Dodd had felt impressed by the Medium to take the maston test a year early, so when they arrived to arrest him, he was able to claim sanctuary at Muirwood as a maston. They had left empty-handed, thwarting the king's will. There was a bounty on his head if he were even caught wandering outside the abbey grounds. So far the lad had harkened to Sanford's wishes for him to stay in Muirwood. He knew his youngest son wished to join his mother and other Family back in Forshee, but any attempt to escape to Billerbeck Abbey would be fraught with peril.

"He is young and has much to learn," Sanford said, brushing his hands together. "I only hope he does not do something foolish. If he listens to the Aldermaston and his wife, he will do well. If he were impetuous like Mennion, I would be more worried." He grinned.

Tobias smiled as well. "I miss Dodd. Do you know, Father, why he chose to study at Muirwood instead of Billerbeck?"

"Of all you lads, Dodd is closest with the Medium," Sanford said. "Sometimes it seems as if he is in a daydream. Billerbeck Abbey serves our Hundred, which is why all of you studied there, but Dodd felt that he needed to be in Muirwood. I had no reason to refuse him."

Gates ambled up to join them. He always wanted to be included. He walked to the window and pressed his fingers against the glass.

"What day is it?" Gates asked, gazing out the window. "Does anyone remember?"

"It is Twelfth Night," Mennion said, chewing and talking at the same time. "I heard a guard say that several days ago. It is the winter festival. What does it matter, they will not share any of the pastries with us."

"It looks like they set up a maypole."

"Really?" said Elder.

Gates pulled on the window latch and then shoved the window open. The wind outside was cold and knife-sharp. It was midmorning already, though due to the late season, the sun was having trouble breaching the height of the walls. With the window open, noises from the greenyard filtered up. People were gathering below, and Sanford noticed the gates were open. A scaffold had been erected, which was the shape his son had seen.

"What is happening?" Tobias asked, staring down.

"I know not," Sanford replied.

"I cannot see," said Mennion, who had finally abandoned his bowl and was shoving at his brothers. "Make room!"

"Be still!" snapped Sanford angrily. His sons quieted.

The crowd slowly filled the greenyard just below their room. Those in attendance reflected many different social classes. They were milling about, their voices murmuring with a thousand discussions. The scaffold was wide enough to fit no more than a dozen people.

A trumpet sounded and the noise suddenly hushed. There was a creak of wagon wheels, and the crowd jostled enough to open up a path, permitting a small wagon to pass through it.

"Who is that?" asked Gates.

"I cannot see," Mennion growled.

It was not a full wagon, just a small cart that would normally be used to transport vegetables or the like. Standing in the cart was a man with a faded brown cloak and tattered pants. The hair was unkempt, but Sanford recognized him.

"It is Tomas Morton," he said in dismay.

"The king's chancellor?" Elder gasped.

"Was, not any longer. He resigned his post. Crabwell is chancellor now. There he is." He pointed. "I did not see him before, wearing the black cloak and gold stole. Do you see him?"

"He's an ugly man," Gates said. "Give me a sword and I will—"

"Silence!" Sanford hissed.

The crowd parted to create a path to the scaffold. That was when Sanford noticed the man in a black hood standing by the short ladder that led to the top of the scaffold. His blood went to ice in his veins. There were several members of the king's guard gathered around who helped lift Morton from the cart. He walked, a little drunkenly, to the edge and went to the ladder, which wobbled when he tried to climb it.

"Is he . . . is he . . . ?" gasped Tobias.

Sanford stared in dumbstruck amazement. The crowd had fallen silent below as a hush settled over it.

A woman pushed through the crowd and approached Morton, her voice pitched with anger and scolding. "Sir! Sir! There were papers my husband left in your hands when you were chancellor. Please, sir! Where are they?"

The prisoner looked confused. "Good woman," he replied, "have a little patience. Give me an hour, and the king will rid me of any care I have about lost papers. And everything else, for that matter!" He shook his head at her in disbelief and then made another attempt to climb the ladder, which rattled in place.

Sanford's sons were silent, their eyes widening with growing terror as they took in the scene unfolding below them.

Morton turned to one of the soldiers. "Good sir, can you see me safely up the ladder? As for coming down, I daresay I will need your help again."

The soldier helped steady the ladder and several men assisted Morton in climbing to the top of the scaffold, and a few clambered up after him. One of the soldiers who had stayed below handed up a huge block of wood with a notch cut out of it.

"By Idumea," Sanford whispered.

Tomas Morton stood before the assembled crowd and started to speak. "I am here to face justice and the king's will," he said in a firm, loud voice. "I have been tried and—"

"No speeches!" shouted a man in armor astride a huge warhorse. "I am the sheriff of this Hundred. No speeches, Morton. You refused to sign the Act of Submission in a court full of witnesses. Lay your head down and suffer a traitor's fate. If you be man enough."

Sanford recognized the captain. His name was Trefew. He was one of the king's new sworn men. Descended from the Naestors, he was a brutal man rumored to have no conscience at all.

"Well, then," said Morton, his voice quavering. "I make no speeches. I am a humble servant of the king's will. I did refuse to sign. That is true. I am a man, Captain Trefew. And I die a maston of the chaen, a faithful servant both to the Medium and to the king." He carefully knelt in front of the block.

The man with the hood stepped behind him and loosened his tunic collar, exposing the bare flesh of his neck and the silver chaen. Sanford stopped breathing.

No, no, no!

Morton laid his head down on the block, but then held up one hand, staying the executioner as a soldier handed him an axe.

"A moment, let me put my beard aside. It committed no treason. There we are. Do your office, Master Headsman. I forgive you."

The four sons watched in horror as the headsman lifted the axe. There was an audible gasp from the crowd.

When it was done, Sanford pulled the window handle and shut the glass, blocking out the grim sight with his body. His sons' eyes were wide, their cheeks pale. Mennion scurried over to a privy bucket and vomited up his breakfast.

A maston murdered in daylight before a crowd under the pretense of law. Not even in Colvin Price's day had a king committed such an egregious act against an innocent man.

Sanford turned to his sons. "We must find a way to escape," he said in a low, urgent voice. "Captain Trefew looked up at our window. He wanted to be sure we were watching."

CHAPTER TWO

Binding Sigil

The dinghy glided down the river, cutting through the waters like a slick fish. The air was thick with strange smells and gnats that shimmered and glided in the waning afternoon sun. Maia felt a sheen of sweat on her brow, and her heart bubbled with anticipation as the docks loomed closer. The *Holk* waited back in the estuary, a massive black shadow moored alongside a wharf built against the fenlands, near a cabin made of stone blocks.

Maia hunched on the small bench, feeling anxious and excited. For so long, she had wished to go to Muirwood Abbey and become a maston. The faint buddings of hope inside her heart were so delicate and fragile, she was frightened even to breathe on them lest they be snatched away.

Jon Tayt worked the oars tirelessly. His boarhound, Argus, had settled along the bench near Maia, his muzzle resting on her lap. Next to her, clutching her arm, was her grandmother Sabine

Demont, the High Seer of Pry-Ree, who gazed up at the abbey grounds with a curious smile, as if she were seeing something that Maia could not.

Muirwood was beautiful. The abbey rose above them, its steep gray walls covered in a web of scaffolding, and even from the river Maia could hear the sound of hammers striking chisels and see the ropes and pulleys strain as stones were added to the structure. There were dozens of workers around and on the abbey.

Maia squeezed Sabine's arm. "I thought construction had been halted," she said, her mouth widening in amazement. "I heard my father order it."

Sabine grabbed her hand to squeeze it. "He did, Maia. But we answer to the Medium's will. Can you feel it here?"

Maia nodded humbly. "From the *Holk* as we approached. I have never felt so calm and peaceful. I could feel the abbey . . . *welcoming* me."

"When Lia drove out the Queen Dowager and her people after Muirwood was burned, she set protections on these grounds and fixed them by irrevocare sigil. The Myriad Ones cannot dwell here, and neither can any who serve them. You will be safe here, Maia. You must prepare yourself to take the maston test so you can fulfill Lia's prophecy and open the Apse Veil again, restoring the abbey's full rites. The dead must be freed from this world, and the mastons who are still in Assinica need to escape. It is the only way." She pointed to the scaffolding. "The interior work is already finished. The exterior is nearly done as well. The scaffolding is a disguise to make others believe the abbey is still far from completion. We should never judge by what we see on the outside."

"I was wondering what was left to do on it," Jon Tayt said gruffly. "It looks nigh well finished to my eyes."

"It will be done by Whitsunday," Sabine said. "It has taken many years to complete, but it was built faithfully in the style of its predecessor. I can see the old abbey in my mind, Maia."

Jon Tayt pulled one of the oars in and began maneuvering the skiff to the dock post. There was a man there with a pole and hook, waiting for them. As they came nearer, Jon Tayt fetched a coiled rope and flung the bulk to the man on the dock, keeping hold of one end. He quickly tied a knot to secure it to the bollard and then stepped onto the dock to confront the man who was fastening the other end.

"You are doing it wrong," Jon Tayt said angrily, shooing him away. "Let me."

Maia smiled. Jon Tayt was very particular about how things ought to be done. He was short and squat, with wavy copper curls covering part of his balding head and a bushy pointed beard that held on to the crumbs of his various meals. Argus bounded from the dinghy onto the dock, and the boat rocked slightly, earning the dog a curt whistle from his master.

"Welcome back to Muirwood, my lady," said the dockman to Sabine. "I sent the page running to the Aldermaston as soon as we spied the *Holk* upriver. He wishes to see you right away."

"Thank you," she replied. Maia went to cross to the dock on her own, but Jon Tayt finished with the rope and reached out a meaty hand to pull her across. She wore a pale blue gown that marked her as a wretched. Not that the dress would actually disguise her, but it would offer her more anonymity, making it easier for her to blend in with those living at the abbey. Her stomach trembled with nerves as she thanked Jon Tayt and waited for Sabine to be helped onto the dock.

Her grandmother was sprightly in her movements, considering her age. Her long hair had gray streaks through it, but the natural buttery color was still evident, and her wise eyes and lovely smile commanded more attention than her wrinkles and crags.

"This is your new home as well," Sabine said, turning back to the hunter. "The hunter's lodging is ready for you. But please come with us to meet the Aldermaston."

Jon Tayt sighed. "I would rather walk the grounds and get a feel for this bog. The Bearden Muir, you called it? By Cheshu, I miss Pry-Ree! I do see a lot of oak trees, though. Will be good for throwing my axes. They look hardy enough."

Taking Maia's arm, Sabine led her down the dock to a series of stone steps that led them up the hill. Jon Tayt followed behind, carrying their gear like a pack horse, and Argus padded next to him.

As they mounted the steps, the grounds became suddenly visible, and Maia smiled to see so many people about. Sabine walked close to her, pointing out the various sights. "There is much to see, but let me quickly explain what I can. The cloisters are over there, the lower wall next to the abbey. That is where the learners study reading and engraving. The boys study there during the day, but after the gates are locked at night, the Aldermaston's wife brings the Ciphers there to study."

"Do the boys know? Surely someone must see them?"

"There are tunnels beneath the abbey grounds, Maia. The Ciphers enter the cloisters from the tunnels. Not even the gate porter knows what goes on after he locks up each night. The tunnels connect the Aldermaston's manor to the abbey, as well as to several other locations, including one in the village beyond the walls. Leerings protect the passageways. Over there, that is the laundry where lavenders scrub the clothes. And there is the duck pond. One of my favorite places is the Cider Orchard, where the Muirwood apples grow. It is lovely in the spring." Maia's heart thrilled at the sight of it. She had heard dozens of stories about her ancestors Lia and Colvin and how special the Cider Orchard had been to them. How she longed to visit it.

"Are there any apples?" Maia asked.

Sabine shook her head. "It is not the season yet. Wait until spring. The Aldermaston's kitchen. Do you see it over there with the steep roof and the cupola? That is where you will eat, Maia. It is the same as when my great-grandmother lived there many years ago. When my mother returned on the ships, it was still standing. So was the orchard, though it had grown rather wild! After many years of taming and tending, it was restored. The Aldermaston's manor is next to the kitchen. The learner quarters are over there, but you will not be staying there."

Maia looked at her in concern. "Where then?"

"You will stay in the Aldermaston's manor, Maia. Your father may have disinherited you, but you are still a king's daughter. I have asked the Aldermaston to choose one of the Ciphers to be your companion. She will stay at the manor with you."

Maia nodded, biting her lip. Her emotions continued to bubble inside her—a strange brew of nervousness and anticipation. This was really happening. For years she had longed to come to Muirwood and see her mother. A pang of sadness stabbed her heart, which she concealed from the others.

As she gazed at those wandering the grounds, she could easily discern the difference between the wretcheds and the learners by the style of their clothing and bearing. Young men and young women walked the grounds, some wearing the finery of nobility, others wearing pale blue gowns and girdles or blue tunics and belts. She saw several—of both classes—look her way curiously. Some began whispering and pointing. Some looked very young.

"How many learners are here?" Maia asked, keeping her voice low.

"Forty or so. Many start when they are twelve or thirteen, but few make it to their fourth or fifth year. If someone has not passed the maston test by the end of their sixth year, they are sent away."

"I am nearly nineteen," Maia said, feeling the twist of anxiety in her stomach. "I have not had enough time to prepare."

"Lia passed the maston test when she was younger than you, and she had never studied a tome in her life. Strength in the Medium comes from your Family. You already know how to read, and you speak multiple languages, which gives you an advantage over many of these learners. Some struggle to speak a sentence of Dahomeyjan, yet you are fluent. You have had *more* training than most of the learners. And your experience in the world . . ." Her voice trailed off.

Following her gaze, Maia saw a man and woman were approaching them from the Aldermaston's manor. Then she recognized the pair's gray ceremonial robes and realized it was the Aldermaston and his wife. She was not certain what she had been expecting, but she had not imagined that she would be *taller* than the Aldermaston. He was short and stocky, with wispy gray hair that receded far up his scalp. His ears were large and pronounced and his jowls slightly drooping. She had expected a beard, but he was clean-shaven. He did not look imposing, the kind of man who could call thunder out of the sky. His wife was bird-thin and frail, with silver hair that was short and bobbed.

As the distance separating them closed, what struck her next about the Aldermaston were his eyes. They were light brown in color, yet they were the most piercing, intense eyes she had ever encountered. As his gaze shifted from Sabine to her, she felt as if he was reaching inside her soul and examining her deepest secrets, her hidden shame. The eyes were full of wisdom. They were compassionate. They were deeper than the depths of the sea. She felt stripped of all concealment by the time he came to a stop in front of her.

The Aldermaston's warm hand reached forward and found hers. He clasped her hands within his and brought her closer. "Welcome," he said in a sincere, ponderous way. "Welcome to Muirwood. We are so pleased you have come. You are the daughter of mastons, and now you will become one yourself. You are most welcome, Marciana."

"Thank you, Aldermaston," Maia said, her voice trembling with emotion from the tenderness of his greeting. He looked at her as if she were his own daughter. She could feel the power of the Medium radiating from him like ripples of steam off a hot kettle.

As soon as the Aldermaston released her hands, his wife pulled her into a hug. Maia could feel the bones of the woman's shoulder blades through the fabric of her cassock, and her nose was flooded with the welcome scent of purple mint. When the woman pulled away, she gazed at Maia with unmistakable warmth. "Hello, Maia," she whispered. Then she patted her cheek.

"Come with us to the house," the Aldermaston said, and then gestured to Jon Tayt to approach. "There is much we must discuss. You are Jon Tayt, our new hunter? Welcome, sir. Come with us."

Maia did not understand the whirlwind of emotions inside her, but she nearly started weeping. There was a feeling in the air, something thick and tremulous and unidentifiable. It weighed almost painfully on her heart.

They reached the manor house and entered it, drawing the gaze and whispers of the learners and helpers all around the abbey grounds.

There was a very tall man with thick graying hair waiting for them in the Aldermaston's private chamber. He wore simple yet dignified robes of office, and he greeted the Aldermaston as soon as they entered.

"I brought her, Aldermaston," the man said, bowing respectfully. The difference in their heights was almost startling. "She awaits in the anteroom."

"Thank you." He motioned toward the man. "This is Tomas, my steward. We have served together for many years. He is a faithful counselor and taught engraving in the cloisters for many years. And Tomas"—this time he flourished an arm toward Maia—"this is our new guest."

"Welcome, Lady Marciana," Tomas said with a smile that flashed two large dimples in his cheeks. He had a large graying mustache to match his thick hair, and he stroked it absently. "Would you like anyone else to be here, Aldermaston? I can send for the healer?"

The Aldermaston gave a subtle shake of his head and only lifted his palm slightly. "No, Tomas. Thank you. We are enough."

As soon as Tomas shut the door, enclosing them all in the room, the Aldermaston turned to look at Maia, his face serious and sad. "Marciana, I have grievous news."

She swallowed, feeling her insides ripping. "My mother is dead," she said softly, the words thick in her throat.

The Aldermaston nodded heavily and Sabine put her arm around Maia's shoulders.

Grief sent cracks through Maia's heart. The truth had come to her in a dream, so it was no surprise, yet the announcement still felt like a blade stabbed between her ribs. She flinched, trying to master herself.

"Three days ago," the Aldermaston said, walking forward and taking her hand. "I tried to Gift her with healing. I sought the Medium's will to Gift her with life, but it was not to be. The Medium took her from us." He shook his head with sorrow. "Sadness, disappointment, and troubles are inescapable, Marciana, but there is more to life. Of course, I do not seek to diminish how *hard* some of these events are. Words cannot always comfort grief. As has happened in your life and the life of your mother, troubles can last a long time. But try to remember this, Marciana. You must not allow them to consume you."

Maia knew from the look in his eyes that he too was intimate with suffering.

"I wish I could have seen her one last time," Maia said, her voice choked.

"You *will*," the Aldermaston said fervently, tightening his grip on her hand. "Death brings sorrow. It always will. But you will do something important here, Maia. You will open the Apse Veil again. The dead are grieving all around us because they are condemned to linger here in this world. You will open the gates of their prison. Your mother knew it. I know it. You were foreseen to do this. Someday, you will see her again. You are bound together by irrevocare sigil."

Maia looked away, unable to gaze for long into his intense eyes. He was so quiet, so soft-spoken, yet he was filled with certainty and conviction that was harder than stones and stronger than storms.

"Thank you, Aldermaston," Maia said haltingly.

He led her over to a chair and helped her sit. Then he took his wife's hand and guided her to a table heaped with scrolls, quills, ink, scriving tools, a small tome, and various other tools and implements. Once she was seated, he sat down himself. Sabine settled into a chair near Maia, and Jon Tayt slouched on the window seat against the wall.

"Tomas," he said, "would you explain to the High Seer what we heard from Comoros?"

"Yes, Aldermaston." Tomas stayed standing, hands clasped in front of him. He sighed. "Chancellor Morton was . . . I do not know how to say this delicately . . . he was beheaded at the greenyard of Pent Tower for not signing the Act of Submission. This was done in the morning in front of a crowd of at least five hundred witnesses, including all the prisoners in the tower. Those are the facts as I understand them." He sniffed, his jaw clenching with pent-up anger.

Maia stared at him. She had heard the news first from her husband, Collier. It had happened less than a fortnight ago. Thinking of her husband made her sick inside. She had fled Naess, and he had been imprisoned for her treachery.

Jon Tayt snorted. "They killed a man for not signing a piece of parchment?"

Tomas nodded, rocking on his heels. "The Act of Submission places the king's authority above the Medium. Abbey lands now fall under the king's tax. All Aldermastons will be appointed by the king and not the High Seer. In short, he is a bloody, raving lunatic!"

"Tomas," the Aldermaston said gently.

"I should not have said that," Tomas said immediately, his cheeks flushing. "I neglected to remember that his daughter has just arrived. Lady Maia, I beg your pardon, but I do not have kind feelings toward your father at present."

Sabine leaned forward. "He will be surprised when he learns I am at Muirwood."

"I would think so," Tomas said, rocking on his heels again.

Jon Tayt sat at the window seat, scratching behind Argus's ears. "He had better not come here," he said gruffly. "I may lose my temper with him. To think, he *beheaded* the man in full daylight?"

The Aldermaston leaned forward and folded his arms. "We

cannot let the current situation distract us from the Covenant of Muirwood. When the queen died, and I believe she was poisoned, we sent a message to the palace to inform the king. I am expecting news imminently of what is to be arranged for the state funeral. We may very well have a royal host descending on Muirwood." He lowered his voice. "That would be most inconvenient. The king would learn that the abbey is nearly complete and that construction was not halted as he ordered. What do you advise, High Seer?"

The thought of seeing her father again, especially so soon after her mother's death, made Maia grimace and clench her fists.

Sabine stared hard at the Aldermaston. "Maia does not have much time to pass the maston test."

"I agree," the Aldermaston replied, only adding to Maia's concern.

"Who have you chosen to be her companion?"

The Aldermaston turned to his wife and gestured for her to speak.

"High Seer, we have many capable girls among the Ciphers," she said. "Some are highborn. Some are wretcheds. I feel impressed by the Medium to choose Suzenne Clarencieux as Maia's companion."

"Tell me of her," Sabine said thoughtfully.

"This is her final year of study, and she is to pass the maston test herself come Whitsunday. She is of a respectable Family, the oldest of three children. She helps the others learn, and does not have airs. She is well respected by the other learners and has influence among them. I believe she will be discreet in this matter. She is a Cipher, so she can be trusted with secrets."

"Send her in," Sabine said. Tomas smiled, flashing his dimples again, and left to get her from the anteroom.

"You prepared the tome, I see," Sabine said to the Aldermaston once the door had been closed once more.

"As you instructed," he replied thoughtfully, indicating the tome in front of him.

"That tome is for you, Maia," Sabine said, reaching out to squeeze her hand. "I asked the Aldermaston to engrave a page. The final page."

The door opened, and the tall steward returned to the room with a young woman, nearly Maia's match in age and height. She was a beauty, Maia saw, and wore a silk-and-brocade gown that must have cost at least a thousand marks. A jeweled choker circled her neck, and her hair was braided into a long golden rope. Her appearance made Maia feel a prickle of envy, as she was once more dressed in plain clothes that did not speak of her station. The girl's expression was one of alarm, especially when she saw she had been brought into a crowded room.

Sabine rose from the chair and greeted her. "Welcome, Suzenne. Be at ease."

Her eyes widened. "You are the High Seer," she gasped, then did a deep curtsy.

"Have you told her, Joanna?" Sabine asked the Aldermaston's wife.

"No."

Sabine nodded, then reached out and took the younger woman's hand. "You are probably fearful. Be at ease, truly. You are here because of your merits, not as a punishment."

The girl flushed at the compliment. "Thank you."

"Suzenne, you are here because the Medium wills it. I asked the Aldermaston to choose a learner of great ability and discretion to assist us. The Medium impresses upon my mind that they chose well. I have a duty for you to perform that will require the utmost secrecy and discretion. Before moving forward, I must ask if you will willingly accept this charge."

Though she looked overwhelmed, and her eyes were shiny with held-back emotion, the girl did not hesitate to reply. "Yes, High Seer. Of course! I will serve however the Medium wills."

Sabine nodded and released her hands, then walked over to Maia and gestured for her to rise. "This is my granddaughter, Lady Marciana . . . Maia."

Suzenne looked at Maia, her eyes widening with shock. "The king's daughter?" she gasped.

"Yes," Sabine said, stroking Maia's arm. "She will be studying at Muirwood. She is to become a Cipher before she takes the maston test. I need your help to teach her, Suzenne. The fate of the abbey rests on her."

"Yes," Suzenne stammered. "Of course. If you wish it, High Seer."

"There is one thing you must understand. It is knowledge that you must protect above all else, Suzenne. Everyone in this room will know, but no one else can know. Do not be frightened. Maia . . . please show her the mark on your chest."

Maia's stomach lurched and she felt herself go pale with shame. Obediently, she tugged at the bodice of her blue gown and exposed some of the shadowstains on her chest, the whorl of tattoos that had afflicted her since she first wore the kystrel, which now hung around her husband's neck.

Suzenne's eyes widened with fear.

"This you must keep secret," Sabine said, motioning for Maia to cover the marks. "It is written in a tome on the Aldermaston's desk."

Maia felt the flush of the Medium engulf the room. A small stone Leering on the desk began to glow red-hot. The Aldermaston produced a set of tongs and set them on the Leering, heating them up.

The Aldermaston looked at the trembling girl. "Suzenne, you must safeguard this secret. It is the Medium's will. Maia was deceived by the Dochte Mandar and tricked into becoming a hetaera. You will understand what that means when you take the maston test shortly. You must know that she did not make this choice willingly. She will carry the mark the rest of her life, but she is not evil. I want you to know that I trust her implicitly, just as I trust the High Seer . . . just as I trust the Medium. That is how I know Maia belongs here. This place is her only refuge, her only sanctuary. You must guard her secret, Suzenne. Will you do so?"

Suzenne sniffled, dabbing tears from her eyes. "I will, Aldermaston."

With that, the Aldermaston nodded and pulled the tongs from the burning Leering. His wife fixed a band of solid aurichalcum across the bottom of the tome, pressing together the final page and the page above it, which was blank. With the tongs, he gripped the ends of the bands, allowing the heat to fuse it around the pages. Then he set down the tongs and pushed the tome away from him.

Sabine took up a scriving tool from the table and drew a symbol into the molten gold. The Medium thrummed in the chamber, making Maia feel strange and wonderful.

"This is a binding sigil," Sabine said softly, setting down the tool. "No one will be able to speak of Maia's secret." She looked at Maia. "Not even our enemies."

Or your husband, her eyes seemed to say.

We all face difficulties, but they should not become our core. We grieve, we suffer, we weep. Challenges are experiences that help us to grow, like the winds that help strengthen the roots of the apple trees in the Cider Orchard. Storms are always temporary and should never distract us from the beautiful days that were before or will come after. Do not become so fixed on a single injustice that you can no longer remember others may be suffering near you. Like the healing of the body when it is ill, the healing of the heart requires patience.

—Richard Syon, Aldermaston of Muirwood Abbey

CHAPTER THREE

Suzenne

A gentle hand on her shoulder awoke her.

"Maia, it is time."

Her eyes blinked open to smothering darkness, the shadows dispelled by a single fat candle. The room in the manor house was like a cave, the darkness thick and oppressive. Maia struggled to remember where she was. For the past few weeks, falling asleep had meant a Myriad One might wrench control of her body and plunge her mind into vivid dreams of the past. But now she was free of the being that had taken root in her. She could not remember any dream, nor could she remember falling asleep. The last thing she remembered was lying awake, listening to the sound of Suzenne's breathing.

"Thank you," Maia said, brushing strands of hair from her eyes as she sat up. There were two small beds in the room, both set into tall wooden stands with sculpted poles and gossamer veils. A large hearth was against the far wall, a Leering carved into it. She remembered Suzenne dousing it with her mind before they had climbed into their respective beds. The two had not spoken at all before they had gone to bed, as Suzenne had needed to pack her belongings and move them to the room. She had several chests, and she had spent hours hanging beautiful gowns in the wardrobe. Suzenne was so quiet and busy that Maia had felt a sense of awkwardness in speaking to her. She hoped they would get a chance to get to know each other later.

After setting the candle down on a nearby table, Suzenne quickly removed her nightgown and chose one of the many elegant gowns from the wardrobe, though she examined several before deciding on one. Maia had nothing to wear but the clothes that had been given to her—the wretched gown and a nightgown for sleeping.

"May I borrow a comb?" Maia asked softly.

Suzenne startled and then nodded, gesturing to the small table where an assortment had been set out the previous night. Maia quickly combed through her hair, pausing a moment to finger her earrings, which had been part of a jewelry set given to her by her husband. She had left the rest of the jewels behind when she fled Naess, but she had been unable to part with these. For a moment, she was lost in the memory of how Collier's fingers had trembled as he tried to put them in her ears. Sighing, she let her hand fall, wondering where he was sleeping at that moment, deep in the northern kingdom of Naess. What would *he* feel when he woke up? Did he hate her?

After dressing in a gown just as opulent as the one she had been wearing earlier, Suzenne quickly scooped some water onto her face, dried it with the towel, and reached for the candle.

"We must go and light the Leerings," she said to Maia. "I always go to the cloisters a little early to make sure things are ready." She paused, her expression uncertain. "If . . . that is all right with you?"

"Yes, of course," Maia said, feeling the awkwardness stretch between them.

Suzenne smiled. "We bring our tomes," she said, grabbing a heavy leather satchel with a strap, which she slung around her shoulder. Maia had been given one as well, so she did the same, and was impressed by the weight of it against the small of her back. Suzenne then led the way down the darkened hall to the Aldermaston's private chamber. There was not a soul moving about, and their feet crunched softly on the fresh floor rushes. After delivering a short knock on the door, Suzenne opened it and Maia followed her inside. A small Leering provided illumination for the Aldermaston, who sat at his desk, poring over a tome.

"Good morrow," he bid them, motioning to the anteroom door.

Maia smiled at him and he gave her a tender look. Then he glanced back down at the tome, his eyes scrutinizing the glimmering page.

The anteroom was a small waiting chamber with a padded bench and a side table. There was a nice carpet on the floor, which Suzenne lifted, revealing a trapdoor. She handed the candle to Maia and then pulled the handle to open the door. She started to hurry down the steps. Maia reached down to return the candle to her and started down after her.

She was about to close the trapdoor above her head, but Suzenne stopped her. "Leave it open for when we return. We must always be very cautious and quiet and not raise suspicion that we are learners."

Together they walked down a darkened corridor that smelled of earth and must. It was a strong smell, but not an offensive one. The tunnel was long and narrow, just wide enough for them to walk side by side. Partway down, another pathway intersected theirs.

"That way is to the abbey," Suzenne said, pointing. "Our path will bring us to the cloisters."

Her words had been very efficient so far. Not condescending, yet certainly not inviting. Suzenne reminded Maia of some of the little girls she had known as a child, playmates who'd let her win at every game. Always there had been awareness of who she was, who her father was. She had been sent to live in Pry-Ree and help administer her father's policies when she was still very young—younger than Suzenne had been when she first started learning at Muirwood. Her contact with others her own age had been even more limited there. And then she had been banished and no one had dared befriend her. Throughout her life, her closest relationships had always been with those who were older than her. Except, of course, her husband. Maia's mind cringed at the thought and she pushed it away. She did not want to think about Collier at that moment; she could not bear to. She bit her lip and said nothing.

Eventually they reached the tunnel leading to the cloisters and ascended a steep, narrow set of stone steps to reach the floor. The trapdoor was open, and voices could be heard from above, the sound of other girls.

Suzenne sighed, and Maia could tell it bothered her to be late to her duties.

"There you are," said a pretty dark-haired girl when they climbed into the room. "You are *never* late, Suzenne. Were you sleepy? It was quite dark when we came." Her smile was impish.

Several of the girls held candles. There were six young women, eight including Maia and Suzenne. Maia stared at the room in amazement, taking in the sight of the sturdy shelves full of gleaming tomes and the low study desks equipped with squat legs to support the weight of tomes, each surrounded by four chairs.

Against one wall was a shelf of scriving tools, clamps, tubs of wax, and so forth. One of the younger girls, who looked to be about twelve, was standing in front of a Leering that slowly started to glow. Leerings always had a face carved into them, and in this room, all the faces were female. Maia thought it interesting that this was where all the boy learners received their lessons.

Suzenne answered the teasing with seriousness. "It is a farther walk from the Aldermaston's manor, Maeg. I can do that, Sissel," she said, brushing aside the young girl who was slowly lighting the Leering. The look of strong concentration on Sissel's face proved the Leering was only barely obeying her. Suzenne stared at it and the brightness grew more quickly.

"I was only teasing," Maeg said, giving Suzenne a look of annoyance. Then she looked at Maia, sizing her up quickly, her look superior. "So you are the new girl," she said, a little chuckle in her voice. "Another *wretched*."

Suzenne walked to a different Leering and it started to awaken slowly, the glow chasing away the shadows. "She is not a wretched," Suzenne said over her shoulder. "She is Marciana, the king's daughter."

"Princess Murer's half sister?" Maeg said, surprised. "I mean, her *step*sister? The banished one? I always heard they dressed you as a servant."

Maia felt a prickle of heat enter her cheeks at the girl's condescending tone.

"Maeg," Suzenne said warningly. "Be nice."

"I thought I was," Maeg said, the impish smile returning to her face. "This is your new companion, Suzenne? Poor thing."

It was not clear which girl she pitied more.

"Pull out your tomes," Suzenne said firmly. "We need to be ready when the Aldermaston's wife arrives. Where are Jess and—ah, here they come." Three more girls came scampering up the stairs, making it eleven, one of them rubbing her eyes sleepily. She glanced at Maia, smiled, and then joined the other newcomers at a table. Maia saw the uneven match in numbers. Of course it would be that way, she realized. Every girl had been assigned a companion before her arrival. She was upsetting the order of things.

"She is right behind us," one of the girls said breathlessly. They opened their leather satchels and lifted out their heavy tomes. Maia stood awkwardly, not certain where she should sit as she watched the others quickly assemble in their usual places. Maeg looked her over again, a small smile curling her lip.

Suzenne looked flustered as she hurried over to the third Leering, obviously distraught that the Aldermaston's wife might arrive before her duties were complete.

Maia did not understand why she had not simply lit all the Leerings at once. With a flex of thought, Maia bid the others to awaken, and light spilled down from the walls. Suzenne gasped in shock, startled, and the other girls reacted the same way.

"Did you see *that*?" one of the girls whispered.

"Suzenne, how did you . . . ?" another said.

"I did not," Suzenne said, shaking her head, backing away from the Leering. She turned and looked at Maia, her eyes widening with . . . was it fear?

"That was *you*," Maeg said from her table, her expression altering from curiosity to contempt.

"Not even Jayn could light so many at once," another girl tittered.

There was the sound of footsteps, and the Aldermaston's wife appeared in the cloisters, wearing her gray robes and a white shawl.

Suzenne quickly walked over to Maeg's table, where every other seat had been taken. She fumbled with the straps of the satchel as she seemed to realize that Maia was still standing awkwardly alone and there were no empty chairs at the desk. A flush of scarlet bloomed in her cheeks.

"It is all right, Suzenne," the Aldermaston's wife said gently, walking up and putting a frail arm around Maia's back. "She will work with me today. I am the lucky one this time." Her voice was gentle and soft, yet it had the power to quiet the room to absolute stillness. "This is Marciana, the Princess of Comoros. Her mother, as you know, has passed on. Treat her kindly, as you would wish to be treated yourself if you were in a new situation. She is here to study with us."

One of the younger girl's hands shot up.

"Yes, Ellzey?"

"Is she a Cipher too?"

The Aldermaston's wife smiled patiently. "Yes, but she will serve in a different way since she is a princess. Most Ciphers will become ladies-in-waiting or perhaps chambermaids. Many of you will join a royal household in some manner. You study so you may gain wisdom, so that you may be a counselor and advisor to those you serve. There are great gems of wisdom in these tomes. To find them, you must be able to read. Even though that is forbidden by the Dochte Mandar, it is the way of the mastons. Many of you will marry men of a higher rank. They will choose you not because of your beauty, your cleverness, or the way you play a lute or a harp, but because you have passed the maston test and they value the wisdom of your mind. As I have told you before, Ciphers keep secrets. You must keep the secrets of the lady you serve. You must keep the secrets of your lord husband. And you must keep the secret of what we do here in Muirwood Abbey. Some of you may have the privilege, someday, of serving even a king or a *queen*." The hand on Maia's back increased pressure, just a little. "Let me introduce you to the Ciphers, Lady Marciana."

"Please, call me Maia," she said, uncomfortable with being the focus of their intense scrutiny. Some she could see stared at her with interest. Others, like Maeg, with jealousy. Suzenne's look was the most guarded, but it was not a look of approval. It was serious and solemn.

"If you wish it," the Aldermaston's wife said. She brought them to the first table, which seemed to have the youngest girls sitting at it. "We only choose a few girls from among the newcomers who are sent to learn at the abbey," she explained. "Many of the girls come to Muirwood for lessons in languages, embroidery, healing, and music. The Aldermaston and I watch them their first year to see whom we can trust. These are all second-year learners the Medium has sent to us. This beautiful young woman is Haven Proulx from Caspur Hundred. She is the daughter of the Earl of Caspur. Next to her is Joanna Stay. I like her name, because that is *my* true name." She put her hand tenderly on the girl's shoulder. "My husband and I were not always Aldermastons of Muirwood. She is also from Caspur Hundred. This is Ishea Haut, a transfer from Claredon Abbey, a third-year learner but a first-year Cipher. I love her braids. And this is Keresia Draper from Norris-York Hundred. She is a wretched."

Maia nodded to each one, and the Aldermaston's wife took her to the next table, quickly introducing her to each of the girls, who came from a variety of Hundreds. One of them wore an apron and smock that Maia recognized immediately. "You are from Hautland," she said curiously. The girl blushed and nodded, saying nothing. Maia's experience in Hautland had indicated there existed a profound division between the sexes in that kingdom; women there were treated with great suspicion.

One by one Maia was introduced to them all.

"This is Maergiry Baynton," the Aldermaston said when they reached Maeg. Her impish look had not diminished one bit. "She is an accomplished dancer and musician. I love hearing her sing, and she is quite adept at the harp. She is from this Hundred, the daughter of the sheriff of Mendenhall. That makes her position as a Cipher very dangerous for her. If her father were to find out, the situation would be perilous for all of us. But the Aldermaston and I trust her very much." Maia nodded to her, but Maeg did not nod in return.

"And this, as you know, is Suzenne Clarencieux from Kent Hundred in the south. She has the most elegant writing of all of us, myself included. Really, there is little else she can be taught, and she helps me instruct the younger girls when they first start engraving. I will *miss* her after Whitsunday." She squeezed Suzenne's shoulder, who flushed at the compliment. "Now, continue engraving what you were working on yesterday, girls. I will not be checking your work today, as I need to instruct Maia. Suzenne, would you please?"

"Yes, I would be happy to help."

Maia watched the girls' quiet demeanor dissolve as they pushed away from chairs and quickly scurried to the shelves, each one picking out a tome she would bring back. The Aldermaston's wife led her to the bench along the far wall with all the scriving tools. Maia observed discreetly that Maeg was speaking quietly with several of the other girls, directing them to give her covert looks while making comments behind her hand. Her heart squirmed with disappointment.

Maia knew she should not care. Having spent years suffering at the hands of her stepmother and her stepmother's Family, she was used to being treated poorly by others of her sex. Used to being judged, weighed, and scrutinized. She realized, too late, that her display of lighting the Leerings must have injured Suzenne's standing amongst the girls. She promised herself to apologize later. She had hoped to form a friendship with Suzenne. But she realized that the girl already had her friends, that she had been studying for years at Muirwood, and that her final months were being disrupted by a girl who, quite probably, terrified her.

Maia stared down at the band of aurichalcum around the lower portion of her tome. None of the other girls had a binding sigil on theirs. None of the other girls carried a dark secret like hers. Maia had been the vessel of Ereshkigal, the Queen of the Myriad Ones. She had done things, unwillingly and under that being's terrible influence, which she would regret all the rest of her days. These girls had been raised under the protective shadow of two loving Aldermastons, a tender man and his equally kindhearted wife. They had learned to read and engrave from a young age.

Part of her heart wanted to resent them for all the benefits they had enjoyed while she had been locked away in the attic of her stepmother's Family manor. She smoothed her hand over the polished empty page of her tome.

"We practice with these," the Aldermaston's wife said, pushing a wooden sheet toward her with a sheen of clear wax set inside a frame. "Before you scrive in gold, you must practice your hand until you can write flawlessly. This will not be difficult for you, Maia, but it will be tedious at first. You must spend a portion of time each day *reading* as well as *practicing*. My husband will teach you the doctrines of the Medium during the day. I will instruct you at night on how to hear its whispers." She closed her hand on Maia's arm. "I look forward to this opportunity, Maia," she said in an undertone so the others could not hear. "I love you already. I spoke with your mother for many long hours over many painful years. I will share with you everything I knew of her. She was, in my view, one of the most noble women who ever lived."

Maia felt her heart quiver with pain as tears stung her eyes.

"She sacrificed her life and happiness," the woman continued, her throat thickening, "for yours. You may feel out of place, Maia, but you were meant to be here. These girls are your family now. You are the oldest. And they are your sisters."

Maia wiped her eyes quickly. She did not like to cry, but her grandmother had taught her that she needed to learn to accept her emotions rather than bury them. Her father had always urged her to do otherwise, so it was a hard lesson to learn.

"I do not think Suzenne likes me very well," Maia said softly, watching the other girl as she went from table to table and coaxed the other girls in their efforts. "She is afraid of me."

The Aldermaston's wife patted Maia's hand and wisely said nothing.

CHAPTER FOUR

The Queen's Garden

With the sun came a different schedule—a different life. The first official lesson was in languages, and though Maia sought to remain in the background, the teacher, who was from Dahomey, knew who she was. In his excitement to converse with another fluent speaker, he had addressed her immediately, speaking fast and excitedly. Maia had answered him as briefly as she could, but her response still showed her ability with the language. The lavish way he praised her in front of the class made her wince. Maeg's eyes narrowed with envy, and throughout the class she whispered to some of the other Ciphers behind her hand, undoubtedly spouting unpleasant things about Maia.

Maia met some of the boys at the school in the language class. While she recognized some of the Family names from her youth, none of the students themselves looked familiar. There was one boy who was aloof from the others and seemed rather impatient with the pace of the class. She was too uncertain of herself to ask who he was.

Languages was the only class shared with the boys, as they were busy reading and engraving tomes in the cloisters for the rest of the day. Maia found embroidery to be painfully tedious, but the archery lesson was enjoyable. The studies on law, medicine, and history were also quite interesting.

When the classes were finally over, the students were allowed to wander the grounds and enjoy themselves, unless the weather was blustery. The days were short and the wind brisk and scented with pending rain. Suzenne walked alongside her as they left the classroom, and Maia saw several young men waiting for the girls at a cluster of trees.

Maeg had a mischievous smile as she began bantering with some of the youths. Then she turned to look at them. "Suzenne, are you coming, or must you tend to the poor waif *all* day?"

It was a deliberate cruelty, Maia knew that at once, and Suzenne's cheeks flushed with discomfort. These were her friends, and it was clear from Maeg's tone and word choice that Maia had not been invited to join them.

Suzenne looked flustered with indecision, and Maia could see that while her heart longed for one thing, her sense of duty and propriety urged her to do something else.

Maia touched Suzenne's arm. "Go with them," she said softly. "I am tired and would rather walk the grounds by myself. Thank you for showing me where to go today."

Suzenne hesitated, and Maia could see the strain in her brow. She was doing battle with herself.

"Will you be all right?" Suzenne asked in a concerned tone.

"She can fend for herself well enough," Maeg said spitefully. "Come, Suzenne! It will be dark soon. The days are so short now."

Maia smiled, patted Suzenne's arm, and turned and walked away, her cheeks burning from the slight.

"Is she *really* the king's daughter?" one of the boys muttered.

"Yes," said Maeg wickedly. "I will tell you all about her. Come on, Suzenne!"

"Poor lass, I pity her," said another boy.

Maia kept right on walking, anxious to be away from their gazes. There was a certain petulance to youth, she realized. She had been exposed to it before from her stepmother, Lady Deorwynn, and her stepsisters, but she had expected something different in an abbey. It baffled her that people who studied the Medium and knew how sensitive it was to thoughts and desires could be so callous in their treatment of one another.

She sighed. She had borne the torment of Lady Deorwynn and her girls. Compared to that, what were Maeg's saucy looks? She determined to bear it without becoming vengeful. She would try and earn Suzenne's trust over time.

The weight of the students' behavior eased off her shoulders as she started to explore the grounds. Her eyes drank in the structure of the abbey beneath the sturdy scaffolding. She longed to strip away the wood and see the abbey as it was meant to be. A memory fluttered in her mind of climbing the scaffolding of a towering abbey in the city of Rostick in Hautland. As she walked in the soft grass, she remembered that city's clean cobbled streets, so crammed and narrow, yet pristine. Before coming to the abbey, she had fled from one kingdom to another, crossing perilous mountains and facing storms, avalanches, and the sea.

Maia walked into the Cider Orchard, where the leaves were turning yellow and falling off due to the cold. As she trod through the soggy remnants on the grass, she smiled to herself, feeling as if she walked amidst ghosts. She touched the gray branches, running her hands over the bark, and breathed in the musty smells of moldering leaves and early winter. In truth, she was not troubled by solitude. It was pleasant being by herself.

After she emerged from the orchard, she veered away from the areas where the learners had gathered, and circled around to the laundry. There were no lavenders there at this hour, since their work had been done earlier in the day. Beyond the roofed shelter, she saw a field of purple. Two workers were kneeling amidst the plants, using small knives to cut sprigs. She walked closer, wanting a better view, and was startled to realize that one of the laborers was her grandmother.

Sabine and the girl, both wearing dirty aprons to cover their dresses, were conversing in low voices. As Maia approached, Sabine smiled warmly and quickly brushed the dirt off her hands and rose.

"There you are," she said, shaking loose dirt from her apron. "You are done with your studies?"

"Yes," Maia said, giving her grandmother a hug.

"I wanted to show you something," Sabine said. Then she turned to the girl kneeling beside her. "Thank you, Cybil. It was thoughtful of you to take the time to teach me your craft."

"My pleasure, my lady."

Sabine took Maia's arm and steered her a different way.

"Does she know who you are?" Maia asked softly, glancing back at the girl.

Sabine shook her head and said nothing. She pointed to a walled section of the grounds just ahead.

"What is it?" Maia asked. The wall was thick with ivy, so thick that the stone beneath could hardly be seen. All the walls were quite high, and one corner had a roof edge visible from below. They walked along the path to the portion of the wall with the sloping roof.

"Your mother had this built," Sabine said, nodding toward it. "It was her private garden. They call it the Queen's Garden. She did not allow anyone in here except the gardener. It was her place of refuge. Her solace."

As they approached, Maia noticed a sturdy wooden door hidden behind the drapes of ivy, and felt the presence of a Leering. As she approached, its eyes began to glow in warning. She felt a pulse of fear start inside her.

"It will obey you," Sabine said, "for you are of her blood. She built this garden in the hope that you would come study at Muirwood one day. She would often come here and spend hours inside, thinking of you."

Maia's heart pulsed with sadness. But it was also comforting to hear how much her mother had loved her. She stared at the small carving set into the stone beside the door and silenced it with her mind. The stone slowly moved, making a grinding noise.

"It is open now," Sabine said, pushing on the door.

As it opened, the fragrance of flowers gushed from the gap and filled Maia's nose with a pleasant perfume. The garden was beautifully tended, with low stone benches, boxes to add a variety of heights, and beautiful trees and trimmed hedges. There were flower boxes everywhere, each filled with a different varieties of rosebushes.

Sabine took Maia's arm as they explored the garden together. The front corner near the door was covered by a sloping roof, providing a small covered shelter for when it rained. The walls were high enough that sounds from the grounds outside disappeared and only the trilling of the birds nesting in the branches could be heard.

"It is lovely," Maia said with a smile, patting her grandmother's arm. "Did she choose all the plants herself?"

"Yes, every one. It is yours now, Maia. I spent a little bit of time today tending it. There are weeds to pull and hedges to trim. That will be your job while you are here. I thought you would like it."

Maia did. It would be a refuge, a place that was her own. She touched one of the walls of the flowerbeds, feeling the grainy texture of the stone. Warmth for her mother glowed like an ember in her bosom. "It is perfect."

"I have been mulling something today," Sabine said. "I hope it is not uncomfortable for you, but I wanted to discuss it. Let me know if it is too painful."

Maia turned and looked at Sabine curiously. "What is it?"

"Your marriage."

The word sent a shard of pain through her left breast. Maia bit her lip.

"If it is too painful . . ."

"No, it is all right. What do you wish to know?"

Sabine held her hand and walked with her around the footpath inside the garden. "Based on what you told me on the *Holk*, your wedding happened rather quickly. It was in the King of Dahomey's tent, it was performed by a Dochte Mandar, and there were multiple witnesses. In my mind, it is a valid ceremony, and you made your promise." She sighed. "It is not what I would have wished for you. King Gideon of Dahomey never passed the maston test. I learned from the Aldermaston of his abbey that he had no real intent to pass it. My understanding is he spent more time trying to escape his studies than he did seeking to gain wisdom from them." She fell silent. "But what is done is done, Maia. As your grandmother, I may not like your . . . choice in a husband, but there is no denying he *is* your husband. I would advise you not to tell anyone. I would also advise you not to pretend you are free. There are many young men here at the abbey who may take a fancy to you."

Maia was surprised that the first emotion she felt in response to her grandmother's words was relief. She had wondered, and worried, if the marriage would be easily annulled because of the circumstances. Maia felt *bound* to Collier, even still, and worried how he might feel about their union. She had never considered herself free to choose another.

"I think not," Maia said. "I am quite a pariah already."

Sabine squeezed her hands. "Yes. But you are also the Princess of Comoros. There are powerful men in this kingdom who would seek to use you to dethrone your father."

"I suppose I had not thought much about it," Maia said uncomfortably.

"It is not a supposition," Sabine replied. "While your mother was here, she received several visitors. Many came in secret and urged her to rise up against her husband. Even though she was a foreign queen, from Pry-Ree, they told her that the people respected her because she was faithful to her maston vows. They admired her example and the dignity and elegance with which she had suffered the humiliations of her position. They offered to summon armies to fight for her. These stirrings of rebellion were no small concern for your father."

"But she refused them?" Maia asked, amazed at what she was learning. "I never heard of any insurrection."

"Of course you would not have heard of it. You were kept so close to your father, then watched over so carefully by Lady Shilton, Lady Deorwynn's mother. You were always a political risk to your father. As his firstborn and lawful daughter, you could . . . in theory . . . inherit the throne. I say in theory because it has never happened before. As you know, no queen has *ever* ruled Comoros in her own right. There was one who tried generations ago, but it caused a civil war. Ultimately, her *son* ruled. This kingdom has a deep history of contention and strife, which is once again reaching a boiling point. That is why I must warn you. As much as we will try, we cannot keep your presence here a secret for long. You must pour all your energy into passing the maston test yourself. Maybe within a fortnight. When your father learns you are here, I assure you he will send soldiers to fetch you."

Maia swallowed. "I do not want to see him," she said darkly. "I cannot help but think that *what happened to me* is his fault."

"I know, child. I know." Her voice was soothing, comforting. "Just be wary, especially if any young men approach you and try to share a degree of . . . intimacy with you. There are several noble Families who have sent their learners here. Many of them oppose your father but are too afraid to speak out because of what happened to the last Earl of Forshee."

"I was there when the earl spoke out," Maia said. "What Father did to him was terrible."

"Can I ask you something else?" Sabine said.

"Of course. You can ask me anything."

"Thank you." Her brow furrowed. "Did you and your husband have intimate relations?"

Maia flushed and was grateful that the sun was setting quickly, filling the gardens with shadows. "No." She squirmed uncomfortably.

"Then there is no risk that you are with child. I say this not to upset you, Maia. But even though your marriage did not begin under the maston rites, it does not mean that it *cannot* someday. You will pass the maston test yourself. If he chooses to take it again, then you can be united under irrevocare sigil as your maston oaths encourage." She put her arm around Maia's back, hugging her. "Someday you will want to have children. They are truly a blessing from Idumea. You will have to be very careful, Maia. Very guarded with your expressions of intimacy. Your kiss would be fatal to your husband or even your children. I am sure this will cause you grief and hardship throughout your life, but there is no reason for you not to experience the joys of having a family."

Maia's heart ached at her grandmother's words. Her regrets

stirred within her like a hive of bees, ready to sting, and she tried to calm her feelings. She was grateful she did not have to bear the secret all alone.

"What if my husband decides to divorce me?" Maia asked, her voice thick.

"Do you think that he might? From what you have said, it sounds like he is ambitious and he married you for your station. Through you, he claims legitimate right to Comoros. I do not think he will abandon that because he feels you betrayed him."

Maia nodded. "You are right. I wish . . . Grandmother, I *wish* we could have brought him with us!"

"I have been mulling on that myself," she replied. "It was not the Medium's will. I felt certain at the time. But it weighs heavily on me."

"It burdens my heart," Maia said miserably. "He was a hostage for years in Paeiz after his father lost a war there and he was ransomed at great cost. I could tell the imprisonment changed him. It made him who he is today, made him reluctant to learn the maston ways." She winced sorrowfully. Her heart was tangled with conflicting feelings—sympathy, frustration, dread. "What will he think of me now?"

"Shhh," Sabine said soothingly. "You have enough worries of your own without taking on his. I do not think the Dochte Mandar will hold him ransom for long. They know he has the coin to pay them. It was money he was going to spend invading Comoros. Now the Naestors will use it to invade Assinica." Her expression was bitter as she said this last part.

"Yes, but how resentful will he be?" Maia said. "This is a heavy burden." She remembered something Collier had told her, how when he was imprisoned in Paeiz he had hoped her father would pay his ransom in honor of the plight troth that had existed between him and Maia. "I wish *I* could help him," she whispered miserably. "But I have nothing."

All those who offer an opinion on any doubtful point should first clear their minds of every sentiment of dislike, friendship, anger, or pity.

—Richard Syon, Aldermaston of Muirwood Abbey

CHAPTER FIVE

The Aldermaston's Kitchen

Awarm light shone from the kitchen windows as Maia and Sabine approached. A figure detached from the shadows around the building, and Maia immediately recognized Suzenne wringing her hands and looking flustered.

"Oh, there you are," Suzenne said with a look of relief. "I am so sorry I lost track of you after studies." She looked at Maia's companion, and her expression twisted with regret. "Forgive me, High Seer, I did not recognize you. I am very sorry I abandoned your—"

"Do not trouble yourself," Sabine interrupted graciously. "I was showing her part of the grounds. Have you had supper yet?"

"No," Suzenne replied, still wringing her hands. "I remembered on my way to the learner kitchen that I was supposed to start coming here for my meals. I checked inside and Collett said she had not seen you yet."

Maia wondered why Suzenne looked so disturbed, but she smiled and said nothing about the friends who had beckoned the other girl to join them. Perhaps she was feeling guilty about her choice. Together they opened the door to the kitchen, and a delicious spicy smell wafted out.

As Maia gazed inside the opening, she was struck by how immaculate it was. This was not a kitchen full of flour dust and spilled seeds. The floor was swept, the trestle tables were perfectly aligned, and every pan, ladle, and crockery was hanging from a measured peg or sturdy shelf. The kitchen had a vast aroma of wonderful smells—yeasty bread, cinnamon, cloves, salted stew. The head cook, Collett, was an older woman who wore a clean apron and her hair pulled back in a tight bun. She stood when they arrived, and her expression was quite sour and grim. She gripped a wooden spoon like a sword hilt.

"Well, your supper is half cold now, I suspect," she said primly in a slightly raspy voice. "I serve meals at sunup and sundown. It pleases the Medium when we are on *time*."

"I beg your pardon," Sabine said, smiling at the other woman with obvious affection. "I made us late and bear the blame. What is that delicious smell, Collett?"

She fidgeted a bit, trying not to look pleased. "A cobbler for the Aldermaston and one for us. They are nearly done."

"It smells divine. I miss your cobbler, Collett. What fruit did you use?"

"I had some moldering apples in the cold storage," Collett said with a sniff. "Not much good for anything else."

"Even better," crooned Sabine. "This is my granddaughter, Maia," she said, taking the younger woman's arm. "And her companion, Suzenne Clarencieux."

"I know Lady Suzenne, of course," Collett said with a dignified air. "Welcome to the Aldermaston's kitchen, Lady Maia."

Maia gazed around, remembering the stories she had heard

of how her ancestor, Lia Demont, had been raised in this very kitchen. There were large ovens in the corners and a high sloped ceiling that ended in a cupola, supported by struts. The heat from the fires hung warmly in the air, and the wonderful smells from the kitchen entranced her. Two scullery girls, probably the same age—around eight or nine—sat eating on a bench in the corner of the room. They were talking in very low voices and pointing at the new arrivals with wonder.

A sturdy loft had been erected on one side, and Maia could see it was packed with barrels and sacks. Every article in the room had been arranged just so, all a declaration of Collett's keen sense of organization and discipline. She was taken aback when she spied an older gentleman with snowy white hair, and a mustache to match, sitting on a barrel by the ovens. He was eating a bowl of soup, his leather cap resting on his knee, but he was so quiet she had not noticed him.

"Well, I will not allow you to stand idle and unfed," Collett announced firmly. "There are bowls and spoons over in that cabinet as you see them. I do not waste food, so I did not serve you yet." She waved a hand at a large pot. "I need to tend to the cobbler."

Maia fetched the dishes and ladled herself a generous helping of the savory stew. She then took her bowl and walked over to the two empty chairs near the bench where the younger girls sat. "May I sit with you?"

One of the girls had light hair with reddish streaks, braided into a crown, and she nodded vigorously, her gray eyes bright with interest. "Yes. Are you a wretched like me? You serve the king's daughter?" she asked, nodding her head toward Suzenne, who was following with her own bowl. Suzenne's face went scarlet with shame.

"I am the king's daughter," Maia said, smiling at the mistake. She mussed up the girl's silky hair, loosening some of it from the braid. "And yes, I do feel a little like a wretched sometimes."

"You should not have said that, Aloia," said the little girl's companion, a girl with dark hair and blue eyes and rosebud lips. "You are always saying silly things."

"Is she now?" Maia asked, then took her first bite of stew. It was a tantalizing blend of onion, carrots, potato, and venison. The broth was creamy and salty. It was delicious.

"She is always saying too much," said the dark-haired girl. "She never stops talking."

"That is unfair," the girl said, pouting. "You like to talk as much as I do."

"What are your names?" Maia asked, looking from one girl to the other. Suzenne settled on a chair next to her, blinking with surprise that Maia was speaking to the younger girls. Sabine and Collet spoke in low tones about one of the cook's recipes.

"I am Davinia," said the dark-haired waif, smoothing her skirt. "She calls me Davi."

"I am Aloia," said the braided girl. "And I am not stupid."

"Of course you are not," Maia said, reaching out and pinching her nose softly. "Have you always lived in the kitchen?" she asked.

"Always," said Davi. "Since we were left behind. It does not happen so often now. There are only five wretcheds in the entire abbey."

"Most of the helpers are children from the village," added Aloia, trying to get her share of the attention. "You are really the princess, though? Everyone says that Lady Murer is the princess, but we know the truth at Muirwood."

"Do not talk of such things!" Davi complained.

"Why not? She is talking to us! So you are the princess? Truly?"

Maia swirled her stew around and took another bite. "This is wonderful. Collett is a splendid cook." She poked the stew a bit. "Yes, Aloia. I *am* the Princess of Comoros."

Both girls tittered with eagerness. "But the king has tried to make you deny it," Davi said, lowering her voice conspiratorially.

"In every way he can, yes," she answered. "He took away my jewels and my gowns. He took away my servants and all my coin. He signed a law giving everything I owned to my stepsister. He can do that—he is the king." Talking about him made her heart ache; she knew his hold on the throne was a result of his riches and power, not his subjects' goodwill. Although he did not deserve the title, she did not feel it was her duty or the Medium's will to overthrow him.

"But," she added, wagging her spoon at them, "it is not jewels or dresses that make a princess. And laws cannot change that my mother was a queen and my father is a king. Even if no one else believed it, I would still be a princess." She fished a nugget of venison from the stew and ate it with relish. Glancing over at Suzenne, Maia realized the other girl was watching her rather than eating.

Maia smiled at her, trying to set her at ease.

Suzenne flushed and raised her spoon to her mouth.

"Who is the man sitting by the ovens?" Maia whispered, leaning toward the girls. "Why is *he* in the kitchen?"

"That is Thewliss," Aloia said, matching her conspiratorial tone. "He is Collett's husband. Shhh! He even sleeps here at night."

"Scandalous," Maia said, grinning. "They do not sleep in the manor house?"

"Oh no," Davi said. "That is their bed underneath the loft. You see it, over there."

"I see it," Maia said. "So they live here with you?"

"Oh yes," Aloia said with a bubbly voice. "We are too young to be left all alone here."

"I wish they would leave us alone here," Davi complained.

Maia finished her stew as the girls continued with their chatter.

Aloia nodded seriously. "Do not talk to Thewliss. He is very shy. He never talks to anyone."

"He is the gardener. He keeps the grounds," Davi added.

"He is planting winter bulbs right now. In the spring—"

"They will blossom and bloom! He is a wonderful gardener. He talks to the plants more than he talks to us."

"I think they can hear him. Some of them answer him."

"I saw him talking to the birds once!"

"You did not!"

Collett's voice rose over the conversation. "Girls, quit your prattling! You have been chattering away all day long! Hold your tongue for half a moment and take the cobbler to the manor house for the Aldermaston."

The girls sprang from the bench and promptly obeyed, taking their stew bowls for cleaning, and quickly arranged the dessert to bring to the Aldermaston. Before they scurried off into the night, they brought small, still-steaming dishes of cobbler to Suzenne and Maia.

Maia took a bite from her bowl and murmured with delight. There was a treacle, oat, and cinnamon topping and the apples were soft and mashed at the bottom.

"This is one of the desserts she sells at Whitsunday?" Maia asked.

"Yes," Suzenne replied meekly, taking a taste herself. "She believes in carrying on the traditions of old." Her face darkened a bit. "I am sorry for leaving you earlier," she apologized. "I should not have. We are companions now."

Maia reached over and patted Suzenne's arm. "You have my permission," she said. "I do not mean to take you away from your friends. Besides, I was with my grandmother, so I was not alone."

Suzenne stared at her bowl, as if she were not enjoying it.

"What is wrong?" Maia asked softly, keeping her voice low so that the others would not hear. Sabine and Collett were talking over tea and keeping their conversation quiet as well.

"I appreciate your permission," Suzenne said, not looking at her. "But I feel I disappointed the Medium today. I offended it. I am to take the maston test soon." She bit her lip. "To be truthful, I am a bit nervous about it. It would grieve me if I failed because I did not show you proper respect."

Maia smoothed some hair behind her ear. "You should be the last person at the abbey to fear failing the test. You have studied here for many years. I have already seen that you are strong with the Medium."

Suzenne looked up at her, then glanced back down. "Not as strong as you."

Maia sighed. She reached over and squeezed the other girl's hand. "I understand a little of how you feel, Suzenne. I am also afraid to take the maston test. Because of . . . *what* I am. Will the Medium reject me because of it? My heart tells me it will not. But there are those little crumbs of fear that linger in the pan." She picked a little crumb out of her treacle to emphasize the point. "We can only do our best to clean our inner vessels. To make ourselves worthy to receive the Medium's will and power. My grandmother believes I am the one who must open the Apse Veil to allow the dead to return to Idumea and to save the people of Assinica. No one in her generation has been strong enough to do so. Even my mother failed." She sighed again. "I feel great pressure to succeed."

Suzenne looked up at her, her expression softening with sympathy. "That is a heavy burden."

"Well, if you face your fears, then I will face mine. We will take the test together."

Suzenne smiled, a very small one, but it was a start. "Very well." She fell silent again, unsure of herself. "What should I call you?" she asked with a hint of nervousness. "My training says that I should always refer to you as *my lady*. Or Lady Maia."

"Just Maia," she replied, taking another bite of the wonderful cobbler. It melted on her tongue, the apples still hot enough to burn a little.

"It would not be . . . proper," Suzenne said haltingly.

"What about my situation strikes you as overly proper?" Maia said with a laugh. "I have been banished from my father's court. I possess nothing save two gowns and my new tome. I have blisters on my feet from walking from Dahomey to Hautland in the company of a hunter, his dog, and the kishion my father hired to murder me in case I was captured." Memories swirled inside her mind, thick with emotions. "I have endured storms, avalanches, hunger, a thousand indignities, and the pain of loss." Maia stared hard in Suzenne's eyes. "I do not care what Maeg or anyone else thinks of me. I came to Muirwood to become a maston and to fulfill the covenant Lia made when she left these shores. From what I understand, she lived simply and always looked for the good in everyone and everything. So please do not feel guilty for how I am treated. You did not ask for this, Suzenne. If you wish to see your friends, by all means, please do."

Suzenne was very quiet, staring down at her hands as Maia spoke. She set aside her bowl and laced her fingers together. "I cannot begin to understand the hardships you have faced."

Maia shook her head. "There was something in a tome I once

read. What is the good of dragging up sufferings that are over, of being unhappy now just because you were then? I am grateful to have you as a companion, Suzenne. Do not worry about me. I have been alone for quite some time. You are preparing to leave the abbey and must find a suitable situation for yourself. I am certain my arrival has *diminished* your expectations."

Suzenne looked at her sharply, as if Maia had read her mind.

"Is that it?" Maia asked softly. "Do you worry that my disgrace will impact you?"

Suzenne's eyes widened with surprise and she looked miserable.

"Do you think I judge you for feeling that way?" Maia asked sympathetically. "I do not. What you have studied and learned about court propriety and etiquette has prepared you to marry an earl someday or serve a great lady. I hope my presence here will largely go unnoticed for now and not hurt your future. Here at Muirwood, we are equals—just two girls who wish to learn and then pass the maston test. I have done too many wrongs myself to ever judge someone else for theirs." She stifled a yawn. "It is early still, but I am tired from the day. Are you?"

Suzenne nodded. "May I ask you something first?"

"Always. What is it?"

"Well, I noticed during languages today that you are fluent in Dahomeyjan. Would it be acceptable to you if we . . . if we practiced a bit each day? I would like to improve in that language. Would you mind?"

"Not at all," Maia replied, switching effortlessly to the other tongue.

"You are not . . . what I . . . expected," Suzenne said, tripping over her words again. A little flush rose to her cheeks.

"I hope we can become friends," Maia said, patting her hand.

As Suzenne started eating her cobbler, Maia walked over to the ovens and found a clean bowl and served another helping. Grabbing a spoon, she brought the bowl to the barrel where the quiet Thewliss was still sitting.

"Have you had any cobbler yet, Master Thewliss?" Maia asked gently, offering him the bowl.

He looked startled, his blue eyes blinking rapidly as she stood over him.

"No . . . not yet . . . no, my lady."

"Call me Maia," she said, offering him the bowl. "Tomorrow, if the weather is pleasant, can you meet me at the Queen's Garden after the studies are over? I would like you to teach me the different plants and which were my mother's favorites."

Thewliss turned beet red under his snowy hair and mustache and nodded vigorously without being able to utter a reply.

"Thank you, Thewliss," she said, patting his shoulder. "I will see you tomorrow."

CHAPTER SIX

Celia Lavender

Several days later, a thick mist shrouded the grounds of the abbey. It brought with it the smell of the Bearden Muir, an odd pungent aroma that fascinated Maia and made her consider seeking out Jon Tayt to find out what he had learned about the area. She had seen him several times in passing and knew where his lodge was. She knelt by the washing trough of the laundry with Celia, one of the few Ciphers who was also a wretched. The trough water was warm, and the suds tickled her fingers as she scrubbed the garment against the ripples of stone.

"Does Suzenne know you are helping me wash her clothes?" Celia asked, peering up from her veil of flaxen hair. She was examining a small stain on a chemise, squinting at it and then using her knuckles to rub the fabric.

"Of course not," Maia said, smiling. "Please do not tell her. If I could do it without *you* knowing, I would."

"When you told me you wanted to help, I thought it was a sign of mock humility or something. I did not think you actually *knew* how to wash clothes."

Maia pulled up the wet garment and twisted it hard, wringing out the moisture. "I spent the better part of two years at Lady Shilton's manor in Comoros. Do you know who she is?"

"I have not heard the name," said Celia apologetically.

"She is Lady Deorwynn's mother. I was a servant in her household. Lower than a servant, actually. I did many chores there."

"Even though you are the king's daughter?"

"Even so," Maia said. "The difference now is I am choosing to help. Before, I did not have a choice. There is dignity in working hard. It helps me think. As much as I like poring over the tomes, I also want to *do* something."

"Like what, Maia? Besides washing clothes, that is."

"Washing clothes is something tangible I can do to serve Suzenne. She has given up so much for me, willingly or not. But there are other things I wish to do . . . so many things. That hill over there, for example," Maia said, straightening and pointing. "There is a tower or something on the crest. I want to see it."

"That is the Tor," Celia said. "It is not a short walk to get there, but the vista is beautiful."

"The Tor," Maia said. She had heard the name before, but she knew not where. "But what was built on it?"

"A tower. When the ships returned from Assinica, a tower was built to honor two Aldermastons who died on that hill. There is a walkway that goes up the side of the Tor . . . a path with paving stones. When folk visit for Whitsunday, it is a popular place to stroll and climb. There are watchers on the tower, though. Watchers for the Aldermaston who look for approaching ships or soldiers."

"I wondered what it was," Maia said, dunking the dress again and scrubbing. "Can you make the water warmer, Celia?" she asked.

The wretched flushed. "I am not as Gifted as you with the Medium."

"Try."

Celia paused in her work. She set the chemise in the basket and turned to the Leering at the head of the trough. Clasping her hands and bowing her head, she shut her eyes. The eyes of the Leering slowly started to glow. The girl's cheek muscles bunched up, and her forehead wrinkled with intense concentration, then little gurgles of water started to drip from the Leering. The trickle increased slowly, beginning to churn the water still in the trough. A haze of steam began to rise up from inside. Maia waited, silently, watching as the girl struggled to tame the Leering. It must have felt strange for Celia to use her talent here. Her studies with the Ciphers were kept secret, so she could not practice in front of the other lavenders.

Finally Celia opened her eyes, looking at Maia with chagrin. "You would have done it much faster."

Maia shook her head. "Well done, Celia. Why do you close your eyes?"

"Habit, I suppose. We are not allowed to see the maston sign when a Gifting happens, so I have always felt that when I call the Medium . . . I should be . . . I suppose . . . reverent is the right word." She started washing another one of Suzenne's garments. "Do you think I should not?"

"If it works for you that way, why change? The Medium works with all of us differently."

Celia sighed. "Sometimes I am not even sure I understand what the Medium is. The Aldermaston's wife says that you can feel it in your head and in your heart. When I use it, I do feel a little . . .

tingling inside my breast. But I have not heard any voices in my head. I wish I knew for certain what it felt like for the Medium to talk to me. It is confusing."

Maia smiled and chuckled to herself. "You know, the Aldermaston has been tutoring me in the evenings," she said. "These last few days have been a feast of learning for me. Maybe this will help you understand. He explained that light and dark cannot exist at the same time. You can be in a dark room but once you light a candle, the darkness is chased away." She stopped scrubbing the clothes and set down the work. She looked at Celia seriously. "The Medium is *everywhere* here in Muirwood. I sense it not only in the Leering right there, but in the trees of the Cider Orchard. I sense it in the gardens and trails. I sense it in the bread that Collett bakes. In the birdsong that comes each morning. The Medium is all around us, Celia. It is even right here," she said, clutching the damp cloth.

"In the laundry?" Celia asked hesitantly.

"Yes, the Medium is in the laundry. It is in the work that we are doing. We are serving someone else. We are washing another's clothes. And the Medium is *here*, right now. With us." Maia's heart burned inside her with the passion of new certainty. "You are uncertain about it because you have lived without darkness. You were abandoned here as a baby and have spent your entire life within the Medium's glow." She shook her head. "It was not until I came to Muirwood that I realized such a place existed. I have visited other abbeys, to be sure. But never for long, and I have never lived in one. I realize now that I felt the Medium as a young child, back before my mother began to lose her babes. I vaguely remember it. For most of my life, I have been living in a box, nailed shut, and thrown into a well." Maia stared down at her hands. "Only now do I see what light truly is. You will understand it yourself once you leave Muirwood. You will long for this feeling . . . this place."

Celia stared at her with great interest, her eyes wiser than her years. "Then I shall never leave," she said, folding the wet clothing. "I always wanted to visit Comoros. Not anymore."

"I only wish," Maia said passionately, "that the rest of the kingdom could understand what we have here. So many live in squalor and suffering. The abbeys are a refuge from that state of desperation. But can there not be a way to bring the peace of the Medium back into the cities and towns?" She scratched her arm. "To spread the light so that others may enjoy it?"

Maia wrestled with her feelings. She treasured the time she had spent studying with the Aldermaston and his wife and her own grandmother. Had she been sent as a learner to Muirwood, she would have been given these lessons in dribs and drabs, but they were trying to prepare her for the maston test as quickly as possible. Her grandmother had explained that she was protected from the Myriad Ones while inside the grounds. They could no longer hunt her. But if she were to leave, she knew she would hear their whispers again and feel the tendrils of their thoughts beckoning her to embrace the ways of the hetaera. Her best chance for safety was to pass the maston test and receive a chaen. Wearing the chaen would allow her to bring part of the Muirwood with her to the outside world. How she longed for that safety. Never again did she ever want to be under the sway of such malevolent beings. The Medium would protect her if she honored her oaths.

The two worked quietly again, comfortable in silence as they finished off the load. Maia saw a young man walking in the misty field of purple mint, his hands tousling the stems and flowers as he slowly walked through them. He was the boy she had noticed in her first day of learner classes—the one who never spoke and always stood so aloof from the rest. He was tall and well-built, with broad shoulders and unruly dark hair with tawny streaks of gold in it.

"Who is that, Celia?" Maia asked, nodding to the young man.

She looked over her shoulder. "Oh, that is Dodd."

"Dodd?" Maia asked, confused. "Is he a learner?"

"I am sorry, I keep forgetting you are new. I have trouble pronouncing his full name. Dodleah Price. Everyone calls him Dodd."

"Oh," Maia said, nodding. "I have heard of him. He has many brothers?"

"Yes, he is the youngest of the brood. His Family is from the north, as you know, and all of his brothers studied at Billerbeck Abbey. He came to Muirwood for some reason instead. As the son of an earl, he was quite popular his first few years here. But since his father was banished to Pent Tower, the Price Family is all in disgrace. The chancellor sent soldiers to arrest him, but he passed the maston test and sought sanctuary here. He cannot leave the grounds or he will be arrested by the sheriff."

Maia nodded. "I am sorry for him. His father was disinherited and the earldom of Forshee was given to another man who is my father's right hand these days. I loathe the man."

Celia finished the cleaning and helped Maia stack the folded clothes back inside the basket. "I am sorry for Dodd," she said. "He and Suzenne were going to marry."

Maia stared at her in surprise. "Truly?"

"Yes, or so everyone said. They arrived the same year as learners. There was much bantering between them for the first two years. He would give some offense to win her attention, but she would rebuff and deliberately ignore him. When they were old enough to dance around the maypole, he shocked everyone by asking her, though she had widely declared she would refuse him. She did not, and the two danced and became close after that. There was even talk about her Family visiting *his* Family in Forshee Hundred."

Celia lifted the basket and rested it against her hip. "When his Family met their disgrace, things *changed* between them. She stopped walking with him after studies. He passed the maston test, you see, so though he still takes classes, he is not really a learner anymore. He did not know she was a Cipher. It has been painful to watch. He roams the grounds, restless."

"Of course he is restless," Maia said, her heart aching for the young man. He had banished himself to Muirwood. His father and brothers were in Pent Tower, and their lives would be in mortal danger if they did not sign the Act of Submission. What a torture his life had probably become, and if what Celia said was true and Suzenne truly had abandoned him, his pain had to be all the more poignant. That rankled Maia to hear. She had betrayed Collier because the Medium had not provided a way to bring him with her. Every day she spent free reminded her of his confinement.

They left the shelter of the laundry and started back toward the manor house where the washing would be hung to dry. The mist kissed Maia's face as they walked. Sometimes the fog lasted the entire day, but she could make out some brave wisps of blue sky trying to peek through before the sun set.

"He is following us," Celia said, casting a glance over her shoulder.

"He is," Maia said, observing Dodd's stride increase. He wore a dark leather jerkin that covered a cream-colored padded shirt, belted at the waist with a thick, silver-studded leather belt. His hair was dark and unruly, his chin and nose a little pointed. It was a handsome face, but his mournful countenance sullied it.

He caught them without much difficulty and seemed as if he were about to pass them when he seized the basket from Celia's arms instead, hoisting it onto one shoulder with a flexing arm.

"Allow me," he said gallantly, his brooding expression softened by a kind smile. "You walk to the Aldermaston's manor?"

Celia was completely flustered. "Well . . . for certain . . . I see . . ."

"Yes, that is our destination," Maia said, returning his smile. "Thank you."

He walked for several steps without saying anything further, but he did interrupt the silence eventually. "You are Lady Maia."

"I am," Maia replied. "You are Dodleah Price."

"Call me Dodd," he said in an offhand manner. "I have often seen you wander the grounds, but I had then failed to summon the courage to speak with you."

Maia felt a little startled. She glanced at Celia, who had flushed a shade of pink.

"Is that so? Why should you fear to speak to me? We are cousins to degree, after all."

"Notwithstanding, I was afraid you would think it an impertinence," he answered. "Since we have not been introduced. You knew my father, but we have never met."

"There is no need to be so formal, Dodd." She looked him in the eyes so he could read her earnestness. "Do you wish to ask me something? I will not take offense."

He smiled, looking relieved. "Thank you. That does lessen my anxiety. I am normally quite forthright and I like to say what I feel." He frowned, as if swallowing something quite bitter. "A habit of my Family, I fear. Do you think your father will execute my Family if they do not sign the act?"

The question struck her in the pit of her stomach. She flushed with shame. "I do not know," she answered truthfully. "I hate to cause you further pain, but you must understand . . . I do not know my father very well anymore."

"I see," he said, grinding his teeth. "Thank you for being truthful." He sighed, apparently wrestling with himself.

"I hope he will not," Maia continued earnestly, feeling a sharp pang for him. Celia continued to walk alongside them, listening, although she had been struck silent at the approach of the young man.

"I have been chafing here," he said, staring off into the mist as they walked. "Not knowing is the hardest torture. If they were all to be killed, I would prefer to die with them. Part of me says I am a coward for staying here."

"You are not a coward," Maia insisted. "My *father* is the coward for not being brave enough to hear the truth spoken by a trusted ally. But then do not the Aldermastons teach us that men are slow to believe anything that will hurt their feelings?"

"Quite true," Dodd said with an aggrieved chuckle. "To hear you say that about your own father is a balm to my wound. Thank you. I feel a little better."

Maia gave him an awkward smile. "I was there, Dodd. When your father shamed the king publicly. He said nothing more than what everyone felt but was too cowardly to put it into words. Once something is said, it cannot be unsaid, unfortunately. Even if it is true."

"How right you are again," Dodd said with a small chuckle. "You are meek *and* wise, Lady Maia."

"Please, call me Maia," she said, smiling. "So you were stalking the mint flowers waiting for a chance to talk to me?"

"And summoning my courage," he admitted. "I am grateful

that I did. I would have carried the basket regardless. Is ... Suzenne your companion? Have I heard that correctly?"

"She is."

He frowned at that, his look brooding once more. Celia risked a look at him, but she said nothing.

"Why do you scowl?" Maia asked, trying to keep her voice light.

He looked at her with a certain solemnity. If she had not known he had passed the maston test early, she would have guessed he was a man grown already. "Because she abandons you each day," he said with a reproving tone. "I had thought her better than that."

"I gave her leave to see her friends," Maia said, trying to defend her.

"One cannot give a person leave from doing his or her duty," Dodd answered a bit sharply. "But then, perhaps I have my own reasons for judging her harshly. Thank you for speaking with me, Maia. I have wanted to approach you since you arrived, but felt it would be awkward for us both. I was wrong."

It was as obvious as rain that he still harbored deep feelings for Suzenne. Maia could not help but lose respect for her for abandoning such a worthy man due to his ill fortune. She was a proud, pampered girl who had not faced many difficulties in her life. Maia had already noticed her strong tendency for perfection and propriety.

"Someone is coming," Dodd said, slowing as they approached the manor house. Through the mist appeared a young lad, sprinting hard toward them. It was the Aldermaston's page, a boy named Owen. He was a sturdy lad of about fourteen who looked as if he could have worked in the forge with the smiths.

"There," he gasped, running up to them, panting. "Come with me, straightaway. Come quickly, 'fore you are seen! Celia, take the basket inside. I was sent to find you two," he said, looking at

Dodd and Maia. He glanced through the fog behind and around them. Celia looked worried and bit her lip, staring at the basket in Dodd's arms.

"What is it, Owen?" Maia asked, her stomach twisting with concern.

"From Comoros," he said, shaking his head. "Follow me, and I shall tell you all. Riders from the king. They just arrived, I tell you. The Aldermaston said they must leave their swords at the gate or they cannot enter."

"Who, Owen?" Maia pressed. "Who did my father send?"

Owen's eyes darted to Dodd's stern face. "The new Earl of Forshee. With a retinue of thirty men *and* the sheriff of Mendenhall. The Aldermaston told me to bring you to the tunnels so you both cannot be seen. Oh filth, there he is!"

The failure to master anger is the most common one among mastons. It is a wall that prevents the Medium from reaching us. For he that will be angry for anything will be angry for nothing.

—*Richard Syon, Aldermaston of Muirwood Abbey*

CHAPTER SEVEN

Forshee

Maia recognized the badge on the soldier's tunic—the swooping eagle of the Forshee earldom. The soldier approached them through the mist, followed by two others.

"I found him!" the soldier shouted. He had an unkempt beard and a scowling face. "Here is the lad, cavorting with wretcheds. Drop the basket, son. You are coming with us."

Dodd's face went taut with controlled anger. He swung the basket down and handed it to Celia.

"I obey the Aldermaston's summons, not yours," he answered evenly.

"You will *obey* the Earl of Forshee's summons, lad, if you know what is best for you."

"I have sanctuary on these grounds."

The man snorted. "Not for long, cub. We are taking you *to* the

Aldermaston." He stepped closer, his face menacing. "Come freely if you will, or I am just as pleased to drag you. What shall it be?"

Maia's anger kindled at the disrespect being shown to Dodd. Neither of the men saw past her wretched gown.

"I will come," Dodd said.

"Wise choice. Best if we did not shame you in front of the girls. Begone!" he snapped at them. Celia flinched and darted away. Maia followed, her heart pounding fast with fury. By her side was Owen, who wrung his hands and muttered to himself.

"Not fast enough," he said. "I ruined it."

Maia put her hand on his shoulder. "It is not your fault. I am going to the tunnels. Tell the Aldermaston I will be waiting in the antechamber. Where is my grandmother?"

"She is already at the manor."

Maia nodded, walking vigorously. Celia, who had started out ahead, was hard pressed to keep up. "Do you think there will be violence?" Celia asked worriedly.

"I would hope not. Violating an abbey's peace risks summoning its defenses."

"What do you think the soldier meant? He said Dodd would not have sanctuary for long."

"I do not know," Maia replied, her mind whirling with possibilities, none of them good. She parted company with Celia and steered toward the manor house in the fog. There were several other soldiers walking the grounds, but the wretched's dress she wore ensured they also ignored her. As she neared the manor, she heard voices through the mist, but the words were garbled, and she could make no sense of them.

When she reached the manor, she quickly maneuvered through the underground passageway to the anteroom just off the

Aldermaston's personal chambers. As she carefully and quietly climbed the ladder up to the ground floor, she heard raised voices coming from his room. She pushed on the trapdoor cautiously, barely enough to budge it, but it suddenly swung open. Someone above her had pulled it. Her heart leaped with fear before she realized it was her grandmother waiting there, her finger on her mouth in a gesture for silence.

Maia climbed the final rungs, and they set the trapdoor down softly.

"I will not go with you," Dodd's voice declared angrily. "I have chosen refuge in Muirwood, and here will I stay."

"Your decision is foolish," returned another voice, a voice she recognized. The new Earl of Forshee was the one who had driven her out of her father's palace. He was a towering, bearlike man, grizzled in age, and utterly ruthless—loyal only to her father. After seizing the earldom, he had immediately begun to purge all of his predecessors' supporters. She had heard him occasionally referenced as the king's hammer.

"How long have we known each other, Richard Syon?" the earl asked. "Since we were lads?" His voice dripped with malice.

The Aldermaston's reply was devoid of emotion. "We have known each other for the better part of forty years, Kord. We passed the maston test at the same abbey."

"You always wanted to be an Aldermaston," sneered the earl. "You could have been a lord of the realm. A privy councilor. Instead you chose this swampy land and its sulfurous bogs."

There was silence. "I did not choose it, Kord," the Aldermaston said simply. "I answered a call to serve. The court suits your personality better than it ever would mine."

"Ah, Richard. Always so sanctimonious. What a coward you

are. But then you have always been short and fat. I suppose a soldier's life would never have suited you."

"Probably not," the Aldermaston replied humbly.

"Well, hopefully the life of a wayfarer does. I come bearing news from the king."

"Thank you. I see you brought the sheriff of Mendenhall with you. Greetings, Rupert."

"Hello, Aldermaston," came the reply, in a voice devoid of any emotion.

"Will you begin an inquest into Queen Catrin's death?" the Aldermaston asked.

"That is treasonous language," Forshee said with a growl of anger. "The queen, Lady Deorwynn, is in excellent health and awaits the birth of her baby. There was no queen here at Muirwood."

"The ruling from the High Seer was quite clear. The king's marriage to Lady Deorwynn is unlawful."

Maia looked at her grandmother, whose eyes had narrowed as she listened to the argument in the other room. The Aldermaston's voice was perfectly calm and controlled when he spoke next. "Regardless of your politics, it is my feeling that Queen Catrin was murdered. An inquest should be started to determine the facts of the case."

"Whoever murdered the old waif did the king a service," Forshee replied dispassionately. "Are you suggesting the king ordered it?"

Maia's blood raged in her veins and she stiffened. Sensing her discomfort, Sabine put a hand on her arm.

"I did not suggest who the killer might have been or what could have motivated them to act," the Aldermaston said. "My only suggestion was to start an inquest. I assumed that was why you had brought the sheriff."

"You assumed incorrectly, Richard. I tell you, the king and his queen *rejoiced* when your letter arrived. I believe he called for a special dance to mark the occasion. Now that she is dead, there can be no more objections to Lady Deorwynn's queenship and the legitimacy of her heirs. Let me speak plainly, man. I am here on a charge from the king. He commands that the construction of Muirwood commence immediately. I have learned from the dear sheriff, who has discreetly observed the work being done, that the structure is practically finished already. The king and queen intend to celebrate Whitsunday at Muirwood—the most ancient abbey of any realm—and you are to prepare for their arrival a fortnight prior to the celebration. The entire king's court will descend on the abbey, and a tournament will be held. At that occasion, Richard, you will be removed from your office and a *new* Aldermaston will rule."

A stunned silence descended after that statement. Maia saw Sabine flinch, her eyes widening with concern. "He cannot do that," she whispered faintly.

"Speechless. At last!" Forshee sneered. "You will prepare your servants for the arrival of their new master. The king has already made his choice. Aldermaston Kranmir from Augustin. He is, as you know, Lady Deorwynn's uncle. The Crown will be seizing all abbey lands, all wealth appertaining, and revoking the rights of sanctuary. So you see, my young boy, your residence will shortly be moved to Pent Tower, where you will join your lord father and your brothers. And if you do not swear your loyalty to the Act of Submission, you will be executed as a traitor to the realm." This last ended as a growl. "The sheriff of Mendenhall will be staying here until Whitsunday to oversee the final construction of the abbey and to ensure a *smooth transition* to the new Aldermaston. It will be an impressive ceremony, I assure you. The king's lawyers are writing the procedure as we speak. The king will be the one to invest the Aldermaston with the stole of office."

There was another period of silence. "That sounds very interesting," the Aldermaston said. "I wonder what the High Seer will do when she learns of it?"

"The king does not care a shriveled fig what she thinks," Forshee snarled. "He will not allow Pry-Ree to countermand his authority. Our kingdoms have been at peace for many centuries now. If she interferes, you can expect it to awaken the ancient enmity between our kingdoms. I would relish that. Do tell her, Richard. I know you will."

"Thank you for your visit, my lord earl of Forshee. And welcome to Muirwood, Sheriff. It seems we will be seeing more of you. I shall have guest quarters arranged for you on the grounds, if that would be to your liking, or do you plan to stay at one of the marvelous inns in the village?"

"I will be staying on the grounds the entire time," said the sheriff flatly.

"Very well. You are most welcome. Is that all, my lord earl?"

Forshee's voice was low and cruel. "Does nothing provoke you, Richard?"

"Will that be all?" the Aldermaston repeated gently.

Forshee muttered under his breath. "Well, lad, enjoy your misty months at Muirwood. My next errand from the king will not be to your liking. I am summoned to Pent Tower to give your father one last chance to sign the Act of Submission. The headsman is sharpening his axe every day, but I may be inclined to recommend he keep it dull for this one. Good day."

***

When the guests had departed, the Aldermaston gathered his counselors together in his private chambers. They were the same people as before, except Dodd was included instead of Suzenne. He paced nervously as the others took seats around the table, and Maia felt rage in her heart for the injustice being shown to him. She had finally found a place of sanctuary, and her father and Lady Deorwynn were already undermining it.

Jon Tayt's eyes burned with suppressed anger as the news was quickly shared. "I was sorely tempted to loosen one of the shoes of the earl's stallion before he left. Or slit part of the saddle strap. And that was before I knew any of this."

"There is no need for that," Sabine said, her brow furrowed. She sighed. "I am grateful the Medium led me to Muirwood before he arrived. There are only a few months until Whitsunday, and the king has left his spy in our midst."

"I will ride out tonight," Dodd said angrily, still pacing. "While that . . . abominable man is riding for Comoros, I can rally my father's retainers and all those loyal to my Family and summon an army—"

"That is exactly what he is trying to goad you into doing," Sabine said cautiously, shaking her head. "His measured intent was to provoke us into rash action. You can be certain the grounds will be watched. If you were to leave this circle of safety, you would be captured."

He wheeled on her. "How can I sit here and do *nothing*?"

She looked at him with compassion. "Do you trust the Medium?"

His lips quivered with pent-up emotion. "Of course I trust it."

"Do you?" she asked in an even softer voice. "Is that the feeling that compels you to ride north? Or are you listening to your rage?"

His jaw clenched in anguish. "How can I not feel anger, High Seer? He threatens my Family. The king would murder my father for speaking the truth. Is that just?"

Sabine shook her head. "No, it is not just. But we cannot see the end of all things. Only the Medium can. We learn the Medium's will when our hearts are calm, our thoughts untroubled. You must not allow your emotions to rule you, Dodd. Then you will know the Medium's will for you. All of us will die eventually. We must not be afraid to *live*."

She turned her attention to the Aldermaston. "The Medium compels me to leave. It has been weighing on me since I arrived." She reached over and gripped Maia's hand. "As much as I desire to remain here and help tutor my granddaughter for the maston test, I must depart. Aldermaston, the exterior works of the abbey are done. I will need a dozen of the workers to come with me on the *Holk* with spades and shovels."

"Where?" Maia asked in concern.

Sabine shook her head. "I cannot tell you. But I feel its urgency. I must leave you."

Maia felt her heart constrict with pain, but she understood that the news the Earl of Forshee brought had irrevocably changed the situation. Her father had cast out the Dochte Mandar, and now he was putting himself above the order of the mastons. He was becoming like the kings of old who had persecuted and hunted the mastons. Her stomach filled with dread, remembering what had happened to that king, and fervently hoped the Medium would not compel her to do battle with her father. Violence always spawned more violence.

"What would you have us do after you leave?" said Tomas, the steward. He looked as shaken as Maia felt.

"What you have always done," Sabine replied. "All of us must seek the Medium's wisdom in this situation. Jon Tayt, I entrust you with my granddaughter's safety. Right now, her presence here is not commonly known, though it will not remain a secret for long. I have a sense that a confrontation between you and your father is coming, child. He will try to make you sign the Act of Submission. You must not, Maia. One cannot attempt to force the Medium to obey without dire consequences. His decision may trigger a devastating Blight on this kingdom. We must do all that we can to persuade him to abandon this folly. We *must* persuade him."

"You may as well try persuading a stone," Jon Tayt muttered darkly. "He will not heed."

Sabine stood to leave and Maia rose and pulled her grandmother into a tight hug. Their time together had been painfully short, and she already felt the keen edge the absence would bring. At least she could say good-bye. She had lost her mother without having that chance. She still had not resigned herself to it, and the news that her father had celebrated such a tragedy sliced into her already scarred heart.

She glanced over and saw Dodd staring at her intently, his eyes blazing with emotion. She felt the weight of her duties crushing her shoulders, growing heavier moment by moment, like watching a rockslide gain new stones as it tumbled down a hill. How would the descendants of her ancestors feel about the world to which they returned? They would be joining a corrupt kingdom led by her father, a faithless king. Yet it was that or face the armada of the Naestors who sought to destroy them.

She felt Sabine's thumb on her cheekbone, brushing away a stray tear. "You are not alone," Sabine whispered, her voice urgent.

"I do not want you to go," Maia said, a sob threatening to choke her.

Sabine's eyes glistened with tears. She leaned forward and touched her forehead to Maia's. "I do not know what will happen," she said. "My gift of Seering is of the past. Our ancestors faced hard trials like this one. Lia's father knew he was going to die, knew that he would never be able to raise his daughter. He still obeyed the Medium's will." She bit her lip. "Perhaps the Medium will expect us to give our lives to this cause. I do not know, but I do know this. It is scriven in Lia's tome over and over. Trust the Medium. Trust the Medium. Even when the present becomes unbearable." Her fingers tugged gingerly in Maia's hair. "Seek the Medium's will and then do it. I will do *all* that I can to return before Whitsunday. But no matter what happens, you *must* redeem the abbey, Maia. You *must* fulfill the Covenant."

Maia stared into her grandmother's eyes. "I will."

CHAPTER EIGHT

Alone

The cloisters were perfectly quiet as Maia set down her scriving tool and stared, tear-stricken, at what she had just engraved. She experienced a twisted mesh of feelings as she brushed the tiny shards of aurichalcum away. Next to her tome lay her mother's, open to its final sheet, her last entry, the one Maia had just engraved into her own. Blotting her tears on her sleeve, she read the passage again. A passage Catrin had written to her husband.

My most dear lord, king, and husband,

The hour of my death now draws near. The tender love I owe you now forces me, as my illness also compels, to commend myself to you and to remind you of the maston oaths that you made in peril of your immortal soul, which you should regard in higher esteem than the honors of this second life. You have brought many calamities upon yourself, my dear husband. For my part, I pardon you everything. I will not accuse

*you when the Apse Veil is opened at last and we stand in judgment
before the Medium. Remember our daughter, the symbol of our love.
I entreat you most earnestly to restore her to favor and not to punish
her for loving me most faithfully. I entreat you also, lord husband, on
behalf of my maids, they being but three in number. They served me
faithfully. They are wretcheds all. Lastly, I make this vow. That my eyes
desire you above all things.*

> *Yours in truth and honor,*
> *Catrin*

Tears gathered on her lashes as she read the words one last
time, amazed at what a person's heart could endure. Her mother
had been a banished queen in Muirwood for the final part of her
life, but despite Maia's father's inexorable cruelty to her, she had
loved him to her last breath. There was something strong that
bound two hearts together. Love was a power indeed.

She felt her heart begin to burn with the Medium, spreading feelings of warmth and love and sympathy throughout her
body. The words her mother had written had been scribed with
a human hand—a hand of flesh and bone and blood—yet they
seemed to be wreathed in flames. The woman's body was now
resting in an ossuary, a hull. But there was part of her that existed
independently. Maia felt it, almost like a ghostly hand that rested
on her shoulder. The feelings spasmed in her heart, stronger and
more urgent.

Mother, are you here? Maia thought.

There was a scuffle on the steps, and the feeling vanished as if it
had never been. Maia quickly dried her eyes as Suzenne ascended
into the cloisters, her face drawn and pinched with concern.

"I saw your note," Suzenne said. "How long have you been here?

I did not hear you leave." She glanced around the cloisters, looking for signs of disruption.

Maia tried to smile, but her mouth would not cooperate. "I could not sleep, Suzenne. I did not want to wake you."

The Leerings were already lit, and Suzenne rubbed her arms as she walked around the tables, approaching Maia cautiously. There was a small disapproving frown on her face.

"What is it?" Maia asked, summoning her patience.

"You should have woken me," Suzenne said, standing next to her table. "We are not allowed to be alone in the cloisters." She seemed like a queen in state herself, her hair brushed and perfect, her gown washed and pressed. There was always a hint of haughtiness to her, though she tried to conceal it—or so Maia thought.

"I did not know that. I was restless since my grandmother is leaving this morning. We stayed up late talking and I came here to avoid waking you." Maia had also spent a good portion of the night trying to write a letter to her husband to explain herself, her regrets, and the true reason she had abandoned him. But finding the right words had been particularly painful and difficult, and she knew getting a letter to him in a dungeon would be all but impossible, not to mention life threatening, since women were not allowed to read and write. Still, she needed to do this thing—both for him, even if he never got to read it, and for herself. She would work on it again later.

"You have not slept at all?" Suzenne asked, surprised.

Maia shook her head. "I wanted to be alone. And I do not have much time to prepare for the maston test. I learned that my father is coming to Muirwood for Whitsunday."

Suzenne gasped. "Truly?"

"Yes, truly. The entire court will be descending in a few months."

"How do you . . . feel about that?" Suzenne asked.

It was a good question, but one Maia was unwilling—perhaps even unable—to answer truthfully. How *did* she feel about her father? He had done so many ill deeds . . . and a part of her still had to wonder if he had purposefully sent her to Dahomey to become a hetaera. Was it possible to hate and love someone at the same time? Her feelings were a jumbled mess.

"My father does not know I am here," she said, twisting a strand of her hair. "He will not be pleased when he finds out."

An uncomfortable silence descended between them.

"I would think so," Suzenne said, forcing the words out. She looked flustered.

"I am sorry if I worried you," Maia said, hoping to steer them into safer waters. "I did not know about the rules. I will tell the Aldermaston what I did and see if he will grant an exception for me."

"I would not . . . *mind* coming with you," Suzenne said, gazing down at the floor. "Coming earlier to the cloisters, that is. I would enjoy learning from you. I appreciate the Dahomeyjan you practice with me at night. What is that tome you were copying?"

Maia sighed. "It was my mother's."

"Oh." She fell silent again. Her expression was pained. "Maia . . . I heard the Earl of Forshee was here. Do you know if that is true? Was there any word about . . . the prisoners in the tower?" She glanced up at Maia, her emotions clearly at war with her curiosity.

"It is true," Maia said. "And yes, there is news. Why do you ask?"

The look of torture on Suzenne's face was exquisite. Maia could tell she wanted to ask about Dodd's Family, only she did not know how to do so without revealing herself. Maia did not relieve her of her discomfort by volunteering the information. She felt that she owed as much to Dodd.

"One of the learners . . . well . . . not exactly anymore. His father was the former Earl of Forshee. I just wondered if there was any news about his father or brothers."

Suzenne was still trying to mask her interest, but she seemed genuinely concerned—enough so to risk embarrassing herself.

"They will be given one last chance to sign the Act of Submission before they are killed," Maia said flatly, watching for Suzenne's reaction.

"Oh no," Suzenne gasped, her expression crinkling with sorrow. "Poor Dodd."

Maia looked at her in surprise. "You still care for him then?"

Suzenne blinked away tears and covered her mouth. She tried hard to regain her composure, but Maia could see the strength of her feelings slipping free of the mask of indifference. "Yes," she finally gasped. "I always have."

Maia rose from her chair. "Then why did you abandon him?" she asked. Though she did not seek to harm the girl, she could not keep herself from asking. Her own guilt at betraying Collier was sufficient motivation to pry.

Suzenne was miserable. "My parents," she choked. "Oh, Maia! How can I make you understand? After Dodd was disinherited, my parents forbade me to even speak to him. They had been supportive of our . . . relationship . . . I was surprised that they would . . . but what else could I do? Do we not owe obedience to our parents? I trust their judgment. But in this thing . . . I wonder if they are more worried about *their* position in court than they are about *my* feelings." She shook her head, burying her face in her hands.

Now Maia understood. Suzenne was from a well-bred Family, one whose position was answerable to the state of rank. Seeing how far the noble Prices had been cast down, her parents had done what they believed to be in their best interest.

Maia put her arm around Suzenne's shoulders and hugged her as she wept softly, her shoulders convulsing.

"Have you told no one this?" Maia whispered, stroking Suzenne's beautiful hair.

The other girl shook her head with anguish. "I dared not," she gasped. "The girls gossip and murmur and tease. I am sorry to give you yet another burden, Maia. You understand my situation, do you not?"

"All too well," Maia said. "We love our parents, yet we are hurt by them. Loyalty, when divided, is sharper than a blade and cuts both ways." She tipped her chin up. "I will not tell." She observed her closely. "So Dodd does not know how you feel?"

Suzenne shook her head no.

"I see. Well, I can say he suffers as greatly as you do."

There were sounds of approaching girls from the passageway below as the other Ciphers began to arrive.

"We can talk later," Maia said, patting Suzenne's arm. "For now, we must dry our eyes."

Suzenne nodded, smiling. A burden shared was easier to endure. Maia could see the relief spreading across Suzenne's entire countenance. A warm prick of heat came into Maia's heart. She felt more respect for her companion now that she knew the truth.

Maia greeted the younger girls as they entered, unusually chatty considering the early hour, while Suzenne walked around and arranged the chairs into straight rows. Every now and then she dabbed her eyes on her sleeve.

Maeg came in with a gaggle of other girls, all chittering excitedly like little ravenous birds. "You will never guess what I heard!" Maeg said proudly, her eyes bright and gleaming.

"What is that?" Suzenne asked, not facing the other girl as she approached.

"The king and queen are coming for Whitsunday!" Maeg said with obvious delight. "The entire court is descending! Suzenne, is it not wonderful news! This is our last year, our last dance around the maypole. We will not have to suffer smelly blacksmiths or sniveling first-year learners—"

"Or that *fat* hunter!" chimed in another girl with a wicked chuckle.

"Yes, especially not *him*," Maeg said with disdain. "Suzenne, this is perfect! Not only do we have a chance of finding a suitable husband, but likely a position as well! I would *love* to be in Lady Deorwynn's household. I hear all of her ladies-in-waiting wear the finest gowns and are given jewels and perfume. That is where Jayn is serving. Oh, I could just laugh. We could end up together, Suzenne! All three of us again! It would be perfect."

Maia's cheeks flushed, but she kept her back turned so that they would not see her face. Serving Lady Deorwynn was not as glamorous as Maeg made it out to be. Maia knew firsthand of her caprice; she could not bear it if another girl was prettier than her or her daughters, and any spark of spirit was ruthlessly crushed in those who served her. Perhaps Maeg deserved such a fate, but not Suzenne.

"You are not thrilled?" Maeg said with a tone of surprise. "What is wrong, Suzenne? This is the most wonderful thing that could have . . . oh no, I see." The tone suddenly changed and shifted, turning darker. "I see why you are not as excited as I am. Yes, how could I forget. Your new *companion* is the *king's daughter*." She said the words with utter derision.

Maia could hear the girl approaching her and steeled herself to face her petty abuse. She remembered the Aldermaston and how he had faced down the Earl of Forshee with quiet calm and an unflappable manner. And the last words of her mother's letter to her father resounded with her too—after all his ill treatment of her, she had shown him only love. If they could do that, surely she could face one pompous brat.

"Yes," Maeg said, circling around the desk to face Maia directly. "I can see why you are sad. It is pitiable, indeed."

"No, that is not it," Suzenne said, her voice flustered.

Maia lifted her gaze and stared at Maeg calmly, as if she were nothing more annoying than a bothersome fly.

"You should have been born a wretched," Maeg said tightly, her face betraying her animosity at last. "You certainly look the part. You come in here with your airs and your languages and your reading. You look like a wretched. Do you obey orders like one?"

"Maeg," Suzenne said plaintively.

"You may have been the princess once," Maeg said, dropping her voice low. "Used to giving commands and orders. Snap your fingers," she said, snapping her own sharply to add force to the words. "But look at you now."

Suzenne approached and tugged on Maeg's arm. "The Aldermaston's wife is coming," she whispered in an urgent voice. "She will hear you!"

Maeg stared at Maia coldly, her eyes blazing with heat, with power, with the desire to humiliate. Maia had seen such looks before. There were some women in the world who could only grow in their own eyes if they crushed another girl beneath them.

Maia pitied her, truly. Maeg had been born to privilege and groomed as a member of a favorable Family, but she would have to earn her place in the kingdom by manipulating the feelings of her betters. Glory was a tottering ladder to be climbed—one lie and half-truth and well-placed compliment at a time. The higher one ascended the rungs, the more exhilarating and nerve-racking the view . . . and the more devastating the fall.

Not giving in to the taunt, not giving in to the vengeful thoughts, not surrendering to the goading . . . Maia discovered a reservoir of power inside her, a calm placid lake that was undisturbed. The Medium soothed the hurt as she looked away from Maeg and slowly took her seat.

There was an expression of satisfaction in Maeg's eyes—she had wanted to see Maia humbled and speechless, though she clearly did not understand her reasons for not reacting. Maia saw the other girls staring at Maeg in horror and fear. Yes, they were all afraid of her turning her claws on them next. Maeg strutted through the class, found her place, and sat there primly and elegantly, as if she were the queen of the world. Maia smiled to herself and shook her head, picturing the other girl atop that trembling ladder.

Suzenne sat down next to Maia, her cheeks flushed. "I am sorry," she whispered.

Maia felt nothing but serenity. Maeg's barbs were too dull to stick inside her.

The Aldermaston's wife mounted the steps and entered. The girls were restless with the energy of the impending news. Their eyes hungered for word of the changes coming.

Maia said nothing, knowing already that the Aldermaston's wife would tell them very little.

"Girls, we have a new guest staying at the abbey. He arrived last night. The sheriff of Mendenhall will be spending the winter with us until Whitsunday. He will be monitoring the progress of the work on the abbey before the arrival of the king and queen." Her eyes were very serious. "Celia."

All the girls looked startled. The wretched's face grew grave. "Yes?"

"You will be assigned to wash the sheriff's clothes. You will also go through any correspondence he gets from court. Memorize it and report what you learn to the Aldermaston. That is your assignment. The others will support you in any way you see fit."

Her voice was stern and iron hard as she stared at each girl in turn. "Many of you will be assigned to serve different households when the court arrives. The fate of the kingdom will be decided before the year is out. This may be the end of the Ciphers or the beginning of your usefulness to the Medium's will."

As I have studied the tomes of the ages, I have discerned that our behavior flows from three main sources. Desire. Emotion. Knowledge. Is it not the sign of a true maston when all three are harmonized? When they are, great power comes from the Medium to aid us.

—Richard Syon, Aldermaston of Muirwood Abbey

CHAPTER NINE

Guilt

When she was younger, Maia had enjoyed her music lessons the most. There was an inherent magic in creating music, in coaxing sounds from different instruments, freeing the peculiar possibilities of each. At Muirwood Abbey, she found that portion of the instruction to be the most disappointing, if only because Maeg made each lesson her own personal performance.

Since their confrontation in the cloisters before dawn, Maeg's callousness and spite had only bloomed with the rising of the sun. Though Maia had continued to ignore her barbed attacks, it had only made them worse. Maia waited with painful anticipation for the studies to end, especially the dreaded music session, so that she could wander the grounds and try to scrub the ill thoughts from her mind like one would attempt to wash smoke fumes from a garment.

The time ended and Maia put away her lute, pausing to stroke the curved bowl fondly, wishing she could disappear with it back into her room. There was still a little blue in the sky outside, but the sun was setting earlier and earlier as winter set in, providing less time to wander the grounds after lessons.

Maeg finished a beautiful string of chords on the harp—her favorite instrument—and some of the girls tittered words of praise. Hoping to escape before she was seen, Maia moved quickly toward the door.

She was not quick enough.

After being praised by one of the younger girls, Maeg lifted her voice mockingly, "Well, I may not have been born a *king's daughter*, but I did learn to play from my mama. She was excellent at the harp. I was not showered with gifts as a babe like Maia, given the best instructors from Paeiz or Dahomey. What a waste. Fleeing so soon, Maia? Off to scrub clothes again with Celia? You really *are* a wretched."

Maia ignored her, not even looking at her, and fled the room into the afternoon air, trying to subdue pangs of loneliness and anger as her feet padded on the soft grass. The air smelled like rain and the sky was full of brooding clouds, beginning to turn orange in the dimming light. She *was* going to find Celia, it was true, but how did Maeg know? Maia had not realized anyone had witnessed her helping the other girl. Another thing to be used to torment her. She shook her head and sighed, but what she heard next stopped her in her tracks.

It was Suzenne's voice.

"Stop it, Maeg. Stop it! How can you say such things?" Her voice was full of scolding and pent-up emotion, and the words trembled as they came out of her mouth. Maia blinked with shocked surprise. "Maia deserves our compassion, not scorn. You have tormented her since she arrived. Enough! It is not right with the Medium to treat someone this way, especially to strike a girl who you know has decided not to strike back. It is cowardice, Maeg. Stop it. We are the oldest and should set the example."

To Maia's surprise, Suzenne came marching out of the music room, her cheeks livid with emotion, moving so fast she almost collided with Maia. She took Maia's arm in hers and started to march across the green, her eyes flaming with passion, anger, and defiance.

"I am so *sorry*, Maia," Suzenne said, the words tumbling out of her mouth in a rush.

"It is all right, Suzenne. I do not let her taunts stick in me."

"No, I am sorry for not having defended you the day you arrived," Suzenne said, shaking her head. "I have been a terrible companion. I have abandoned you; I have stayed silent *too* long. This is not what we are taught in the tomes." She squeezed Maia's arm, her voice dropping lower as the reality of what she had done seemed to finally work its way into her mind. "I do not care how she treats me because of this. She is a vengeful girl, and no one likes to be insulted in public. But I could not bear it another moment, not when you are always so patient and kind. You talk and listen to Davi and Aloia in the kitchen. You even draw out shy Thewliss, who does not usually speak to anyone save his wife! You are truly a princess, Maia, regardless of what your father says or has done to you. I admire you and I am even envious of you." Suzenne looked into her face, her eyes bright with tears. "You carry so many troubles, yet you cared about mine and sought to comfort me this morning. It has been a fishhook wriggling in my heart all day." She swallowed, her look pleading. "I lost my best friend a year ago when she left the abbey. Her name is Jayn Sexton and she serves Lady Deorwynn now. She is miserable in her position because Lady Deorwynn is much like Maeg. She does not have a friend in the world. And neither do I." She looked down. "And the more I thought about it, the more I realized that you are truly alone too." She stopped, tears dripping down her cheeks. "We must be companions, Maia, but I would be your friend too, if you would let me."

Maia was shocked by the girl's words and the raw need they awoke inside of her. She saw the sincerity in Suzenne's eyes and knew she was a girl who did not change her opinions easily, that she had consciously made a stand by scolding Maeg—one that would earn her the girl's enmity.

Tears pricked Maia's eyes. "I would," she whispered thickly and hugged Suzenne.

The two smiled as they wept together, and suddenly the clouds above them did not look nearly so oppressive. The sunset, when it came, was glorious.

***

The clouds glowed with the warmth of the fading light, turning orange and pink and a thousand dappled hues as Maia and Suzenne walked together in her mother's garden. They talked and listened, sharing the first intimacies of friendship with the knowledge that whatever they said would be kept a treasured secret.

Maia explained the troubles of her parents' marriage: how the stillborn births following her birth had poisoned her father against her mother; how Chancellor Walraven had used his kystrel to tame their feelings instead of letting the couple learn to work through the sadness and comfort each other. She talked about her years in Pry-Ree as the heir apparent, of making decisions in her father's name and learning the intricate dance of politics and negotiations between kingdoms. Suzenne's grandfather had once been part of the Privy Council to Maia's grandfather when he was king, so she had knowledge of her own about the political world.

The conversation then went on to Maia's banishment and disinheritance, though Maia spent only a little time talking about her horrible time living in the attic of Lady Shilton's manor and the torment she experienced there. Although she did not share all the details, what she did say affected Suzenne greatly and she had hugged Maia, soothing many unspoken hurts.

Finally, Maia explained about her father sending her to Dahomey to seek out the lost abbey. She had described getting the kystrel and what it felt like to use one, especially in comparison to the sensation of being surrounded by the Medium at Muirwood. The difference was so stark she wondered how she had ever been confused, but Suzenne explained that in big cities like Comoros, it was always more difficult to feel the Medium, which abhorred human suffering. Maia talked about the protector her father had assigned her, the kishion who had been sent to watch over her and even to kill her if necessary to prevent her from being captured. She spoke vaguely about her journey through Dahomey, only mentioning that she had managed to escape after being abducted by the king.

She did not reveal the truth about their marriage, feeling the friendship was still too new for her to share such an intimate secret. As it was, thoughts of Collier haunted her sleep and made her worry during the day. She dreaded meeting him again, dreaded seeing the accusatory look in his eyes. Yet she desperately wished for a way to explain herself to him. She still labored over perfecting her letter to him.

They walked arm in arm away from the garden, watching in the distance as Thewliss pushed a cart of tools back toward the kitchen. They followed in his wake slowly, their heads bent low in conversation.

"I understand you much better now," Suzenne said, smiling with genuine affection. "I will admit I have been harboring fears.

I knew the Aldermaston trusted you. I knew your grandmother was the High Seer and that if *she* trusted you, so should I. But I worried that during the night, you might talk in your sleep or groan or make noises that would frighten me."

"You did?" Maia asked, smiling. "My nightmares ended when my grandmother saved me. I fear they will return once I leave the abbey." Her look hardened. "I must prepare myself in case they do."

"Then I will go with you," Suzenne said, patting her arm. "The men you traveled with. You could not be your true self with them. I know your secret; although a binding sigil prevents us from talking about the particulars, it is enough. I am grateful the Aldermaston trusted me. Thank you for sharing what you did."

"I have never had a friend before," Maia said. "I am sorry you had to lose one to gain one."

Suzenne shook her mane of golden hair. "The only true friend I have had is Jayn Sexton. With her, I could share my secrets. I have been cordial and respectful to Maeg, but that is all. She honors me because of my rank."

"And your beauty," Maia said, nudging her.

Suzenne smiled demurely. "My father once said that beauty is a test that most fail. He said his Aldermaston once taught him that the most unhappy couples he ever knew were the handsomest pairs."

"Is that so?" Maia said, laughing softly.

"Indeed. Things come easier to those with beauty. Respect and attention are more freely given. Is that respect earned? Is that attention worthy? Often not. No, my father said to be plain is more of a blessing, though I could tell, as my father, he was proud of me. But he always praised me for my character, not my accomplishments. I love my father deeply. He is very wise and once served faithfully as one of the king's advisors. Your story about your own father's cruelty cuts me to the quick. I should not have behaved as well as you did, I think."

"Thank you," Maia said. As they drew closer to the kitchen, Maia heard someone call out her name from the shadows of a looming oak tree. She recognized the voice instantly. It was Dodd Price. Suzenne's body went rigid next to hers.

"Yes?" she answered, stopping.

"I was looking for you after the music lesson," he said, approaching them. He nodded briefly to Suzenne, his mouth quirking into a smile. "I heard about the rebuke you gave Maeg, Suzenne. Well done." He turned his gaze back to her. "Maia, I need your help."

"What is it?" She could hear the sound of pots clanging and the voices of the two kitchen helpers streaming out from the small building. Thewliss finished stowing his cart and walked through the kitchen doors, doffing his cap and nodding briefly to Maia and Suzenne. The light and smells caused her stomach to growl.

"I will not detain you long," Dodd said, glancing at the door, "but I was hoping you would introduce me to your hunter tomorrow?"

"He is the abbey's hunter now," Maia said.

Dodd shook his head. "They call him Maia's hunter. He arrived with you, and everyone knows he is here to protect you. I wish to speak to him. Will you do it?"

"Of course," Maia said, "but what do you wish to speak to him about?"

"He has been spending every day in the Bearden Muir with his hound. I want him to take me with him. To show me the land."

"Why, Dodd?" Maia pressed.

Though he attempted to conceal it with a smile, she could tell Dodd was nervous. "Because I may need to leave rather suddenly."

"No!"

It was Suzenne who had gasped it. He looked at her, his brows furrowing.

Maia squeezed her arm. "You are worried about your father and your brothers," Maia said firmly.

"Of course I am," he answered. "I may be the only one who can save them."

"Do not leave," Suzenne said, her face flushing. "Dogs bark to frighten the hare into running. That is when they snatch it."

"Am I a hare?" he snapped, sounding offended.

Maia keenly felt the awkwardness of the situation. Part of her wanted to save Suzenne and Dodd from an embarrassing moment, but she felt she should hold back. The two had not spoken to each other since Suzenne's parents had ordered her to spurn him. Defying her parents was not something she was used to doing.

"I did not intend it to sound that way," Suzenne said, her voice trembling. "What I meant was that they are attempting to frighten you into action. Never do something out of fear. That is not the way of the Medium."

"Now you are lecturing me about the Medium?" he said with a choked breath. Maia could almost hear his thoughts—part of him was straining to tell her that *he* was the one who had passed the maston test already. He did not say it.

"I was just trying to remind you," she said imploringly.

"Thank you," he said flatly. "Maia, will you help me?"

"I will talk to him," she answered, keeping her tone neutral. She agreed with Suzenne and did not think it wise to leave the grounds in a hurry. "Meet me by the laundry after studies tomorrow. I will arrange it if I can."

"Thank you," he told her, with much more warmth. He gave Suzenne a confused look, then wandered back into the darkness, muttering something under his breath they were not meant to hear.

The iron grip from Suzenne's hands finally loosened. There would be bruises.

"What did I do," Suzenne said miserably, "beyond making everything even worse?"

Maia patted her hand, feeling the blood beginning to return to her fingers. "You must come too. I think the two of you are overdue a long talk," she said.

The look of pain in Suzenne's face convinced Maia she was right.

CHAPTER TEN

Resentment

The wind tossed their hair as Maia and Suzenne left their learner studies. The air had a pungent smell of soggy leaves and wet grass. The ground was a bit mushy as they tramped together toward the laundry, moving through the brisk and cutting wind.

"If I was ever under the sway of delusion before," Suzenne said with a low voice, "it is over now. Maeg will have her revenge and today was just the first taste of it."

"I am sorry," Maia said, trying to comfort her.

"Do not apologize," Suzenne responded. "I have seen the lengths she has gone to belittle others. I have never been the recipient before. Did you see how quickly Clara stepped in to fill the void? I suspect she has hated me for some time."

Maia patted her arm, brushing away the strands of hair that blew in front of her nose. It had rained earlier in the day, but thankfully the rain had paused before the studies were over.

"My stepsisters are like that," Maia said. "Ignoring them is the best possible remedy. Though the snubbing smarts."

"I do not regret speaking up. The truth is, my stomach is a hive of bees right now, and not because of Maeg and Clara." She sighed sharply. "I do not know what I am going to say to him."

"Jon Tayt is really friendly. He is easy to talk to."

Suzenne butted her with an elbow. "You *know* that is not who I meant."

"Oh, you mean Dodd? The young man watching us over there?"

"Is he? Oh, Maia, why am I so nervous?" Her voice wrenched with dread.

The young man stepped away from the shelter of an oak and approached them through the squishy grass, his boots spraying flecks of water. He really was handsome, his tawny brown hair a little damp from the wet. He looked about as uncomfortable as Suzenne, his expression a mixture of anguish and delight.

"Hello, Dodd," Maia greeted.

He nodded to her, but his eyes were on Suzenne's face. "Hello," he said softly. "Are you unwell?"

"I am well enough," she replied, flushing darkly.

"You wanted to see Jon Tayt," Maia said, steering them across the grounds toward the hunter's lodge. "The clouds look as if they might burst any moment. We had best hurry."

"Of course," Dodd replied, falling in next to them. He deliberately walked alongside Suzenne.

The silence between them was fraught with unspoken emotion. "How is your Family?" he finally asked her. "Is your sister ready to become a learner?"

Suzenne looked at him sharply. "You remembered."

"I knew there was a gap between your ages. Is she going to study at Muirwood as well?"

"Yes," Suzenne replied. "I love this abbey. It is like home to me. I will be sad to leave it . . . after Whitsunday."

The words added another jolt of tension to the moment.

"Yes, I may be leaving as well from the look of things," he said angrily. "Potentially in chains."

Suzenne bit her lip. "I am sorry, I did not mean to—"

"Of course not," he interrupted. "Maybe I should leave the abbey before I am compelled to do so. This is not a home to me. It is a prison." He raked his fingers through his tousled hair. "The moors oppress me, but perhaps I will grow to like them. In the past, when the king's army was defeated at Winterrowd, soldiers skulked in the Bearden Muir for months. Perhaps I shall do that, if Jon Tayt will teach me. I can live off skunks and weeds." He chuckled tonelessly.

Suzenne frowned, her forehead furrowing. "Do you really think the abbey's sanctuary will be revoked? Surely the High Seer will do something."

"What can she do?" Dodd said. "No offense, Maia, but your grandmother does not have an army at her command."

"Armies are not the only way to change things," Maia said softly.

"But they are the *one* sure way," he answered stiffly. "Did not Winterrowd change the destiny of men and kings? The mastons did not just lie down and die that day . . . they rallied under Garen Demont, and not a single man who fought with them was killed. Would that I had been there."

Maia could see the restlessness teeming inside of him. He was weary of biding his time, of waiting for outside events to dictate the course of his life. She could see the impetuousness of his character, his hunger for action.

Suzenne, on the other hand, looked increasingly worried by his rash words, his hunger to fight. As she walked alongside him, her fingers knotted together and he fidgeted.

Maia gave Dodd a probing look. "You have trained to be a soldier?" she asked.

"I have trained with the sword," he answered, his tone ruffled. "My older brothers sparred with me."

"But do you know anything of military tactics or of how to provision soldiers? Soldiers who do not eat do not fight."

"Well, no, but I have read stories about armies in the tomes. I think if I left Muirwood and went to Forshee, many would rally to me as they did to Garen Demont."

Maia shook her head. "But Garen Demont was a seasoned battle commander, was he not? He had fought with his father at Maseve. During his exile, he fought in foreign wars. People rallied to him because he knew what he was doing."

"Are you calling me a fool then?" he challenged.

"Of course not, Dodd. I am seeing if you are speaking with your heart or with your head. Before you lead men to their deaths, you must first exhaust all other options. War should be a last resort."

She could tell Dodd was not taking her words kindly, but she could not regret them. "So you are saying," he said through clenched teeth, "that we must continue to submit to your father's authority, even if he breaks all oaths and covenants?"

They were approaching the hunter's lodging now. It was a comfortable little dwelling nestled in a grove of oak trees with a pen nearby to house horses. As they advanced, they could hear the sharp crack of an axe splitting wood. A paltry drizzle of smoke came from the chimney atop the thick thatched roof.

"You have no confidence in me," Dodd said petulantly as they neared the dwelling.

Maia stopped and faced him. "Please do not say that," she said, touching his arm. "I have sympathy for your situation, Dodd. Truly I do. Remember that I was there when your father spoke up to mine. Although what he said was true, your father may, even now, regret acting so rashly. If you are going to confront a king with his armies, his vast treasury, and his anointing, it should be done from a position of strength. Even Garen Demont was surprised by how quickly the king summoned an army to repel his invasion. There is wisdom in counseling with others who are on your side. Do not feel as if you have to act alone."

Dodd just nodded, seemingly at a loss for words, and Maia led them around the side of the dwelling. They found Jon Tayt standing amidst a huge pile of split lumber, his face glistening with sweat. The axe swept down again, a powerful stroke that shattered the log and sent fragments clattering in all directions.

Argus was nestled by the hut, and when Maia and the others came into view, the boarhound leaped up and charged Maia with frantic wags of its tail. She dropped to her knees and embraced the dog, fending off its pink tongue as best she could.

"*Chut*, Argus!" Jon Tayt growled in jest. "She is *not* your master. I am!" He flicked his meaty wrist and effortlessly stuck the axe blade into the splitting stump. "By Cheshu, you are spoiling the dratted beast! Every time you leave, lass, I have to kick him repeatedly to earn his respect again and keep him from pining after you. Ungrateful cur."

Maia went up and hugged the sweaty hunter, ignoring the reek. He had bits of bark in his beard and his retreating copper locks were damp with perspiration too. He mopped his forehead on a red scarf and stuffed it back into his belt.

"I got your message; now which of these two needs my advice?" he asked Maia, shoulder to shoulder with her and sizing up Dodd and Suzenne. "*Ach,* do not they look like a pair of forlorn lovebirds. *Druwy un glust ac druwy relall.* Advice most needed is the least heeded, as they say in Pry-Ree."

Dodd and Suzenne both went scarlet with mortification.

"Never mind my jesting," Jon Tayt said, breaking into a grin. "I know you did not come here for lessons in love. I, a sworn bachelor, would be poorly officed to help you with that. It was the lad you wanted me to speak with, Lady Maia?"

"Yes," she said, scratching behind Argus's ears as he sat dutifully next to her, panting.

"Well, we talk as we work," Jon Tayt said. He plucked the axe from the stump and tossed it to Dodd, who caught it in surprise. Jon Tayt sniffed and walked over, pulling up another round of wood and dropping it on the stump. "Go ahead, lad. Break it up."

Dodd stared at the hunter in amazement, hefting the axe awkwardly in his hands. "You want me to cut wood?"

"By Cheshu, do you have wax in your ears? There are chores to be done! Break it in half. Go, lad. The wood will not cut itself." He dug his thumbs into his wide belt and watched as Dodd approached the round. Gripping the axe, the younger man moved around the stump and then stopped in front of it, standing with feet apace, and hefted the axe over his head.

"That is not the proper stance," Jon Tayt said, waving at him. "You will knock yourself over. Feet apart this way, one in *front* of the other. You are going to use your legs, your hips, your shoulders, *and* your arms. Starts in your back foot over there." He walked up to Dodd and adjusted his hips to show him how to grip the axe. Dodd looked uncomfortable, obviously unused to such work, as he corrected his stance.

"Now, you are going to try and aim the blade here," Jon Tayt said, pointing to the base of the block. "You do not aim for the top of it. You want the blow to go all the way through it. Start the swing way back. Then up and over your head. Every muscle goes into it. Big wide swing. Give it a go, lad."

Jon Tayt stepped back and gestured surreptitiously for Maia and Suzenne to step aside.

Dodd gripped the axe hard, his face pinched and serious, and swung back. The axe flew backward from his hands and clattered into the woodpile.

Jon Tayt wiped his face, grimacing. "You hold onto the *haft*, lad."

"I know," Dodd said heatedly, stalking over and fetching it. Even his ears were pink with shame. He came back, took the stance, and then brought the axe wheeling down. Maia startled, just slightly, as the blade clove the round in half with a crack like thunder.

"Good swing. Now fetch the pieces, one at a time."

Dodd was frowning with impatience and frustration as he quickly planted one of the halves on the stump. He stepped back, checked himself, and split it with a powerful stroke, the pieces flying away like startled rabbits.

"Smaller," Jon Tayt guided. Dodd complied and soon the round had been reduced to a small stack of kindling.

"And why are you two standing there?" Jon Tayt said to the girls. "Do you not see the wood littering the ground? You must not have failed to notice that stack over by the side of the lodge. Get to it!"

As they started to collect the fragments of wood, Maia saw the confusion and surprise on Suzenne's face. She was delicate in lifting each piece and Maia could see she was very uncomfortable with doing physical work. Maia had long been a servant, and her wretched's gown was loose about the arms and wrists, making it easy to maneuver. She was able to grab several fragments into a bundle and move the pieces much faster than Suzenne could.

A drop of rain splashed on Maia's nose. She stared up at the darkening sky, and soon the rain began pelting them. It was not a gentle drizzle, but a rumbling downpour. The wind began to keen through the trees. Argus padded over to the grass and lay down, his fur soon soaked through.

"Did I tell you to stop cutting?" Jon Tayt said, annoyed. "It is only a little rain, and the work must be done. Another!"

Maia smiled at the determined look on Dodd's face as he mopped the rain from his eyes and went back to the block. He started to work in earnest, bringing down the axe in powerful, confident strokes and splitting the logs into pieces that Maia and Suzenne then fetched and stacked.

"Our gowns are ruined," Suzenne complained, staring at her sopping sleeves and bedraggled hair. Though Maia was equally soaked, the physical work made her feel alive. A part of her reveled in the dampness of her hair and freshness of the rain.

"It is only water," Maia said, lifting her face to the sky and feeling the rain on her nose and cheeks.

Suzenne did not look convinced, but after a while she got into the rhythm of the work. Jon Tayt showed them how to stack the wood properly, of course, since he was an expert in all things. Despite being wet from nose to tail, Argus looked tranquil in their company, and his tail wagged contentedly. They had built up quite a pile of wood when Maia noticed Suzenne staring at Dodd. He had doffed his tunic and his padded shirt was soaked through, the sleeves bunched up at his elbows. His hair was sticking to his neck and he looked as if he were enjoying himself.

"You two run along," Jon Tayt said in Maia's ear. "A little work is good for the soul. He will be more open to what I have to say to him now. Go on with your friend."

"Thank you," Maia answered, patting his shoulder. She gestured for Suzenne to follow. Her friend looked torn between the prospect of staying behind to talk to Dodd and getting into dry clothes, but she nodded after a moment and took Maia's arm.

The cold was beginning to intensify with the setting sun and the chill wind, so they clung to each other as they walked back to the Aldermaston's manor. The grounds had been abandoned in the storm, and it was just the two of them, sloshing in the mud and grass as they wound their way back to shelter.

"I have never been this wet or cold," Suzenne said, her teeth chattering. "But was that not . . . exciting?"

"I enjoyed it," Maia said. "It is not as cold as a blizzard, I can assure you of that."

"You are so brave," Suzenne said, shaking her soggy tresses. "I did not think he would make us work in the rain."

Maia patted her arm. "Yet we command our helpers to do it," she said. "As if their discomfort is a lesser evil than ours."

"I will remember that the next time I ask Celia to do the washing," Suzenne said. "Should we go to the kitchen first? What will Collett say if we arrive like this?"

"Thewliss will say nothing, of course," Maia teased.

"I know, he never speaks." Suzenne laughed. "Who is that?" she asked, looking ahead.

A figure had emerged from the gloom, a tall man wearing a dripping mantle that covered him almost completely. He was walking toward them from the kitchen.

"Do you recognize him?" Maia asked, her stomach knotting with concern.

The hooded figure approached them, and as he drew near, Maia recognized him as the sheriff of Mendenhall. She frowned.

He stopped in front of them, his face sallow and scrutinizing. He had cunning eyes, a goatee, and a long hook nose. She remembered from her first morning with the Ciphers that Maeg was his daughter. The thought made her uneasy.

"You are quite soaked through, girls," he said solicitously. "I hardly recognized you, Lady Clarencieux."

"We were caught in the storm," Suzenne said, trying to look presentable and failing. Her face wilted with mortification.

"Best to get indoors," he advised. "You must have wandered far to have gotten so wet." His tone was measured and nuanced. "I would advise you, young ladies, not to wander off the grounds. It is easy to get . . . lost."

"Thank you, my lord," Suzenne said, flushing.

He nodded and was about to leave, but he paused and took a close look at Maia. "I thought you were my daughter's companion, Lady Clarencieux. It seems you have a new one?"

Maia's insides shriveled with dread as she awaited Suzenne's response. The sheriff had not addressed her directly, which was not unusual given that she was clothed in a wretched's gown.

"Yes, the Aldermaston made the change," Suzenne said. "Good evening." She tugged on Maia's arm and pulled her toward the kitchen door.

How much more grievous are the consequences of anger than the causes of it. A single word, spoken in enmity, can scar a heart for a lifetime.

—Richard Syon, Aldermaston of Muirwood Abbey

CHAPTER ELEVEN

Gallows

E ven your shift is wet," Suzenne said to Maia, nodding to the wet clothes hanging from the hooks by the fire Leering. "Here, take this instead of your nightgown if you are ready to get out of the bath. You can sleep in it tonight." She offered her a white chemise of the softest fabric, one of several Suzenne had stored in her trunk.

Suzenne had already bathed, and her hair was freshly combed but still damp. The fire in the hearth licked with greedy tongues and the entire room was cozy and warm, smelling of the fragrant soaps and bath salts Suzenne had provided for their use. Maia had not felt so luxurious in years, and she tried to stifle the little pricks of envy that needled her heart. Suzenne's Family had provided for her. Her wardrobe was bursting with gowns and slippers and shoes, and she had a locked jewelry box on the table.

"That is very kind," Maia said thoughtfully. "Would you hand me the blanket to dry myself?"

Suzenne draped the blanket around Maia's shoulders as she stepped out of the tub. The rush matting underfoot was soggy and damp. Cinching the blanket around herself, Maia turned to thank Suzenne. Her friend's eyes were wide, her nostrils tightened with fear. She had seen the brand from the serpent Leering. Hot with shame, Maia tightened the blanket around her body and took the proffered chemise without saying a word, disappearing behind the changing screen to put it on.

There was a knock at the door, and Suzenne answered it while Maia changed. The two girls from the kitchen bubbled in, their voices chattering away.

"It is warm as the bread ovens in here," said Aloia. "We should bake a loaf or two by the fire. Here is your supper."

"Thank you," Suzenne said.

"I will carry it, my lady. Do not fret yourself. Over on the table? Come, Davi, carry the pitcher of cider."

"I *am* carrying it," Davi replied, halting and catching herself. The cider sloshed. "Move! I almost spilled it."

"You are so clumsy," Aloia said, holding the door wide.

"You are so slow. Move on!"

The smell of trencher bread and stew filled the room, making Maia's mouth water. She finished adjusting the strings on the chemise and emerged from around the changing screen. The two girls were jostling each other with the tray and pitcher, but they beamed when they saw her.

"Can we have another story?" Aloia asked imploringly.

"She has not eaten yet!" Davi said, stamping her foot. "Tomorrow. Be patient."

"I am not very patient," Aloia confessed. "Tomorrow, then?"

Maia nodded. "Thank you for bringing it in the rain," she said, noticing the wet spots on their cloaks.

"It was no trouble," Davi said. The girls curtsied and scurried back through the door, which Suzenne locked behind them.

Maia longed for her warm dinner, but her hair was tangled and damp and she knew she should comb it first. She walked to the stand where Suzenne kept the combs.

"Let me help you," Suzenne offered. "It will go faster, and then we can both eat together."

Maia was especially touched by the friendly gesture considering Suzenne's reaction to seeing the hetaera's mark. "Yes, thank you." They each took a comb and started working through Maia's dark tresses. Unbidden, a memory flooded inside of her, of warm hands and a comb. A creaking ship. The smell of him, standing behind her, fingers gliding through her hair. His face came unbidden to her mind, the scar on his cheek, his dark hair and blue eyes. Collier. Feelings came with the memory—confusing, painful, yet they caused a warmth inside her as well. Some part of her core was burning.

"What are you thinking of?" Suzenne asked, combing through another strand.

Maia had not realized her arms had stopped moving and that she was just sitting there, letting Suzenne do all the work.

"Forgive me," Maia said, quickly resuming. "I was lost in a memory."

"What of?"

She cringed, wondering how much she should reveal. Their friendship was still very new, and she was not yet ready to share such a treasured memory. To do so would make it less hers. "When I sailed to Naess, I was promised more than a kingdom if I would yield my . . . my mind. Yet yielding that would mean yielding my body, my actions, even my sense of self." She sighed. "It was tempting, Suzenne. I was used to wearing rags and was offered the chance to be the empress of all the kingdoms." She looked down at her hands. "I am ashamed at how tempting it was. I did keep the earrings, though. Just to remember why I left." They were also a reminder of something else . . . *someone* else, but Maia was not ready to speak of that.

Suzenne was quiet, thoughtful. Her effort with the comb quickly loosened the tangles. "I had noticed the pretty earrings and wondered about them. We are all ashamed to feel the lure of power and beauty. Do not the tomes teach us that the Myriad Ones tempt us with their thoughts? That they invite us and entice us to yield to them? The same words are also used by the mastons to describe the Medium. It also invites us and entices us. But to different ends."

"It is true," Maia said, increasing the vigor of her brushing.

"I am proud of you," Suzenne said, her voice sincere. "For the *choice* you made. We may be ashamed of feeling swayed by such things, but we need only be ashamed of our choices. There is power in choice." She paused, wriggling loose a stubborn clump. "I feel changed after standing up to Maeg. I am the same person, but I feel different inside."

"Persecuted?"

"Quite the opposite. I feel self-worth. I know Maeg will make me suffer. That is who she is. She cannot help herself, just as Celia cannot help being so kindhearted. Or you, Maia, cannot help being wise. I respect you a great deal."

Maia felt a flush of pleasure, but it did little to contain her guilt. She did not deserve praise. Had things gone differently, she would have become a monster, a terror to all the kingdoms. The thought made her shudder.

"Are you cold?"

"No," Maia answered softly. She turned in the chair and looked up at Suzenne. "Are you . . . afraid of me?"

Suzenne bit her lip. "You saw me staring."

Maia nodded. "I am not angry. You can speak the truth."

"I know I can," Suzenne said, putting her hand on Maia's shoulder. Her *right* shoulder. "I do not wish to hurt your feelings."

Maia smiled. "Believe me, many women a thousand times more provoking than you have deliberately sought to injure me. You are not of that kind, Suzenne. Be honest."

"I am a little fearful," Suzenne said. "I thought at first that the Aldermaston chose me as your companion to keep a watchful eye over you. To warn him in case you began to . . . slip. But I have observed your actions, Maia, and I know you to be thoughtful, meek, and quite accomplished. There is much *I* can learn from *you*, which wounds my pride a little. Only a little," she added teasingly. "I had almost forgotten that you were a . . ." Her mouth suddenly twisted, as if she were in pain. "I forgot, I cannot speak it. The binding sigil has frozen my lips. When I saw the mark on your shoulder, a *feeling* came over me. I do not know how to describe it, but it was not a good feeling. Not a proper feeling. I was almost . . . jealous of you. It is a symbol of great power, Maia."

"It is," Maia responded, her thoughts darkening. "If there were any possible way to be rid of it . . ." She sighed. "But the Aldermaston and my grandmother say it cannot be undone."

"You are safe from the curse while you are at the abbey," Suzenne said. "Must you always stay here? Is that the only way you can be protected?"

Maia shook her head. "No, if I pass the maston test, I will be permitted to wear the chaen. The chaen will help protect me from the influence of the Myriad Ones. If I were to leave the abbey without one, I would have no such protection. So while they hope I am strong enough in the Medium to reopen the Apse Veil, I must also pass the maston test to protect myself."

"I know it *must* happen before Whitsunday, but will it be soon?"

"I do not think so," Maia said. "I have been meeting with the Aldermaston often. He feels impressed by the Medium that I need longer to prepare myself. It is still too near to the time when the Myriad Ones had sway over me. I must first . . . distance myself from them, both physically and in my thoughts. He says they will test me again. The Myriad Ones do not relinquish their prey willingly."

"He is wise," Suzenne said thoughtfully. "Some people are afraid to speak to him. His eyes . . . it is as if he can see through to your very soul. I always feel at least a little guilty when I talk with him."

"You need not," Maia said, squeezing Suzenne's hand. "He is the most gentle, mild soul I have ever met. Even with the Earl of Forshee railing on him, he did not flinch, did not raise his voice. The man is absolutely immune to anger."

"The stew is getting cold," Suzenne said, setting down the comb.

They sat at the small table they shared and began to devour the tasty stew and warm trencher bread. After their efforts stacking wood, Maia had certainly worked up an appetite. They ate in silence, savoring the flavors and the warmth of the hearth. Maia watched as Suzenne's damp hair quickly dried in proximity to the heat. She was a beautiful girl, but her looks were only accentuated by her kind soul and her genuine wish not to harm anyone. So different from Maeg's beauty.

"Tell me about Maeg," Maia asked, breaking off another hunk of crust. "She is the daughter of the sheriff of Mendenhall, is she not? I thought the Aldermaston's wife had said as much when I first met the Ciphers."

"She is," Suzenne answered. "Her father does not know she is a Cipher."

"Truly?"

"Indeed," Suzenne answered with conviction. "The sheriffs of Mendenhall have all been loyal to the Aldermaston for generations. But Maeg's father was installed a few years ago after your mother was banished. He was her jailor, so to speak, and he visited often to make sure she was still here and not running amok elsewhere in the kingdom."

"How do you know Maeg keeps it secret from her father?" Maia asked.

Suzenne smiled. "She has boasted of it often enough," she answered. "She is training to be a courtier. She and I both were, which is why we were chosen as companions. Only our mothers know we can read and engrave. Both of them were Ciphers too."

Maia nodded. "So there is a strong tradition of secrecy then. That is good. I worry that she may tell just to spite you."

Suzenne shook her head. "She would not do that. Not in a world that slaughters its daughters for daring to read. I have been told that I must not even tell my future husband."

"You mean Dodd?" Maia asked playfully.

Suzenne went crimson with embarrassment. "I do not yet know . . . whom I will marry." She gazed down at her hands.

"But you love him?" Maia asked softly.

"I cannot answer that," Suzenne whispered.

"Why not?"

"My parents have . . . they have forbidden me . . ."

Maia shook her head. "I did not ask what they had commanded you do. I only asked for your feelings. It does not take great wit or imagination to see it, Suzenne. You love him."

The look of painful misery on Suzenne's face said it all. Her voice was strained with anguish. "I will not say it. Words have meaning and power if you say them. I have never *told* anyone what I feel."

Maia reached over and grasped Suzenne's hand, reminded of the proverb she had read recently in the tomes. *We often want one thing and pray for another, not telling the truth even to ourselves.*

"I will not say it," Suzenne repeated with determination.

"I will coax you no further," Maia replied.

"And what of you?" Suzenne said, shifting the burden back on her. "I know your father has forbidden you to marry. Will you defy him?"

It was only fair for her friend to make her blush in return. "Mine will be a political match, I think," she said softly, looking down.

"Were you not promised to the heir of Dahomey when you were little?" Suzenne pressed. "I remember hearing there was an alliance of some sort long ago. He was a baby. I think we were born the same year, if I recall. Prince Gideon."

Feint Collier, Maia wanted to correct her. She sighed and leaned away from the table. "Yes, we were betrothed as infants."

"Did you ever meet him? I know your father eventually abandoned the suit."

"Yes, it was abandoned long ago," Maia said, the memories beginning to churn and foam in her heart. She remembered awakening from a trance to find herself kneeling in front of a wooden altar, swearing before a Dochte Mandar that she would become the King of Dahomey's wife. She was, she realized, ostensibly still the Queen of Dahomey—a fact that made her cringe.

"Did you meet him?" Suzenne pressed.

Maia was saved from having to answer when a firm knock sounded on the door. Eager to escape her friend's relentless questioning, she lurched to her feet and hurried to open the door. In the hallway beyond were the Aldermaston and his wife.

"Good evening," Maia stammered, still feeling a little flushed.

"A quick word with you both," the Aldermaston said in a kindly voice that was at odds with his expression. He looked so solemn and grave.

Maia backed away from the door to give them room to enter. Suzenne rose from the table and quickly fetched a shawl to cover her shoulders, even though the room was stifling. Maia sent a thought to the Leering and damped down the flames. She felt awkward meeting the Aldermaston in her nightclothes, but nothing could be done about it now.

The Aldermaston's wife closed the door.

"What is it?" Maia asked, feeling her stomach twist with anxiety.

"Ill news came on the heels of this storm," the Aldermaston said, his voice deep and unworried. "I wanted you to know instantly, Marciana, and it is appropriate for your companion to know as well. Please sit."

Maia was too nervous to sit, but she obeyed him and joined Suzenne back at the table. Dread had driven away their earlier frivolity.

"We received word from Comoros," the Aldermaston continued, "that your mother, the queen, is to be interred here at Muirwood in a simple ossuary and with no ceremony. The sheriff of Mendenhall is to observe the service and no one else is permitted to attend." His voice was so tender. "The sheriff made inquiries about Suzenne's new companion today and pressed me for information about you. I think the rain and wet made it more difficult for him to recognize you. Be on your guard. He is cunning and persistent. He seeks to curry favor with your father by being dutiful to his orders."

Maia's heart panged. "So I cannot attend my mother's interment?"

The Aldermaston shook his head no. "It would not be wise to reveal your presence at Muirwood too soon, my dear."

"There is more," the Aldermaston's wife said. She gave Suzenne a sad look. "The sheriff received word today from Comoros. Celia told us this afternoon after finding the letter. One of Dodleah Price's brothers attempted to escape Pent Tower. It was the eldest, Tobias, who had not seen his newborn babe. He was caught before he could leave the city and executed on the tower green in front of his father and the rest of his brothers." Her voice strained with emotion. "The sheriff was given orders to account for Dodleah's presence here at Muirwood daily. He was instructed to watch vigilantly for news of the pending executions of the rest of the Prices. If Dodleah attempts to flee, he is to be hunted and killed on the spot."

Suzenne's face went white as her chemise. "Oh, no," she breathed, her face twisting with grief. She covered her mouth to stifle a sob.

The Aldermaston turned to Maia, his face a composed mask. His voice dropped even further. "There is also news from Hautland that the King of Dahomey was captured and is being held for ransom. One hundred and fifty thousand marks. It is said the amount would more than deplete Dahomey's treasury. It exceeds the ransom requested when his father was captured in Paeiz."

Maia's heart sank. One hundred and fifty thousand marks. It was her fault that he had gone to Naess in the first place; his ship had taken her there. She remembered the look of desperation on his face as he had pleaded with her not to double-cross him.

"Maia, do not betray me. Forget my other promises. I should have asked for this one first. I was too afraid to ask. The hetaera always betray those they love. Do not love me then. I could not bear it if you betrayed me . . ."

This settled it. Collier would never forgive her.

CHAPTER TWELVE

Kishion's Threat

It was anticipated that on the day of the execution there would be snow, but it was a mild winter's morning, all blue sky and icy air—the kind of day where children would be flinging clumps of slushy ice at each other under normal conditions. Instead, they had assembled on the green to watch men die.

It was cold enough that Lady Deorwynn's nose stung, but she had layered herself in thick velvets and a heavy mantle to ward off the chill. The mantle had cost five hundred marks and was exquisitely designed, with gold stitching woven throughout, a costly fur lining around the fringe, and tiny glittering gemstones that flashed when the light struck them just so. She wore silver fox-fur gloves, and though the jewels around her throat, ears, and wrists were unseen, she felt them. Their presence reassured her.

Murer stood next to her, dressed in a flattering gown that showed off her trim figure. That gown had nearly cost two thousand marks. Instead of a large cape and hood that would have hidden her immaculate dress, she wore a fox-fur shawl that she had let down around her shoulders, revealing the twisting curls of her elegant hair. The effect was somewhat ruined by her constant fidgeting.

"Be still, Murer," Lady Deorwynn chided.

"I do not understand why we even need be here," Murer said sullenly. "I pray I shall not *faint*."

"That is the very reason. You must show strength and courage. These men are traitors to your lord father."

"My lord *step*father," Murer whined under her breath.

"Be silent!" Lady Deorwynn sidled up closer to her daughter, her voice dropping low and dangerous. "Some words are not to be toyed with, Murer. You must get that into your head. Our Family has never been as vulnerable as it is right now. Crabwell is undermining me with the king. The earls are starting to show their teeth. I must show *them* who has sharper teeth!"

"But it is so cold. I thought this shawl would do."

"You should have thought of that before coming out in the snow like that. By the Blood, Daughter, you can be such a fool."

She watched Murer's cheeks flush, and not from the chill, and the girl's eyes burned with anger and resentment. Lady Deorwynn hated to reprimand her girls in public, but truly she wondered if neither of them had inherited her wits. By the time she was Murer's age, she had already accomplished some grand schemes.

"Where is Father?" Murer asked after a while, searching the assembled nobles. "Oh, there he is. With *Jayn*."

Her tone grated on Lady Deorwynn's already fragile nerves. She cast a surreptitious glance and her blood began to seethe. She blinked, trying to keep her expression neutral, but her thoughts were black with rage. On the day of his enemies' execution, the king was flirting with one of his wife's ladies-in-waiting. She gritted her teeth, trying to stop herself from storming over and banishing the interloper to the darkest nights of Naess. She knew her husband had a wandering eye. He was a *man*; he could not help himself. She had hired Jayn Sexton after dismissing the last girl who had attracted him, hoping a woman as young as his daughter would be less of a temptation.

It was Jayn's own shy coyness that probably appealed to him—in a world where there were so many courtiers seeking his notice, she had achieved it by not seeking it at all. There was a studied innocence in her youthful expression, but she was a girl with secrets. Lady Deorwynn had recognized that too late. Well, she would ferret them out.

"Who do you think Father will choose to be my husband?" Murer asked, disrupting her chafing thoughts. "Now that all the Price boys will be put down, that is. I had my heart set on Gates, but he will die. I had hoped to persuade Father to let me entreat for his life. He would have been so grateful."

"You are truly a fool," Lady Deorwynn said testily. "As I have told you before, you will not marry one of the nobles of Comoros. You are a princess, Murer."

"But cannot a princess pardon someone who is at fault? Why could I not pardon Gates?"

"A princess does not have that power. Are you really so naïve? No, I see by your smirk you are toying with me. You get pleasure from vexing me."

"Not at all, Mother," Murer said, leaning over to kiss her cheek. "So who is my husband to be?"

"Your lord father is considering Dahomey, to divert their attention from war."

Murer furrowed her brow. "But the king is being held prisoner! If he pays the ransom, he will be penniless!"

"Yes, and all the more pliable as an ally if your father provides you with a generous marriage portion. Money persuades people, Murer. Surely you have not forgotten that lesson. Marks are seeds that produce prosperity."

Which was why, she realized, she was at such odds with Crabwell. The chancellor's aim was to seize all the wealth of the abbeys for the Crown. There was no telling how much coin was being wasted on the frivolous reconstruction of the abbeys. Each one cost a sizable ransom! But Lady Deorwynn knew that men were best kept in check when *their* wealth was connected to the success of their ruler. The men of Comoros would grow resentful if her husband accumulated the rewards for himself. Resentment turned into disloyalty, which turned into treason. Much better to buy the people's good faith with ample land grants, manor houses, ranks, and privileges. Then, periodically, topple one of the nobles who fell out of favor and give his rewards to another. Surely that was the best way to keep men in check. Crabwell disagreed. As a greedy man himself, he wanted control of the finances in the king's name.

Lady Deorwynn rubbed her swollen abdomen. Surely part of her worry was a result of the pregnancy. It had always been an awkward time for her. Her moods shifted mercurially. Her ankles were fat, her cheeks a little puffy. She was used to the sway she normally had over her husband, and seeing him fawn over a child infuriated her.

She watched as the king patted Jayn's hand. A sharp spasm of jealousy shot through Lady Deorwynn. The Sexton Family was a rising one, a Family who sought greater prominence in the affairs of the realm. Did they really think they would prosper by dangling their daughter in front of her husband in such a manner? Did they not realize that so many favors and bequests came as a result of *her* influence on the king's mind? There were so many powerful, headstrong men in this kingdom, but all of them were blind. A woman ruled them, and they did not even know it. Men *needed* to be ruled.

The gates of the tower creaked and groaned loudly, and a hush fell over the snow-strewn grounds. Murer ceased her fidgeting, and the king ceased his flirting. An ominous stillness filled the air, marred by the squeaky axles of the cart being used to transport the condemned.

Lady Deorwynn tried to suppress a look of triumph as the cart rumbled past the royal entourage. The crowd silently parted, making way for it to pass. There was the aged earl, his scowl evident even at a distance. He stood erect, proud, and defiant as a Price would. He had watched his son die with grim solemnity. Even after the execution, he had refused to sign the Act of Submission. This was the moment the realm needed to see. It would force the rest to submit. For if the Price Family fell . . . what chance did they have?

Some whispered that the Medium would save him, that it always preserved valued mastons. What rubbish and nonsense. History was replete with examples that proved the theory false. The Medium did *not* save mastons. It served only those who compelled it to serve. It delivered to them their most intense thoughts and desires. It had delivered the King of Comoros into her bed. It had made her the queen of the realm.

The only thing it had not delivered to her—yet—was her accursed stepdaughter, Maia. It was only a matter of time.

"It is so quiet," Murer whispered.

Lady Deorwynn wanted to smack her. The cart reached the edge of the gallows, and the Price sons and father were escorted to the scaffold, where the headsman awaited them. They had watched their eldest son and brother murdered on that very spot. Nothing had saved him—not their prayers or their faith or his maston chaen.

Only the father was allowed to speak. He stood on the gallows, his arms hanging limp at his sides. He wore a thin shirt, despite the cold, and his breeches were scuffed and dirty from his long confinement. Lady Deorwynn could see the glint of the chaen peeking from his collar. Her mind wandered to his youngest boy, Dodleah, who was sniveling and hiding in Muirwood. She wondered how long it would take before he learned of the death of his Family. Once he did, she was certain he would be quick to leave his sanctuary and join them in an early grave.

Finally the old man was done. Lady Deorwynn was sick of his little speech, although she had listened to but little of it. She was anxious to be inside again where it was warm. The babe inside her squirmed anxiously, as if it too could feel the danger. Would it be another son? Or a daughter?

The father was brought to the block, his sons standing by gravely. Was one of them weeping? None of them flinched. The father knelt in front of the block. Lady Deorwynn wondered if someone would need to restrain him, but he faced his death with courage and dignity. He had blathered something about the Apse Veils, so perhaps he did not believe this to be the end.

Lady Deorwynn's attention shifted to the executioner. He was hooded, of course. They all were. But there was something familiar about him. The one who had executed Tobias Price had had a beard, but this one had naught but a little stubble about the chin. He was sturdy and strong, and he held the axe comfortably, with confidence. The angle of his shoulders drew her eye. How she loved sturdy men. She admired the presence and power of a man who could steady a cart, lift something heavy, or duel with a blade. She had always been drawn to such men, though she had never indulged in the temptation to surround herself with them.

The headsman reminded her of someone. Yes, she knew it

now. He reminded her of the kishion. The very thought of him sent shivers of fear down to the soles of her feet. When one murders for a living, it puts one beyond the sentimentalities of normal people. The kishion was not a man to be controlled, which terrified her.

The headsman was looking at her.

A growing realization filled her heart with dread. It *was* the kishion. He stood there, staring at her, holding the axe meaningfully, as if he meant to threaten *her* with it. *It will be your turn soon*, he seemed to whisper in the silence. Lady Deorwynn began to tremble.

"Are you cold, Mother?" Murer asked.

He had not visited her since the night he had infiltrated her bedchamber. Every time she thought back on it, she shuddered with dread. Despite her guards, despite her power, he had slipped into her private chambers as quiet as a shadow and delivered an ultimatum to her. Restore Maia to the king's favor or else suffer the consequences. How could Lady Deorwynn do that when no one even knew where the girl was? She had her spies searching for Maia constantly. The ship had never returned from Dahomey, though the kishion had been with her and had vouchsafed that she had survived the cursed lands.

The father of the Price clan knelt in front of the block.

"This is a horrid practice," Murer whispered. "I hate watching. Why do we have to watch?"

"To prove we are strong. To prove we are not cowards. Do not shame me, Murer."

The eldest Price laid his head down. The stroke was swift and sure. There was an audible sigh from the crowd. With their father having set an example of courage, his sons could do no less. Each faced the block without shrinking. Lady Deorwynn had to credit them with that.

Chancellor Crabwell had a little speech prepared. As soon as he finished, it would be over. He stood from the podium where the nobles sat.

"Thus is the fate of traitors to the realm," Crabwell said in a booming voice. "Let no man or woman defy the king's will and live. Fix the heads to the tower spikes as a warning to others!"

Lady Deorwynn frowned. Why had he added the part about women? No woman had ever been executed for treason before, so what could Crabwell mean by saying that? She looked to her husband and saw him comforting Jayn Sexton, who seemed to be weeping quietly. His arm was around her shoulder! Lady Deorwynn clenched her fists in seething rage. The girl had not even been a lady-in-waiting for a year. If she were dismissed, it would send a signal to the other girls. Yet she had the irrational suspicion that if she did dismiss Jayn, her husband might countermand her. That would be intolerably humiliating.

"So much blood," Murer whispered, staring at the scene with wide eyes and a haunted look. "So much."

Ashy flakes of snow began to fall, startling Lady Deorwynn. The sky had been so clear moments before, but now it was gray and veiled. The snow came down in thick sheets, silent yet substantial—a benediction on the event.

"Can we go now?" Murer asked, and Lady Deorwynn turned without answering and approached her husband. He offered her his arm, having the courtesy to look a little guilty.

Later that evening, she found a bucket on the table in her bedchamber. A red cloth was stuffed in it. It was so strange and curious, she unthinkingly reached inside and lifted the rag. Only then did she realize it was soaked in blood. The earl's head was nestled beneath it.

It took all her strength of will not to scream.

It is said the greatest remedy for anger is delay. For mastons who cannot restrain their anger will wish undone what their temper and irritation prompted them to do.

—Richard Syon, Aldermaston of Muirwood Abbey

CHAPTER THIRTEEN

Winterrowd

The earth in her mother's garden was hard and thick like frozen clay, and Maia worked her muscles hard to get the harrower to break it up. Suzenne knelt beside her, fingers stained with dirt, her gown covered with an apron just as Maia's was. The breath came out of their mouths in a mist as they continued to work in the bone-aching cold. Maia wiped her itchy cheek on the back of her hand and looked up as Thewliss clomped up with an armful of small black buckets.

"These will grow in winter?" Suzenne asked him, gazing at the sheet of snow covering everything in the garden.

"Um-hum," Thewliss grunted, still shy to speak. He nodded in satisfaction at their razing of the flower beds and proceeded to pull tufts of roots and stubs from the buckets.

"What are those plants?" Maia asked, watching as he gently detached the roots. She had visited Thewliss in her mother's garden several times. Each time she tried to coax him out further.

"Cyclamens and winter heath," he said shortly. His nose was bright and pink and his snowy drooping mustache fluttered as he spoke. "They are pretty."

"Did my mother like them?" Maia asked, feeling a stab of pain in her heart. The interment of her mother's body was happening at that very moment in another part of the grounds. Her bones would lie at rest in an ossuary and be buried in the cemetery.

"She did," Thewliss replied softly. His eyes were shy and reserved, yet full of compassion. "She liked . . . to help plant things too. You remind me of her." A timid smile flickered across his face.

Maia felt tears well in her eyes, and she reached over and gripped his dirty hand in her own. Sensing her mood, Suzenne reached out and touched her shoulder.

"What else do you plant in winter?" Suzenne asked the old gardener.

"Quite a few things," Thewliss said, easing his hand away and deftly planting the roots in the freshly churned earth. "Leeks, garlic, onions, asparagus . . ." He sniffed and brushed his nose on his sleeve. "Asparagus . . . I already said that one . . . cabbage. Parsnips too. Those are good. Sometimes peas. Winter lettuce." He sniffed again. "You can always plant something." Then he fell quiet as they worked together to plant the flowers.

After finishing, Maia thanked him for allowing them to help. He turned pink with embarrassment, as he always did when thanked or given a compliment. He stared at her for a moment, his eyes blinking, looking like he wanted to say something but could not find the words.

Maia was about to leave, feeling overwhelmed by the heaviness of her loss. She needed a good cry, she decided, and it would be better to go away and do it secretly, but something in Thewliss's eyes forbade her to leave.

"Do you miss my mother too?" she asked him.

His eyes were red-rimmed. He took off his cap and crushed it in his hands, his snowy hair spilling about his head. He nodded vigorously.

Maia sighed and put her hand on his shoulder. "You are a good man, Thewliss. You built her a wonderful garden. I am sure it helped her bear the loneliness. Thank you."

A tear trickled down his cheek. He looked down at his muddy boots, shifting uncomfortably. Then he pulled off his dirty gloves and stuffed them in his belt, reached into one of his pockets and withdrew a linen napkin. At first she thought he was going to blow his nose on it, but he handled it as delicately as he had the fragile roots. He slowly unfolded it and she saw it was an embroidered kerchief. He handed it to Maia.

"What is this?" she asked, taking it. Each corner was decorated with a design of little flowers and vines. It was beautifully wrought, intricate and lovely. Maia stared at the tiny flowers. "Did my mother . . . ?"

Thewliss nodded. "Never dared wipe my nose on it," he mumbled. He stared her in the eyes. "You can have it."

Maia held it like a relic, her amazement too great for words. Her mother had fashioned this small gift of affection and appreciation for the aging gardener. It was his only reminder of her mother. The way he had handled it showed it was his greatest treasure.

"I cannot take this," Maia said huskily. "It is yours. She gave me something that I have treasured. Her tome. That is treasure enough. This was made for you, for a tender gardener." She folded it reverently and then put it back in his hand. She wanted to kiss his snowy brow, an instinctual act, but she caught herself, realizing that to do so would be as grievous as murder.

She could never, ever kiss anyone again. Something about this simple moment—the innocent impulse that might have led to disaster—brought the harsh reality of her situation home to her. Her grandmother's words echoed through her head: *Your kiss would be fatal to your husband or even your children.*

She took Suzenne's arm, and together they left Thewliss in the Queen's Garden and started off across the grounds together, their shoes crunching in the fresh snow. Maia's feet were cold, and she longed to be in the shelter of their room.

"Thewliss was chatty today," Suzenne said, her tone teasing.

Maia sniffed and nodded, trying to let her friend cheer her, trying not to drown in her thoughts. The regret in her heart was as heavy as a cold iron anvil. She could never be rid of it permanently; she could only move it from corner to corner.

"I cannot imagine how you are feeling," Suzenne said, squeezing her middle. "Today was going to be hard, no matter what."

"I know," Maia said. "That is why I thought about helping Thewliss in the garden. The work was helpful, but it stirs memories. The knave sheriff of Mendenhall gets to attend my mother's funeral and I cannot. Some things are just not fair, are they?"

"Indeed not. Do you want to go warm ourselves by the Leering in our room? Maybe we can help someone else so you can keep your mind off it? Look, there is Celia."

Maia was impressed by how much Suzenne had changed in so short a time. She had stopped wearing her jewelry and fancy gowns so much, choosing instead to favor high-quality garments of the plainer variety. She had offered many times to let Maia wear her gowns, but Maia felt it was important to maintain her disguise as a wretched.

"She is crying," Suzenne said, her voice concerned.

When Maia looked closer, she saw Celia kneeling by the laundry trough, her face buried in her hands, and her shoulders were shaking.

"Celia, what is wrong?" Maia asked, wondering if Maeg had been rude to her again. She looked up when she heard their voices and almost ran to them.

The girl was trembling with emotion. "Oh, Maia, Suzenne! My heart is breaking." Tears streamed down her cheeks. Maia gave her a fierce hug, trying to calm her.

"I just read the sheriff's latest messages from the Crown." She swallowed, hiccupping. "I must tell the Aldermaston and his wife, but they are overseeing the interment ceremony." She tried drying her eyes on her sleeve. "Poor Dodd! Poor Dodd!" She broke down weeping again.

"Celia, what is it? What has happened?" Suzenne implored with new urgency, squeezing the other girl's arm. "Tell us!"

Celia sniffled, trying to master herself. "I thought . . . *hic* . . . that during the ceremony would be a good time. No one was around. I read the messages." She sniffled. "Suzenne, the Prices have been executed. All of the men. The father first of all. Dodd is the only son left, and he is the youngest. I thought . . . I truly thought the Medium would prevent this from happening." Her shoulders shook again as fresh tears spilled out. "Why would the Medium let them die?"

Maia's pain at losing her mother was overshadowed at that moment by the gravity of Dodd's loss. The ache of it made her gasp and her mind spun with tortured rage. Her *father* had done it. Her *father* had executed so many innocent men, guilty of no crime but the so-called treason of refusing to abandon their consciences at his command. How could a maston do such a thing? This was murder. There was nothing else to call it.

Suzenne was weeping as well, covering her mouth with her hand as she always did when she was upset. Her eyes radiated absolute misery.

"We must tell Dodd," Suzenne gasped. "Maia, we must tell him before the sheriff does!"

"We cannot," Maia argued in despair. "How will we say we learned of it? We cannot betray the secret."

Suzenne shook her head. "This is too painful. He must know! Celia, you must tell the Aldermaston straightaway. He must know at once!"

"I will wait for him in his study," Celia said, nodding and hurrying away.

Maia and Suzenne clung to each other as they walked aimlessly through the snow, both too upset to decide where to go or what to do. Maia stared up at Muirwood Abbey—still hidden beneath a shell of scaffolding—her heart burning in her chest. How could the Medium have forsaken them? What did it want them to do? She had learned to listen for its frail whispers, but at the moment she was too upset. One of the lessons the Aldermaston had taught her again and again was that anger masked the feelings of the Medium.

The silence of the wintry grounds was disturbed by the sound of an axe splitting wood. She tugged on Suzenne's arm and started for Jon Tayt's lodge, wanting to tell him the news so he would keep his eye on Dodd. The two had become friends, and Maia knew that Dodd had taken a liking to the hunter and valued his counsel.

"I am heartsick," Suzenne said, shaking her head. "When a dog goes mad, one puts it down. But what do you do to a king?" She stared at Maia desperately. "We have enemies aplenty, kingdoms that want to invade our realm and rob our wealth. If we do not stand united, Comoros will fall like ancient Pry-Ree. Oh Maia, do you think the Blight will come now?"

"I do not know," Maia said, feeling a devastating conflict churn within her. Her father was the king. If he were to fall, then Lady Deorwynn and her brood would rule.

Rebellion.

The thought twisted in her mind, dangling in front of her like sharp daggers. In the long-ago past, a wayward king who murdered mastons had been defeated on a field called Winterrowd. Was there a Garen Demont they could call upon now—a leader of men who had been banished to another realm? No, there was not. But there was her husband, the King of Dahomey. And he was festering in a dungeon in Naess, betrayed by his own wife.

They rounded the end of the lodge as another piece of oak shattered into kindling. She expected to see Jon Tayt swinging the cleaving axe, but the hunter was nowhere to be seen. It was Dodd, his tunic cast aside, his padded shirt open at the collar, exposing the glint of his chaen. He had a look of murderous rage on his face as he kicked away the scraps of wood and hefted another thick round on the block. He grabbed the axe again, his arm and neck muscles bulging as he swept it over and around, splitting the log in a jagged line.

They both knew at once that Dodd already knew, and Suzenne gasped at the sight of him. His mouth was tightened in an animal snarl, his teeth exposed and clenched together. Hate blazed on his face. Trickles of sweat trailed down his cheeks as he stepped back and swung the axe again, a loud crack echoing in the small clearing.

One of the standing pieces of wood tottered and he kicked it off, then stuck the axe blade into the stump and went for another round of wood.

"I see you have heard too," he snarled, grunting as he lifted the heavy round. He twisted the axe free and stepped back. His face scrunched with fury as he swung the blade down again, the wood splitting into pieces, the loud thunder of it echoing.

"My brothers are all dead," Dodd said, moving another piece into view. "My father is dead. My mother is a widow. And I . . . I am the greatest coward-maston who ever walked Comoros." Another crack of thunder as pieces of wood clattered about.

"No, Dodd," Maia said. "You are not a coward."

He stared at her, eyes lit with wild rage, gripping the axe as if choking it. "Do not coddle me, Maia. I can bear the truth. I am a coward and a fool. If I were a man, I would have Jon Tayt use this axe against me and then send my head to the king's table, just as my father's head was delivered to the false queen's. I *hate* your father, Maia. I *hate* him more than I have hated anything other than my own self." His cheeks quivered. "I should have left Muirwood. Why did I stay here so long!" He flung the axe aside and it landed in the snow with a hiss.

Maia knew there was nothing she could say to calm or comfort him. In this moment, in his red streak of rage, he probably saw her as being complicit in her father's crimes.

"You are not a coward, Dodleah Price," Suzenne said angrily. Tears streaked down her cheeks as she marched up to him. "You never wanted to be a soldier. Your older brothers did. Your ambition was to be an Aldermaston someday. And I admired you for it. You came to Muirwood because you wanted to study under the best Aldermaston of the realm. The kindest, most thoughtful man in the whole world. You can feel the Medium's whispers better than anyone I have ever known. *I* am the coward, Dodd! I abandoned you because my parents were worried the king would despise us if I were to marry you." She started sobbing, but she struggled through her tears to speak her words. "You are the kindest, wisest, most patient man I have ever known. And

I left you, abandoned you—disappointed you when you needed me most." She swallowed. "I am the coward, Dodd. But I have found my courage at last. Forgive me for deserting you. I will not desert you now. Dodd, I *love* you!"

Maia's heart burned at the unexpected, beautiful words, and she stared at her friend with mute amazement. The look of transformation on Dodd's face was like the metamorphosis of a butterfly. He stared at her, eyes wide with shock. His mouth parted, too dumbstruck to speak.

Suzenne marched up and hit him in the chest with her fists. "Say something!" she begged him, her brow bending with worry.

Maia watched as Dodd seized her in his arms and crushed his mouth against hers. It was a hungry kiss, a greedy kiss, and Maia's heart twisted with jealousy watching it, watching them cling to each other like two drowning souls—a release she herself could never have. She was so happy for them, she wept. But the tears hurt.

Dodd pulled back to stare into Suzenne's face, using his thumbs to brush away her tears. "You truly mean it?" he gasped in disbelief.

"Yes, you fool!" Suzenne cried with bittersweet joy. "Now please tell me you still care for me as well. I am fit to burst . . . or . . . box your ears!"

"How can you not know?" Dodd said with a tortured sigh. "I have *always* loved you. My heart has *always* been faithful to you."

"He says it *at last*," Suzenne drawled, shaking her mane of golden hair and pulling him into a hug so tight it had to hurt.

Dodd pulled away, his look brooding and a little accusing. "What about your parents? Will you push me away again if they object?"

Suzenne shook her head vehemently, imploring him with her look. "Listening to them has been my utmost regret. I will defy them if I must, but perhaps seeing me suffer has made them soften. Let me prove my loyalty to you."

"I forgive you. Let us never speak of it again." Then, pulling her into his embrace, he nestled his cheek against her hair and they held each other, swaying. Maia stood quietly, transfixed by the achingly sweet moment.

"Do not leave," Suzenne murmured. "It is death if you leave."

"As you command me, my lady." He stroked her hair. "I was going to summon the courage to murder a king. I am sorry, Maia. In my heart, I believe he deserves to be slain."

"Not by your hand," Maia replied softly.

Suzenne dipped her head against his chest. "Whitsunday," she said.

"What?" Dodd asked.

"We will marry on Whitsunday."

He pulled away, staring at her as if she had uttered the most sacred of words. "Your parents?"

She nodded. "That is when I will tell them. And nothing they say or do will alter my decision. If the king is displeased with me, then I will claim sanctuary here as well. Maia and I will pass the maston test together soon." She reached up and touched his lips. "Whitsunday."

CHAPTER FOURTEEN

Chancellor Crabwell

I t terrified Maia how quickly the season turned. One moment, the earth was hard and frozen and spikes of ice clung from the eaves of the abbey's kitchen. The deepest part of winter was like a stifled breath, a gasp, and then—it was spring. Her father was coming. The Apse Veil was still closed, and the Aldermaston did not yet feel she was prepared for the maston rites. Every day she stalked the grounds, visiting the promontory and looking for signs of the *Holk*'s return. She missed her grandmother and worried for her safety.

The skeletal branches of the Cider Orchard were now white with blossoms, not snow. It was a beautiful sight, and she loved roaming the grounds with Suzenne and Dodd. Their relationship had deepened since the tragedy, but they always welcomed her to join them on their jaunts, including her warmly and openly. It was a little painful, watching them squeeze each other's hands as they strolled the apple orchard. She imagined what it would be like to walk that way with Collier, to wander the grounds alongside him, holding his hand. Still, she was happy for them, happy for something so good to have come out of so much pain.

One spring day, they were out for one of their walks in the Cider Orchard. Maia was listening to the chirping larks and the drone of bees as she looked at the abbey. The scaffolding had all been removed, and only the interior work continued. The spires reached high enough to pierce the huge cotton clouds above it.

"I have given some thought to something," Dodd said in a low voice.

"It is always dangerous when a man thinks too hard," Suzenne replied, nudging him.

"I know—I start getting ideas and who knows where they will lead. If the king succeeds in revoking the sanctuary of Muirwood, this will be a haven no longer. I think we should flee to Pry-Ree, to Tintern. Jon Tayt has shown me several ways to escape the abbey grounds unnoticed—"

"I do not speak Pry-rian!" Suzenne interrupted, looking concerned at the thought of sneaking into the Bearden Muir.

"But Maia does. Surely your grandmother would grant us exile. I could get us there safely. Jon Tayt has taught me much about surviving in the woods and hiding our trail."

Maia nodded and ducked beneath a low-hanging branch full of blossoms. "He has taught me as well. And I have no doubt we would find sanctuary in Pry-Ree if we sought it. But I hope my grandmother returns soon. I do not think she will surrender the authority of the abbey willingly."

"Do you expect to see her?" Suzenne asked.

"I expect it every day, but she is delayed for some reason, and we have heard nothing still. There is much she must do, being the High Seer . . . especially now. But I cannot see this ending any other way than in a confrontation with my father, and I believe with all my heart she will return in time."

"I hope it does not come to that," Suzenne said worriedly. "Comoros has a nasty heritage of civil war. Why must we feud so?"

Dodd sniffed. "You know very well, my love. You cannot rule a kingdom through fear alone. When people stop being afraid, they become angry. I am grateful I did not pursue my revenge, but though patience is a virtue, it is not a satisfying one."

"Is that so?" Suzenne said in a playful tone, swinging around and grabbing his hands, looking up at him. "Whitsunday will be here soon. Will not your patience be rewarded then?"

He smiled and leaned down, kissing the corner of her mouth. "I am wrong, as usual. It will be well worth the torture of delay. Do you fear the maston test? Either of you?" He glanced at Maia as well.

Suzenne shook her head. "My parents have always told me it is nothing to fear. There are Leerings that cause that emotion, but they can be silenced. Taking the maston test is more a test of commitment than anything else. I am quite ready to take the oaths."

Dodd looked back at Maia.

"Compared with what I have seen and done in my life," Maia said with pursed lips, "it holds no terror for me either. I have met with the Aldermaston these many months, and together, we have examined the life I once led." Dodd had no idea that she had once worn a kystrel. He looked at her gravely, but there was sympathy in his gaze as well. "I am more than ready to commit myself to the Medium's will," she added. "I always have been."

Dodd nodded in approval. "Some people think it is a surrender of a bitter kind. That it is restricting to constantly stifle your thoughts and bridle your passions. My father explained it to me differently, through a story about his ancestor Colvin Price, who had a great love of horses and a deep respect for the dangers of the Bearden Muir. When he and Lia were wandering the swamp together, the Cruciger orb led them to the safest paths. When they lost the power of the orb, they wandered aimlessly. Some people demand the freedom to stumble into ditches. I prefer following a guide to the safest road, even if it *is* through a swamp."

Suzenne and Maia nodded in agreement. Their sojourn in the trees was interrupted when Owen hurried toward them. His cheeks were flushed, and it was clear he had been looking for them for some time.

"What news, Owen?" Maia asked.

The page bowed meekly. "The Aldermaston bids me tell you that the lord chancellor just arrived. He is staying at the Pilgrim Inn outside the grounds, but will dine with the Aldermaston tonight."

"That *is* news," Dodd said. "Chancellor Crabwell?"

"Aye," said Owen. "I did not see him myself, but his retinue took control of the inn when they arrived, and many a man saw him enter."

Suzenne looked to Maia in concern. "What could he be doing here? I would not have expected him to arrive for another month, or maybe a fortnight before Whitsunday. Do you know him, Maia?"

"Yes," Maia said, her stomach churning with nervousness. "He would recognize me."

"That is what the Aldermaston thinks as well," Owen said. "He suggested you stay away from the manor. The sheriff of Mendenhall has been snooping as well."

Maia and Suzenne looked at each other. "Jon Tayt's lodge?" they both said at once.

"A good plan," Dodd said. "Stay away from the manor for now, even the kitchen. I will warn Jon Tayt you are coming to the lodge. If you cannot go there safely, I will come warn you." He squeezed Suzenne's hand and then departed the Cider Orchard.

Owen bowed his hat to them and left as well.

"How well do you know Chancellor Crabwell?" Suzenne asked, linking arms with Maia as they started to walk toward the hunter's lodge on the outskirts of the abbey.

"He replaced Tomas Morton as chancellor before the man was executed. He is loyal to my father. He may be here to see what sort of resistance the king can expect from the Aldermaston."

Suzenne shuddered. "Do you think your father would murder an Aldermaston?"

It was so painful to consider the man her father had become. His ruthlessness as a king was apparent and reviled. And what he had done to her and her mother was deplorable. She still had memories, though, memories of the time before the stillbirths, when they were a real family. A slender part of her hoped against hope that he would remember himself, that he would forsake the monster he had become.

"I hope not," she murmured softly, unable to see the beauty of the blossoms any longer.

***

Jon Tayt's lodge was not the proper lodging for a princess or her companion. There were axes and long knives set in racks on the wall. There were torches, coils of rope, snow shoes, blankets, kegs, longbows, arrows in abundance, at least four pairs of rugged boots, pots of all sizes, wooden spoons and ladles, and an assortment of forks, paring knives, and animal skins. There were no chairs to sit on, but enough barrels of varying sizes to be used as substitute seating. There was a hearth, naturally, which was well stocked with wood that Dodd had helped split and stack during the winter, and Jon Tayt had arranged the stones to encourage the fire to provide more heat than was necessary, making the lodge quite stifling.

They ate meat from small pans, enjoying the sumptuous fare. Jon Tayt rattled on incessantly about the virtues of ovens versus stoves, and the heat and food and constant talking combined to make Maia a little drowsy.

Argus's ears shot up and a low snuffling growl issued from his mouth. Someone was there. Maia felt the chill of fear grip her heart.

"*Chut,*" Jon Tayt warned, rising from the bearskin mat and setting down his tray. He reached the front door just as a timid knock sounded. It was Owen again.

"The Aldermaston has called for Suzenne," Owen said nervously, wringing his hands. "The chancellor wishes to speak with her."

Suzenne's face went ashen. "Me?"

Owen nodded dumbly. "He said he must see 'one Suzenne Clarencieux.' Those were his exact words, my lady. The Aldermaston sent me to fetch you."

Jon Tayt scowled. "I like that not. By Cheshu, what is he after? Does he know your Family, lass?"

Suzenne blanched. "I would think not. We are a noble Family, but not one of great importance."

"He's sniffing like a dog, looking for a scent. Owen, take her to the Aldermaston. Maia, you stay here with me."

Brushing off her hands, Suzenne rose and looked very nervous as she headed into the dark with Owen.

"What is your guess?" Maia asked Jon Tayt as he shut the door behind them. "I can tell you are thinking."

Jon Tayt rose and did not answer. He began stuffing supplies into a rucksack. After a moment, he looked at her pointedly. "Yours is over there, lass. Fill it!"

"Am I not safe on these grounds?" she asked.

"Are you a maston yet?" he snapped. "Until you are, you have no protection, and cannot call for sanctuary even under the old law. Quickly. I sense an ill wind blowing."

Maia nodded and rushed over to the rucksack, which she began stuffing with food, a water flask, and a blanket.

The door opened without a knock and Argus started to bark fiercely. The sheriff of Mendenhall entered. Argus nearly leaped at him, but Jon Tayt whistled, and the dog stepped back, scaling back his barks to a low-pitched whine that showed he was sensitive to the tension in the room.

The sheriff's eyes were gray. She had never noticed that before, but now that he was staring at her so pointedly, she could notice little but their cold, cunning color. He wore his noble's clothes, a fine leather tunic, and the collar of knighthood visible around his neck. His sword pommel showed the maston symbol, but that could mean any number of things. His eyes were calculating, and he stared at her deliberately.

"Thank you for quieting the dog," the sheriff said, releasing his grip on his dagger hilt. "I am grateful I did not have to."

"Never threaten a man's hound," Jon Tayt warned. He had an axe haft in his hand, poised to throw. His eyes were deadly earnest.

"I seek no quarrel with you, hunter," the sheriff said.

"You may have found it regardless," Jon Tayt replied. "How many men do you have outside?"

"Enough," the sheriff answered.

Jon Tayt's eyes burned with fury. "You think so?" His voice was full of challenge.

"Let us go outside and you can count. How high *can* you count?" The last was added as a deliberate insult.

"What do you want?" Maia asked, stepping forward. A part of her—a dark part of her—wished she still had her kystrel. She felt the need slipping in through the door cracked open by her fear and wariness. This was what the Aldermaston had warned her against. Temptation. She licked her lips, trying unsuccessfully to quell her fear. Fear of the unknown, fear of the future, it did not matter—fear was the reason many turned to the powers of the Myriad Ones. She did not feel them nearby. That was impossible on the abbey grounds. But she could practically feel them scratching at the invisible walls that kept them out.

"You," he replied simply.

"I do not understand you, Sheriff. What do you mean?"

"I came for you, my dear," he said, a long, nervous smile playing across his mouth. "I have a theory, you see, and I summoned Chancellor Crabwell to Muirwood to help me test it. He left Comoros in secret two days ago and told no one where he was going. He was most interested in my news."

Maia swallowed, trying to contain the nervousness blooming inside her. "What news is that?" she asked, but she suspected his answer.

"Every spy in every kingdom is searching for the King of Comoros's missing daughter. All reports suggest she was taken to the Dochte Mandar in Naess, but no one has seen her there these many months. There are many rumors, my lady. Rumors that Lady Deorwynn had her poisoned." He snorted. "The people have been demanding to see her. There are riots in the city, my lady. You may wear the robes of a wretched, but you cannot conceal your beauty."

Jon Tayt hefted the axe, his eyes brooding with intention. Maia held up her hand, forestalling him.

"What is it you want?" Maia whispered.

"You admit it then?"

"I have admitted nothing. You are the one telling the story, Sheriff. What is it you want?"

A crooked smile crossed his face. "What many people want," the sheriff answered, his voice harsh and cold. "Lady Deorwynn's downfall. You are the true heir of Comoros, not Deorwynn's brood." He almost spat out the word. "There are many who seek her demise. I suspected your secret months ago. I have been very patient. Very discreet. You will find those traits distinctive about me, my lady. I know someone has been rifling through my correspondence. Someone here at the abbey. Someone not quite subtle enough." His eyes burned into hers. "It may even be you. I summoned Chancellor Crabwell to Muirwood to test my conclusion. I believe you are Marciana, the king's daughter, our *true* princess. How you came to be at Muirwood, I do not know. But this I will tell you. Chancellor Crabwell wishes to speak to you. He sent for Lady Clarencieux to help me locate your presence on the grounds. I am to bring you to him immediately."

Maia stared at him, her insides twisting with confusion and dread. "What does Chancellor Crabwell have against Lady Deorwynn?"

The sheriff gave her that same crooked smile again. "They both seek to whisper in the king's ear at night. They are bitter rivals and implacable enemies. She seeks his downfall and wishes to put one of her kinsmen in his place. It is a matter of great importance which of them will have the other killed first. The chancellor has used your disappearance to foster the rumors of your murder at her hand. So you see, Lady Maia, that locating you is a matter of supreme importance." His eyes narrowed coldly. "Now come with me."

The Medium is intent on your personal growth. That progress can be quick when you willingly allow it to lead you through every experience you encounter, whether it initially be to your individual liking or not.

—*Richard Syon, Aldermaston of Muirwood Abbey*

CHAPTER FIFTEEN

Alliance

Maia had first met Chancellor Crabwell when she was living in the attic of Lady Shilton's manor in the most contemptible of circumstances. Even the poorest servants of the manor had been treated better than her. On that particular day, her father had come to visit, and Maia had been locked in her room to prevent her from seeing him. The only visit she had gotten that day was from Chancellor Crabwell and Captain Carew, one of her father's personal knights, who had attempted to persuade her to renounce her titles. She had refused.

Chancellor Crabwell had aged—his dark hair was streaked with silver now, his brow wrinkled from the constant strain of stress, and his mouth puckered into a permanent frown. He wore a velvet cap with a badge on the fringe as well as the ceremonial stole of his office as chancellor. Crabwell was the man responsible for implementing her father's wishes—no matter how depraved.

It was taking its toll on him.

"Out with you, hunter. And Sheriff, bar the doors," Crabwell said with a sneer of command. They were in a private chamber in the abbey, away from the main hall. The full darkness of night had descended hours ago, but a few flickering lamps provided light.

Jon Tayt took a step forward, his hand gripping the axe haft, as it had been doing since the sheriff's arrival at his lodge. "By Cheshu, you will have to throw me out, my lord. I do not obey you, and I am *not* leaving her here unprotected."

Crabwell turned and looked at him with petulant annoyance. "And who are you, my good man?"

"He is the abbey hunter and my protector," Maia said, stepping forward.

Crabwell's brow furrowed into even tighter wrinkles. He snorted. "If I snap my fingers, the sheriff's men will drag you from the abbey grounds and quite promptly remove your head. Do not meddle with me, sir. You do not want to provoke my enmity."

Jon Tayt flushed, his eyes searing with fury. He stepped forward suddenly, before any of the guards could move, seized the chancellor's wrist, and slammed it on the nearby table. He hefted the axe. "Which fingers were you intending to snap, my lord?" he said.

"Jon," Maia said coaxingly, delicately.

Crabwell's eyes widened with fear. A trickle of sweat went down his cheek. Several of the men had hands on hilts, but no one drew a weapon with the hunter so near the chancellor.

"You send men to the gallows often, do you not?" Jon Tayt leered. "Well, I am good with an axe. And I am not from this country, nor do I hold any loyalty to it. Send the sheriff and his men away."

Crabwell coughed and then nodded to the sheriff to leave. "You are most persuasive, Master Hunter."

Jon Tayt snorted. "I figured you would not be keen to spend the rest of your life scratching your nethers with a stump."

Chancellor Crabwell nodded affirmatively. The door shut, and Jon Tayt released his arm. He walked over to the door and locked it.

"I am a student of history as well as the law," Crabwell said, rubbing his wrist. It was clear he was not used to being handled so roughly. "I have a deep respect for the sharpness of Pry-rian arrows. And their uncanny aim."

"It is in the fletching," Jon Tayt said snidely. "Now to business. Did you come here to threaten her?"

"Of course not!" Crabwell said, incensed. "Lady Maia, the king's daughter, you have been missing for some duration. Have you been hiding in Muirwood all this time?"

"I am not hiding in Muirwood, Chancellor," Maia replied. She folded her arms, feeling the delicacy of the situation press in on her from all sides. Chancellor Crabwell was intimate with her father. Yet it appeared he had come to Muirwood in secret, summoned by the sheriff's message. Without knowing the intricacies of the situation, she did not want to reveal too much.

"The facts seem to the contrary," he said. "Look at you, wearing a wretched's robe."

"The last time we met I was wearing a scullery maid's rags instead," Maia replied. "You tried to persuade me to accept the Act of Inheritance. Now there is another decree. Are you here to persuade me again?"

"I am here," Crabwell said, his voice throbbing with emotion, "because you are found at last!" He wiped his smooth mouth and then flicked away the trail of sweat. "My spies have been searching for you throughout all the realms. There are a thousand different rumors as to your whereabouts. Some say you were secretly wedded to the King of Dahomey. Some say you murdered a Prince of Hautland. Others that you destroyed an abbey. Rumors that I can scarcely credit."

Maia felt her stomach lurch at the words. Dizziness washed over her, but she tried to keep her expression calm.

"What did my father tell you about my departure?" Maia asked, her mouth very dry.

Crabwell rubbed his eyes. "Very little. He said he was sending you away for a time and that when you returned, you would be more . . . docile. That was his very word. You seem to be the same headstrong girl I met years ago. But let me test it. Do you accept the Act of Inheritance?"

"No," Maia answered flatly. "I am a princess."

Crabwell continued. "Do you swear to uphold the Act of Submission on pain of treason?"

"I do not," Maia said, shaking her head. "The king has no authority over the maston order. He was anointed by an Aldermaston. He cannot rise above the one who raised him."

Crabwell smirked. "Yes, *docile* is not the word I would use. Where did you go, Lady Maia?"

Though she had managed to hide her reaction, the chancellor's words had affirmed her darkest suspicions. Her father had sent her, deliberately, into the hetaera's lair. Suppressed rage and crushed love bled inside her heart. Truly, her father had broken every vow.

"If my father did not trust you with that information, why should I?" she replied. "You are his chancellor."

He stepped forward, his eyes glittering with emotion. "But I may not be for much longer," he said in a low voice. "There is a . . . rivalry between Lady Deorwynn and myself. She seeks to undermine my authority and bring me down."

"You seek the same for her," Maia replied. "Why should that concern me?"

"I think it does," Crabwell said, dropping his voice even lower. "I am not the only one who despises Lady Deorwynn and her ilk.

Her relations have been so grasping. It is her uncle, you know, who is to become the new Aldermaston of Muirwood. He will be arriving in a fortnight, before Whitsunday, to prepare for his new domain. Much is transpiring in the realm right now, Maia." Wiping his mouth, he turned aside and began to pace.

"Tell me," Maia said, watching him. She schooled her emotions, keeping her expression wary.

"My spies have seen someone entering her chambers at night," Crabwell said. "A man. I believe he is a hired killer."

Maia frowned. "A kishion?"

He looked surprised she knew the word. "Indeed. Very secretly, I have been investigating Lady Deorwynn's actions. Remember when you were poisoned? I received a report from Doctor Willem regarding the incident. I interviewed some witnesses, and I have reason to believe this kishion was brought to Comoros and paid for by Lady Deorwynn herself. You were his first target. Her husband, your father, is his second. You see, she wishes to rule Comoros herself. I believe she may be a hetaera. Do you know what that is, child?" He stopped to look at her as he said it.

Maia swallowed and nodded, her throat constricting with shock. She had always felt unsettled by the knowledge that her father had hired the kishion to protect her or destroy her. But had Lady Deorwynn used the same man to try and poison her? How could she hope to distinguish the truth from so many lies and evasions?

Crabwell wiped his mouth again and continued pacing.

"Why would she kill my father?" Maia asked hoarsely, still wrestling with the implications.

He looked at her in surprise. "Because he has fallen in love . . . again."

Maia lowered her gaze, her heart twisting with anguish. *Not again, Father. Please, not again!* "Who is the girl?"

"One of Lady Deorwynn's ladies," Crabwell said with a shake of his head. "He was flirting with her during Lady Deorwynn's pregnancy. When she miscarried, the king seemed to lose all interest in her and began to pursue—"

"What?" Maia asked, confused. "Lady Deorwynn lost the babe?"

Crabwell nodded. "The day after . . ." He stopped, swallowing. "The day after she caught her lady sitting on the king's lap. Their marriage is crumbling into ashes before our eyes."

Maia sighed, shaking her head in disbelief. It was happening again. She had little compassion for Lady Deorwynn, but she was not surprised to hear the woman had become frantic to prevent the collapse of her power.

"Oh, Chancellor," Maia said, disheartened. "We have so many enemies without. Enemies who seek to prey on our kingdom. Yet we squabble within like children."

Crabwell sniffed, stifling a chuckle. "Well said, Maia. The intrigue goes deeper. Lady Deorwynn is pushing your father to make an alliance with Dahomey. You may not know this, but the King of Dahomey was recently imprisoned and held for ransom."

Maia's brow crinkled and her heart raced. She struggled to keep her interest concealed. "I had heard this. You imply that he is free?"

Crabwell nodded vigorously. "The ransom is paid. I am certain he bankrupted his entire treasury and probably secured loans from Paeiz or Avinion for the remainder. It was truly a king's ransom. He is an ambitious young man who owes a great debt, and he is agreeing to an alliance with Comoros. Lady Deorwynn seeks to marry him to her eldest daughter, Murer. He is arriving shortly to consummate the alliance and to be invested as an earl of the realm." He snorted. "He will be given the earldom of Dieyre with its lands and income. That alone is worth fifty thousand marks. Ironic, is it not?"

Maia paled, her heart shuddering from the disappointing news. "Is it . . . is it certain?" she asked tremulously, struggling to maintain her composure.

"Your father needs allies and Dahomey needs money. The negotiations are still under way. As you can imagine, King Gideon is trying to squeeze this situation as best he can. If Lady Deorwynn succeeds, it will entrench her power even further. Her son will become a king, her daughter a queen, and her uncle will rule all the abbeys."

Her heart burned with silent agony. Of course . . . Collier was furious. She could only imagine how injured he was by her betrayal. The thought of him divorcing her and marrying Murer caused unbearable pain, yet she kept her countenance and tried to think.

She forced herself to respond to the chancellor without revealing her upset feelings. "And what will she do with you, my lord?" she said in a small voice.

"She will have me executed, no doubt," he said with venom. "And she will name the new Earl of Forshee as chancellor. He has been insufferable to me of late, no doubt relishing the prospect of gloating over my downfall."

"By Cheshu," Jon Tayt muttered, shaking his head. "You are a dead man, I think."

Crabwell shot him a murderous look. "The dance has not finished the final chords yet, Master Hunter. There is time yet. As you see, the king no longer favors Lady Deorwynn. I have been trying to convince Lady Sexton to *encourage* the king's affections. He is weary of quarreling with Lady Deorwynn. Lady Sexton is very meek—his wife's opposite in every way. He tries to persuade her that she is saving his soul and bringing him back to the maston cause. I am not certain she believes him, but he can be quite charming when he wants something. Now, this is where you come in, Lady Maia."

Lady Sexton. The name sounded familiar, and she realized it was Suzenne's friend who had left Muirwood the previous year.

He rubbed his hands together like a little child about to receive treats. She abhorred the gesture, but it revealed the delight he took in his machinations.

"I have been preparing evidence to charge Lady Deorwynn with murder. I have assembled enough evidence to charge her with hiring the kishion. And I have been fomenting rumors and gossip about your possible death throughout the realm in order to get the people to demand to see you. The king has been quite unsure of the situation, having lost you somewhere himself. His men have been searching for you as eagerly as mine. I plan to tell him that I have found you at last, that you were here all along, seeking to be reunited with your mother and pursue your studies to become a maston yourself." He waved his hand. "Whether or not it is true does not matter. Lady Deorwynn has sensed my ploy and has been arguing, most forcefully, that your father should restore you to favor and give you your dower lands. She does this, of course, because she does not want to be blamed for your death. By arguing publicly for your restoration, she wets the flames crying in riot for *you* to become the heir of Comoros once again."

Maia blinked, startled.

"Yes, my lady." He grinned at her, his eyes widening with pleasure. "If we ally together, you and I, we may be able to right the ship of state and prevent it from crashing on the rocks. I do not want Lady Murer to wed the King of Dahomey. The more besotted the king becomes with Lady Jayn Sexton, the more fragile Lady

Deorwynn's hold will be. I have guards watching the king night and day to prevent his assassination. If he were to fall, we would all be ruined, including you. You are Lady Deorwynn's biggest threat. While I trust you have a capable protector in this axe-wielding Pry-rian, I would not wager he would survive if a kishion came hunting you."

She exchanged a glance with Jon Tayt. Before answering, she needed time to mull over all that Crabwell had told her. She pushed a lock of hair behind her ear. "What are you proposing, Chancellor? I have not agreed to anything yet. Do not interpret by my silence that I do not have serious doubts regarding some of what you have told me."

"You always were wise and insightful," he crooned. No wonder her father enjoyed him so much. He was oily, duplicitous. She did not trust him one bit. "If I tell your father you are here, then Lady Deorwynn will know at once. She will send the kishion to murder you." He shook his head seriously. "Let us continue to keep your presence here a secret. The sheriff has enough men to guard and watch over you. He owes his position to my influence, so he will do as I order him. Your father and Lady Deorwynn will arrive shortly to celebrate Whitsunday at Muirwood, confiscate the revenues of the abbey, and install a new Aldermaston. That would be, in my estimation, the perfect opportunity to reveal your presence. It will not give Lady Deorwynn enough time to react."

He walked over to the table and lifted a cup, drinking thirstily from it. He glanced at her, his eyes still scheming. "What say you, Lady Maia—Princess of Comoros once more?"

CHAPTER SIXTEEN

Counsel

fter she told her tale, Maia felt the power of their silent
gazes on her. She looked around the room and registered
the different ways her friends had reacted to the news.
The Aldermaston looked wise and brooding as always, his eyes full
of sympathy for her. His wife looked grim, and seemed particularly
upset over the news that Jayn Sexton was the king's new favorite.
Tomas, the steward, sat quietly in the council chamber, shaking
his head with surprise. He looked like he wanted to speak, but he
deferred to the Aldermaston. Jon Tayt was sullen and had a murderous look in his eyes, as if he wanted to go out, find the chancellor, and take off his head instead of just his fingers. Suzenne was
there too, her face pale with dread and worry—Maia could tell she
was concerned about Jayn, for they had been very close.

How Maia wished her grandmother were there with them. The
Aldermaston's counselors were an able group, but the situation

was so fraught with political peril that she herself was unsure of what to do.

"What answer did you give Chancellor Crabwell?" the Aldermaston's wife asked.

Maia breathed in through her nose and glanced at Jon Tayt. She nodded to him.

Jon Tayt fidgeted in his seat. "She thanked him for his keen interest in her welfare and said she would mull over the matter with her counselors before responding. A good answer for a precarious situation. By Cheshu, he was like a spider seeking to wrap her up in webs."

"His news must have been painful for you," the Aldermaston said earnestly.

Maia had always been struck by the depths of the man's compassion. He was about to be evicted from his stewardship as an Aldermaston, yet he showed greater concern for her than he did for himself.

"It was," Maia said, glancing around the room again. "I still do not know what I should tell him, though." The chancellor did not want to linger in the abbey and implicate himself further. He had retired to his room at the Pilgrim Inn and said he would await a message from her until morning before he departed back for Pent Tower.

The Aldermaston leaned back in his chair and the leather cushions creaked. He set one hand on his belly and the other on the desk. "That is the purpose of a Privy Council, my dear. I have found the practice to be most helpful. Before I seek to understand the Medium's will, I seek the advice of others whose opinions I deeply respect. After I have listened to that counsel, I form my own opinion on the matter. Then I bring that opinion to the

Medium for further direction. What would you ask of us?" His deep eyes were penetrating.

Maia bit her lip. "I admit I am tempted by the chancellor's offer. It would seem to be within my best interest to accept an alliance with him and seek his help in restoring my rights through the law. If that were to happen, I might be able to help protect Muirwood and prevent the changes my father plans. However, the chancellor seems very motivated to preserve his own power. I may be lashing my destiny to a ship ready to sink."

"Aye," Jon Tayt said, nodding vigorously. "You are wise for one so young, lass."

The Aldermaston held up his hand, silencing Jon Tayt. He took his wife's hand in his and then turned to his steward. "Tomas? What do you think Maia should do?"

The steward smiled as if a silent joke had passed between them. His dimples appeared. "He always does this," he said confidingly to Maia. "He seeks my input before sharing his own. I am more impulsive, I think, than the Aldermaston. He listens to me so as to know what *not* to do." He chuckled softly. "Maia— let me just say that I regard you truly as if you were my own Family. I have watched you since your arrival at Muirwood. You give service to others with nary a concern for yourself. I think you would make an excellent queen, and I would support you with all my heart." He smiled at her, trying to convey his sincerity. Then his look became more serious. "I would not trust Chancellor Crabwell with anything more important than cleaning dishes. He is plotting against his king. He is plotting against you as well. If you sail a ship by changing direction every time the wind blows a different way, you will not reach your destination. I think it would be very foolish to trust him."

Maia stared at the steward, grateful for the counsel. "But what should I tell him, Tomas? There will be implications if I say something or not."

"You are quite right," he said, nodding. "I would thank him for his offer and remind him that it is your intent to pass the maston test at Muirwood Abbey, and you would like to keep your thoughts focused on that." He held up his hands.

The Aldermaston nodded, then looked at Jon Tayt. "What do you say?"

Jon Tayt leaned forward, putting a meaty arm across his knee. "By Cheshu, you know I do not lack for opinions, Aldermaston. The man, quite simply, is a coward and a knave. He is riddled with fear—I could see it deep in his eyes."

"You threatened to chop off his fingers," the steward reminded him.

"Of course . . . and it was just that, a threat. I wanted to see how he would react. A man with power would have pulled his hand away or ordered his guards to kill me on the spot. When you kick a dog too oft, it barks at strangers and flinches from its master. Crabwell is a kicked pup. A drowning man thrashing in the waters, clutching at anything. If you want to save him, you must bash him up a bit first to calm him." He lifted a finger and then pointed it at Maia. "He may also have been testing your loyalty to your father. Should you send a message to your father first, letting him know where you are? Your father may have sent him here to tempt you—to see where your loyalties be. Men like Crabwell lie as easily as they butter bread. He said what he wanted you to hear, not necessarily what he really felt. I advise you send word to your lord father and spoil his game."

Tomas shook his head. "A steward . . . or a chancellor in this case . . . gets the king's messages first. He will be sure to have controlled access to the king."

"Why do you keep interrupting me?" Jon Tayt said, wrinkling his brow.

"I beg your pardon," Tomas said, bowing his head.

"It is fit that we challenge all ideas," the Aldermaston said. "Do not be offended. Intelligent men can disagree on the interpretation of the facts at hand. Continue, Master Evnissyen."

Jon Tayt nodded, brushing his nose, and turned back to Maia. "It may also be wise to take Maia away from Muirwood before the king gets here. I could bring her to Tintern, and we could send word and await the High Seer there."

"The grounds will be watched even more scrupulously now," the Aldermaston's wife said softly.

"I have slipped by the sheriff's men dozens of times already," Jon Tayt snorted. "They do not know where the secret passages let out. All I would need is Argus and the cover of darkness."

"Well enough. Any more input?" the Aldermaston asked him.

"No, my lord. I am keen to hear yours."

The Aldermaston nodded and turned. "Suzenne Clarencieux."

The young girl looked terror-stricken. "Me?"

"Yes, what would you advise?"

Suzenne twisted her hands together, looking pale and worried. "I just wondered something."

"What is it, Suzenne?" the Aldermaston's wife asked softly.

Suzenne looked up at her, eyes crinkling with concern. "I am worried about Jayn. Has there been word from her recently? Perhaps she could corroborate part of the tale? I cannot believe she is . . . seducing . . . the king." She looked down, ashamed.

The Aldermaston's wife glanced at her husband, who nodded. "I *have* heard from Jayn Sexton," she announced. "She has written to me secretly, and her information does confirm much of what the chancellor told you, Maia. There are ill feelings between the king and Lady Deorwynn at the moment. Jayn has found herself in the position of receiving gifts and attentions from your father, though she knows not how to interpret them. Since she left Muirwood, she has explained how difficult it is to feel the Medium, even as a maston, outside the grounds of an abbey, especially in the court of Comoros. There are few mastons left, most having abandoned court to stay on their own lands. The king is surrounded by people who tell him what he wishes to hear, thus giving him the false notion that he can offend the Medium with no consequence. She does not trust her own judgment at present and has solicited my advice, which I have given her freely. The attentions of a powerful man can be very . . . confusing."

Maia sighed, sick at heart to hear more of her father's depredations. She remembered studying the history of the past, the time before the Scourging. The King of Comoros' wife had died and he had wed the young, beautiful daughter of the King of Dahomey, Pareigis—not understanding who she truly was. The gap in their ages had always sickened her, and she had hoped her father would not make an alliance for her with a much older man.

"Poor Jayn," Suzenne said, her face wilting with concern. "I am grateful she has confided in you," she added.

"I share this information with you since you are part of this counsel," the Aldermaston's wife said. "Please do not share it with others. She abhors the king's attentions, but she is in a dangerous position. Her mistress is still Lady Deorwynn, who does indeed conspire to unite her daughter to the King of Dahomey."

"Was there any mention by her of the ransom paid?" Maia asked, leaning forward. "I wondered if the chancellor was being truthful about that."

The Aldermaston's wife shook her head.

"Any other thoughts, Suzenne?" the Aldermaston bid her.

"No, Aldermaston," Suzenne said, shaking her head.

Maia looked at the Aldermaston and his wife. "What would you advise me to do?"

The Aldermaston's wife spoke first. "I think we should wait for your grandmother to arrive. She knows the dangers we face, and she will hurry as fast as the winds can bring her. If you must leave Comoros, I would prefer it to be on the *Holk* instead of wandering in the Bearden Muir. But my heart tells me that your destiny is still here, Maia. You are the one who must open the Apse Veil. Despite the political changes, that is still your charge. The Myriad Ones know you are here. They may prowl the borders like wolves, but they cannot enter. I would also advise not telling Dodd about the chancellor's visit until after he has left. He may do something rash, since the chancellor is responsible for overseeing executions ordered by the king."

"I had not thought of that," Maia said, nodding. "I agree." She looked at the Aldermaston closely. "What do you counsel me to do?"

The Aldermaston smiled sadly. "You must pass the maston test. Each day, I have sought the Medium's approval to bring you into the abbey walls. The maston rites will give you knowledge you desperately need as well as protection you do not now enjoy. That is my first priority for you, to help shield you against the influences of Ereshkigal and the Myriad Ones." He looked at her sternly. "When you leave Muirwood, child, you will be afflicted by them again. Pay particular notice to the words of Jayn Sexton. She can hardly *feel* the Medium's influence at court. That is a discouraging reality. I have brooded *constantly* since you arrived, wishing to bring you *immediately* into the abbey. But the Medium forbids it still. You are not yet ready."

Maia felt a twist of sadness in her heart and tears sting her eyes. "Because of what I have done," she said in sorrow.

The Aldermaston shook his head. "I do not know that, child. I only care about doing what is right for you. The time is approaching when you will enter the abbey and seek the rites. But it may not be until *after* the king arrives." He shifted in his seat, leaning forward, his eyes so deep and full of soul. His jowls trembled. "You may yet be tested by the Medium, to see if you will forsake all things in defending the maston order. You may be offered gold, jewels, rich gowns, and handmaidens to tempt you into surrendering your heritage. You have already survived such a temptation." His voice dropped even lower. "Your greatest test may come from your father himself. He has treated you most cruelly." Tears gathered in the old man's eyes. "Our greatest pain in this life often comes from those who should love us the most. Prepare yourself to accept the maston oaths. I have no doubt that you will tame the Leerings inside the abbey. The hardest thing you will ever be asked to tame is your own heart."

Maia felt a burning sensation in her chest at his words. It was like a feeling of heat, but it was also a feeling of grief and of love— as if she could sense the true feelings the Aldermaston held for her. *This* was how a father should feel toward his daughter.

"Thank you," Maia whispered softly, trying to contain the surge of feelings inside her. She looked from face to face again, feeling the power of love and sympathy. Inside this council room in the Aldermaston's manor, she felt embraced by these wonderful people. But there was something more. It was almost a whisper, a breath that could be felt but not heard. The room, she realized, was full to the brim. There were others with them as well, unseen spirits.

The Aldermaston stiffened suddenly, breathing out sharply. "They are with us," he sighed.

His wife nodded, squeezing his hand. The room throbbed with energy and emotion, with the thoughts and feelings of dozens of unseen minds and hearts. This room had been built on the grounds of the previous abbey. The Aldermaston before it had burned to the ground, Gideon Penman, had sacrificed his life to save the abbey, to save Lia. Maia could not see the dead, but she sensed them in the air around her, thick like swirling leaves in an autumn windstorm. She could feel their determination and intensity.

The Covenant of Muirwood must be fulfilled, she could hear them whispering. This moment was not about her and the rights that had been unjustly stripped away. It was about thousands of the dead who had been banished as well . . . banished because the Apse Veils were closed. She could feel them staring at her, willing her to succeed, trying to imbue her with the strength to open the gates so they could move on to Idumea. There were countless unseen hosts of the dead and she felt the awful weight of the burden they placed on her shoulders.

Free us, they seemed to whisper to her. *Open the Veil.*

Maia put her face in her hands, quivering under the pressure of it. How could she face such a task? Such a burden? She was a hetaera, her shoulder scarred with the brand. How could she, of all people, face such a challenge?

She looked up, tear-stricken, and realized the others were staring at her in compassion. "I do not know how I can do this," Maia said, her voice trembling. *There are so many . . . so many counting on me.* The enormity filled her mind, making her weak and doubtful.

"You will not do it alone," the Aldermaston's wife whispered.

But in Maia's heart, she realized the Aldermaston's wife was wrong.

***

Jon Tayt escorted her to the abbey just before dawn. A deep fog had settled over the grounds that night, shrouding everything in gray. Argus padded at her heels, sniffing the grass and flower-beds as they passed. They reached the gate and saw a solitary man standing there, holding a torch to dispel the gloom. By his bulk, she could tell it was the chancellor.

As Maia walked toward the prick of light, she continued to feel the burden that had settled on her shoulders the night before. She had not slept at all. She was surrounded by ghosts, and she felt them with her at that very moment, keeping step with her, plead-ing with her. The strain on her mind and her emotions was intense.

The gate was closed. Maia stepped up and touched the cold, wet bars. The chancellor approached, eyeing her warily. She could hear the nickering of horses farther back, but the mist was as thick as soup.

The chancellor studied her face, looking for signs of what her answer would be.

"Thank you for coming all this way, Chancellor," she said, try-ing to sound brave. "I came to Muirwood to become a maston. My parents both were and so were my ancestors. I feel a great . . . obligation to continue in the order. I will do my duty, Chancellor. I do not seek to be distracted by the politics of the court. Farewell."

He stepped closer, his head nearly touching the bars. "Are you quite certain?" he hissed in a low voice. His jaw quivered with pent-up anger. She would not be his tool, his ally, the rope to pre-vent him from drowning. His eyes were accusing.

"I am," she replied simply and turned to walk away.

"And what if you are cast out of your precious abbey?" he sneered at her, then checked his tone and made it more respect-ful. "These gates cannot protect you long, Lady Maia. Even *if* you become a maston."

Maia heard a trickling sound and turned, seeing Argus, leg lifted, relieving himself on the gate post, the mess splattering onto the chancellor's boots. His expression turned to disgust, and he scowled at the dog, backing away angrily.

Maia turned away to cover her smile and started off into the mist full of ghosts.

"Well done, Argus," Jon Tayt muttered, right behind her.

Mastons learn that a peaceful conscience invites relief from anguish, sorrow, guilt, and shame. It provides a foundation for joy. It is of immeasurable worth. It is also incredibly rare.

—*Richard Syon, Aldermaston of Muirwood Abbey*

CHAPTER SEVENTEEN

The King's Captain

S tudies ended and Maia was anxious to breathe the fresh spring air and roam the grounds a bit to stretch her legs before supper. The learners were all gossiping about the upcoming Whitsunday festival and what would take place. The king's boon companion and captain of his guard, Captain Carew, had arrived to settle the king's accommodations. Maia learned her father would be staying at the Pilgrim Inn, just outside the grounds, and Captain Carew had come with a small cohort to inspect the inn and prepare it for the arrival of the royal visitors. He had brought a fat purse with him and was lavish in spending in the king's name. There was much speculation as to why her father had chosen to stay outside the abbey grounds, but it was on everyone's mind that a change in leadership at the abbey was under way.

Maia and Suzenne linked arms and started walking toward Jon Tayt's lodge, for that was where they normally met Dodd for a walk in the gardens. They had not gotten very far when Maeg called after them.

Suzenne and Maia both turned to look, surprised.

Maeg did not have her typical sneer. In fact, she looked almost . . . *worried*.

"What is it?" Suzenne asked her, wrinkling her brow.

Maeg swallowed and pulled them both aside. "News from my father," she said in a low voice. "I should have told you this sooner, but he asked me to account for both of you each day and to warn him if either of you ever left the abbey." She looked pointedly at Maia. "There are rumors that . . . that a killer has been sent to murder you. The same man who poisoned your mother."

The words unleashed a sudden shock of coldness in Maia's heart. In her mind, she could see the kishion's partial ear, his angry frown. Maeg looked very ill at ease, though her eyes were on Suzenne. Any danger that threatened Maia would also threaten her one-time friend.

"Thank you for telling me," Maia said.

Maeg nodded, glancing down at her shoes. "Just do not wander far. I told Father that you spend a good deal of time in the Queen's Garden. I think it would be wise if you stayed out of sight." She glanced at Suzenne and frowned, her words stalling. She turned to leave, but then stopped to look back. "Captain Carew," she said. "He is the captain of the guard. Father said he is here to protect you. He is inspecting the grounds. Do not be surprised if he speaks to you. He is loyal to your father, to be sure, but he is also loyal to Crabwell. You should know that."

She turned to leave again, but Maia caught her sleeve.

"Thank you, Maeg."

The other girl shrugged off the thanks and walked away, joining her friends and leaving the pair with their worries.

A strained silence descended between them as they walked to the lodge. It was strange. Maia's father had hired the kishion to protect her on her journey to Dahomey, yet also with instructions to kill her if she were captured. They had traveled together a great distance, his moods often mercurial and savage. Would he seek her out to murder her now, after so much had passed between them? Then again, the kishion himself had warned her that he was not to be trusted.

When they reached Jon Tayt's lodge, they heard the sound of splitting wood. They rounded the corner to find Dodd putting another piece of wood on the stump. He paused when he saw them, wiping sweat from his brow. Maia had noticed a difference in him since he had started working with Jon Tayt. He was more tanned, his shoulders were broader, and his confidence with the axe as a weapon had also increased. Of them all, he could stick the throwing axes better than anyone except Jon Tayt himself, which he demonstrated often in the little competitions they had outside the hunter's lodge. His collar was loose, exposing the glint of the chaen beneath his shirt. He hurriedly set down the axe and brushed his hands on his pants.

"Always wood to be split," he said with a grin. "Jon Tayt is out riding with Captain Carew, hawking, I think. One of the escorts rode back early looking for some arrows, which I fetched for him. He thought I was a helper." He chuckled at the mistake. "It is strange seeing so many soldiers on the grounds, most of them armed. I am grateful Jon Tayt showed me how to escape the grounds quickly. That knowledge may prove crucial very soon."

"Maeg just told us that a kishion was sent to kill Maia," Suzenne said worriedly. "Captain Carew is here to protect her."

Dodd looked troubled and surprised. "So am I," he said. "And so is Jon Tayt. I would like to see a kishion get through all of us. Do not fret, Maia. The Medium often warns of danger before it happens."

"It did not warn my mother," Maia said, still feeling conflicted over the situation. "We were going to the garden, Dodd," she said tiredly. "Come with us. The flowers are blooming, and the blossoms are nearly gone. It is beautiful."

"Of course," Dodd said with a smile. Standing between them, he hooked his arms through theirs, and they all walked to the walled garden Maia's mother had had constructed.

The air smelled of daffodils and purple mint. Bees were everywhere, tasting the sweet nectar of the blossoms, and the sun hung lazily in the sky, barely beginning its descent. The oaks surrounding the grounds were full of fresh green leaves. The last whispers of winter had vanished almost overnight, and the Cider Orchard was full of apple buds, each day swelling larger and larger. Spring was a magical time of year, a time of renewal and rebirth. Birds and chicks, feathery nests, tottering lambs—the world made new again.

They reached the walled garden and Maia used the Leering to open the door. The garden was in full bloom. All the effort they had poured in with Thewliss over the winter had resulted in a beautiful spread of plants and garden vegetables that ripened under the warm rays of sun. The door shut behind them, bringing an immediate feeling of peace and serenity.

"What kind of flower is that?" Dodd asked, stepping forward to one of the garden boxes full of tiny blue flowers with intricate yellow middles.

"Thewliss called them mouse ears," Maia said. "They have a formal name, but I do not recall it." She remembered "mouse ears" because it reminded her of the brush she had discovered in the mountains of Dahomey, mule's ear, which smelled strongly of mint. The little blue flowers were a favorite of her mother, and the bed was thick with the small, five-petal flowers.

"No, I remember mouse ears. This one is different. I do not remember seeing it yesterday. It is white."

Maia came closer and looked at it. Her heart galloped in her chest and a flush came to her cheeks. It was a white lily, sitting amidst the blue. Transfixed, she approached the box, her stomach clenching, her heart pounding. She had not seen it growing in the garden before. She reached out and touched it, and it toppled over, not connected to a stem. It had been placed there.

The sound of boots thumped on the ground behind her.

"Maia!" Suzenne warned.

Dodd rushed in front of her to confront the intruder.

"Oh, *that*," Collier said with a slight accent, "is a Dahomeyjan lily. The blue are not called mouse ears, by the way. They are called forget-me-not in Dahomeyjan. *Ne-mou-blie*." A small chuckle came from his mouth then, almost an exasperated snort.

Dodd stiffened with anger, his muscles tensing. "Who are you, sir?" he challenged, reaching for the throwing axe stuffed in his belt.

"You do not want to do that, friend," Collier warned, his deep blue eyes narrowing. His sword and dagger were also in easy reach.

Maia stared at Collier in wonder, shock making her cheeks flush and her wits scatter like gnats. He wore the rider's garb he favored for his Feint Collier persona, his dust-spattered pants and light shirt. He was full of seething energy, his eyes bright and accusing. Though he smiled, his mouth was sardonic, accusing, injured. His dark hair was a little unkempt, still long and thick. Her eyes went to the scar on his cheek, just below his eye—the one she had always noticed. He stared at her full in the face, his lips curling slightly.

"You stalked us here? Or you were waiting for us?" Dodd said, whipping out the axe to defend Maia.

Maia put her hand on his arm. "No, Dodd. He is not the kishion."

"If I *were*," Collier spat, "the three of you would be dead right now. Put down the axe, friend. I will not warn you again."

"Dodd," Maia insisted, tugging on his arm. She could see the muscles clench in Dodd's neck, his cheeks flushed with anger.

"Who is he?" Dodd asked angrily. "He has a foreign accent."

"I have tried to lose all hint of it," Collier said with a chuckle, "but I see I have not succeeded. Yours is from the north. You are Forshee's boy. Not the new Family, the old one. I think there is a rivalry between our Families," he added with a smirk.

"Put it *down*, Dodd," Maia urged, pulling harder. "I know him. He will not harm me."

Collier raised his eyebrows at that, as if to challenge her statement.

"I beg your leave to speak with Lady Maia alone," Collier said, bowing slightly.

Dodd's face tightened with suppressed anger. "You may beg all you like," he said testily. "But—"

"Suzenne, take Dodd outside. I will join you shortly."

Suzenne looked as if she had been commanded to clutch a serpent to her bosom. Her eyes were full of concern. "Maia, this is not wise," she whispered.

Maia tried to control her breathing. Her heart was afire with emotions. Her knees were trembling. She had assumed, she had desperately *hoped*, that there would be time to prepare for their first reunion. Her stomach cramped with worry and concern. Collier looked furious—tightly controlled, but furious still. He looked as if he hoped Dodd would attack and give him an excuse to run him through with his blade.

"Maia, you cannot be serious," Dodd said, looking at her as if she were stark raving mad.

"I am quite serious, Dodd. Please. I know this man. I must speak with him alone. Please wait for me outside the garden. Go."

Suzenne nodded in deference and started for the garden door.

"What is your name?" Dodd asked Collier angrily.

"Feint Collier," he replied with a wry twist in his voice.

"*Faint*?" Dodd asked with a chuckle.

"Would you rather I call you Dodd or Dodleah? Both are equally bad."

Dodd bristled at the words and Collier looked smug.

"Go," Maia repeated in his ear, squeezing his arm. He stared at Collier with undisguised contempt, but he marched to the door with Suzenne, letting them both out.

A breeze fluttered through Maia's hair, and she swept the strands away from her face. He was still as handsome as she remembered, but it hurt to look at him. A jagged wound of pain was clearly festering inside him. She could see it, and it only made her anguish expand. She did not know what to say to him.

"I am—" she started.

"I hoped—"

They had both spoken at the same time and stopped short, their feelings too raw to be expressed smoothly.

They eyed each other warily, and Collier snorted again before closing the distance between them. It had been many months since she had seen him. But the damage was visible. The feelings of distrust, anger, and betrayal were evident on his face. There was no tenderness there, which hurt even though it had been expected. She prepared herself for a storm.

"If you thought no one would recognize you in wretched robes . . ." he said, daring to speak "let me just say that it is a flimsy disguise. You are too beautiful not to be noticed. *This* only calls more attention to you. Have you no other clothes to wear?

I gave you a rather nice gown recently. Too fancy perhaps for an abbey? You kept the earrings, I see."

Maia closed her eyes, trying to steel herself. "Why are you here, Collier?" she asked.

He spread his arms and began to pace around the garden. "I am celebrating Whitsunday here, my dear. I know how you love to dance."

The words were meant to hurt her, and they did. She stiffened.

"I am still a little shocked . . ." he went on. "Forgive my emotions, but are you truly such a simpleton as to walk around unprotected? I came with Carew today to help test the abbey's defenses. There are none!" He sounded outraged. "There were no stern Leerings giving us frowning looks to warn us away. I told Carew to go hawking with Tayt to see how vulnerable it would leave you. I have been talking to many on the grounds, learning what I could about you, and it should *shock* you how easily I found out about your affection for this place. The garden is beautiful, Maia," his voice rising almost to a shout, "but if I had been sent here to murder someone, it would have been too easy! The Leering at the door did not stop me from climbing the wall. Are you truly such a fool?"

Maia swallowed, feeling unnamable emotions raging inside her. Her words were all lost to her in that moment. He looked angry, certainly, but he also looked . . . *worried* about her. As if he actually still, to some small degree, cared about her safety.

She wiped her nose on her knuckle quickly. "I am glad you are here," she said, trying to calm herself. "I have longed to speak with you."

"Oh, I have been *longing* for this as well," he said bitterly, his eyes flashing. "The ransom is paid, my dear. My kingdom is bankrupt. I am in debt, and I know not even the interest to be paid." He dropped his voice lower. "If I topple your father and claim all his taxes, it may not be enough to relieve the burden. It will probably take years, but I will repay every last farthing, pent, and mark. I will owe no man anything." His voice was almost a growl. Then he huffed and turned away from her.

Tentatively, she reached out and touched his arm. He flinched and jerked away from her.

"I am sorry," Maia said, struggling to speak through the tears stinging her eyes.

He held up his hand. "Please, spare me the humiliation of enduring your apology," he said. When he turned toward her again, his eyes were raw with fury, his mouth tight with emotion. His voice fell even lower. "I *knew* what you were. There is no apology needed. It was your right to betray me. Maybe even your duty. I allowed that possibility when I forced you to marry me. I knew what . . ." His voice became strangled, his eyes sparking with unsuppressed fury. "*Goch*, I cannot even say the word any longer!" he snarled venomously. "Whatever spell you put on me is still working. I cannot name it, but we both *know* what you are." His hand shot out and gripped her left shoulder, his fingers digging into her skin. He did it deliberately, his eyes locked on hers.

His touch on her brand caused a queasiness to rupture inside her stomach. For a moment, she felt a veil of blackness darken her mind. She heard a hiss of pain, of terror, of compulsion—from herself?—and then the dark feelings skittered away. Maia blinked, feeling dizzy, but she did not totter or fall.

She deliberately looked into his eyes as she pushed his arm away. "Please do not touch me there," she said, her voice surprisingly steady.

Collier looked at her in surprise, his eyes widening. He had obviously expected a different reaction.

Maia licked her lips, trying to find enough moisture to speak.

"Do you still wear the kystrel?" She could not see the sign of a chain around his throat.

He shook his head no, then tugged at the front of his shirt, revealing the whorl of the tattoo on his skin. "The Victus took it away, saying you wanted to give it to another man. I have not worn it for many months, but the taint, as you can see, is permanent. Who has your kystrel now? The axe boy?" he asked with a hint of jealousy.

"I do not know," Maia said, shaking her head. "I am here to become a maston, Collier. I never . . . I never *wanted* to be anything else."

He chuckled softly. "And here I thought you came to burn this abbey too."

The stab drew blood and Maia flinched.

He cocked his head, hearing the sound of people approaching the gardens. He gave her another scathing look, then jumped onto the edge of the flower bed, sprang onto the wall, and nimbly climbed it. After reaching the top, Collier gave her one parting glance—a look full of retribution—and then slipped over the edge and disappeared.

Maia's heart was breaking. The pain made her nearly crumple to the ground, but she stayed firm, willing herself not to cry. She heard the Aldermaston's voice as the door to the gardens opened again, punctuated by Dodd's invective.

Maia turned to the plot of flowers, seeing the white lily amidst the blue. She carefully cupped it in her hand and then slipped it into the pouch at her waist.

CHAPTER EIGHTEEN

Confessions

Who was that man?" Suzenne asked softly, standing behind Maia and combing her hair gently. "A collier is a stablehand, is it not? A horseman? Is he with the king's retinue?"

Maia heart had churned all throughout supper, and she had eaten no more than a bite, her stomach too twisted to permit food. She had known she would not be able to escape talking about it forever. The teeth of the comb dragging through her tresses and the warmth of the fire from the Leering were both sensations that normally soothed her, but tonight they could not.

"Yes," Maia whispered. "He did ride in with Captain Carew."

"He was very angry," Suzenne said.

"He deserves to be."

Suzenne stopped combing and stared down at Maia's neck. She waited.

Maia swallowed. In a very soft voice she said, "That was my husband."

Suzenne gasped and threw down the comb, coming around to kneel in front of Maia. Her eyes wide with astonishment, she grabbed Maia's wrist and squeezed it. "You are . . . you are married? Why did you not tell me before? Oh, Maia, I almost would not believe you but for the look on your face. Who is he?"

Maia pulled her arm away and quickly untied the pouch at her waist. She withdrew the white lily delicately, staring at it in her palm.

"The flower from the garden?"

"Yes," Maia said. "It is a white lily. The royal flower of Dahomey."

Suzenne looked at her in confusion.

Maia sighed. "Feint Collier is a disguise he wears. Collier is my nickname for him. He is the King of Dahomey. When I told you my story, I left out an important part." She twisted the flower slowly, staring at the glow of the firelight on the petals.

"You married *him*?" Suzenne asked in wonderment. "You are saying, Maia, that you are the Queen of Dahomey?"

"You make it sound so grand," Maia said, chuckling quietly. "We were not married by irrevocare sigil, Suzenne. We were joined by a Dochte Mandar. He can divorce me if he chooses. He may do that." She was so conflicted. Her parents had been wed by irrevocare sigil, yet their marriage had proved a disaster. No glaring clues had told Maia's mother what her husband would one day become, and the thought of unwittingly binding herself to someone like him for all eternity made Maia cringe inside. Still, marrying a maston by irrevocare sigil was a long-held dream for her. "What a mess this is," she continued, pressing a hand to her throbbing temple. "I am not saying the words very well. Here, let me try this instead." She rose and set the lily down on the table. Then she went to the small chest that contained her few possessions. She pulled out a thick folded set of papers. "I have not sealed it yet, for I did not know when I would have the chance to send it to him. All I knew was that he had recently been released from his confinement. I did not suspect for a moment that I would see him today."

Maia stroked her palm against the smooth paper as she carried it over to Suzenne. "It does a better job of explaining the situation. Right now, my thoughts are fluttering like butterflies and I can barely contain them. I cannot stop thinking of the fact that he is here, somewhere on the grounds. And he hates me, Suzenne. I betrayed him. But not in the way that he thinks. I wrote this letter for him, hoping to find a way to get it to him in secret. I have been hoping this for many months." She wiped a tear from her eye before it could fall. "The Medium truly does heed our innermost thoughts. I did not believe it would deliver him to me in such a fashion. I can scarcely believe it now."

Suzenne gave her a look of awe and concern as Maia handed her the letter. She seated herself on the chair by the lily to read it. Maia knew the words almost by heart.

My lord husband,

I know that by writing this, I risk my death. I was taught to read and write when I was very young by Chancellor Walraven, who tutored me in the customs of the mastons and the Dochte Mandar. He believed my parents were not able to conceive and deliver more children, so he felt it my duty as the future ruler of Comoros to understand the arts that are strictly forbidden of my gender. He gave me a kystrel when I was fourteen to protect me from the influence of the Myriad Ones when my father banished the Dochte Mandar from Comoros. I did not realize that in doing so, he put me in their power.

Revealing this, I put my life in your hands.

I have long regretted not expressing my true feelings to you relating to the circumstances of our first meeting and our subsequent marriage. In all honesty, I did not believe I could trust you. You are a vain and ambitious man. What you saw in me was not love, but an opportunity to expand your influence, wealth, and power. You are more than what your reputation holds, however. As I have grown to know you, I have come to understand you better. We were both very small when our parents agreed to our betrothal. It was my father who spurned that treaty. He has a difficult time keeping his oaths, I have learned.

Here is what I must confess. My father sent me to the cursed shores of Dahomey to find a cure for the evil of the Myriad Ones infecting my kingdom. When I discovered the lost abbey, I was attacked by my father's soldiers because they learned I wore a kystrel and they feared me. They were right to fear me, but I did not become what I am deliberately or even knowingly. When we spoke in your tent the night we were married, I still did not know the truth about myself. You were wiser than I and perceived what I could not. When I made my marriage vow to you, I was not acting under my own volition or my own conscience. I have only ever desired to marry a maston, to become one myself, and to strengthen my Family's bond to the Medium by irrevocare sigil.

When we reached Naess, I was not myself. I am frightened of the creature that ruled me . . . the one who is still bound to me. More than anything, I seek to banish it from my body forever. In the palace of the Naestors, I was offered a chance to become everything you desired me to become and to name you as a ruler at my side. But doing so would have meant surrendering who I am. I would have violated every principle, every spark of good, and every tender feeling I rightly possess. In giving you what you desired, I would have betrayed you more fully than I did . . . and in ways too evil to mention. I was rescued by my

*grandmother, who I learned is the High Seer, and have come to Muir-
wood Abbey to fulfill my destiny.*

*By making that choice, which I did freely and of my own will, I
knew that I condemned you to be a prisoner. This was painful to me,
Collier, for I know your history. If there was a way I could have rescued
you from Naess, please believe me that I would have. I am grieved at
what you have had to suffer because of me, and I have thought of it
constantly these past months.*

*Now that I have spoken the truth to you, insofar as I know it,
it may change your feelings about our marriage. Despite all that has
happened between us, I do not see the future as being entirely without
hope. You and I were plight trothed when we were infants. Perhaps,
in time, you can forgive the unintentional deceptions involved in our
relationship. I truly seek to make amends any way that I can.*

Please forgive me, Maia

Suzenne looked up from the letter and gently handed it back
to her. Then with a quiver in her jaw, she stood and pulled Maia
into a firm embrace. The two held each other, weeping softly, and
Maia felt the healing balm that comes from having shared a confidence with a friend. Suzenne pulled away first, wiping her cheeks,
and shook her head.

"I did not consider," she said, choking, "how painful it must
have been for you when Dodd and I . . ."

Maia shook her head. "I am grateful the two of you are happy.
He is a maston, and you will soon become one. I am not too envious."

Suzenne wiped her nose. "But how can you have a husband?
Did you not . . . consummate the marriage on your wedding night?"

Maia shook her head. "No, we did not. It was a political
union, and he knew I was on a mission elsewhere. Collier swore I

would not leave him until I had agreed to the marriage and said my oaths. But I think as we spent time together, got to know each other, he started to have feelings for me . . . just as I did for him. At times it seemed he did not believe the legends."

"Yes, but believing something is not true does not make it untrue," Suzenne said, wrinkling her brow. "Many leave the abbeys because they do not *want* to believe the Medium is real, despite all the evidence."

"Evidence indeed," Maia said, shaking her head. "Somehow the Medium brought him here."

"I know! It is more than a coincidence."

"What shall I do?" Maia said, wringing her hands. "I need to talk to him, to tell him the truths that are in that letter. But he is so angry, Suzenne. He is so hurt."

"I could see it," she agreed. "I did not know the situation at all, but that much was clear to me. Was he hurtful to you in the garden?"

Maia nodded, not wanting to repeat some of the accusations he had made.

Suzenne started pacing, tapping her lip with her finger as she walked. "Do you think he is staying at the Pilgrim with Captain Carew?"

"Yes, but it is outside the abbey. If I went there, they would seize me at once."

"But the tunnels go beneath the walls of the abbey," Suzenne said. "There is one that goes to the Pilgrim. I know it does!"

Maia's eyes widened. "I had not thought of that."

"Let me call for Owen to fetch Jon Tayt. He can deliver your letter."

Maia's heart began to skip. "Collier and Jon Tayt know each other."

"I will send for him right away."

***

Jon Tayt leaned against the wall and walked his thumbs into his wide belt. Argus sat on his haunches next to him, his tail wagging rhythmically. Maia and Suzenne watched the hunter closely, waiting for him to speak. The firelight from their Leering glinted off his coppery hair.

He sighed dramatically. "If it must be done, it must be done. But by Cheshu, Lady Maia, I am not suited for such wooing."

Maia suppressed a smile. "Do you think my intention is wrong?"

"I do, indeed."

"Then what would you advise?" Maia asked.

"Burn the letter. Right now. Once it leaves your hands, it is irretrievable. It is enough evidence for him to have you butchered by those pigs, the Naestors. Collier may resent it. He likely will. You used too many words. He is a man. He understands two things. One—whether he is hungry. And two—whether he can best another man with a weapon. All this talk is romantic nonsense. He is no love-smitten fool."

Maia's shoulders slumped.

"Your advice is appreciated," Suzenne said, but she cocked her head. "May I ask, Jon Tayt, how many times you have been married or been in love?"

"Nary a one," he said proudly, beaming.

"Then perhaps another voice should prevail. Yes, it was a political match that can be ended with a scribe's quill and ink. But it is still a legal marriage, for it was performed in front of witnesses, as Maia said, and sworn before a Dochte Mandar. It will not be easy for him to cast aside such a binding union. Maia is still the Queen of Dahomey."

Jon Tayt shook his head. "No, she is not."

Suzenne looked confused.

"Must I remind you of such things? When does a prince become a king? When he has been anointed such by one in authority. By the Aldermastons. Maia is his wife, but she is not his queen, not until a coronation is done in the presence of mastons, knights, and the populace." He raised his hands. "It is not too late for him to end the marriage."

"But Maia is the king's daughter! He will still want the union." Suzenne's cheeks were flushed.

"He appears to be making other arrangements," Jon Tayt quipped. "Lady Deorwynn's daughter. He needs money, and she has it. Maia has nothing but her pretty looks and her wits. I do not mean to insult you, lass, but that is the truth. You know he has no intention of becoming a maston, which is what you want from a husband. Perhaps the wise course would be to see what he does. From what you told me, he escaped in a hurry. He has no desire to be arrested under the Aldermaston's authority. Wait for him to speak to you again. If he tries, I promise I will not let Argus bite him, though I am tempted."

Suzenne shook her head. "He is still angry with Maia. What he believes about her is false."

Jon Tayt shrugged. "A fool is born every minute. Most of them live. Whitsunday is almost upon us. The dice are being cast. This is no time to make foolish errors."

Maia nodded to Jon Tayt and started to pace the room. She cleared her mind of all its troubles and tried to seek the Medium's will. She paused by the fire and stared into the flames, her eyes meeting the red-hot eyes in the carved face of the Leering. There was no wood in the hearth. Nothing to consume. Yet the fire was real, just as water Leerings gave off real water. Such simple yet undeniable evidence of the Medium's power. Why could Collier not see it?

She closed her eyes, drawing into herself, listening for the whispers from the Medium.

There was nothing.

Her emotions were in turmoil, but as she breathed deeply, they were slowly calming. The Aldermaston had taught her that she needed to be still, to be small within herself, to be open to the Medium's guidance.

Still, there was nothing.

She opened her eyes and stared at the flames again, feeling the heat on her cheeks and smelling the soot and ash so near. She reasoned it out in her mind. Jon Tayt was right. It was political and likely personal suicide to give Collier her confession. She had not begged or pleaded with him. She had not tried to soothe him or stroke his vanity. She had merely wanted to be honest with him at last. To speak the truth, even if some of that truth would wound him.

She closed her eyes and leaned her forehead against the stone wall above the hearth. The stone was pulsing with warmth. She had betrayed him so many times. How could he ever trust her again?

She opened her eyes wide.

What better way to win his trust than to make herself vulnerable? To give him a weapon to hurt her with? He might use it as such. He had already injured her repeatedly with his words in the garden. Though they had been spoken in anger, justifiable anger, they had still hurt. Let him see her remorse in the letter she had written after coming to Muirwood. Let him know her for who she truly was, not the illusion. If he turned from her then, at least he would be turning from *her*.

Her resolve hardened. She turned away from the hearth, feeling some of the fire still in her eyes.

"Thank you both for your counsel," she said. She had decided. She waited to see if the Medium would contradict her. She felt nothing but the iron of her determination. "Please bring my letter to Collier, Jon Tayt. Tonight. Right now."

The hunter frowned. "How about I let him read it and then I make sure it is cast into the fire? That would be more cautious."

She shook her head. "No. I want him to keep it. He is still my husband."

An ancient Aldermaston once said this, which has helped me tame the feelings that offense inspires: When you are offended at any man's fault, turn to yourself and study your own failings. Then you will forget your anger.

—Richard Syon, Aldermaston of Muirwood Abbey

CHAPTER NINETEEN

The Holk

The Aldermaston's kitchen was frantic in preparation for Whitsunday. There were trays of sweet rolls, platters full to brimming with delights. The two kitchen helpers were dusted with flour and despite the long hours, they were both giddy with excitement for the upcoming festival. Every day brought news, wagons, and people from throughout the realm come to celebrate Whitsunday with the king. Beyond the abbey walls, tents were springing up like an army camp as hosts began to arrive.

"They have not put up the maypole yet," Aloia said to Maia, scraping the side of a bowl with her spoon. Davi came and dipped her littlest finger into the bowl over the other girl's shoulder to snitch a taste. "Davi!" Aloia whined.

"Of course they have not put up the maypole yet," said the other girl. "It will be hung the day before. Oh, would that we were fourteen already! You know the maypole dance, do you not?" she asked Maia.

"I do," Maia replied, smiling, yet her heart stung with pain. Lady Deorwynn had ensured that no one would ask her to dance on her first Whitsunday after coming of age. Now she dreaded the holiday for a different reason. If the Aldermaston did not declare her ready to take the maston test before Whitsunday, the change in Aldermastons might prevent her from taking the test at all.

"Did you see the lists?" Aloia asked Davi, rounding on her excitedly. "There will be jousting! The field is cleared and staked off so that no one can put a tent up near it. Owen said that Captain Carew was practicing there earlier today. He knocked down three knights. No one could unhorse him!"

"Do you know Captain Carew?" Davi asked Maia.

"Yes, I have met him before, but have not seen him for several years."

"I asked Owen if he was handsome and he did not know what to say," Aloia confided.

"Of course not. He is a boy. What would he know?"

Maia smiled, finishing her bowl of soup quickly. Suzenne was sharing a meal with Dodd across the kitchen, their heads bent low in conversation.

"He is handsome," Maia said. "He speaks three languages, and he is good with a bow as well as a blade."

"Do you think Jon Tayt will win the archery contest?" Aloia asked, eyes wide with interest.

"I do not know," Maia said. She was about to set the bowl down, but Davi took it from her and went to rinse it.

The sun was lingering longer and longer each day, but Maia could see the dying light beyond. She kept looking at the door every time someone arrived carrying a large sack of milled grain or additional ingredients. All day she had hoped to hear from Collier. Jon

Tayt had delivered her letter the previous night, but Collier had coolly dismissed the hunter, refusing to read it in his presence.

"If you girls spent as much time working as you did pining," Collett said sagely, "we would have been ready for Whitsunday three days ago. Strong minds discuss ideas, average minds discuss events, weak minds discuss people. Now back to work, you two." Collett looked at Maia, rolled her eyes in exasperation, and went back to the trestle tables, her hair still tight in its bun despite her daylong efforts. She was a fastidious woman and worked harder and longer than two teams of oxen combined.

The girls sighed and went back to their work, leaving Maia alone with her thoughts for a moment. Her father was coming. She could almost hear, deep in her mind, the sound of hooves, the jangle of spurs, the fluttering of banners. With so many guests arriving at Muirwood, the kitchen had not been much of a refuge. Maia thought about sneaking off to the Queen's Garden again, hoping to find Collier there, but she had done so earlier to no avail. Soon the entire court would descend on the grounds and there would be no time or space to think.

Maia's future remained a murky mystery to her. What would it be like to see her father? She wanted to talk to him, but she was also afraid of him—afraid of who he had become.

The door of the kitchen opened again, and Maia looked up and started with surprise when Captain Carew entered. He was a bull of a man, with freshly cut reddish-brown hair. His nose was prominent, but not ugly, and a dusting of pleasant freckles covered his weather-burned tan. He was indeed a handsome man, one who had, according to rumor, caroused with her father.

He was followed by Collier and three other men, one of whom was Jon Tayt. Collett was quick to scowl at the intruders.

"This is the Aldermaston's kitchen, not a feeding trough," she warned. "Your supper will be ready when it is ready." She walked up, folding her arms imperiously. "I do not have time to fix anything extra when men are hungry."

Captain Carew smiled and gave her an elegant bow. "My lady cook, I will break the fingers of any man who attempts to snitch your delights before they have paid for them. I was seeking Lady Maia, and I have found her."

Suzenne and Dodd glanced up. Dodd rose from his seat on a barrel and set his bowl down, looking to Jon Tayt for guidance.

Maia rose too, dusting off her skirts. "You did, Captain."

He smiled at her. "Your travels have only heightened your beauty, Maia. Well met. Would you walk with me in the Cider Orchard?"

Her stomach twisted, but Jon Tayt looked at her from behind the captain's shoulders, his eyes narrowing. He nodded subtly.

"It will be dark soon," Maia said, hedging.

"It will not be a long talk," Carew said, inclining his head. "We may not have another chance to talk before your father arrives."

He had a message for her then. She clenched her hands into fists, nodded, and followed the men out of the kitchen. The air was brisk outside, and she felt Collier's eyes on her, the pressure of his gaze making her cheeks tingle with heat. Argus, who had known better than to enter Collett's kitchen, wagged his tail and padded up to her as soon as she came outside. She reached down and scratched his head.

"The beast does nothing but growl at me," Carew said. "I heard he piddled on Crabwell's boots." He snorted with laughter. "He will walk on that side of you, if you please."

Maia said nothing as they crossed the grounds together and approached the dense apple orchard. There were small ladders set about and the workers were busy culling fruit from the low-hanging branches.

As they reached the borders of the trees, Carew turned back to their escort, the two guardsmen who were walking with Tayt and Collier. "Jeppson, over on that end. Rowen, that side. Collier and Tayt—wait here for us."

Maia hesitated. "We go on alone?"

"Yes, but within their sight," he answered. "I am here to protect you, Maia, not abduct you. I will not risk the Aldermaston's wrath. If it even exists," he added with a chuckle. "Pardon me, I can be irreverent at times. The result of being your father's companion. We were friends, you know. Have been friends all of our lives. I was there when he wed your mother. We passed the maston test together." He extended his arm, gallantly, and she took it and entered the grove of apple trees. Glancing back, she saw Collier watching her warily, his expression very neutral and composed.

Carew patted her arm. "Thank you for coming willingly," he said softly. "What I have to say I must say discreetly. Your father knows you are here, Maia. He sent me deliberately. There are rumors that someone is seeking your life. Someone Lady Deorwynn paid to kill you."

Maia stiffened.

"Do not be afraid," Carew said. "It will be difficult since there will be many guests at Muirwood, but you will be watched at all times." He turned to gaze at her, his expression serious. "You must not come to harm, Lady Maia."

"If the Medium wills it," Maia replied. "I do not fear death, Captain. I have been to the land where death was born."

He sniffed, frowning at her words. "Indeed. The cursed shores?"

She nodded and then stopped. "I think we are far enough. What did you hope to tell me?"

He released her arm and turned to face her. "Crabwell failed to convince you. I thought I would give it a try."

"You?" Maia challenged.

"Why do you chuckle?"

"You are my father's boon companion. You are one of his favorites. The last time we met, you attempted to persuade me to renounce my rights of inheritance."

He held up a finger. "Actually, I did not. I saw you stand up to Crabwell. The little spleen beetle. I am a courtier, Maia. I have no illusions about my station. I was there when you stood up to Crabwell. As you *ought* to have done. I was proud of you, lass. You refused to give up your rights and privileges. How can you give those up? You cannot." He stepped closer to her, his voice dropping lower. "You are the only one of us to have defied the king and survived. Tomas Morton—dead. Forshee—dead. A host of others—dead. Why did they die? Because of Lady Deorwynn and her vengeance. She is the one poisoning the mind of the king. We thought," he added surreptitiously, "that she was . . . allied with the Myriad Ones. That she wore a kystrel. Crabwell has an informant in her household, one of her ladies-in-waiting. A maston girl even. She saw Lady Deorwynn bathe not long ago, and she had nary a shadowstain. In the past, some girls from Dahomey were immune to the taint of kystrels, but I do not believe that is the case now. Using that magic leaves its mark. Lady Deorwynn is cunning and ambitious, but she is no het—she is no emissary of evil."

Maia's heart was pounding. She wanted to clutch her own bodice more tightly, wondering if Carew suspected her.

His voice was smooth and persuasive. "Yes, you are the only one who has stood up to your father and survived. Your father still *loves* you, Maia." His eyes glittered with intensity. "He may rage and he may threaten. But he will not kill you. Believe that. You have power over him. No one else does. Listen to me! Crabwell seeks to overthrow Deorwynn and her brood. Who will be the next heir if not you?" He reached out, and she was afraid he would touch her shoulder, but he only set his heavy hand on the curve of her neck. "*You*, Maia. Crabwell is a scheming power-monger." He snorted. "We all are, myself included. But let me speak plainly to you, girl. Your father seeks to throw down the maston order. He is goaded by Crabwell to seize the wealth and riches of the abbeys. Our treasury is flush, to be sure, but it is not enough to sate Crabwell's lust for wealth. With enough coin, your father believes he can summon mercenaries to defend us from Hautland. I have been to Hautland, my lady. So has Master Collier." He shook his head. "We are on the verge of being invaded. Now is not the time to cast aside the old beliefs. I am a terrible maston. I forsook my oaths many years ago. But I still *believe* in it. So do many others. You are here to become a maston yourself. I applaud you! Help us bring down Lady Deorwynn. Help us reclaim your rights by birth. Crabwell has overreached himself. He is tottering and will fall. Another will take his place, but there is only one you . . . and you are the last best chance of convincing your father to do what is right."

Maia stared into his hazel eyes and saw the deep cunning there. Carew's approach felt so different than Crabwell's. So many were scheming for power. So many wished to use her. Though there were no other witnesses, she knew she needed to be careful what she said.

"You are loyal to my father?" Maia asked him pointedly.

"I am. He is my best friend, and he has rewarded me amply for my loyalty." He dropped his hand. "But he made a terrible mistake when he left your mother. And you, Maia, have suffered for it. I cannot bring your mother back from the dead. I think it is possible to reclaim his soul."

Maia closed her eyes, wondering what to do, what to say. A sharp feeling of insight came to her. "You disagreed with my father about divorcing my mother, and yet you said nothing. Even when the High Seer pronounced the marriage lawful and the divorce invalid."

"You are correct," Carew agreed. "Anyone who spoke against your father's wishes was severely punished. Look no further than what happened to Forshee."

"So now that my mother is dead, you are free to speak your conscience? Is that it?"

"Exactly so," Carew answered. "Accept the truth, lass. He hated your mother at the end." He shook his head and looked sad. "He rejoiced when he learned of her death."

"My mother, the lawful Queen of Comoros, was murdered by a kishion in the very heart of the realm," Maia said with growing indignation. She sought to control her voice, but it trembled with emotion. "Has there been any kind of inquest? Has this kishion been found? Now you say he seeks to kill me. Why are you not hunting him then? You cannot, because you know my *father* hired him! He allowed the man into his realm. Now look at the consequences of that action. Captain, I appreciate the honor of your visit and your intention to keep me safe so you can use me for your own ends as you have so wickedly used my father." She stepped toward him. "I am not to be bargained with or persuaded. You, sir, are a coward." Her lip trembled. "You may be fearless on a horse with a lance, or with a sword in the arena. But you have forgotten the tomes, Captain Carew. You have forgotten the words of Ovidius. No maston can hold his virtue too dear, for it is the only thing whose value will ever increase with its cost. Our integrity is never worth so much as when we have parted with our all to keep it."

He stared at her, his eyes widening with shock. "How do you know that phrase?" he whispered.

Maia realized she had blundered, that she had quoted from a tome. Maia straightened her skirts. "I have always had a prodigious memory, Captain Carew," she answered with a thick voice. "You should remember that."

With the threat lingering in the air, she turned and walked away from him, feeling her cheeks flush with heat. As she emerged from the orchard, she saw Collier eyeing her closely, but he said nothing to her, looking a little bored.

Jon Tayt motioned for her to join him and Argus, which she did. His voice was low as they walked. "The captain did not look very pleased with you, lass. By Cheshu, I could almost hear the scolding you gave him from here. Keep walking. The *Holk* was sighted earlier today. We must go straight to the Aldermaston's study. Your grandmother should be there by now."

CHAPTER TWENTY

Simon Fox

Maia squeezed her grandmother and felt the embrace returned with equal vigor. Sabine smelled of salty sea and wood stain, and her hair was wild and windblown. She looked as if she had traveled a great distance.

"My dear one," Sabine whispered, pulling away to cup Maia's cheeks in her hands. She smiled at her with such tenderness it made the anxiety and ache of their separation even more poignant. This was Family. This was what she had craved.

"You were gone for so long," Maia breathed. The Aldermaston and his wife smiled at them. Jon Tayt was there as well, off to the side talking to a younger man dressed in black with a felt cap that matched his clothes. The young man was stern, and he listened complacently as Jon Tayt prattled on.

"I am sorry, dear one," Sabine said, taking Maia's hands and squeezing them. "I have been at sea a great deal, giving directions to various Aldermastons to help them prepare for what is coming."

She sighed, wiped a few strands of hair from her eyes, and shook her head. "My son-in-law is making things rather difficult."

"Where have you been?" Maia asked, drawing her over to some stuffed chairs in the corner of the room.

"Pry-Ree, Hautland, Dahomey. Other places as well." She patted Maia's hand. "I most recently visited Dahomey to seek King Gideon, only to discover that he had changed ships immediately to come to Comoros."

"Then you have heard?" Maia asked, staring into her eyes.

"I have heard a great many things," Sabine answered. She gestured for the others to draw near. As the young man dressed in black left the shadows, Maia saw that his velvet tunic was actually a very deep burgundy color, so dark it had appeared black. It was expensive and exquisitely styled, with ribbed sleeves that were black, and gold fringes at the sleeves and collar. Though he was a young man, he had a wispy forked beard paired with mild brown eyes that held a contemplative expression. He looked to be only a few years older than Maia.

"This is Simon Fox," Sabine said. She rose and walked over to the young man, then bowed her head slightly to him.

"Greetings," he said as he bowed in return, his accent distinctly Dahomeyjan. "It is a pleasure to meet you all."

Sabine touched his sleeve and then gestured toward him with her other hand. "Simon is part of the Victus."

Maia's eyebrows lifted and a worried feeling bloomed in her stomach.

"He is also one of the spymasters of King Gideon of Dahomey. He was trained and mentored by Chancellor Walraven personally. There are some among the Victus who cannot condone the planned murder of the mastons in Assinica. Like Walraven, Simon risks his life to aid us with information. He has come here to speak with his master at Whitsunday, but I wanted to introduce you all to him first, so you would know where his loyalties truly lie. To the world at large, he is known as a wine and cider merchant whose Family is responsible for shipping barrels throughout the kingdoms. He has contacts within most of the noble Families, knows ship captains of every allegiance, and receives messages from all the kingdoms with surprising regularity. His most recent assignment was serving under Corriveaux in Dahomey, and he has since been reassigned, through Walraven's influence, to the Court of Comoros to spy on Maia's father. What he learns he will tell the Victus, King Gideon, and us."

Maia stared at him with distrust as she rose from her seat, her mouth pursed.

Sabine took a moment to gaze at each of them. "I wanted to introduce you to Simon personally. I trust him, and his information has proved timely and invaluable. He has already assisted me in one very urgent matter. He has studied the maston ways and lore and, along with others in his situation, feels that the order of the Dochte Mandar is corrupt and is bringing harm to the people. Show them your kystrel, Simon."

The man sighed and quickly undid the buttons on his tunic front and collar, opening the material of his shirt. He was of slight build, the tunic giving him a deceptively broader girth. The sight of the chain around his neck and the whorl-like tattoo on his skin made Maia sick inside.

"Show them," Sabine insisted.

"As you may know, the kystrels were forged in the past," Simon said, his voice slightly accented. "They were handed down from hetaera to slave. In the Dochte Mandar tradition they are believed to allow us to commune with the spirits of the dead. In truth, they commune with the Unborn, the Myriad Ones. This is not a kystrel, but a replica. There are missing segments of the pattern, here and here," he said, pointing to the markings. "This was crafted to look as if it were of ancient origin, but in truth it was created by a clever metalsmith whom I hired to perform the work. The shadowstain you see on my chest . . ." He dabbed his tongue with his finger and then rubbed at the stain. Part of it came away and left a blot of ink on the young man's finger. He held it up to them. "It is ink, not a tattoo."

Sabine smiled and patted his arm. "Simon would like to become a maston. Most of those who live in Naess dread the maston order. But some of the young men and women in the rising generation have studied alongside mastons and read the tomes; they have seen that power should not be constrained and forced through the hetaeras' amulets." She squeezed his shoulder. "There are some in Naess who can hear the true whispers of the Medium, despite the near-darkness that rules so far to the north. Simon joined the Victus to help thwart it, and was led by the Medium to Walraven. At the time, he believed him to be an enemy and not our ally, but he trusted the Medium's guidance and learned that they supported the same cause. Men like Corriveaux are part of the old order. Simon hopes, someday, that there may be an abbey built in Naess."

As Sabine said the words, Maia felt a familiar warm feeling in her bosom, a sense of peace and contentment. She found herself smiling. She had seen the dark city full of Leering lights. She remembered the enormous cliff face that rose behind the port city, jutting from the waters like a mountain-sized Leering itself. The possibility that an abbey might exist there someday filled her with wonder and hope.

Sabine stared into Maia's eyes and nodded. "You feel the Medium as well. That is how I came to trust Walraven. It is how I trust Simon. You see, the lad has no true kystrel. He cannot force the Medium to obey him. But it listens to him nonetheless. He can activate a Leering with his thoughts, just like we can. Even though his bloodline comes from Naess, enough Family blood flows within it to give him access to the Medium's power. It grows slowly, patiently. The same as it has been doing with us all." She patted his arm again and returned to Maia's side.

"Simon, tell the others about the armada."

Maia watched as he quickly buttoned his tunic, concealing himself once more. His expression was grave and guarded. There was a glimmer in his eyes that Maia recognized. A hunger and thirst for knowledge. She had a feeling he knew more languages than she did.

"The armada sailed from Hautland weeks ago," he said blandly, his voice devoid of any emotion. "The common belief is that the armada was sent to invade Comoros and will sail around Pry-Ree, turn south, and strike the heart of the kingdom from the south. That is one of the reasons the king is coming to Muirwood. He cannot win a battle at sea against such a force, so he will allow the city to be sacked and ravaged. Most of his army has been drawn away from the city, leaving it undefended. But that is not the aim of the armada. While Comoros frets and waits for the invasion, the fleet sails for Assinica."

He stroked the wisps of light brown beard. "The fleet is well equipped and stocked with provisions. It does not expect or need reinforcements. Its only goal is to crush the mastons. Our spies have informed us that the mastons sailed up navigable rivers in the land that opens to a vast lake. That is where their city and abbeys were built. It was wise, because an entire fleet cannot engage all at once. That will be helpful, but they cannot resist such an overwhelming force. Our spies indicate that they have not been training in war and are quite peaceful and prosperous. There are no castles or keeps or strongholds. The abbeys are the most impressive structures, but they are not defensible. In a word, they will be slaughtered unless the Medium intervenes."

Sabine nodded, her eyes determined. "I do not think that it will," she said softly. "I have felt the strong impressions from the Medium to save those people. They are peace-loving and will not rise to defend themselves, even against those who come to slaughter them. They will be massacred. The Medium compels me to save them, but I do not have enough ships. Nor do I have enough time. I have pleaded with the Medium to tell me how to save them—by attacking Naess ourselves, by treaty. All that I hear in return is that the Apse Veil must be opened. There are abbeys there, and the people can use the network between the abbeys to cross into these lands for safety. We have been trained in war. We must be their defenders." She turned and looked at Maia. "Have you taken the maston test?"

Maia shook her head, her stomach churning with concern for the defenseless mastons. "No, Grandmother. The Aldermaston felt I was not yet ready."

Sabine turned to the Aldermaston, who met her gaze unflinchingly. "My lady, I have sought the Medium's will each day to bring her inside to take the rites. My own desires have continually been thwarted. I have assumed it was because you were not yet here."

"I am here. We will go tonight. It will take time to remove all the people from Assinica. We may need to open more than one Veil to hasten the work. The spirits of the dead are restless, especially in Muirwood. I can sense them with us now. It is not just for the living that the Apse Veils must be restored. The dead brood over us with their thoughts." She clasped her hands behind her and began pacing. "I sought out your husband in Dahomey, Maia," she said sadly. "When he did not come, the Cruciger orb told me that I should return to Muirwood. The Medium brought him here ahead of me, it seems." She chuckled. "Perhaps you will need *his* strength to open the Veils. Have you spoken to him yet?"

"I have," Maia said. She lowered her eyes to hide her confused feelings. "It did not go very well. He is hurt and angry."

Sabine frowned. "He hurried too soon. He does not even know yet."

"What do you mean?"

She waved her hand, not giving an answer, and turned to Simon Fox. "You must make sure he learns about it quickly, Simon. You came here today under a cloak, and you shall leave through the tunnels. Jon Tayt will show you the way. You must arrive through the gates as expected when the king's host comes."

Maia was determined to learn this secret, but she knew it was not the time. She would ask her grandmother later.

"My lady," the Aldermaston said. "As you remember, the king is bringing the new Aldermaston for Muirwood with him. You know him as well as I do—Ely Kranmir from Augustin. I received a message that he is to arrive imminently. What would you have me do?"

Sabine looked at him, her eyes widening. "So many snakes in the woods. How to walk without being bitten by one?"

"Is it a sin to thrash an Aldermaston, by Cheshu?" Jon Tayt said gruffly. "We could bar the gates against him."

Sabine smiled. "Lia did that to his predecessor, I recall. The story is famous." She began pacing again, shaking her head thoughtfully. "Mutiny at sea, treason by land. If he succeeds in naming his own man Aldermaston of Muirwood, the oldest abbey of the realm, where will his ambitions end?"

"In a grave," Jon Tayt said with a snort, "as it always does. Even the mastons of the past had to rebel against their fallen king."

Sabine looked at him and shook her head. "Not without a warning first. The Medium always warns before it destroys."

"If I may?" Simon Fox said in a deferential voice.

The others looked to him. "Yes, Simon?" Sabine replied.

He stroked his wispy beard again. "There is no easy answer to this conundrum. The stakes are high and the jeopardy is real. Lady Maia, if you will excuse me not using your given name? Thank you. Lady Maia is the only person who has defied the king's authority without being executed. Many have signed the Writ of Submission—or the *Act* of Submission . . . pardon me . . . for fear of their life, including Aldermaston Kranmir. Do you believe the king will execute his own daughter? I do not. Therefore, I suggest that as soon as he arrives, we focus the king's attention on his daughter's presence. She is lawfully married to my master, King Gideon. If we legitimize the marriage in the eyes of the people and have Lady Maia proclaimed Queen of Dahomey, her father will not be able to overthrow the customs on his authority alone. That is my counsel."

Sabine looked at him, her brow furrowing. "You are asking me to trust my son-in-law with her life."

"Yes," Simon replied, bowing meekly. "In my opinion, the king cannot overthrow the maston order unless Maia submits and signs the act. He was anointed king. His true wife, Lady Catrin, is dead. But Maia's royal birth means she has the same authority, the same benefit, as her father. Yes, she has been disinherited. Unlawfully. Yes, she has been a pariah. Unpardonably. But she has more right to the throne than any other person besides the king . . . and even he knows that. Think of the mastons in Assinica. Who will they look to as their rightful ruler? Him? Or her?"

Maia felt her knees begin to tremble. Her voice was hoarse in her own ears. "I will not rebel against my father."

Simon shook his head. "I did not suggest you should. Yet. All I am suggesting is that you do not give in to him. Even if he threatens your life. If you are a maston, even *he* cannot evict you from these grounds. Perhaps the world should see what happens if he tries."

Maia swallowed, feeling her stomach twisting into knots.

"I am certain the Medium will not allow Muirwood to fall without a struggle. Let us go," Sabine said with a determined nod to the Aldermaston and his wife. "Prepare the abbey. It is time Maia took the maston test."

Belief and character are intermixed. Following the Medium's whispers over time will forge a strong character that can be called upon in times of desperate need. Character is not developed in moments of temptation and trial. That is when it is intended to be used.

—Richard Syon, Aldermaston of Muirwood Abbey

CHAPTER
TWENTY-ONE

Forbidden

The nervous feelings inside Maia's stomach made it difficult to concentrate. Darkness had fallen across the abbey grounds, a solemn darkness that brought with it a weighty silence. Maia and Suzenne sat next to each other in the Aldermaston's study, wearing simple white learner robes and outer cloaks with veiled hoods. They were to take the test together.

"Are you as nervous as I am?" Suzenne whispered, clutching Maia's hands.

Maia could not speak. She only nodded.

Suzenne stroked her arm. "Jayn told me the maston rites are nothing to fear. They are . . . solemn. Symbolic. She was . . . different after passing the test. More thoughtful and serious."

"You are already serious," Maia teased, nudging her shoulder.

Suzenne smiled, and Maia admired her friend's regal beauty and good nature. Such a contrast to Maeg, she thought. Maeg and the other learners who were finishing their studies at Muirwood would be taking the maston test the next day. There was so much change coming. A new Aldermaston—what would he do about the Ciphers if he learned of them? Each girl had taken a tremendous risk to be taught to read and engrave. If the Dochte Mandar were to find out, they would all be hunted down.

"That has always been my temperament," Suzenne said. She sighed. "My parents will be arriving on the morrow. I must tell them I plan to marry Dodd. They will not be pleased, to be sure!"

"It is your choice, is it not?" Maia whispered sympathetically. "And you love him."

"I do love him . . . so much that it hurts. After tonight, everything will change. When you open the Apse Veil . . . oh, Maia, all will change! I think of the mastons waiting across the ocean. They have been waiting for so long. Will we speak the same language? Will they feel like . . . lost cousins?" She smiled broadly, head cocked.

Maia's stomach twisted even more. "That is assuming that I *can* open it."

"It begins with a thought," Suzenne reminded her sternly. "This is no time for doubt. You must do it, Maia." She squeezed her arm. "I believe you can. I believe the Medium prepared you for this moment."

"Well, so long as I can lift such heavy expectations," Maia said with a smirk. "I do feel . . . uneasy. I suppose that would be the case under normal circumstances, but tonight is oppressive with . . . I do not know the right word. Even the air feels different."

"I do not feel it any differently," Suzenne said. "Does it feel more solemn for you?"

Maia shook her head. "*Brooding* is the word I was thinking of. I have read in the tomes that the Medium gets like this at times. Especially before something significant happens. I can see my grandmother feels it as well. So does the Aldermaston."

There was a tap on the door, and the Aldermaston's steward, Tomas, entered. He wore long cream-colored robes and a matching cloak. He was so tall that they would have recognized him even with his gray hairs covered. He looked very much like an Aldermaston, except for the dimples in his cheeks, which lent him an altogether jolly air.

"Are you both ready?" he asked, flashing the dimples with a pleasant smile. Suzenne and Maia nodded and both rose from the bench.

"Cover your faces," he instructed gently, gesturing toward the veils and hoods they had been given. They did so and followed him down the hall illuminated by a lantern he held in his strong hand. Because of the late hour, the corridors were abandoned. Their slippered feet padded softly to the doors.

The night sky glittered with stars, interrupted only by a fringe of clouds on the western horizon. The grass was soft and damp as they trod the short distance from the manor house to the abbey. As Maia gazed up at it, her stomach flipped as if she were staring off a cliff. The scaffolding had all been dismantled, and the polished stone seemed to glitter in the starlight. It was massive, impressive, and the sight of it filled Maia's heart with deep reverence. She could sense the Medium rejoicing in its freedom from the timber cocoon. As they approached the huge pewter door inset into the side of the abbey, Maia saw another person, also veiled and waiting in the shadows. The figure detached from the darkness, and by the walk and grace, she recognized it as Sabine, who had also covered her hair and was wearing a veil.

The nervous feeling inside Maia only increased. The abbey rose like a mountain, giving her the same sense of wonder she had experienced looking at the various mountain ranges she had trekked through in Dahomey and Mon. Memories of Cruix Abbey, which she had unwittingly destroyed, flashed in her mind, making her cringe with anguish and regret. Taking a deep breath, she tried to master her feelings, though worry hung heavy in her stomach. She could not bear it if anything harmed Muirwood. She loved the abbey and the grounds, having found a peace in the few months she had lived here unlike any she had felt throughout her life.

Sabine approached her and took her hands, squeezing them. "Are you ready?" Maia could hear the emotion in her voice.

"I am," Maia replied, desperately trying to feel it was true.

Sabine touched Suzenne's arm, stroking it affectionately, and then turned toward the abbey. They all started to walk toward the pewter doors. All except Maia. Her feet were rooted in place, her legs seized with trepidation.

After several steps, the others noticed she had not followed.

"What is it?" Sabine asked, looking back at her.

Maia's heart hammered in her chest. Sick fear had leeched into her blood. Her legs would not move. Her tongue felt swollen in her mouth. She willed herself to close the distance. Her body would not obey.

Sabine walked up to her and took her hand. "There are Leerings set into the doorway. You must silence them to pass," she whispered.

Maia nodded, trying to wrestle her terrors into submission. The very air was suddenly oppressive. The abbey glowered down at her, and she felt so insignificant and small in comparison. She bowed her head and reached out to the Leerings in her mind. *Let me pass*, she pleaded.

There was a voice in her mind, a whisper that cut through stone and bone.

You are forbidden.

Trembling, Maia felt herself faltering, her vision blackening slightly. Dizziness washed over her. The feeling nearly drove her to her knees.

"Go on ahead," Sabine told Tomas, motioning for him to take Suzenne. Her friend stared back at her in surprise and concern, her brow wrinkling, but the steward took her arm and they both walked effortlessly up to the pewter door and opened it. A shaft of light momentarily blinded Maia and then it was gone and they were inside.

Maia panted with panic, gazing up at the looming spire. Every crenellation, every slant had been meticulously carved. The stones thrummed with power. She could sense it, overpowering and awful in its majestic omniscience.

"I cannot enter," Maia said huskily, clutching her grandmother's arm.

"Was it the Leering?" Sabine said with concern in her voice.

"No, it is more than just a Leering," Maia said bleakly. "I heard the Medium's whisper forbidding me. I am not worthy yet."

Maia bowed her head and started to cry, feeling the disappointment and despair crushing her so low that she could not contain the tears. She, Maia, who still hardly ever cried! The internal pressure to succeed had created this waterfall of anguished tears, which flowed unrestrained. Sabine wrapped her in her arms, hugging her close. It was the mark on her shoulder, she thought. And the tattoo on her chestbone. It was too soon. She was still vulnerable to the Myriad Ones. The abbey must be condemning her.

"Shhh," Sabine soothed. "I felt tonight was the right time. The Medium moved me to bring you here. Maybe there is another reason. Do not despair."

"How can I not?" Maia said miserably. "The abbey was my last comfort. I have given up everything . . . power, jewels, fine gowns . . . friendships. I have abandoned my father. I have lost my husband. Yet it is still not enough. The taint from the Myriad Ones afflicts me still." She clutched Sabine's hands. "I am willing to do anything the Medium asks of me. What more must I give?"

Sabine raised her veil and cowl and then lifted Maia's. She looked into her eyes with compassion and sympathy, which made Maia's heart burn with shame at the depths of her own despair. No, she had not lost everything. She had gained new friends. She had discovered her grandmother. She was still alive in spite of a myriad of attempts to crush her. As she tried to quiet her emotions, she felt a subtle, gentle soothing from the Medium.

"Walk with me," Sabine said kindly, hooking arms together. "There is one more thing you can give. Perhaps something we neglected to consider. For such an occasion as this, we should hold vigil. Giving up sleep will help us be more sensitive to the Medium's will, and it will communicate the urgency of our need for direction. I will hold it with you, beginning tonight, and then tomorrow, and then however long it takes."

Maia stared at her pleadingly. "But my father is coming."

"I know," Sabine said, radiating an inner calm that Maia marveled at.

***

They walked the grounds together all night, and when morning came, they stood and stared across the moors wreathed in fluffy mists. A vigil was about more than giving up sleep. It was a demonstration of willingness to heed the Medium's direction, a sacrifice of comfort and rest to request aid for a specific need. Normally it was held alone, but Maia and her grandmother had roamed the grounds from one end to the other, visiting the Cider Orchard, the duck pond, and the laundry. At one point they encountered Argus and Jon Tayt, who had tracked their footprints and complained loudly of being led on a merry chase through the grounds.

Maia was exhausted in the morning, but she was not as depressed in spirits as she had been at nightfall. She still did not have a clear reason why the Medium had forbidden her entrance to the abbey. Sabine had counseled her to not assume, but to use the time and the quiet to ponder and reflect and open herself even wider to knowledge and wisdom from Idumea.

"The sun has come," Sabine said, patting her arm. "I must prepare for the day. I will change before we meet for breakfast in the Aldermaston's kitchen."

Maia gave her a final hug. "I wish to see my mother's garden and watch the flowers open."

Sabine smiled and walked with her to the garden. "I am so thankful your mother left this piece of herself for you. Till breakfast, dear one."

The Leering responded obediently to her thoughts, and Maia sealed the portal shut behind her. The interior was full of shadows, for the sun had not fully risen yet. Maia was a little chilled, but it was a lovely spring morning, and the flower beds gave off delicately sweet aromas.

"You startled me."

Maia flinched and whirled around to see Collier emerge from behind a tree. He looked haggard and wary, and was rubbing his eyes. He traced a gloved hand along the edge of a branch. "I normally hear the gardener's clacking cart from a way off first."

"Have you been in here all night?" Maia asked, her heart pounding a ragged rhythm.

"I could not sleep," he answered evasively. "I have been mulling over secrets and trying to make sense of them."

"Have you had any success?"

He shook his head. "Only failure. But I am persistent. It would amaze you how patient I can be," he said meaningfully.

The words caused a shudder through Maia. "Corriveaux said something like that to me."

"No doubt he has read my ancestor's tome," Collier said flippantly. "Well now . . . this is an unusual schedule for you, Maia. You normally do not visit the gardens until *after* some of the lessons. Did you have trouble sleeping as well?"

Maia nodded uncomfortably, looking down at her wet slippers. "I am sorry I startled you, but this garden *is* mine."

"Are you forbidding—?"

"No," Maia interrupted, shaking her head. "I was apologizing. You have come here since our last meeting."

Collier admitted ruefully, "Until the gardener arrives, of course. It is quiet. Out of sight. My mother had a garden like this," he said, gazing up at the vine-strewn wall. He was closer to her now, approaching slowly and warily, like a cat. "I received your letter of apology," he said. "I have been pondering how to best answer it." He scratched the stubble at his throat.

"Do you have any questions?" Maia asked softly, staring at him in spite of herself. His eyes were so blue, they reminded her of the flowers nearby. The forget-me-nots. Collier's raw attractiveness both pierced and alarmed her. All her life she had distrusted handsome men. A man like him would catch the eye of many ladies . . . would he even be capable of fidelity?

"I have many questions," he said guardedly. "But I cannot trust answers from you. I must seek them from other sources. From other harbors." He turned away from her and walked over to the wall. "You are either incredibly devious or utterly sincere. Or . . . quite possibly . . . both, depending on who is . . ." He regarded her significantly and tapped his forehead.

"I am myself right now," Maia said resolutely, her insides twisting with suppressed feelings. "And I hope to be myself forever after. That is why I seek to become a maston."

"Yes, I know," he said in almost a pained voice. He shook his head. "I never wanted to marry a maston. Too sanctimonious. Too many scruples. Too . . . good. I admired my father as a man. He was a king-maston and he taught me to trust the Medium and surrender my will to it." He grit his teeth in frustration. "To what end? He was vanquished by the King of Paeiz. His coffers were gutted by a ruthless neighbor seeking more land. Half of Dahomey is cursed anyway, and fighting border wars is tedious business. I crave land. I crave power. I already told you this, and I thought we had an understanding between us."

She saw his ambition again, saw the gleam in his eye that said he would not be satisfied without conquest. It repelled her sensibilities.

"What good are fortunes and land when so many of your people are suffering in poverty, Collier?" Maia responded.

"What good is giving alms after you have given away everything and they are *still* poor?" he retorted. "You said in your letter that you seek to marry a maston. I am not one. I do not believe in Idumea. I think our forefathers chained our minds with their practices and beliefs. But let us suspend our opposing doctrines for a moment and say, just for argument's sake, that you are the girl described in your letter. I assume you still do not want me to overthrow your father?"

Maia nodded once, briefly, and braced herself for his incredulity. The truth was, she was sorely conflicted, and each time she heard more about her father's depredations, the feeling only worsened. But unless the Medium commanded her to, she would not depose him. Collier was the kind of man who could do that, but would he risk *becoming* like the man he despised in doing so?

"Of course not!" he said with a harsh chuckle. "So if I continue to uphold our marriage, I have shackled myself to a girl with no ambition and a father-in-law who is quite likely the most lecherous and tyrannical ruler in history! Yet I cannot topple him and do the kingdoms and you a favor." He threw up his hands in frustration. "I have married a girl who is a simpleton, who would plead peace against logic . . . and thus thwart me in achieving my goals. To make matters even more insufferable, she is beautiful, and yet they say her kiss is death." His jaw trembled with suppressed emotion. He breathed in heavily through his nose, calming himself deliberately. He shook his head wonderingly. "By what power, *Wife*, do you allure me? For I am half tempted, darling, to prove it wrong right now. I do not believe a kiss will be fatal, despite what the tomes say. If I am wrong . . . maybe I deserve to die."

He took a step toward her, his gaze both a challenge and a question.

Maia shrank and retreated. "No, Collier," she said, shaking her head to clear her own mind. Her heart thundered in her ears. How she wanted to kiss him. She could feel the temptation twisting inside of her. But she knew what would happen if she relented. She knew from personal experience that he was wrong, that a hetaera's kiss was deadly. She still grieved for the dead Aldermaston of Cruix Abbey.

The sound of a rickety cart could be heard approaching the garden, could be heard as Collier stopped in front of her. Beyond the wall, Maia heard her grandmother's voice greeting Thewliss warmly.

Collier stood in front of her, trembling, his eyes fixed on her face. A half-mocking smirk twisted his mouth. "You have not told your father yet about our marriage."

"I have not," she whispered. "Few know."

He nodded. "Good."

She closed her eyes, feeling sick inside. "What are your intentions?" she asked him. She desperately wanted to hear a rejection of the plans for him and Murer.

He pursed his lips and shook his head. "That you will have to learn for yourself, just as I must learn for myself who you truly are."

Collier started toward the wall to escape, but stopped himself. He glanced at her over his shoulder, his eyes gleaming. "You are not very good at making allies," he said simply. "You offend Crabwell and then scold Carew. Maybe you truly are this naïve." His eyes narrowed. "I may be slightly younger than you, but do not underestimate me. I cannot trust you, Maia. Nor should you trust me. We are allies at the moment. But that may change come Whitsunday."

CHAPTER
TWENTY-TWO

Princess of Comoros

When Maia was reunited with Suzenne at the Aldermaston's kitchen, she could tell her friend had experienced something transforming. Her countenance had altered, and her eyes were filled with a wisdom that had not been there before. The kitchen was tumultuous with preparations for Whitsunday, but the whirl seemed to still as their eyes met.

Suzenne set down her dish and hurried to Maia, brushing strands of Maia's dark hair away from her forehead. "What happened to you last night?" she whispered, bringing Maia with her to a secluded spot beneath the loft. Sabine, who had come in with Maia, nodded at Suzenne and smiled, then greeted the two kitchen girls with hugs and accepted breakfast from them. Collett oversaw the kitchen bustle while sternly punching a mound of dough at a nearby table.

"The Medium forbade me to enter." Maia lowered her eyes,

her stomach still churning from the confrontation with Collier. She was tired as well, from not sleeping that night, and her clothes were damp and uncomfortable.

"Oh, Maia," Suzenne whispered. "I was afraid it was something else. That . . . you were feeling . . . tempted."

Maia shook her head. "I have felt nothing like that since coming to Muirwood," she replied.

"But why is that? You went to another abbey before."

"I know. There is something different about Muirwood. There are protections here that Lia set up on these grounds all those years ago. The Myriad Ones cannot trouble me here. But I have no illusion that they *will* trouble me should I leave." She sighed in misery. "I had really hoped I would be allowed to take the test last night." She tried to smile through a frown. "But what about you, Suzenne? You passed it. I can see it in your eyes."

Suzenne nodded timidly and clasped Maia's hands. She was silent for several moments, choosing her words carefully. "It was like nothing I expected," she said falteringly. "I cannot describe it. There is little that compares to the sensation. The knowledge I gained there is forbidden to write in tomes. But more important than the knowledge is the . . . feeling. Maia, I have never felt so close to the Medium before. It is a beautiful reminder and a privilege to wear the chaen." She touched her bodice reverently. "What I do not understand now is how anyone could experience the rite and walk away from it. How could they break the vows they made? I shudder to think of it."

"You mean my father," Maia said in a sad voice.

Suzenne waved her hand. "Not just the king . . . all those who insinuate themselves in the high court. Men like the new Earl of Forshee and the Aldermaston of Augustin! How can he replace our Aldermaston without the High Seer's approbation?" She bit her lip. "Now that I have felt the Medium so powerfully . . . their actions are incomprehensible to me."

Maia patted her hand. "Is it so hard to understand, Suzenne? We see it among the Ciphers. These are girls the Medium has trusted to learn and engrave. Yet despite all the tomes they have read and the principles they have been taught, for some the words remain only on aurichalcum . . . they do not enter the heart." Maia smoothed some of her own hair over her shoulder. "The Medium only has imperfect people to do its will. I am afraid that has always been the case. I can only hope it will accept me as one of them."

Suzenne looked her deep in the eyes. "Maia, you have survived troubles I can only wonder at. I was worried about you when you did not come to the abbey last night. I have been worried sick."

Maia smiled at the sentiment. "My grandmother suggested holding vigil instead."

"You have not slept then? No wonder you look so weary! I took it all for disappointment. How silly I am. I think that is wise, and I shall hold vigil with you as well. Whitsunday is two days from now. We will keep each other awake whatever the cost."

"Thank you," Maia said, feeling her love blossom wider for the other girl. "You are a true friend."

Suzenne reached out, and they embraced. There was a soothing balm in the compassion of a friend. When Maia pulled back she sighed. "And I encountered Collier in the garden this morning."

Maia quickly related the extent of their short meeting. Suzenne covered her mouth, shaking her head in disbelief. "How that must have pained you," she whispered, fidgeting.

Maia agreed. "He thinks me either devious or utterly naïve. He is still very angry."

Suzenne sought to reassure her. "But not quite so much as last time. Your letter helped, I think."

"Did it?" she replied with a hint of despair. "And yet . . . mark how you have your Dodd. A maston himself, and the two of you will be bound by irrevocare sigil. That is all that I have wanted for myself from childhood, even though my parents' marriage was full of sorrow. Collier took the maston test, but he failed it deliberately. He did not want to be bound to do the Medium's will. He has his own ambitions."

Suzenne touched her arm gently. "If I were to give you any advice on passing the maston test, Maia, it is trust. You know the game that children play . . . the one where they fall backward and are caught by someone else? Trusting the Medium is somewhat like that. You cannot see it behind you, but you know it will not let you fall." She smiled into Maia's eyes. "Believe that you will not fail . . . as I do."

Davi approached with a steaming bowl, offering it urgently. "Eat quickly, Maia. The Aldermaston's wife just sent Owen here to fetch the two of you. You must come to the manor at once."

***

All of the Ciphers had gathered in secret in the Aldermaston's study and the tension in the room was as heavy as smoke. The murmuring and fidgeting caused chittering sounds like birdsong throughout the chamber. Finally the Aldermaston's wife had to clear her throat to quiet them all.

"Please, girls," she said calmly. "I know you are nervous. I must share news. Celia, who has been reading the sheriff's messages for us while doing his laundry, has informed me that the sheriff has heard from Lady Deorwynn, offering him an earldom if he will support her against the chancellor."

There was a gasp as this was spoken, and Joanna, the Aldermaston's wife, patiently held up her hand for silence. Eyes turned to Maeg with astonishment, and the girl could not smother a smug look. "Please, let me finish. When the nobles arrive, there will, of course, be a great deal of posturing, negotiations, and alliances made and broken. Do *not* let this distract you from our purpose." She began to pace amidst the girls. "Keep your ears open. Learn what you can from our guests, who are arriving by the hour. Lady Deorwynn and her children arrived last night, and we expect the king and his retinue later today. And Maeg, your father, the sheriff, is Chancellor Crabwell's sworn man, so I would not get my hopes up too soon."

Maeg nodded demurely, but Maia could see the fire of ambition in her eyes.

"Lady Deorwynn also sent word to me that she seeks a new lady-in-waiting."

Again, the girls gasped at the news.

"Jayn!"

"Is she dismissing Jayn?"

"Oh my!"

"She is not dismissing Jayn," Joanna reassured them. "Please, you must bridle your passions, girls. Many of you will take the maston test today, and I know you are nervous. These are exciting times for certain, but we must not let our excitement distract us from what is truly important—the Covenant of Muirwood. Jayn Sexton is still one of Lady Deorwynn's ladies-in-waiting. The new post is for her daughter, Lady Murer. Lady Murer is under negotiations to wed the King of Dahomey, so this position would require girls who can speak Dahomeyjan and are willing to go there if chosen."

Silence struck the room at last. The Aldermaston's wife nodded solemnly and her birdlike frame seem to be forged of iron as she paced in front of the girls. Some eyes glanced at Maia, for all knew that she was the best at speaking languages and many of them had sought her coaching. Maeg went pale with jealousy, but Maia was too agitated to care. She felt Suzenne's fingers tighten against her arm, offering quiet consolation.

"Now, Lady Deorwynn seeks an audience with the girls from the noble Families right away. Haven Proulx, Maergiry Baynton, Suzenne Clarencieux, and Joanna Stay—you will prepare to meet with Lady Deorwynn immediately." She paused and then looked straight at her. "And Maia. Lady Deorwynn asked for you specifically," she added in a soft voice.

They were given a short amount of time to change clothes, put on jewels if they desired, and primp themselves. A knot had twisted inside of Maia's stomach at the news, and she felt her cheeks growing hot with anger, shame, and weakness at the thought of seeing Lady Deorwynn again. That woman was on the abbey grounds at this very moment, along with her daughters and sons. Her father's sons. Maia clenched her fists. The boys were not to blame for their sire, nor for their parents' disastrous upheaval of Comoros. Suzenne looked uncomfortably at Maia out of the corner of her eye. Out of all of the girls, Suzenne was the most fluent in Dahomeyjan, yet she was also the most unwilling to live abroad.

"I will not leave Dodd," Suzenne vowed as they combed through their hair again. Maia was too distracted to pick proper attire, so Suzenne helpfully chose something more formal for her to wear. Before long, a knock sounded to retrieve them, and they clutched each other's hands as they followed Owen to an audience chamber where the guests awaited them.

Maia felt her knees shaking with trepidation, and try as she might to calm herself, she could not. The Aldermaston's wife awaited the girls who had been summoned, outside the room, watching rather nervously as they all gathered together. Maeg was so heavily painted she looked otherworldly in her beauty. Haven was a pretty girl, though not a beauty, but her sneer matched her friend's. Maia stared down at the floor, chafing with discomfort, praying that the Medium would preserve her from the viper's fangs. The door opened, and they were at last admitted.

The first person Maia saw upon entering was Collier, which stretched her nerves even more tightly. He was dressed in all his royal attire today. She recognized his jeweled doublet, black and sparkling with eye-catching gems. He was freshly shaven, his jaw firm and smooth, displaying a statuesque grace. Only his blue eyes moved toward her as she entered, but then she noted a small smirk tug one corner of his mouth. His gaze was challenging, and Maia had to look away, unable to bear his gaze in this moment. To his left stood Lady Deorwynn, standing with hands clasped formally up near her bosom, left hand over right like a dignified salute. Behind her was a train of young women wearing gowns identical to the one Maia had once worn. The ladies were all young, none older than twenty-five, none even close to Deorwynn's age—a few years shy of forty.

Lady Deorwynn wore the strain of her marital relationship in her eyes and the set of her lips; otherwise not a single stray hair was out of place. She wore a gown shimmering with gold thread, which easily cost ten thousand marks. She wore a diadem with a huge ruby inset, and there were more jewels and rings at her wrists and throat. Her elegant finery cast a shadow over her young ladies, making her resemble a single blossom amongst the weeds—the intended effect, no doubt. Lady Deorwynn sought to exert her power over those around her through every possible means.

Maia's heart faltered as she took in the sight of Murer standing to Collier's right. Dressed in a gown almost as exquisite as her mother's, she was clasping his arm possessively and looking superbly satisfied with herself. Dear Aldermaston Syon was farther back, by the wall, speaking in low tones to his steward, Tomas, who looked solemn and nodded deferentially to whatever orders he had been given.

"Well, well, these are surprisingly pretty girls," Lady Deorwynn said in a breezy yet brittle voice. "I was expecting pastier skin due to the swampy climate here in Muirwood. Does the sun never shine, I wonder?" She chuckled disdainfully. Her eyes narrowed when she saw Maia, but she offered no verbal acknowledgment.

"Thank you, my dear Joanna," Lady Deorwynn continued, bowing respectfully to the Aldermaston's wife, "for bringing your brightest girls. I understand that they have been taught to embroider, play musical instruments, speak languages, dance in the latest styles, run multiple households, and manage servants. Fine qualifications indeed. But only the best will be worthy to serve *my* daughter, the Lady Murer. She may be a queen herself someday, I dare suggest"—and here she gave Collier a simpering smile that made Maia want to retch—"so we must choose someone who will show the foreign courts what treasures of beauty and grace exist in Comoros."

"Indeed, my *queen*," Collier said with an affected accent that was heavier than was normal for him. He bowed gallantly and patted Murer's hand. "I miss hearing my native tongue. Let us test languages first. Shall we, my dear?"

Lady Murer nodded haltingly and together, arm in arm, they approached the first girl, Haven. Collier sized her up dispassionately, his eyes studying her face before traveling all the way down to her slippers. He cocked his head and asked, very rapidly, how she enjoyed the muggy rain and festering swamplands of this desolate land, and if she would not prefer the elegant vineyards of Dahomey to such a bleak existence in a stunted apple grove.

He spoke far too quickly for anyone who was not fluent in the language to understand. Maia could see Haven's eyes widen with shock and then disgrace. Her stumbled reply was a plea for him to repeat his question more slowly. Collier sniffed dismissively and moved on to the next girl, Maeg. Maia stared at him, wondering what in all creation he was plotting.

For indeed, Collier appeared to have a special mission. He pretended to be charmed by Maeg's appearance, and he asked her, much slower, about the weather in her Hundred.

"I am from this Hundred," Maeg replied in stuttering Dahomeyjan. "My father is the sheriff."

"Indeed? Do you like hawking? Good. Do you know Paeizian fencing? No? How sad, for I truly love the sport."

He spared no time in moving on to Joanna, with his companion Murer a mute appendage to his brisk interrogations. He asked her about the size of the pigs in the swamplands around the abbey, following up with a question about whether the men of her Hundred were also pigs.

Joanna's eyebrows furrowed, then shot clear up to her hairline as her brain translated his mocking question.

She stuttered incoherently, not sure how to respond to a king's jest, and her cheeks flushed with embarrassment. Collier chose to ignore her distress and approached Suzenne, whom he regarded with a genuine sign of interest. His gaze took in how close Suzenne and Maia were standing to each other, and his eyes narrowed slightly. Murer had obviously not understood most of the dialogue thus far, but she continued to cling to Collier's arm with a possessiveness born of self-assurance. Maia struggled to control her feelings, wondering if Collier intended to torture her publicly. She was concerned for how he would treat Suzenne.

"And what is your name?" he asked Suzenne quite deferentially. It was an easy question any of them could have answered.

"I am Suzenne Clarencieux, Your Majesty," she replied, eyes lowered in a flawless, formal courtesy. Collier's eyebrow lifted in surprise at the sign of respect. Collier then asked her several questions about her father's standing, her Family lineage, and, with a private smile, how she enjoyed wandering about in gardens with axe-wielding ruffians.

Suzenne's chin lifted a small degree as she replied calmly and very fluently that carrying axes in gardens was appropriate when heavy branches could fall from above quite unexpectedly. Collier grinned appreciatively at her reply, looked back at Murer with a nod and an approving smile, and then moved on. Murer looked completely baffled by the exchange, unable to decipher the lightning-quick banter of foreign words.

"And you are?" he asked Maia with a curious tone in his voice, giving her a piercing look that almost dared her to speak the truth. She gazed into his eyes, wondering what he expected of her . . . fact or farce. Before she could respond, Lady Deorwynn appeared at his side.

"She is my lord husband's *natural* daughter," Lady Deorwynn said, intervening, her face a little flushed. "Lady Marciana. She is the one we spoke of recently. There is a little matter I must talk with her about, so I asked for her to be brought with the others. She would not be a suitable companion for Lady Murer, my lord."

"Ah . . . thank you, Lady Deorwynn," Collier said with his facetiously heavy accent. "I must agree with you. She would not be a fitting companion for Lady Murer. She speaks several languages, does she not?"

Lady Deorwynn bristled. "Perhaps, my lord. If she still remembers them all. She has been . . . serving . . . in my mother's household for many years, with little chance to practice."

"What an honor and privilege," Collier said, his eyes afire as he turned to Lady Deorwynn, "to be a . . . how does one say? . . . a servant in your mother's household. In Dahomey, we do not treat our well-born children so kindly. Many are given up as wretched. I am pleased to see the king's *natural* daughter is not treated so *cruelly* in Comoros."

He turned and looked back at the group of young ladies. "Music next, my lady?" and he bowed gracefully to Lady Deorwynn.

"You wish to hear music?" she asked, confused.

"You said they taught music at this abbey, yes?" He widened his eyes in feigned innocence. "Let the girls play!" His arm swept grandly toward the cluster of girls. Then he glanced surreptitiously over at Maia. "All of them."

Anger, if not restrained, is frequently more hurtful to us than the injury that provoked it.

—*Richard Syon, Aldermaston of Muirwood Abbey*

CHAPTER
TWENTY-THREE

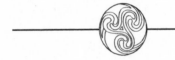

Forsaken

The room was full of unspoken tension, underscored by the quivering notes played by nervous fingers on strings. Instruments had been fetched, and each girl was being asked to perform a piece. Hanging over them all was the knowledge that they were performing in front of a foreign king who had power over their future destiny. Collier was all deference and grace to Lady Murer, who wore an increasingly smug expression as she soaked in the experience of being so graciously doted upon by such a handsome man. Murer's golden curls bounced giddily as she tried vainly to monopolize Collier's gaze and attention. Collier's smile and courtly manners were enough to placate the vapid young woman, but Maia, who knew him perhaps better than the others in the room, saw more. Fire had erupted in his gaze when Lady Deorwynn interrupted their interchange. She could tell his secret objectives were consuming his thoughts, though she was at a loss as to what those objectives were.

Maia sighed and scanned the room to take her mind off his plotting. Lady Deorwynn's five ladies-in-waiting were seated off to one side, and Maia easily discerned which young woman was Jayn Sexton. Covert glances were exchanged between Suzenne and the dark-haired girl with the heart-shaped, demure face—a face that looked even more miserable than Maia felt. Maia could tell the two wanted to speak privately, but it was not possible in such a room with so many eyes to witness.

Joanna was in the middle of her lute piece when Murer's younger sister, Jolecia, appeared next to Maia and pitched her voice very low. "My mother wishes to speak with you privately, Maia."

Maia turned, startled to see her stepsister standing there so uncomfortably. Across the room, Lady Deorwynn looked flushed, almost feverish. She was watching the girl play, but her hands fidgeted with nervousness.

Maia nodded and slowly slipped away from Suzenne's side, walking discreetly around the room to where Lady Deorwynn stood by her ladies-in-waiting. Collier and Murer were seated next to the musicians, listening appreciatively to the melancholy song. He observed Maia's departure, but he betrayed nothing other than a swift glance. Murer whispered something to him behind her hand and tittered softly.

The thought of speaking privately with Lady Deorwynn filled her with strong, unsettling emotions. This was the woman who had distracted her father from his marriage vows. This was the woman who had arranged her banishment from court. This was the woman who had ordered her mother to humiliate Maia by using her as the lowliest household servant. She tried to slow her pounding heart, reminding herself that she was truly a legitimate daughter and princess and she must act with grace and calm.

"Yes, Lady Deorwynn?" Maia said formally, curtsying.

Lady Deorwynn's nostrils flared when Maia did not address her as queen. But Maia had never recognized the marriage; she had only ever referred to her mother as the queen. Lady Deorwynn kept watching the music, holding up her hand to prevent conversation. The song finished and everyone clapped. Maeg took her turn next, seating herself behind a giant harp. She straddled the instrument confidently, her back stiff and poised, her arms hanging loosely. Her fingers began to pluck chords, teasing out beautiful notes.

"Very good," Collier murmured in an overly pronounced Dahomeyjan voice, nodding approvingly. "Lovely *and* talented."

As the music swelled around them, Lady Deorwynn's brittle voice slipped under the sweet sounds, her voice very low and private. Maia could see it pained her to be civil.

"Thank you for seeing me, Marciana. I had hoped for a chance to speak with you before your father arrived."

Maia frowned but said nothing, waiting for the woman to speak.

Lady Deorwynn's eyes flashed to hers, her cheeks flushing with emotion. "We have not always been friendly with each other," she began awkwardly.

"We have *never* been friendly," Maia corrected stiffly. "But that is understandable considering the circumstances."

"Why must you make this more difficult?" Lady Deorwynn seethed, but she caught herself. Her jaw was trembling with suppressed wrath. She swallowed deliberately, attempting to calm herself. "Yes, I have mistreated you in the past. Do you want me to say it? Then I have said it. It was ... beneath me. I am sorry for it, Marciana, truly I am. I do not expect you to believe me. You are young and have a vengeful temperament. Unfortunately that is very common in youths."

"You malign me unjustly, madame," Maia replied softly. "You should get to know me before you claim to judge my character."

Lady Deorwynn looked at her, shocked and angry. "Judge your character? We have all witnessed your character, child. You are the most obstinate, headstrong young woman who ever left her mother's womb! You were spoiled as a child, which made you proud. Any other child would have accepted the diminishment of her station and reconciled herself to it. Yet you have refused to do so despite all reason, dignity, and duty."

Maia felt the angry warmth shoot all the way to her ears, but she bridled her tone. "You do not know me at all," she replied simply. "You have never tried."

Lady Deorwynn bristled. "I know enough . . . witnessed by my own mother. And what I have seen myself." The lady's green eyes closed in frustration. "Marciana, I did not come all this way to argue with you. Be civil, girl."

Maia raised her eyebrows in bemused silence, waiting.

"I came here to celebrate Whitsunday, of course. But there are other reasons. You may not believe me, child, but I have been advocating for you with your father. Yes, it is true. I have told him that I want you back at . . . at court." She licked her lips, and Maia noticed her hands were trembling. Maeg's song wafted through the air, concealing the sounds of their intense conversation.

Maia stared at her, waiting.

"Have you nothing to say to that?" Lady Deorwynn demanded, apparently perplexed by Maia's lack of a joyous response.

"I am not certain I understand you."

"Must we be so coy?" Her voice was low, almost a growl. "I have asked your father to . . . reinstate you. To compensate you with your mother's dower lands. You are to be a lady again, Marciana, if you can yield to common sense."

Maia's brow wrinkled. "What must I do in return for this . . . honor?"

"You *know* what you must do," Lady Deorwynn snapped angrily, her full lips curled back impatiently. "You must sign the Act of Submission. The papers of reinstatement have already been drawn up. The Privy Council has seen them. Marciana, you can leave Muirwood Abbey as a lady with lands, inheritance, servants . . . all will be restored to you. You must only sign the act. What say you?"

There it was. Lady Deorwynn sought to understand in advance what Maia intended to do. She was seeking a confidence, some sort of assurance so she could be prepared to face Maia's father with an answer.

Maia stared at her with distaste. "Tell me, Lady Deorwynn. The new Aldermaston of Muirwood, the one my father has sent. He arrives today, I believe. He is related to you, is he not?"

"I am his niece," Lady Deorwynn said icily. "What of it?"

Maia nodded. "If he is related to *you*, then I suppose his betrayal to the order makes sense." She turned to leave. "I will sign nothing against my conscience."

Lady Deorwynn clutched Maia's sleeve. "*I* did not dismiss you!"

Maia stared down at the white tendons quivering beneath the flesh of Lady Deorwynn's hand. There were rings on her fingers, emblems of power and authority. Gemstones worth thousands of marks, and glittering diamonds set into bold bands. Maia reflected that she had given up the promise of all that when she left Naess, as well as the doom of having a Myriad One trapped inside her for the rest of her life.

"By your leave then," Maia said tonelessly, determined to remain unruffled.

"You are a terrible creature," Lady Deorwynn whispered. "Your stubbornness will kill you. Your father will not relent on this matter, Maia. I know his intentions. He will tread down *any* who stand in his way. The Aldermaston of Muirwood or his wife. The High Seer of Pry-Ree. He will raze Tintern Abbey to the ground. Even you, child. Even you." She flung Maia's hand away harshly.

Maia rubbed her wrist slowly, but said nothing as she stepped back to her seat.

Feeling shame and anger stain her cheeks, she dared not look anyone in the eye, especially Collier. She rested her hands in her lap, feeling the weight of her emotions as a burden too heavy to bear.

It was Suzenne's turn to play next, and Maia used the reprieve to calm her thoughts. The Aldermaston had worked with her for many months to that end. Emotions would dissipate and pass. He had encouraged her to feel them, label them, understand them, and even endure them. She could almost hear his wise counsel in her mind as she sat there quietly, hands folded in her lap, enduring the shame of the moment and trying to prepare herself for yet another, worse confrontation to come with her father.

When Suzenne finished her piece on the flute, Lady Deorwynn strode forward and lifted her voice above the applause.

"Do they not all play well, my lord?" she said to Collier, all hint of antagonism vanished.

"Your kingdom is well versed in music, Lady Deorwynn," he said most graciously. "These young women have been putting their time to good use. But . . . there is one we have not heard from yet."

Lady Deorwynn glanced at Maia, her face suddenly vengeful. "There is no need, my lord." She gave Maia a look that clearly communicated she was no longer welcome in the room.

"Indulge me," Collier said with a charming foreign lilt. "I will not be satisfied until I hear her play."

Lady Deorwynn's color changed, but she mastered herself and did a formal curtsy to the king. "If you insist."

"I do insist," Collier said grandly, taking Murer's hand and squeezing it affectionately. He clapped his other hand on hers. "I have not heard Lady Murer play."

Lady Deorwynn was shocked. "My . . . my daughter?" she asked tremulously.

Murer's eyes widened with surprise and sudden terror. "My . . . my lord?"

Maia almost let a smile slip onto her lips. She stared at Collier, a sense of wonder blooming in her heart.

"Yes! What instrument do you play, my dear?" He chuckled and flatteringly teased, "Or should I ask . . . how *many* instruments, hmmm?"

Murer was dumbstruck. Her mouth parted, showing her teeth, but his request had rendered her speechless.

"She can play . . ." Lady Deorwynn struggled for an adequate answer. "She can play the flute . . . no, the lute. She can play the lute. Right, dearest?"

Lady Murer was pale with misery. She shook her head. "I have not played in . . . some time."

"The lute," Collier said, affecting an exaggerated disappointment. "I see. You do not love music then?"

"I love music!" Murer spluttered to reassure him, blinking rapidly.

"Perhaps you prefer to hear *others* play then. Very well . . ." He quickly stood and fetched the lute from the stand. He struck a few chords himself, his fingers plaintive against the strings. Then he started a little galliard, which was a fast-paced dancing song. His foot tapped as he played. Then he stopped, midchord, and handed the lute to Joanna, who had played earlier.

"If you would, please play again for Lady Murer," he asked her, nodding respectfully. "You know the tune, yes?"

"I do, my lord," she replied, and taking the lute from him, she started to strum the tune he had abruptly cut off.

"I understand in Comoros you have a quaint tradition," Collier said, holding out his hands to Murer and smiling handsomely. "You dance around the maypole, correct? Even a lord may dance with a wretched on that night. Is that not so?"

"Yes, my lord," Lady Deorwynn said through gritted teeth, her visage marred by her vengeful emotions.

"In Dahomey, we dance the galliard around the maypole," he instructed, pulling Murer to her feet. "That has been the tradition. Do you know it?" he asked Murer politely, but with a subtle mocking tone, as if he were in doubt.

"Yes, of course!" Lady Murer exclaimed, coming to her feet, relieved that she could at last do something that pleased him.

He positioned his chair in the room, leaving an open space around it. "This will be our maypole. Not quite as tall, alas, and no streamers. Everyone dances the galliard now. We invented it in Dahomey, you know. But . . . we have a *new* dance there." He dramatically cast his eyes around the room full of ladies, entrancing them with anticipation. "It is called . . . the Volta!"

Lady Murer's eyes widened with growing dread. "Indeed? I . . . yes . . . I believe I have *heard* of it, but I do not *know* that one."

Maia stared at Collier, trying to determine his true intentions and mood. She had never forgotten that one night at the Dahomeyjan inn, when he had taught *her* the Volta. That was the time—long ago, it seemed now—before she learned that he was not a king's collier at all, but was the king himself. Her mouth went dry. It was the first time she had danced with a man since coming of age, and not for practice.

"You do not know it?" Collier demanded of the room incredulously. "It is quite famous in my country." He let go of Murer's hands and turned around, looking across the assembled girls. His gaze settled on Maia. "Do any of you know the Volta?"

His words hung in the air for a moment, his blue eyes searing into hers, demanding that she rise and join him. His hand lifted and reached out to Maia, singling her out.

Unable to resist, Maia stood wordlessly and approached him, causing a chorus of bubbling gasps to escape from the girls assembled. A small hint of a smile flickered on his mouth, such that she could tell he was pleased she had not refused him. Maia's heart skipped irregularly, and she silently prayed his scheme was not to humiliate her through the dance. Joanna resumed playing the tune, and Collier's head kept time to the rhythm. When their hands met, his palms were so warm they almost burned.

"Like before," he whispered, winking at her, and suddenly they were dancing around the chair. She dared not look at anyone else, for fear of stumbling and humiliating herself. Collier was a confident lead as he pulled her along in the intricate dance.

The Volta was similar to the galliard except it included a lift and a turn. She could feel the music swelling to that point, and the memory of soaring through the air in Collier's arms felt as immediate as if it had only happened the previous night. Her legs lost all their tiredness and a spark of lovely giddiness filled her breast. They went around the next turn and then suddenly Collier's hands seized her waist and lifted her high. She planted her hands on his shoulders and pushed, staring down at him, studying the grooves of his face, the scar just below his eye.

His eyes—they pulled her in, almost unwillingly, like shimmering whirlpools. She stared at him, recognizing a look of respect and admiration. There were yet other emotions there that surprised her—tenderness. Protectiveness. The twirl ended and she was back down on her feet, moving to the rhythm once more. It felt like they were flying.

They continued the dance around the chair. The whirling motion of her skirts followed as she swayed to the rhythm.

Then came the next turn. She was ready for it, almost hungering for it when he swept her up again, giving her the same thrill as if she were flying. She felt her hair sweep across her shoulders as she pressed against him, her heart beating wildly. Her mouth was dry, her skin tingling down to the balls of her feet. The turn ended and they swept around the imaginary maypole once more. Everything stilled and slowed and they were the only two creatures who existed in that moment, forgetting the hostile gazes that were surely bent on them.

He brought her down a little slower that time, and their hands fumbled a moment to join again before the next round. She gazed up at him, her feelings overwhelming, yet so vulnerable. She felt as if she were a little bird, cupped in his lean, firm hands—easy to crush and kill or tenderly caress. The sound of the music was overwhelmed by the feeling of her feet skipping, their hands entwined, her pulse whipping inside her bosom with feelings stronger than the dance.

And she suddenly realized, to her horror and dismay, that her feelings for Collier had changed significantly over these months. She startled herself by how deep they were. She cared for him. She ached for his esteem. She *loved* him. And yet she trembled in fear that he would cast her away, an unwanted impediment to his ambitions.

Something connected between their gazes. Could he read her thoughts? His expression swiftly altered from mirth to seriousness. From triumph to warmth. She felt his hands again on her hips, ready for the last twirl. His muscles hoisted her up even higher, his feet slowing and breaking the rhythm as he suspended her above him. Her arms felt weak as she pushed against his shoulders. Her chin dipped as she stared down at him, her hair tickling her cheeks as it veiled her gaze from the others in the room.

Her eyes entreated him pleadingly, her heart in her throat.

The final end of the turn completed and she hung there, poised like a bird on a breeze, and then he slowly let her down. He stared at her as well, his eyes unveiled only to her—filled with a mute plea for her to never betray him again.

I will not, she responded silently, searing the unspoken promise into his eyes with her own.

The chords of music plucked to an end.

In the hush that followed, Maia could not bear to look at anyone else but Suzenne. The expression on her friend's face was rife with emotion, her mouth parted as she stared in wonder, knowing—better than anyone else in the room—the state of Maia's heart at that moment. That Maia had danced with her husband and no one knew it.

CHAPTER TWENTY-FOUR

Kranmir

Collier took Maia's hands in his, bowing his head gallantly to her. "Truly, Lady Maia, you have made good use of your time here." The look of scorn he shot at Murer finished the insult with a sting.

Lady Deorwynn was livid, her teeth bared into an almost wolflike snarl. She glared at Maia with red-hot hatred. "Out," she said with no pretense of civility. "I believe you are wanted elsewhere, are . . . you . . . *not*?"

Before Maia could move, Collier increased his grip on her hand. "Yes, I believe you are right, Lady Deorwynn. She is wanted greatly elsewhere . . . in Dahomey, in fact."

Gasps of surprise sounded behind her. Even Maia looked at Collier in astonishment. What was he proposing now?

"You have chosen *her* to wait on *my* daughter?" Lady Deorwynn retorted, utterly aghast at the notion. "Surely one of the other girls would be better suited. My husband will not—"

"You completely misunderstand me," Collier rudely interrupted. Still holding Maia's hand, he stepped closer to Lady Deorwynn, his jaw clenched in suppressed anger, the guise of the simpering suitor vanishing in a burst of flames. "Surely all can plainly see that Maia is the fairest woman in this room. And to Maia's beauty, add grace, wisdom, and refined talents. She was born to be a queen in her own right and not just trained as a courtier. I can see why you have so jealously hidden her from me, my lady."

Lady Deorwynn's face went scarlet with dawning realization. "You . . . all along . . . you came here for . . . for *her*?"

Murer's composure finally cracked with the knowledge that this handsome king was not to be hers, but Maia's. She covered her mouth and stormed tearfully from the room.

Collier inhaled deeply as he regarded Maia's stepmother. His voice deepened to his richer, truer tone as he dropped all pretense of a heavy accent. "Lady Deorwynn, forgive me, but you are blind. Your power has waned. Maia and I were secretly married in Dahomey many months ago. I came to Comoros to reclaim my wife. And I am not departing these shores without her." His lips quivered with rage as his eyes scorched the vain woman. "And you will *never* harm Maia again." He gazed authoritatively at the stunned group of women. "Leave us," he barked with a tone of command.

The room quickly began to empty, most of the women leaving in a fluster, and some, like the queen, leaving with a look of uttermost loathing. As the ladies hastily filed out, Collier bent his lips to Maia's ear. "Not your friend."

"Suzenne," Maia called, stalling her. Suzenne looked around in surprise before coming forward, her brow knitting together in consternation and fear.

The Aldermaston's wife lingered at the door and then closed it, leaving the three of them alone. The silence was immense. The two friends wordlessly regarded Collier, Maia in admiration and Suzenne in awe.

Collier's aspect had changed suddenly to one of triumph and delight. "Oh my, I must admit . . . that was very satisfactory," he chuckled, tugging softly on Maia's arm and leading her over to the cushioned seat. "The look on her face. I will *always* cherish that memory. By Idumea's hand, how I loathe that woman." He smiled reassuringly at Suzenne and motioned for her to sit near Maia. "How do you fancy traveling to Dahomey, lass?" he asked her.

"What have you done, Collier?" Maia asked, still shocked at the sudden change in events.

"Nothing I had not planned to do earlier," he said, arching his eyebrows. "I was saving the announcement for when your father arrived. I had this little speech prepared—" He shrugged modestly. "But when I saw how Deorwynn was treating you . . . when I saw her contempt and heard her excoriating words, I had to do something, my dove. No one insults the Queen of Dahomey. No one insults *my* wife." He shook his head. "We may not agree on all matters, Maia, but we can assuredly agree that she is a serpentine vixen who thrives on spreading misery. How have you endured her all these years?"

Maia's heart was bubbling with so many emotions she could hardly breathe. She stared at Collier with wonder, not knowing what to say first. "But you humiliated Murer . . ."

"Deliberately!" he crooned, pacing. He went to the lute and plucked a few notes from it. "It was delicious. I cannot feel bad about that, Maia. Do not even ask me to. I vindicated you."

"I know," she answered, "but you caused pain and grief. Murer . . . she really believed in the betrothal . . ."

He smirked and played an inharmonious chord. He winced and then fixed it. "Perhaps if they knew of my subtlety, they would have been better prepared. You remember my name . . . it is *Feint*

Collier." He sighed impatiently. "Murer was a necessary deception, of course. But you were my target all along."

Maia was flattered that he had not been truly tempted to cast her aside; however, questions still persisted in her mind. "But what of our encounters in the garden?"

He wrinkled his brow. "What do you mean? I was completely, even brutally honest in the garden, Maia. I am still angry with you. I am not entirely certain how to make our marriage work." He stood restlessly, and toyed with the lute. "We see things very differently, you and I. But sitting here, listening to that woman berate you, humiliate you—you, who are the rightful heir of this kingdom, and *she*, the usurper! Who is Murer compared with you? I confess that I wanted everyone to see that. Believe me, word of this will spread, and spread quickly. My mortal offense to Lady Deorwynn and her children . . . well, frankly the beauty of it is that it will only increase my popularity among your people! So, believe me, Maia, I have been planning this. I thought our dance would happen at Whitsunday, but it still can." He plucked out a few more notes on the lute, smiling at her impishly.

Maia bit her lip, still whirling from the mercurial shifts of his mood. "What will you tell my father?" she persisted.

"That our marriage has already happened," he stated, nodding to her. "I will probably have to summon the witnesses, and it may decrease the number of earldoms I had hoped to achieve from this visit. He will pay me less than what I deserve. But in the end, he needs an alliance with Dahomey. Brannon cannot survive the armada when it arrives. He needs me and he knows it." He glanced back at Suzenne. "What do you require to join Maia in Dahomey, loyal friend that you are? I understand you may be . . . engaged?"

Suzenne looked down at her lap confusedly, and then back up at Collier. "I am, my lord."

"Yes, to Dodleah Price. The landless son of Forshee." He leaned forward conspiratorially. "He would be welcome in my service, my lady. I could possibly . . . arrange"—he shrugged and frowned—"for lands and titles in Dahomey? If my lady so wishes it?" He winked at Maia, obviously relishing the role of benefactor.

Maia gasped, turning to Suzenne, and saw tears glittering in the young woman's lashes. "Truly, my lord?"

Collier nodded. "Call for Dodd. Let us see how he feels about the matter. Jon Tayt speaks highly of him, and I respect his opinion."

"I will at once!" Suzenne declared, flushing and beaming, and raced out of the room.

A knot had developed inside Maia's chest, a weight that sat heavily. "I cannot possibly go with you to Dahomey," she uttered softly.

His brow wrinkled. "Why ever not?" he asked. He sat down at the edge of her seat, forcing her to make room and bewildering her senses with his nearness. He reached out casually and tucked a wavy lock of dark hair behind her ear. His finger set off a shiver that traveled from neck to spine. Maia struggled to gather her wits and explain.

"I must face the maston test, as I wrote in my letter."

"There are plenty of abbeys in Dahomey," he reminded her. "In the past, the princes and princesses of the realms would come to Dochte Abbey to study. Take the maston test in my country, or any country you choose except for this one."

Maia shook her head. "It *must* be Muirwood."

He remained genuinely perplexed. "But why?"

She stared down at her hands but firmed her resolve and looked into his eyes, even though the depth of their color made it hard to stare at him. "There is a covenant that has been passed down in my Family. A covenant to restore Muirwood Abbey."

"The abbey is built," he said, confused. "It is small compared to some I have seen, but it is beautiful and functional. Deorwynn's uncle is to be the new Aldermaston, I understand. Kranmir."

Maia shook her in frustration. "Kranmir has no authority to be the new Aldermaston!"

Collier shrugged. "True, but it is all politics anyway. The politics of Aldermastons is little different from that of the Dochte Mandar."

"It is more than that! You must understand this. The full rites of the mastons have not been restored. You did not complete the maston test yourself, so you do not know of it, but the Apse Veil must still be reopened. In the past, mastons could travel between abbeys by using the Apse Veil. Now they cannot, and the dead are stuck in this realm."

A look of sardonic doubt shadowed his face, but he said nothing.

"You do not believe me," she said.

"Please finish," he said, nodding to her to go on. "I do not argue about the High Seer's authority to name her own people. The Dochte Mandar do the same. I just do not believe in Idumea and the dead needing to go there. The Apse Veil being closed means nothing to me."

"But it *is* true! No one has crossed the Apse Veil in a hundred years. I know the beliefs of the Dochte Mandar. Walraven taught them to me. They believe they can commune with the dead and the dead are born again. That is a lie. Those who have died yearn to return to Idumea, but they are trapped here. Lia entrusted her posterity with restoring the rites at Muirwood. This will include the ability to cross between abbeys as well as the rites for the dead. My grandmother is the High Seer, and she is not powerful enough in the Medium to open the Apse Veil herself. The Medium has specifically given the burden to *me*."

Collier sighed, nodding with a satisfied smile. "I see."

"I do not think you do."

"So these secret rites must be performed. Mastons can then travel hither and yon. Some visiting Idumea. Well, how wonderful Lia left *that* for you to do. No wonder you came here instead of Pry-Ree. It took a while for you to be discovered." He tapped his mouth thoughtfully, then gave her that maddeningly handsome smirk of his. "So let me understand the implications of this situation. Your father is coming to throw down the authority of the Aldermastons . . . here, at Muirwood. Your grandmother has come to defy him. Did she bring, say, an army with her?"

"No," Maia replied, her stomach churning.

"I thought not. I have been out with Captain Carew, and he has been exploring the defenses of the abbey. They are . . . how shall I put this . . . rather frail. Anyone can walk in or out, Maia. The Leerings are just stones. Some are imbued with power, I grant you, but they obey not just the mastons. How can your grandmother prevent Brannon from seizing Muirwood and throwing out Aldermaston Syon? You may not realize this, but your father plans to perform the investment ceremony himself, making himself in control of the maston order in Comoros. All the revenue the abbeys produce will be confiscated by the Crown. Undoubtedly, Brannon covets the wealth and power of the abbeys for himself, since he has already taken Augustin's treasure, with Kranmir's blessing, no less. And . . . might I add . . . no Medium intervened at Augustin." He raised his eyebrows challengingly.

"I do not know what will happen," Maia conceded, wincing. "But my grandmother plans to speak to him."

He snorted impatiently. "Maia, see reason! Your sainted father has more ambition than . . . well, than me! It will take more than some *holy* scolding to change his mind. What is she going to do to stop him?"

Maia shook her head. "I do not know."

"Maia." He said her name in a gentler tone this time, laying his hand on her arm. "Sabine can do *nothing* to stop her son-in-law. Only force will convince Brannon . . . which is obviously not her intent."

There was a soft knock on the door. Collier glanced up in irritation. The door opened to reveal Sabine and the Aldermaston's wife. The High Seer nodded to the other woman, then entered alone.

Collier rose, his cheeks flushing. "I see the Family resemblance," he said, nodding to her respectfully, but Maia could see the wariness in his eyes, in the subtle frown on his mouth. "Welcome, High Seer."

"Welcome to Muirwood, Gideon," she offered kindly, walking forward. "Word travels quickly in a small abbey. So you have acknowledged Maia as your wife?"

He smiled, though it did not reach his eyes, and bowed curtly. "I have. I was attempting to persuade her to accompany me back to Dahomey, but she claims there is unfinished business here at Muirwood. I hope to convince her that it is fruitless nonsense."

Sabine approached and Maia saw that she was holding the Cruciger orb in her hand. Even from a distance, she could see the writing scrolling across the orb. She burned with curiosity to know what it said.

"Nonsense, indeed?" Sabine replied, her brow wrinkling with amusement. "If you knew what I knew, you would not think that."

Collier looked uncomfortable. "I am sure you are privy to many of the Medium's secrets," he said guardedly. "I am not a maston myself."

"You must become one," Sabine said seriously.

Collier shook his head and chuckled. "I must do as I *choose*," he replied, his voice hinting at displeasure.

"I know," Sabine replied. She was standing very near him now. Her eyes were burning with a loving intensity. "And the Medium sent me here to persuade you to make the right choice."

He cocked his eyebrow. "Did it now? Is this a warning? Have you come to threaten me, as your great-grandmother, Lia, once did my ancestor?"

Sabine was unflappable. She shook her head slowly. "No. Just to tell you a story. Lia had the Gift of Seering. She saw the future. She saw what would result from the Earl of Dieyre's decisions. I know about your ambitions, Gideon. I know you desire to fulfill your ancestor's destiny. But what did it gain him? He ruled an empire of bones and dust." Her eyes narrowed. "I have seen it, Gideon. My Gift of Seering allows me to see the past. The future is a fog that I cannot pierce, and I have no more idea what will happen tomorrow than you do. But I have seen your ancestor. Dieyre walked in misery, alone at the end of his days. When he first met the Naestors, his eyes flooded with hunger; he was desperate to speak to another soul, even though they could not understand one another. If he had *believed* in Lia's warning before it was too late, he would have chosen to exile himself with the mastons. He would have had a very different end."

Collier stared at her with distrust. But he did not speak.

Sabine held up the Cruciger orb. "Do you know what this is?"

"I do," he replied. "They are very rare. The Dochte Mandar have some in their *collection*, though they cannot work them."

"Quite right. This orb was given to me. Lia was my great-grandmother, and she passed on the Cruciger orb to her daughters, who were chosen to be Aldermastons and High Seers. The orb's purpose is to help the one who wields it find the true path. To find what has been lost. I have never regretted my Gift of Seering, even though I cannot see the future. Indeed, I have found it more useful to see and learn from the patterns of the past. There have always been corrupt kings. There have always been those who would persecute the mastons. Let me tell you of one."

Collier breathed out through his nose impatiently, as if he were about to receive a lecture, but he did not leave. He stood silently, gravely, his eyes determined not to believe.

Sabine lifted the orb higher. "During the time of Lia's life, there was a corrupt king ruling Comoros. His wife died, and he later married a daughter of Dahomey, Pareigis. Under her influence, he taught his followers, those most loyal to him, to murder the mastons. Many died, their innocent blood shed. Eventually, a maston rose against him—the son of an earl who was slain. Garen Demont. My ancestor."

Collier nodded, familiar with the story. "Yes, the king was himself slain at the field of Winterrowd. I do not use the word *murdered*, as some do, because I was taught it was the Medium's will that he died. How convenient."

Sabine smiled at him, her eyes narrowing. "The story I must tell you is about that king's father."

Collier frowned.

"Not many know of him. He is a forgotten king, in many ways. His name was Jonas. When his kingdom was invaded by Dahomey, he turned to the High Seer of Avinion for support. He bargained and pleaded for assistance. But because he had betrayed so many, he found few allies, even when he offered gold. King Jonas trusted no one, so always traveled with his treasure. He feared that his own servants would plunder it in his absence. Fatefully, he fled to an abbey, seeking shelter, with the Dahomeyjan army coming from the south and the Pry-rian army coming from the north. While traveling to the abbey, he crossed a swampy fenland and realized that his wagons of treasure would have difficulty crossing, so he sent them another way. It started to rain, and the fenlands flooded. His wagons of treasure were stuck. Before his eyes, he watched them sink into the mire. Because Jonas was pressed upon by the advancing armies, he did not have the men or troops to return for his treasure, and he died shortly thereafter, leaving the kingdom to his young son. The treasure vanished from the earth, taken by the Medium's will. It has been lost these many years to serve the Medium's purpose."

Collier's eyes reflected his confusion. What was the purpose of this tale?

"Gideon," Sabine said, holding forth the orb regally. "When Maia and I came to Muirwood, I knew that you were being held hostage by the Naestors. A king's ransom was the cost. Maia was sick with worry about you. So was I, for you are part of *my* Family now. I sought the Medium's will, trying to seek a way to save you from bondage." Her voice thickened with emotion. "I had a dream . . . a vision . . . and I saw King Jonas's wagons sinking into the bog. I had a clear vision of where this happened." She stepped forward. "So I asked the Aldermaston of Muirwood to lend me workers. I used my ship, the *Holk*, to take us where the Cruciger orb led. We were successful, Gideon. We unearthed the treasure of King Jonas."

Maia stared at her grandmother, her heart nearly bursting with gratitude. Her grandmother had used her resources and Gift to save Collier from the dungeon. And she had done it in secret. Tears stung Maia's eyes and trickled down her cheeks. The feeling of gratitude was so immense she could hardly breathe.

"And with his fortune and other treasure gathered from abbeys across the kingdoms, I secured your release from the Naestors. So you see, my grandson . . . your treasury has not been touched. You are not bereft of funds or means, as you have believed." She swallowed and reached her hand out to clasp his kindly, lowering the Cruciger orb as she did so. "What are gold and silver but heavy burdens? What are jewels but pieces of rock? They will not bring happiness to you or anyone. They never have. I sought you to tell you this truth when you were released. I was waiting for you in Dahomey with your steward to explain, but you came to Comoros directly. The Cruciger orb led me here to find you. You have no debt. You have no obligation to any man or even to me. I do this freely, of my own will, because you are my granddaughter's husband. You are *my* Family! We must stand together in this, Gideon. You must stand with us. I cannot force you to become a maston. I can only ask you to choose it freely. Whether you do or not, you are still a free man. I have bought your freedom. Can you see that I could not have done this without the Medium? Gideon, you *know* the Medium is real. Feel the gentle whispers of your honored parents. The mastons need you to stand with us at this crossroads. We must stand up to a king."

Another knock sounded on the door, and the Aldermaston's steward, Tomas, hurried inside. He blocked the door with his body, holding it shut. His face was drawn with concern. "High Seer, he has just arrived. Aldermaston Kranmir. The Aldermaston is showing him the manor first, then the grounds of Muirwood. They will arrive here shortly."

Sabine turned, her posture rigid with resolve. "Show them in."

In the tome called the Hodoeporicon, *there is a great proverb on anger that has always impressed me. In a controversy, the instant we feel anger we have already ceased striving for truth, and have begun striving for ourselves.*

—*Richard Syon, Aldermaston of Muirwood Abbey*

CHAPTER
TWENTY-FIVE

Apples

The Aldermaston of Augustin Abbey wore the pale gray cassock of the order, but he also had on a fur-lined stole that was all black and a strange-looking three-pointed velvet cap, also black, that looked almost like a mushroom top. He had a solemn face, clean shaven, with a long thick nose and brooding eyes, his expression stern and unimpressed. As he entered the chamber and caught sight of the High Seer, those dark eyes flashed with suppressed anger, but his expression did not change. Richard Syon, the Aldermaston of Muirwood, walked alongside him.

"Sabine," said Kranmir with a flat voice. "I did not know you would be here."

Maia bristled at his informal use of her grandmother's name. He was a master of controlling his expressions, but that look in his eyes sent a shiver through her. Her emotions were still reeling from learning about the treasure and Collier's freedom from debt. She glanced at her husband and could tell he was struggling to control his emotions—his jaw was tense, his eyes were narrowed on Kranmir.

"Hello, Ely," her grandmother replied, nodding respectfully. "You just arrived?"

"It would have been sooner, but the condition of the roads into Muirwood is absolutely deplorable. That is the first of many remedies I will mention to the king. It should be a priority." He cocked his head slightly. "I am altogether astonished to find you here, Sabine. How did you arrive ahead of me? What port did you use? Bridgestow?"

He was deftly trying to ply her for information, and Maia cast a warning look at her grandmother.

"Thank you for your concern. I understand from my travels that the king is appointing you as the Aldermaston of Muirwood. Is that so?" She gave him a hard look, her eyes piercing.

Kranmir suppressed a small smile, almost as if it were a little joke. "Matters such as these are always inflated around a mere kernel of truth."

"How would *you* then convey the truth?" Sabine countered. "There can be no doubt as to how this appears on the surface."

He raised a placating hand. "Sabine, I attempted to explain this all rather concisely in a missive I sent you. By your question, I infer that you have not received it. My servants tell me that you are seldom in one place for very long. I had believed you were still in Naess, so my message may be lingering there unopened."

There was a tone of rebuke in his voice and Maia felt her blood simmering with heat. His fancy words and haughty demeanor rankled her. Aldermaston Syon was stoic, his expression grave but not confrontational, even though it was his domain and position that were in jeopardy. His eyes were fixed on the High Seer, his support for her conveyed in his stare.

"Please summarize the contents of your message," Sabine told him patiently. "I truly wish to understand your position."

Kranmir clasped his doughy hands in front of him after smoothing the sable fur of his stole. "In my letter, I recommended that a new policy be employed throughout the various kingdoms. You bear a heavy administrative burden, my dear, one that frankly overtaxes your capabilities. I am aware of *several* Aldermastons who have expressed a measure of discontent in waiting to hear back from you regarding matters of the utmost importance. My suggestion is that each kingdom be given the administrative duties that you bear, which will then be settled upon a chief precinct. Matters will be treated locally first, thus diminishing the burden that you are clearly struggling to heft. My recommendation is to begin this at Muirwood Abbey in Comoros, as the chief abbey of the realm. All the revenues from the other abbeys will be sent to Muirwood *before being passed on to you, of course,*" he concluded with pronounced enunciation. "This, you must agree, will help centralize the administrative burdens and provide more timely responses to the Aldermastons who cannot hear from you as often as they would like." He smiled when he finished, nodding to her.

Sabine paced for a few moments, letting his words sink in. "Am I correct in assuming, Ely, that in your letter you also requested the privilege of becoming the Aldermaston of Muirwood to help carry this burden?"

Another flicker of a smile crossed Kranmir's mouth. "Of course not, Sabine. I would never take it upon myself to do such a thing." His voice became more sinuous. "But truly, when have you *not* requested input from us as to new positions to be filled? When have you *not* acceded to those suggestions as the Medium has moved you to do?" His eyes were like flint.

Sabine feigned confusion. "So you are not to become the Aldermaston of Muirwood?"

"That is not what I *said*," Kranmir replied, holding up a single finger. "I would never take it upon *myself*. The king has seen fit to endorse my suggestion to you and seeks to implement it immediately through an act of the realm. The language of the act is quite clear that the revenues will be centralized through Muirwood to be dispensed as the Aldermaston sees fit to benefit this realm *and others*. He has chosen me to represent this new ideal in Comoros. I am certain you will see the wisdom of his recommendation in time."

Sabine's eyes narrowed. "You may be sure I will discuss it with the king in great detail." Then her expression softened and her voice was pained. "Oh, Ely. Not you. How I wish you could see that gold is a poor substitute for integrity."

Kranmir's eyes flashed with sudden fury and his lips straightened into a firm line. He said nothing, but he could not mask the hatred in his eyes. "Is there anything I can provide to make your stay more comfortable?" he asked crisply.

Sabine shook her head. "Richard has been an able host. Thank you, Ely. That is all. I am sorry I could not respond to your messages more promptly. I can see how deeply it has hurt you. Forgive me."

His expression smoothed, but Maia could see he was not mollified. "It is a small matter, Sabine. I am not quick to be offended."

"I know," she replied softly, seeing the truth hidden in his words. "I see the wound has actually been long in festering. Your predecessor . . . suffered from it as well." She gave him a knowing look, which caused a little smudge of pink on his cheeks. Nodding to her reverentially, he turned to leave.

Richard Syon stood still, watching Sabine for instructions. She motioned for him to depart and nodded subtly, implying he should carry on the tour. He bowed gravely and followed Kranmir out of the room. The steward delicately shut the door, leaving the three mismatched Family members alone.

Sabine sighed regretfully, clasping her hands behind her back.

Maia rushed to her side, wanting to comfort her, but feeling heartbroken at the same time. "He is no Aldermaston," she said.

Sabine shook her head, frowning. "He *is* still. I will need to replace him in Augustin." Her frown deepened. "That will cause a rift, to be sure. He has already rebelled. Perhaps a schism is unavoidable. I hope not."

Collier chuckled softly. "He deceives so gracefully," he said with contempt. "What a gifted liar. I almost envy him that ability, except it made me want to smack him." He chuffed to himself and shook his head. "And you named him to his position, High Seer? Was the Medium *wrong* to do so?" His eyebrows lifted archly, almost in challenge, but it was clear he truly wanted to understand her side.

Sabine met his gaze without anger. "There is a common misperception, Gideon. If the Medium knows what will come to pass, why does it choose people who will fail? It has been my experience that most of humanity is governed by greed, grief, or glory. The most difficult passion to subdue is pride. Surely you know *that*. What happens if a rotten apple is placed in a barrel?"

Collier looked at her curiously. "A spoilt apple ruins the barrel. Is that not the proverb?"

"Indeed. Before it is spoilt, it can be turned into treats, crushed into cider. But when it is diseased, the taint quickly spreads to the other fruit. If you dump out all the apples, my lord, and put in fresh ones, the taint will affect the new batch." Her eyes narrowed. "There is something about the impurity that cannot be seen with mortal eyes. It requires scrubbing and patience to clean the barrel from within. *That* is how the taint is stopped. But at the time of the choosing, it is not spoiled *yet*."

Collier stared at her, his expression grave. "So you must purge the barrel, High Seer?"

She pursed her lips. "If I do not, the entire barrel will be lost."

He tapped his chin. "How do you purge a barrel that is guarded by a king?"

Sabine smiled, her expression deep and poignant. "You persuade the *king* of the danger."

And Maia realized, in that moment, that her example was meant for Collier, not Kranmir.

***

Maia and Collier walked together, side by side, through the Cider Orchard. She used to think of him while wandering there with Suzenne and Dodd. Being with him alone was a strange and thrilling contrast. The limbs were weighed down by heavy clumps of fruit, the skins a pinkish red. Some were glossy and smooth, others blotchy and darker than others. Each tree showed a variety of colors—pale gray bark, vibrant green leaves, and fruit that varied in shade between yellow, pink, and red. Some of the trees had already begun to drop the fruit, and they found, scattered randomly, fallen apples.

Collier crouched to pick one up and cleaned it on his tunic.

"We grow grapes in Dahomey," he said, examining the fruit critically. "I suppose I will have to get used to the taste of these." He bit into it and made a face. "Rather tart," he said, crunching it.

Maia looked for one that had blotches on it. "I have heard these are the sweetest," she said, plucking one from its stem. The release caused the branch to tremble, and suddenly other apples started plopping down onto the grass. Collier held up his hand to deflect the hail of falling fruit and gave an exaggerated wince, making Maia laugh.

She studied the fruit in her hand, brought it to her nose to smell it, and then sank her teeth into the skin. It was delicious and made her mouth water for more. She had always heard of Muirwood apples, and now that she lived at the abbey, she could not get enough of them. Collier sat down and leaned back against the tree after giving a wary look to the branches.

"I am fearful now," he said. "What if one falls right on my head?"

"Perhaps it would improve your good sense?" she replied archly, raising her eyebrows and making him smile. She knelt down on the grass next to him, smoothing out her skirts so she could sit.

"Apples and barrels and blight," he said after taking another bite. "Sounds like a song that children would sing." He sighed deeply, his expression growing darker as his eyes scanned the orchard.

Maia picked at the grass around her quietly, feeling the warmth of the breeze across her neck. She watched his mood become more somber, and she longed to know what he was thinking. "When you asked me to dance . . . was it . . . *only* to get revenge against Lady Deorwynn and Murer?"

His frown was replaced by a sly smile. "I will admit that I had many compelling motives," he answered. "And I do not regret tweaking their noses. They have treated you unpardonably."

Maia felt a flush of heat at his words. "What have you decided about me, Collier?" She risked a look directly into his eyes, though her fingers still plucked the grass.

"What do you mean?"

"You know what I mean. Do you think . . . I am pretending to be who I am? I cannot say the word because of the binding sigil, but do you believe I am . . . *that* other person . . . still?"

The look he gave her was thoughtful. He shook his head no, and she felt a spasm of relief. "It would almost be easier for me if it were true," he said ruefully. "I may not be as discerning as your grandmother . . . or perhaps I am *more*, depending on how you look at her choice of Ely Kranmir as Aldermaston. Truly, a duplicitous man . . . and no friend of yours, Maia, I can tell you that. When I was visiting your father's court, I had my eye on him as someone not trustworthy. I thought he was just a vain relation of Lady Deorwynn, but I believe he would turn on even her if it benefited his ambitions. He and I are too much alike, I think. Does that not concern you?"

Maia shivered as the wind continued to caress her. "It does, if I am honest."

Collier nodded gravely. "I am so confused, Maia," he said, staring off into the orchard with a faraway look. "Your grandmother is . . . she is truly a special woman. I *want* to believe her, which conversely arouses my doubts and stubbornness! Would she truly have given away a king's ransom with no thought or expectation of obedience? I would have gladly been in her debt instead of someone else's, but she says I owe her nothing . . ." He shook his head in respectful wonder. "I am struggling to even comprehend that."

Maia put her hand on his arm. "She is the kindest, wisest soul I have ever known," she told him sincerely. "One of the oaths an Aldermaston makes is honesty. She cannot lie."

He glanced down at her hand on his arm and then up to her face, hungrily. "Walk with me."

"What?" She was a bit startled by the abrupt request.

"I cannot sit here with you like this. The temptation to kiss you right now is too great. Walk with me." He rose from the trunk, leaving the half-eaten fruit on the ground, then reached down and took her hand to help her up. She left hers as well and took his hand. He did not release his grip as they began striding down the row of apple trees. His hand felt strangely comfortable in her own, and a bubbling lightness shot down to her knees and back up through her chest just from being so near him.

He sighed as they walked, occasionally ducking to pass beneath some of the branches because of his height. "I am tempted to kiss you," he confessed, "because in my heart, I do not believe it will kill me. Yet if what you say is true, if what Sabine has said is true, then I have been deluding myself. I am chafing inside, wondering what would have happened if I had taken the maston test instead of abandoning it. What if I had pressed my father, while he was yet alive, to fight for you and to pressure your father to fulfill the plight troth of our infancy?" His hand squeezed hers with pent-up frustration. "I will admit, Maia, that I am tormented by many thoughts. If you were a . . . if you were *evil* by choice, our relationship would be less . . . tragic, in a sense. If your kiss does indeed bring death, and I am your husband, then how can I *ever* kiss you without coming to harm? I want so much for that to be *wrong*. You were tricked, unfairly, into becoming this thing. Why should you bear such awful consequences?"

Maia listened, both her heart and throat constricting with his words, which mirrored the anguished thoughts in her own mind. She tried to focus instead on the feeling of his hand and on matching his languid gait. She wanted desperately to comfort him, but the futility of their predicament pressed in on her just as it did on him.

"I want it to be wrong," he said again, breathing heavily. "I have taught myself to believe that the maston order is nothing more than a fusty tradition from our ancestors. One used to keep us from doing what we please. There is ample evidence of this. Yet . . . but yet . . . what if I have been wrong?" He laughed bitterly. "I can comprehend why Kranmir looked so angry. How can I judge the man when I have suffered the same blindness, but not for so long? He has convinced himself he is right. But that does not make him right."

"There is a quote in the tomes," Maia said, her voice low. "Ovidius said we are slow to believe that which, if believed, would hurt our feelings."

"I do not remember that one," he said, chuckling. "How true it is, though. What I struggle with, Maia, is the lack of proof. The Medium responds to kystrels just as it responds to mastons. One order says it is wickedness to force the Medium. The other says it is foolish to curb your desires when both aims produce the same results. You have convinced me that you intend to become a maston, that your duty is to stay and open the Apse Veil. But Maia . . . can you tell me how long that will take?"

Maia shook her head sadly.

"I cannot *remain* here," he said disconsolately. "This is not my kingdom. And I imagine your father will be incensed to learn that I have married his daughter without his permission. I cannot trust his hospitality, though he believes I have no coin left for him to plunder. My intention, you know," he whispered conspiratorially, "was to negotiate for lands, titles, and an earldom if I were to marry his daughter. Then I was going to spring the trap and tell him that I had already married you." He clucked his tongue. "Shaming Deorwynn like that was a small price to pay, however. And I will still get an earldom from this. Watch me." He winked at her, some of his good humor returning.

Maia could not help but smile. She looked up at his face. "Thank you."

"For what?"

She grew very serious in that moment, not used to exposing this particular vulnerability. "Thank you for defending me in that room. It has been a long time since anyone has protected me."

His eyes grew soft as he reached out and trailed his finger down her cheek. "You are most welcome." He sighed in frustration. "I am tempting myself again. We had better keep walking." They started once more.

"I also regret what happened to me at the lost abbey," Maia said miserably. "Every part of me wishes it could be undone. I . . . I . . . would understand if you . . . as a husband . . . considering the restrictions"—she swallowed, almost too afraid to say the words— "if you decided to leave me. But I hope you do not."

He looked at her with startled surprise. Then he shook his head slowly. "You rouse my sympathies, Maia. You are most beautiful. Also modest, to a fault. A compassionate young woman, and so wise . . . well, compared to me. Not being able to kiss you . . . well . . . I would be lying if I said it was not a bitter disappointment to me. I am not certain how to endure it . . . but . . . patiently, I suppose."

She ached inside at his words, and the two walked in silence for a while.

"What if your father is not persuaded by Sabine's arguments? What if he does not want to cleanse the barrel? Believe me, the barrel is disgustingly putrid. You cannot be at court for long without smelling the rot."

"How so? I have not been to court in years."

"It would offend your sensibilities," he said enigmatically.

"Tell me, Collier. I am not as innocent as you think. It will sadden me, that is all."

He shrugged and squeezed her hand almost comfortingly as they walked. "Your father has a new mistress, and she is your age. Lady Deorwynn is as sour as milk about it, you can imagine. Yet how she can be surprised is beyond me, since she—as a lady-in-waiting—stole your father from your mother first."

Maia felt the pangs of sorrow. "You mean Jayn Sexton?"

He nodded. "So you had heard of her."

"She is Suzenne's friend. They were companions."

"Ah, that make sense. The court is all aflutter with rumors that the king plans to marry her after Whitsunday. Kranmir has already agreed to do it, assuming the chancellor can get Deorwynn out of the way. It is a messy business, Maia. The court reeks of intrigue." Collier pursed his lips and gave her a hard look. "Your father is truly depraved, Maia. I can *not* understand why you refuse my help with this situation. You even made me *promise* not to intervene! Sadly, Maia, your wisdom has failed you in this matter. Your father will kill you if you do not conform to his accursed plans."

"He is still my father," she replied weakly.

"By the Blood, how can you be so loyal to him?" Collier demanded. "Brannon has done nothing but injure you, humiliate you, torture you. He hired a *kishion* to be your protector! What does that say about him?"

She stopped walking, feeling the conflict burn inside her. She gazed down at their entwined hands, struggling for the words to make Collier understand, yet knowing no simple way to explain such a tangled mess of a relationship. "Because I remember how my father *was*. I cannot forget that. Back when he and my mother were friends . . . well . . . they were like *this*," she said, gazing up at his eyes, squeezing his hand so hard it would hurt. "Their marriage . . . *broke*. Like a porcelain dish. But I can still remember what it was like. And I believe he can come back. He can remember his maston oaths, he can remember what he has lost. I must hope, Collier."

He stared at her pityingly. The look in his eyes said he shared none of that hope with her.

"You will not face him alone," Collier said, shaking his head. "Your father has a rash temper. I have witnessed it. If I am standing next to you, he will watch himself. But clearly you should only confront him on the abbey grounds. He has no legal authority here . . . *yet*. Once he has taken over the abbeys, you may be cast out of here. Then you will come with me to Dahomey. We will open the Apse Veil from another abbey if we must."

Maia shook her head obstinately. "It must be here. This is where the Covenant was made."

"Then perhaps the Medium will give me the evidence I have long desired to see. I will stand by you, Maia, as long as I can. Maybe until one of us is proved wrong."

Maia looked at him, feeling at once comforted and confused. "Tell me about your plans."

He looked away grimly. "You proceed as you think best, Maia . . . and let me do the same. I do not believe the Medium will come and strike down Kranmir or your father. A beautiful orchard can still be razed with axes. And an abbey that has only just been reconstructed can still be burned to the ground. However, I do not think that is Brannon's intent. He wants coin. *And* power *and* youth." He looked at her challengingly. "The Medium will not intervene in this. It gives us what we desire, even to our detriment. My own maston father was the captive of the Paeizian king . . . where was the Medium then? The Medium was on the winning side, as it always is."

Maia bit back her retort when she heard someone calling her name. Recognizing Owen Page's voice, she called out to him, and he joined them in the grove, shrouded by the swelling fruit.

"The Aldermaston bid me to find you both," he said breathlessly. "The king has arrived."

CHAPTER
TWENTY-SIX

The King's Will

B y the time Maia and Collier reached the council chamber, it was already crowded. Davi and Aloia, the kitchen maidens, were hurrying to place more dishes of treats on the serving tables, and many attendees had gathered around to try the delights the cook had made in preparation for the Whitsunday festival. The smell of cider filled the air, and crumbs pattered on the floor rushes like rain. Maia quickly surveyed those in attendance, recognizing most of them. And there he was, talking with the Earl of Forshee, Chancellor Crabwell, and Captain Carew over by the cider cups. As soon as she saw her father, her heart flinched. She had not seen him since that dark night he had sent her away to Dahomey to find the lost abbey. He was heavier now—his cheeks fuller, his chest bigger—and there were streaks of white in his beard. He wore a plumed velvet hat fitted with an eye-catching feather. Glittering rings bedecked both of his hands. He was deep in conversation with Carew, and had not seen her enter the room.

Collier's grip tightened on her arm, and he led her over to where the Aldermaston, his wife, and Sabine were standing, conferring with the abbey's steward, Tomas. The tall steward smiled at her, dimples flashing, but she could tell he was agitated. Sabine nodded to Maia, giving her a steady smile—as if she were steeling herself before entering an arena.

Lady Deorwynn and Murer were there, Maia noticed, huddled in a corner with Aldermaston Kranmir, speaking in hushed tones. Though Lady Deorwynn was pale, her eyes flamed with rage when she noticed Maia and Collier. She motioned toward them, her mouth twisting spitefully as she said something to her uncle. Murer just gave an injured sniff and looked determinedly away from the couple.

There were other onlookers as well, people from court who had come with the king, most of them nobles of the realm. She recognized some of them as earls, but many were young and owed their power to her father's beneficence. She saw Suzenne standing with an older couple who looked to be her parents. There was no sign of Dodd.

Maia was nervous and kept looking at her father, waiting for his gaze to fall on her. When it finally did, his smile melted away, and with a cool, cunning look, he appraised her from across the room. He thrust his goblet into Crabwell's hand and then clapped his hands and strode into the center of the room. The gibbering and laughter subsided instantly.

"Well met, my friends," he said in a loud, commanding voice. "It was a long and tedious journey, to be sure, but we have all arrived at Muirwood as planned. The inns are overcrowded, Richard. The roads are pure muck. This will need to be corrected before we next assemble here."

There was a spattering of clapping, very subdued. Aldermaston Kranmir began to edge closer to where the king stood.

The king smiled and nodded as his gaze fell upon those gathered before him. "When I sent my heralds to announce we would be celebrating Whitsunday at Muirwood, I had not expected certain illustrious guests. Sabine—it is our pleasure and honor to welcome you to Comoros." He dipped his head formally. "If I had known you were coming, I would have prepared a more festive welcome."

Sabine nodded respectfully to him. "I have never been disappointed in the hospitality I have received here. Simple fare is to my liking."

"Ah yes, but not to mine. Thankfully I warned Richard's cook I was coming! Here we are, assembled together before the formal celebrations tomorrow. I thought it might be . . . fitting if we had a little . . . conversation before. I should not like to have any more surprises thrust on me, eh, Gideon?"

He gave Collier a withering look, his expression subtly shifting from pleasure to anger.

"You cannot imagine how surprised I was to find her wandering in my realm, Your Majesty." Collier winked. He hooked his arm inside Maia's and patted her hand. "I was swayed by her beauty and charm. You did promise her to me, after all."

The tension in the room intensified, and Maia could see the rage building in her father's eyes. She swallowed, her heart trembling in fear.

Collier seemed to notice it as well, and his tone softened. "Our kingdoms have always been at odds, my lord. But with a careful union of interests, we have managed to avoid war. Being the weaker kingdom, I did take advantage of the situation. As a ruler, I am sure you can understand why," he said with a wry smile, trying his best to look apologetic. "We can discuss the dowry terms later."

His words had an immediate effect, seeming to soothe some of the fierceness in her father's eyes, which slowly cooled. He still looked displeased, but the fit of passion was ebbing.

"How is my daughter?" her father asked shortly, his eyes glittering as he looked at her.

"I am well," Maia replied thickly, trying to quell her violent emotions. She was so grateful to have Collier standing beside her, but she feared for him too. She feared what could happen to him if were caught in a fit of her father's rage. "It is good to see you, Father."

He sniffed, trying to compose himself, his feelings for Maia obviously as tangled as her own for him. She wondered how much of her mother he still saw when he regarded her. Her mother who had defied his will unto death.

"Did you accomplish your *errand* in Dahomey?" he inquired, his eyebrows arching. "I have expected you to return to the palace to bring me word of your journeys. Why have you not come?"

Maia swallowed down her fear. "Because I learned of a duty I must fulfill here first," she answered simply.

"You have a duty to your father."

"I do," she agreed, trying in vain to console him. "But I also have a duty to the Medium. A charge that was given to our Family." She glanced at Sabine, who nodded discreetly.

"Ah, yes," her father said smugly. "Your mother often spoke of it, to my frustration. The Apse Veil, is it not? What gives you the impression that *you* are meant to fulfill it?"

Maia swallowed again. "It was . . . written in Lia's tome."

Her father nodded, his expression full of intrigue. "Have you read it yourself, Daughter? Or did someone read it to you?" He glanced at Sabine warily.

He was endeavoring to trap her with her own words, she realized. If she were to admit she could read—as he knew she could—it would invite the wrath of the Dochte Mandar on the kingdom. Not just her kingdom, but Dahomey as well. He seemed to take perverse delight in what he was doing.

Sabine stepped forward. "I shared the information with her, Your Majesty. I am the guardian of Lia's tome. It was handed down to me. She saw the future in her visions, my lord. She knew it would take several generations before one of her descendants grew strong enough in the Medium to reopen the Apse Veil. Maia is the one."

"So you say," he replied curtly. He turned to Aldermaston Kranmir and chuckled. "You were right, Aldermaston. He warned me that you would try something like this, Sabine."

"I do not understand," Sabine said, confused but respectful.

"You knew that I intended to overrule your authority in my realm. I have made little secret that I despise the maston customs. I expelled the Dochte Mandar from my realm. I can expel your followers too." His jaw began to gnash with suppressed fury. "The Naestors are sending an armada against me. They think I will be surprised, but I am not. And while they may have supremacy by sea, they will find this kingdom and its castles and keeps to be unconquerable. They may harass the coasts. They may starve us of trade, but if we—Comoros and Dahomey and Pry-Ree— unite against them, we will not be defeated. This is not the time to threaten me with mystical curses and old-fashioned morals. I am the King of Comoros, and I will not yield one span of dirt in this kingdom without fighting for it. Do you think the Naestors will care about your precious abbeys? Do you not think they will loot them and defile them and burn them? I will not let them seize what is rightfully mine. This is for the best, Sabine. I hope you have the sense to see that."

He was nearly growling with anger and determination. Maia could see the purpose in his eyes. He believed in a twisted interpretation of the Medium . . . that a strong will and a determined mind could achieve what it desired. There was not good or evil, only the pursuit of one's desires.

Sabine shook her head slowly. "Your Majesty, your spies have interpreted the situation incorrectly. The armada is not coming to Comoros."

He barked out a laugh. "They are! You are daft if you believe otherwise. We are expecting the invasion imminently. I am celebrating Whitsunday at Muirwood, and let it be known that I was, because it is the most defensible by sea! They cannot surprise us here."

"Your Grace—" Sabine said, "—hear me, please. The armada is not coming. I have it from the highest authorities within Naess itself that the armada sails for the maston homeland—Assinica. They are helpless there. They have been waiting for our abbeys to be restored, for the Apse Veils to be opened so that they might return. Your Majesty, your kingdom is about to swell with refugees from another country." She strode forward, her voice sharp and forceful. "Now is *not* the moment to give in to pride and rash action. These people will come here looking for a king-maston to rule them. You must *be* that man! If the Apse Veils are not opened, these people will be slaughtered. The armada will murder them all to prevent them from adding to your power. These are artisans, my lord. Poets and scholars and artists and musicians. These are people who have lived in a land of peace all their lives. We must shelter them and protect them, and they will add to the wealth of your kingdom a hundredfold!" Her voice throbbed with passion. "Now is not the time to make a schism, Your Grace. Let us heal the breach between us." She reached out her hand, a gesture of invitation. "I forgive you for what you did to my daughter. I bear no malice toward you. The Medium put you on your throne for this very moment, for this very decision." Sabine reached out and gripped Maia's arms, hugging her. "Maia is your rightful heir, Your Majesty. She is the one who can open the Apse Veil. I know it with every feeling in my heart. Please, Your Majesty, I beg you! Do you not *feel* the Medium saying this is true?"

The Medium was there. Maia had felt its tendrils slowly creep into the room as her grandmother spoke. It thrummed in the floor. It burned in Maia's heart. She felt tears prick her eyes, and it was as if a chorus were suddenly singing—not one heard with ears, but with the soul. Maia bit her lip, staring at her father.

"I feel nothing," he said contemptuously. He waved a derisive finger at the High Seer. "You are deranged, Sabine. You *were* right, Kranmir. She is artful. But I will not fall for these emotional tricks." He took a step toward Sabine, his eyes glinting with hatred. "I do not need your forgiveness. I neither desire it nor require it. Your daughter is dead now, and I rejoiced when I heard the news. I will not have *my* conscience dictated to. *I* am the master of this land. *I* am the lord of this land!" He glanced around the room at them all. "Tomorrow morning, I am coming through those front gates and will decree that Kranmir is both the new Aldermaston of Muirwood and the head of the maston order in Comoros. He has already signed the Act of Submission. All who fail to sign will be taken to Pent Tower and tried for treason." He glared at Maia, his look swollen with fury, then glanced back at Sabine. "You might want to be gone when I return, Sabine. Truly, I do not wish to ever see you again."

***

The door of the Aldermaston's study closed. Tomas the steward hung his head, looking as grim-faced as if he were standing at the steps leading to the gallows. Sitting in his usual chair, the Aldermaston seemed disappointed but not surprised. His wife was standing just behind him, her hand on his shoulder, and he reached up to clasp that hand, smiling sadly. Sabine's arms were folded, indicating she was deep in thought. But all the upset around Maia could not compare with the misery and disappointment in her own heart.

Collier escorted Maia to a chair and then turned around to face the others. "And *that* madman is your father," he said flatly. He shook his head and chuckled darkly. "If I tried that in Dahomey, the entire populace would revolt. Power must be balanced, at least slightly. See what it has done to his wits? He rules out of fear and intimidation, not loyalty."

Collier's words stung Maia, making her flinch. She felt tears pressing in her eyes.

"Are you leaving, madame?" Collier asked Sabine. "I know your ship is waiting at the river, so we could all—"

"No," Sabine answered, interrupting him. Her eyes were thick with tears. "No, Gideon. We will stay."

"But you heard him! I tell you, his heart will not be softened in the morning. We must go to another abbey. One in my kingdom . . . or Pry-Ree is closer. Let Maia open the Apse Veil from another abbey."

Sabine shook her head. "No, Gideon. The Covenant must be fulfilled here at Muirwood. That is what Lia foresaw."

Collier looked perplexed. "But did she say what would happen? If she could see the future, as you say, did she not write a warning about what we would face and how we might avoid it?"

Sabine shook her head. "She did not. There were no instructions, no advice about Maia's father or his threats."

"But what are we to do? Surely waiting to die is not the Medium's will?"

Sabine walked up to Collier and put her hand on his wrist. "Sometimes it is."

He recoiled from her words. "How can that be?"

Sabine shook her head. "Do you not understand, Gideon? When the abbeys fell and burned, the dead were trapped in this world. My Gift of Seeing is of the past, not the future. Each day I walk these grounds, I see glimpses of their lives. The Aldermastons of the past. The learners. The wretcheds. They were all people, like us. They had hopes and dreams. Now their bodies molder in ossuaries and their spirits long to be given life again. The dead have been waiting for this moment for centuries. Can you not feel them brooding over these grounds? This is not just about Assinica and saving the innocent there. We must save those who have been waiting in death." She turned and looked at Maia. "Waiting for you."

Maia's heart shivered. The room seemed thick and heavy, as if the hearth had wreathed it in smoke, except there were no fumes. She could feel the writhing despair of the dead.

Collier's eyes bulged. He shook his head with disbelief. "So you are saying . . . so you are saying, Sabine, that we must *trust* the Medium? Without knowing what will happen? Even if we become corpses ourselves?"

She nodded at him. "When Lia was alive, she did not know her fate. She did not know the part she would play in bringing about the great Scourge. If she had, back when she was a child in the kitchen, she may never have had the courage to leave the abbey grounds. In our predicament, we must have courage *not* to leave the abbey grounds." She sighed and looked at Maia. "I do not feel that we should bring you to the abbey tonight, my dear. I think your father has made his decision. I mourn at what that means for him." She swallowed. "In the past, the Medium has removed kings from power."

Maia squeezed her eyes shut and wept silently. The hope she had felt for her father was finally leaving her.

Wars spring from unseen and generally insignificant causes, the first outbreak being often but an explosion of anger.

—Richard Syon, Aldermaston of Muirwood Abbey

CHAPTER
TWENTY-SEVEN

Fog of the Myriad Ones

M aia stood behind Suzenne, combing through the final bits of supple hair. Staring at the reflection of her friend in the mirror, Maia felt a small pang of jealousy. Suzenne wore the supplicant robes again, just as she had the night of her maston test. She looked sweetly nervous, biting her lower lip as she gazed up at Maia's face.

"I am more anxious than I expected to be," Suzenne whispered softly. "My fingers are shaking. Can you help me with the veil?"

"Gladly," Maia answered, walking over to the gossamer veil nestled in a box the Aldermaston's wife had provided earlier. It was just past sunset. Suzenne's parents awaited her inside the abbey, as did the Aldermaston and his wife. Sabine had decided to spend the night in the abbey in the hopes it would help her understand the Medium's will as she wrestled with the monumental doom facing the realm.

Maia removed the veil carefully, and carried the pretty confection over to her friend. She grasped Suzenne's shoulder tenderly. "You look beautiful, Suzenne. Dodd will be so pleased."

Suzenne flushed, unable to conceal a nervous smile. "What a foreboding wedding night," she murmured. "My parents are not exactly rejoicing over our decision, but your husband's promise to bring us to Dahomey with you was received with pleasure. They did nothing more than offer their concerns. I am grateful for that."

Maia smiled and was about to settle the veil over Suzenne's head when her friend stopped her. "Maia?"

"Yes?"

Suzenne began to stammer timidly. "You said . . . you were married in Dahomey . . . in the middle of your husband's army, if I recall. Did you . . . um . . . consummate . . . the marriage later since you did not that night?" She could not look at Maia, as if hoping she had not trodden on an unsafe topic.

Maia bit her lip and blushed. "We have not, Suzenne. I can be of no help to you in that." Her cheeks flamed despite her best attempts to appear unaffected.

Suzenne nodded in understanding and wrung her hands as Maia fixed the veil over her golden hair. Once it was in place, Suzenne's face could barely be seen beneath the gauzy veil.

A knock sounded at their door, and Maia hurried to answer it. She saw the Aldermaston's steward there, and behind him, Collier.

"A mist has settled over the abbey this evening," Tomas said, his cheeks dimpling. "The Aldermaston sent me to bring Suzenne to the abbey for the ceremony. Everyone is already assembled."

Suzenne rose from the chair and joined them at the door. Maia hugged her and touched her cheek through the veil, feeling love for her friend and sadness for herself. She wondered what the morrow would bring for them all.

"And I am here," Collier interrupted, offering his arm to Maia, "because I understand you are still holding vigil. With your grandmother and friends otherwise occupied tonight, I thought I might keep you company?" He offered her a charming smile, which made her flush. She wanted his company, but had been too ashamed to ask for it.

"Thank you," she said gratefully.

They walked together, following Tomas and Suzenne to the doors of the manor house. The grounds were indeed wreathed in damp mists, which was peculiar since the mists normally came at dawn. The air was thick and cool and wet and had a sharp, metallic taste. Dewdrops gathered on her face the moment they emerged into the night air. They could not see the abbey through the fog, even though it was very close.

They walked together until they reached the outer doors of the abbey, and again Maia felt an oppressive feeling warning her not to go farther. She stopped, clinging to Collier's arm, and watched until Suzenne disappeared behind the pewter doors of the abbey. The walls loomed above her in the mist, and although they were invisible in the mist, she had walked the grounds enough times to visualize what they looked like.

"Would you like to walk in the garden?" Collier asked.

"That would be nice," Maia replied, feeling awkward with him so soon after Suzenne's wedding preparations. Much had changed between them since his humiliation of Deorwynn and Murer in the morning. It felt as if the day was a hinge on which the world was turning, and she could hear the groaning creak of a door about to close. "I would like my cloak, though. It is so unusual, this cold and damp."

"Certainly." They started walking back the short distance to the manor. "You are quiet this evening. Are your thoughts as intense as mine after such a day?"

"Yes . . . and I am also tired," Maia said, feeling a fog of sorts inside her head. "I have not slept in quite some time. The abbey has a strange feeling to it tonight." She gazed back at it and saw that even the pewter doors had vanished in the mist. A fleeting fancy slipped into her mind, and she wondered if the abbey would disappear when the mists left in the morning. She could hear different sounds—it was only just after sunset, and learners were walking the grounds preparing to celebrate Whitsunday the next day. The maypole had been erected and the colored streamers affixed. The kitchen overflowed with treats. Yet despite the symbols of festivity, the fate of Muirwood was oppressive and dark. A new Aldermaston would take charge the next day if the Medium allowed it to happen.

"It does feel strange," Collier said, scratching his throat. He glanced around uncomfortably. "I feel as if we are not alone. It is a little unsettling."

They reached the door to the manor and walked down the hall back to her room, both walking faster than necessary as if by silent agreement. Maia opened the door and hurried to fetch her cloak, her arms trembling. She had never felt so dark and gloomy as she did at that moment. Collier stood by the open door, his expression pensive.

The sounds of boots came clipping down the hall. Collier turned and looked, his expression immediately going sour. "What is it, Carew?" he asked, frowning slightly. Maia fastened the cloak around her neck, and when she reached the doorway, Captain Carew had reached them.

"Crabwell wants to talk to you," the captain told Collier. He gave Maia a nod, but otherwise ignored her.

"I am not leaving the abbey grounds tonight," Collier said with a snort.

"He has not left either," Carew explained. "Kranmir has been talking to the king, warning him not to do anything rash. It seems the little man has a spark of conscience left. The High Seer's warning rattled him, I think. Crabwell wants to use the moment to settle him down. A truce or treaty with you might do the trick." He directed his gaze at Maia. "It will not take long, if Gideon is reasonable."

Collier scowled. "A treaty? On Whitsunday eve? Does Crabwell never stop plotting?"

"Does a spider stop weaving webs?" Carew said with a smirk. "A treaty and your dowry negotiations. That is all he asks of you. Then he can work on getting the king a little drunk and hopefully fix his seal to it before morning. Trust me, Gideon, we all want to avoid an open conflict tomorrow."

Collier tapped his chin. "Where is Maia's father now? Is he still at the abbey?"

Carew rolled his eyes. "He left hours ago. He's back at the Pilgrim making eyes at the Sexton girl. Crabwell expects a marriage soon."

Collier grunted in disgust. "Now that he has Kranmir in his pocket, there is no doubt he can arrange the divorce. Your kingdom is a cesspit, Carew. You realize that?"

Carew nodded and grinned. "Our spies in Dahomey say yours is not much better . . . maybe a garderobe if not an actual cesspit. Come, man! I am tired of walking hither and yon. Talk to Crabwell."

A look of frustration crossed Collier's face, but she gave him permission to leave her with a curt nod. He smiled his thanks, cupped her cheek with his warm hand, and stared at her with his piercing blue eyes. "I will be back shortly. Bolt the door, Wife."

"I will," Maia said, squeezing his hand before he left and followed Carew. The two bickered and taunted each other as they walked down the hall. The rest of the corridor was empty, only a few Leerings to illuminate it. The floor rushes looked excessively trampled.

Maia used her thoughts to light the fire Leering in her room and then shut the door, dragging the bolt into place to secure it.

There was a little scuff behind her.

She whirled, heart in her throat, and caught a glimpse of the sheriff of Mendenhall before a black sack was plunged over her head.

***

Maia was trussed up—ankles, knees, wrists, and arms—and a gag covered her mouth. She was wrapped up in smothering sackcloth, the smell of it blocking her other senses. She was being carried by several men who walked briskly and noiselessly. The coolness of the outdoors penetrated the cloth as they carried her outside, and her heart quailed in panic. She tried to scream, but the thick gag in her mouth prevented any noise from escaping her except for small groans. Thrashing in the bonds, she tried to free herself and felt the bands around her wrists begin to wriggle loose. She bunched her legs to kick, but there were easily four or more men holding her captive, and she was no match for their combined strength. The exertions tired her quickly, and the gag made breathing difficult; for a moment she was afraid she would suffocate.

They were walking on soft ground, the boots muffled by the grass. She could hear voices, but it was difficult to make out the words because of the material shrouding her.

"By the Blood, what a night for fog!"

"Darker than usual. We should have brought torches."

"No torches, fool. Easier to slip out this way."

Rage and terror wriggled inside Maia with savage intensity. She had no doubt these men had abducted her to take her to her father, outside the abbey grounds. Even more than confronting her father again, she feared that leaving the abbey's protection would make her vulnerable to the Myriad Ones. She had not passed the maston test yet, so she had no chaen under her dress to guard her from the beings. No kystrel either, not that she would have used one. Feeling a spasm of fear, she wriggled again, trying to buck herself loose.

"She is feisty," one of them grunted disapprovingly.

"You did not expect her to come willingly, surely?" It was the sheriff's voice. "Be still, Lady Maia. We are not sent to harm you, if that is what you fear."

She could not tell them what she feared. She could not utter the loathsome truth to anyone living. Even the thought of doing so flooded her with guilt and shame. She was a hetaera. Even without a kystrel, she was dangerous. And outside the abbey grounds, she could be lethal. Maia shivered with dread anticipation, fearing what would happen next.

"The mist is so thick! Are we going the right way?"

"We are," the sheriff said self-assuredly. "I have trodden these grounds all winter. I can find my way blindfolded."

"The fog is worse than a blindfold. Will the Aldermaston curse us for doing this?"

"Shut it," said another man. "Be quiet for once in your life. See the trees?"

"It's the Cider Orchard," the sheriff explained. "The smells should hide the trail from the hunter's dog. The onion sack she is in will help as well."

So that explained the stench. She bobbed and swayed to the rhythm of their pace, each rut and stumble shaking her bones. She was panting beneath the hood, sweaty and queasy and near to retching.

"The orchard is thick. Almost through. The wall ends just past it, by the hillside. Men will be waiting for us there with lanterns."

The steel hand of fear gripped Maia's heart. She knew struggling was useless, and it was only tiring her more quickly. How could she hope to stop these men?

It begins with a thought.

The jumbling and swaying was dizzying, but she tried to center herself and clear her thoughts. Fear was her enemy. She had to calm down in order to think clearly. *Focus on what you want, burn it to life with your will, and the Medium would help it happen.* As her emotions began to cool, new thoughts awakened in her mind. This was her father's design. He did not want to risk the outcome on the morrow. He did not want to alienate his people by staging a confrontation between himself and his daughter. If she was on his side, if only physically, it would make it easier for him to topple the abbeys of the realm.

What he did not surmise or understand was what would happen to Maia once she left the grounds. Ereshkigal was probably waiting just outside the wall, ready to pounce and claim the body she had previously stolen.

Jon Tayt—I need you!

She sent the thought into the wind, hoping he would hear her. She focused her thoughts, her emotions, her intensity on that one wish, desperate to summon the abbey hunter to her aid. Collier would be blind to the mists. Her grandmother was inside the abbey—what could she do in time? But Argus could use her scent to track her, succeeding where others would fail.

Find me! Cider Orchard, nearing the end of the wall.

Maia felt the rhythm slow. As it did, she could hear the mewling sounds of the Myriad Ones in the distance. It felt as if she were nearing the shores of a vast lake, the waters rippling along the edge. The abbey was the dry ground; the rest of the world was the lake. As her captors continued to move toward the edge of the abbey grounds, she could feel the force of the Myriad Ones' thoughts pressing against hers—hungry, sniffling, greedy to taste her again. Once more, her heart began to hammer in terror, and she struggled against her bonds. She felt the tether burning the skin at her wrists as she struggled to slip her hands through.

They left the protection of the abbey grounds.

Maia knew the instant it happened. The feeling of warmth and protection she had experienced upon coming to Muirwood vanished like a candle guttered by a storm. Feelings of blackness and despair enveloped her, worse than the bonds and the hood and the choking gag. She could feel the voracious, mewling creatures surround the soldiers, who seemed oblivious to the taint of their black presence—perhaps because they were so accustomed to it. To Maia, they felt like smoke that choked her lungs and stung her eyes.

"Thank you, Sheltin," the sheriff said. "The king wants her tonight. I need to return to the grounds to lead the search when it is discovered she is missing, and keep them away from our trail. Graves will go with you to make sure she arrives safely."

Maia felt the nuzzling pressure of the Myriad Ones as they swarmed her body. She began kicking again, not against the soldiers, but against the invasive, violating touch of the Myriad Ones. The ropes and bonds were nothing compared to the awful feeling of the creatures worming against her clothes.

You are us. You are part of us.

Join us, Sister! Choose us! We are your flesh!

We are your bones.
You are us and we are you.
Let me have her first.

Maia wept bitterly as the mark on her shoulder started to burn and her thoughts began to cloud. She focused her will, champing on the gag with all her strength. The Myriad Ones were relentless, and she felt the blackness begin to invade her mind.

"Take her," said the sheriff grimly.

She struck the ground with a heavy jolt. Shouts and grunts sounded all around her. The sudden impact of falling made her unable to breathe, and she blacked out for a moment. As soon as she came to, she wriggled with renewed violence and managed to free her wrists from the bonds. A grunt of pain sounded, and something collapsed next to her head. Maia's wrists stung and felt wet with blood, but she had freed her hands, and she began squirming through the wrappings, trying to loosen the ropes around her arms as she tugged at the bonds around her knees.

"Run! Run for the village! Run for—*och!*" She heard the sound of gurgling breath cut off by a blade.

Another thump followed by another. Maia rocked on her shoulders, trying to change position and escape the bonds. She was desperate to free herself—not just from the Myriad Ones, but from whatever was attacking the sheriff's men.

"I am the sheriff of Mendenhall!" came a scream, the voice warbling with fear. "Stay back! Stay back!" She heard his last breath hiss out of him.

The Myriad Ones were feasting on the death and carnage, their thoughts suddenly loose from her. They lapped up the emotions of the dying, whimpering with pleasure at the taste of the shock, fear, and horror.

A knife slit the ropes around her arms, knees, and ankles. The bags and bonds were flung away from her. She heard heavy breathing, the sound of a man tired by effort. Maia wrenched the hood from her head, her hair sticking to her face.

Crouched over her, sweat dropping down his nose, she saw the kishion holding a bloodied dagger.

CHAPTER TWENTY-EIGHT

Kishion

The Myriad Ones were all around her, thick as the vapors of mist shrouding the air. Although Maia was free from the bonds, she was not certain if she was truly free.

The darkness concealed much of the kishion's expression, but she recognized the size and bulk of him, and he radiated that same awful menace she remembered from the weeks they had traveled together. A shiver of fear went through her body as she watched the puffs of mist from his harried breathing.

"You saved me," Maia whispered, her voice trembling. She was waiting for him to speak, dreading to know his intentions for her. He had poisoned her mother. She could not forget that, nor could she trust him.

"As you saved me," he said with a thick, almost raspy voice. She had not heard him speak in some time and had almost forgotten the harsh timbre of his voice. "On another night . . . in another mist. Do you remember?"

"Of course," Maia answered, struggling to her feet. He lurched toward her, and she flinched from the bloodied knife in his hand, her abdomen still bearing a scar from a wound he had given her as a warning in the cursed woods of Dahomey.

He chuckled derisively and grabbed her arm to help her stand. "I am not here to hurt you, Maia. You need not fear me." There was something in his voice, some strange feeling she could not understand. He wiped his blade on his hip, then sheathed it, still clutching her arm.

The Myriad Ones mewled in the fog, prodding and sniffing at her, enveloping her in determined thoughts, and she felt herself almost faint. Her knees buckled as the blackness threatened to overwhelm her again.

"Are you hurt?" he asked, holding out his other arm to stop her from falling.

"The abbey," she whispered desperately, feeling the multiple wills crushing against hers. They weighed her down like stones.

The kishion gripped her forearm and circled his other arm around her back, then helped her move toward the edge of the wall, toward the thick mass of oak trees and their clawing branches. She felt her left shoulder burn with heat, but somehow, the Myriad Ones could not sink inside her, and she felt them rage in frustration.

The vigil! she realized thankfully. She had been holding vigil for two days, and though she lacked the protection of the abbey, the Medium was still shielding her. As she stumbled forward, she felt the shrieks of the Myriad Ones against her mind, their howls of fury and impotence. Again her thoughts wavered, her vision blackening as if a swarm of dark leaves were spinning in front of her eyes.

"A little farther," the kishion said, his teeth gritted. Could he feel the madness fluttering around them as well? She hunched over, weak, and pressed against him to keep herself upright. Her knees shook with the pressure, and each step became more arduous. It was worse than climbing mountains.

The wall was just ahead. She could sense a change in the Myriad Ones. The sheriff and his men were now dead, and there were no emotions left to suck on. They crowded her again, vengeful and filled with hatred, their thoughts hissing like steam. Maia stumbled, racked with dread and despair. She felt them take control of her arms and legs, turning them into lead.

"Hurry!" she pleaded to the kishion, her mouth starting to lose itself.

Sensing her panic, the kishion hoisted her in his arms and lunged the final steps into the protection of the abbey grounds. It was like coming up for air after being submerged. The blackness of the Myriad Ones was instantly dispelled. They keened with rage at her, furious that their victim had been snatched from their grasp. The walls of the abbey shook with the tremors of their anger, their revenge, their twisted desires. Maia glanced back, feeling unseen sentinels standing there, the ghosts of the dead protecting the hallowed grounds. She breathed deep, almost weeping with relief. The feeling of peace that flooded her heart was such a comfort. She rested her head against the kishion's chest, panting.

"Thank you," she whispered brokenly. "Thank you!"

The kishion carried her, held tight in his arms, and moved through the thick groves of oak trees, ducking occasionally to stay away from the reaching branches. His breath was heavy in her ear, and she could feel the steady rhythm of his heartbeat as he labored to carry her through the trees. The fog shrouded the way, but she knew the grounds intimately now. She thought they were nearer to the kitchen than the manor when the veil of trees parted and they reached an expanse of lawn.

"Set me down, I can walk now," she said, her ebbed strength returning. The weariness threatened to make her doze.

He obeyed and shifted her in his arms, setting her down just past the small twigs and scrub of the grove. The grass was cool and wet against her shoes.

She reached out to touch his arm. "Why are you here?" she asked suddenly.

There was a little more light, diffused from various sources on the grounds. His face was still partially smothered in shadow, but she saw his amused smile. "I have my business, Maia," he said cryptically. "Do not ask what it is. I heard them plotting to abduct you tonight and waited for the sheriff to drag you out. I followed them into the mist. They did not heed my warning."

Her heart filled with wariness and fear. "Did you follow me from Dahomey?" she asked.

He shook his head. "I had to heal from my injury." His hand went down to his waist, pressing his healed wound, and he winced, his lips curling with pain. "The injury still afflicts me. But you saved me, Maia. As I have saved you. We are bound, you and I." His voice dropped lower. "Do not trust your father. He means you harm."

Maia's voice quavered. "I know."

"Then *fight* him," the kishion said, his voice rising with anger.

Maia shook her head wearily. "I cannot. He is my father."

He chuckled coldly. "He hired me to kill you. I told you that."

"Even so, I will not harm him. I wish you had not killed the sheriff's men."

He snorted. "Of course you do." He looked at her with contempt. "Even if the guilty suffer, you grieve." He shook his head. "The king is coming to murder you all tomorrow. Know that."

Maia scrutinized the scarred man. "Did he say this to you?"

He shook his head slowly and cocked his ear. "They are hunting for you. I must go. Can I persuade you to come with me?"

Maia shook her head violently. "I must remain. I am not safe outside these walls."

"You are not safe here either," he said scornfully. "Farewell, Maia. For *now*." He gave her a look full of meaning. He took her hand, just as he had in the past, and gave it a light squeeze before walking off into the mist.

He had not gone far when Maia heard growling and snarling and padded paws crashing through the copse of oak. She recognized the growl as Argus's.

"Argus!" she called. "Argus, come to me!"

There was a savage snarl, the snapping of teeth, and then a yelp of sudden pain.

"Argus! No! Do not hurt him!" She stumbled after the kishion in the fog, her heart racing with panic. The boarhound lay crumpled on the wet grass, whining in pain. The kishion was backing away from it, knife dripping once more.

"No!" Maia screamed, rushing up to the faithful hound. She knelt in the brush, the sticks jabbing her knees and legs, and cradled Argus in her arms as he breathed in spasms and pants. His fur was wet with blood. She hugged him close, tears flooding from her eyes.

"No! Argus, no! Please! Please—you cannot die! Please!"

The kishion vanished into the mist as Maia squeezed Argus tight, burying her face in the ruff of fur. She felt the hound stiffen and stop panting. Tears squeezed from her eyes as the blood dripped from her fingers.

"No," she sobbed, breaking down as she cradled the dead hound in her arms. Her shoulders shook and throbbed.

"Argus!" It was Jon Tayt's voice. He whistled for the dog. In the next horrible moment he was there, crouching next to her. "Maia!" he gasped, his voice choking when he saw her cradling the hound.

"Did you find her?" It was Collier's voice. He rushed up next as Maia wept with despair, clutching the boarhound as her heart split into pieces.

***

It was midnight, the darkest part of the day, and Maia sat next to Collier at the small window seat in the Aldermaston's study. Her gown was still stained with Argus's blood, but she had managed to clean her hands and her face, though her eyes were still red from crying. The fire Leering in the hearth glowed orange, filling the small room with supple flames. Collier pressed her against him, stroking her hair as she stared into the light. Suzenne and Dodd were also there, faces drawn in silent concern and companionship, huddled together and sitting side by side, their hands clasped tightly.

The Aldermaston's steward entered, his gray hair wild from the journey. "The Aldermaston is coming with your grandmother," he informed them. "What a chorus of the bizarre tonight." He walked over to Jon Tayt, who was pacing against the wall, his eyes bloodshot from suppressed grief. He laid a hand on the hunter's shoulder. "I am sorry," he offered in vain.

Jon Tayt shook his head. "By Cheshu, he was only a hound." His face wilted with pain. "But what a hound."

Tomas nodded wisely. "Strangely—Argus's death coincided with some other things."

Maia lifted her head, feeling wooden with fatigue. "What has happened, Tomas?"

"I will let your grandmother tell you." He went back to the door and held it open for the Aldermaston and his wife, Joanna, to enter, followed by Sabine. Then he shut it and took his seat near the Aldermaston's desk.

A sudden thought struck Maia. "Maeg," she said, parting slightly from Collier. "She must be told about her father's death."

The Aldermaston's wife nodded. "I told her, Maia. I was just with her a few moments ago. She was not asleep. She was holding vigil for you tonight."

Maia started, her eyes surprised.

"All the Ciphers were awake," she said. "We were all holding vigil for you tonight."

Maia felt the threat of tears again, even though she had thought there were none left. She looked at Suzenne, who nodded and smiled at her.

"What has happened?" Maia repeated, staring at her grandmother. She looked weary and haggard, but her eyes were full of emotion.

"It is time," Sabine said hoarsely.

Maia stared at her.

The Aldermaston stepped forward, coming to Maia, and took her hands in his. His eyes penetrated her, and when he spoke, his voice was thick with emotion. "Something has happened, Marciana. The abbey is . . . awakening. There are Leerings within that have never responded before. They are all glowing, summoning, calling for you."

Maia's eyes widened as she glanced at Collier and then back at the Aldermaston.

Sabine came up and gripped her arm. "Some test was passed. Some event triggered this. I cannot make sense of it. Was it the blood of the faithful hound spilled for you? Was it you defying the Myriad Ones and not being overtaken by them? Maybe it was all the vigils being kept. *Something* happened tonight. I cannot say what it was. But all the Leerings in the abbey are glowing ... even the hearth fires in the kitchen. The laundry. Every single one is showing its power. The abbey is *singing* for you, Maia." She caught her breath, shaking her head. "The dead have gathered around." Her voice was so thick she could hardly speak. "They are thronging the abbey. They are whispering. They are awaiting something. You must come, Maia." She stroked her granddaughter's arm. "Let us change your gown and put on the veil. It is time. The abbey will not forbid you now."

Maia felt a spasm of doubt ... just a tiny seed of one, like the fluff from a dandelion. She easily crushed it under her resolve.

She turned to Collier. "Come with me," she begged him.

His look changed from surprise to horror in an instant. He shook his head. "I cannot," he said in a choking voice. "With all my heart I wish I could. I dare not." He stood, his cheeks flushed with emotion. "I did feel the Medium tonight," he whispered. "I cannot deny it. When Carew was leading me away ... while we were walking, I heard a voice in my head. I heard the Medium whisper to me what Carew was going to say next. And then he did. Every word he said as we walked, I was told in advance. And then it warned me that Crabwell was going to trick me, that they were coming after you." He nearly choked, his voice thick with tears. "I knew it was the Medium." His hand rested on Maia's back. "You must go. I am not ready yet." He stared into her eyes. "But I will be. Someday. I promise you."

A spasm of hope filled Maia's chest, and she released the Aldermaston's hands so she could hug Collier. She buried her face in his chest, and he embraced her just as fiercely in return. They clung to each other, lost in a moment of time that was fleeting yet seemed to last an eternity. She felt him press his mouth against her hair as he squeezed her hard, crushing her to him. His arms were trembling, and her heart burned with searing heat. She could hear the whispers now, growing louder, calling for her to come.

Like Sabine, she also did not know what it was that had loosened the restraints on the abbey. Perhaps it was Collier's fledgling faith? She was no longer tired, even though she had not slept. Her muscles and joints filled with resolve and courage. She would face the maston test. She would summon all her will, and she would submit to the Medium, giving whatever was required of her.

When Maia finally pulled away from her husband's embrace, she saw tears in Collier's eyes. He seemed embarrassed by them and suddenly looked much younger to her. She took his hand in hers, holding it, feeling its warmth, determined to take part of him with her into the abbey.

"Wait for me," she whispered, clinging to his hand and pressing his fingers with her thumb.

"I promise," he told her. How odd that now, of all times, she wanted to kiss his cheek . . . or his mouth. She could feel the tension between them, the desire to seal the rush of feelings with a kiss. The finality of the curse tormented her: to never kiss him, or their children. She would always suffer for the mistake she had made, even though it had been made out of ignorance.

It was not fair, but she realized that most creatures suffered for mistakes not their own. Argus had suffered from his own instincts. He had been seeking Maia and trying to save her. He could not stop himself from growling and attacking a threat. She did not believe the kishion had maliciously killed the hound. It was his own instinct for self-preservation that had moved his dagger. Just as it was her own instinct to try and save people, even when others thought she was foolish.

Almost imperceptibly, Collier dipped his mouth toward hers. She shook her head, backing away, her heart nearly bursting again with pain.

"No," she mouthed to him, then bit her lip.

His eyes mirrored her suffering, but he nodded obediently and stepped away.

As she let go of his hand, she turned and let her grandmother lead her out of the room to prepare her once again for the maston rites.

There are three things that a maston must do. By these three can one learn to govern oneself and ultimately the Medium. Speak the truth. Do not yield to anger. Give much when you are asked for little. By these three steps will one walk the path leading back to Idumea.

—Richard Syon, Aldermaston of Muirwood Abbey

CHAPTER
TWENTY-NINE

Victus

Even though the night was dark and the fog was oppressive and thick, the abbey shone with light. Maia stared at it through the gossamer veil she wore, amazed by the brightness. In the distance a cock crowed, the creature probably startled by the deceptive glare emanating from Muirwood.

The Aldermaston's steward chuckled and patted her arm. "Poor rooster is going to be surprised when the sun rises later," he said. She could see his dimples flashing. He was much taller than her, and it felt comforting to have him at her side as they approached the doors.

This time she felt only a warm welcome as she advanced.

"Have you ever seen the abbey glow like this?" Maia inquired.

"Not in the twenty years I have lived here," he replied simply. "I do not know what to make of it. This is as far as I bring you. Good luck, Maia. I will continue holding vigil for you. I think everyone is doing the same."

Maia grasped his big hand and squeezed it, then approached the abbey through the fog-kissed grass. She felt peaceful, solemn, and nervous about the duty before her. Strangely, she did not feel any fear. After weeping so heavily for Argus's death, her emotions had calmed, and she could almost swear she felt him padding alongside her in the stillness—a smokeshape in the mist.

As Maia walked, she sensed beings gliding in the stillness all around her. Through the roiling mists, she discerned the peaceful shapes of men and women, fading in and out of view. The dead were congregating at the abbey. She could feel their thoughts brushing against hers. This was the moment they had waited a century for. The opening of the Apse Veil would finally bring freedom. Her heart was struck with the uniqueness of the moment, the whisper of breath before speech.

The Leerings guarding the abbey no longer repelled her. The eyes flared brilliant white as she advanced, greeting her with feelings of welcome, warmth, and determination. Maia tugged on the handle of the pewter door, and it swung smoothly open.

Her heart throbbed with excitement and joy. All her life she had desired to enter an abbey and make her oaths, inspired by her mother's example. She did not fear the oaths. She had a vague understanding of the process—that she would receive a Gift of knowledge first and then be taken to the Rood Screen, where she would take the oaths and receive her chaen. That was where the Apse Veil waited for her.

As Maia entered, she sensed the power of the Leerings inside the abbey flare even brighter. Outside the abbey had been unnaturally bright, given it was after midnight and well before dawn. Inside the abbey, it might as well have been a midsummer day. Everywhere there were vases and pots full of living plants, flowers, and trees. She sensed the Leerings carved into them, each one unique and special, and she was aware of the combination of Leerings pervading the abbey. It was as if dozens of lutes, harps, flutes, and instruments were playing simultaneously—she understood them all at once, in unison, but could also hear the hymn they were playing.

Walking toward her down the hall, she saw the Aldermaston and his wife, Maia's grandmother, Sabine, and . . . there was another woman there as well. Maia squinted and blinked, and the third woman vanished. She blinked a second time, and there she was again, gliding toward her, smiling so brightly it was like looking at the sun. Joy and recognition bloomed inside her heart. Maia had wanted to see her for years, had dreamed of meeting her at Muirwood, and had been crushed by the knowledge of her death.

Mother!

Maia's heart leaped with intense gratitude, and she muffled a sob that nearly ruined her composure. Her mother was there at the abbey with them. She could see that others had gathered behind the group, including a man who was tall, somber, and bearded, appearing as old as the world itself. She could feel his thoughts brush against hers, heavy with purpose, and she realized he was a previous Aldermaston of Muirwood, Gideon Penman— the man her husband was named after. Maia covered her mouth, her eyes brimming. They had all come to welcome her, and she felt their combined hope and joy flood through her, driving away every feeling of unworthiness, self-loathing, and gloom. She was honored to be in their presence, yet she could tell that they also felt honored to be in hers.

The Aldermaston's wife separated from her husband and approached her, taking her hands. Her eyes were wet with tears, but she seemed oblivious to the figures Maia could see so clearly. Perhaps the others could only feel their presence?

"Remove your shoes, Maia. This place is holy."

Maia nodded and quickly pulled off her damp slippers. The humans and specters approached her, all smiling with gentleness and welcome. She had never felt such peace in all her life. The Leerings throughout the abbey thrummed with the power of the Medium. She could feel it penetrating into her bones.

"Do you have any Gifts?" her grandmother asked her, beginning the ritual.

Maia swallowed. "I have," she answered and felt the Medium flood her mind. "I have the Gift of languages. And music. I have the Gift of ruling and deep faith. I hope I am wise."

Sabine smiled at her. "You also have the Gift of Meekness, which is very rare and one you cannot utter yourself. You have others as well, Maia. If you pass the maston test, you will receive more. The Medium has a work for you to do. I think we can all feel that."

Maia shuddered, feeling her knees tremble.

The Aldermaston spoke next. "Do you seek the rites of the mastons?" he asked her.

"Yes," Maia answered, nodding firmly.

"Then first you will receive a Gift of knowledge. Come with us to the chamber below."

Maia walked with them, giddy with excitement and completely at peace. She sensed every Leering they passed and recognized its purpose, whether it was to warm the air with fire or provide light. She did not summon their power. The Leerings seemed to whisper to her as she passed, divulging their secrets. They were all glowing, radiating a forceful feeling of goodness and power. The Aldermaston led her down a series of stone steps, into a chamber that was full of polished wooden benches and had a stone altar at the head.

Sabine sat next to her on one of the benches and held her hands. The Aldermaston's wife sat on the other side of her as the Aldermaston began to explain the history of the abbeys and humanity's exile from Idumea. Maia had been raised by mastons, so she knew much of what they told her. She knew that Idumea was not a person but a world. She understood most of the principles the Aldermaston taught her about the second life, and how, in order to tame the Medium, she needed to first let herself be tamed *by* it. That was a concept that most struggled with, and she could see why. She knew people assumed that surrendering their will to something else was a lessening of themselves, but in Muirwood she had realized it was quite the opposite. The more she gave, the stronger she became. While wearing the kystrel, she had constantly been haunted by fears and self-doubt. A secret shame had clung to her, a sense of concealment and evasiveness. She felt only pride when she thought of wearing a chaen. Being in Muirwood, she had finally, for the first time in her life, felt free to breathe and be herself. Here, she felt accepted for who she was. Her worth was intrinsic, and she learned it had to do with her potential to become one of the Essaios, the race of immortal beings who lived in Idumea. Even a lavender like Celia would have the same opportunity as she, a princess of the realm. For in Idumea, there were no ranks or stations.

The Aldermaston also spoke of the hetaera, and Maia felt part of herself shrivel in shame as he explained the history of the order and their devotion to Ereshkigal. She knew much of it already from what she had learned in Chancellor Walraven's tome, but she understood it much more fully now. And she understood also why Ereshkigal hated her Family so much. It was Maia's ancestor Lia who had cursed the hetaera Leering, which had been a crippling blow to the order.

The hetaera of the past had chosen their fate, had chosen the brand willingly. Maia had not . . . and she now realized anew how wearing the kystrel had helped lead her down that dark path. The whispers she had assumed were from the Medium were not, but were whispers from the Myriad Ones. She shrank with growing horror when she realized the true impact of her journey to the lost abbey. It made sense to her now in ways she could not have imagined before.

Even the dirge of the Dochte Mandar reeked of the hetaera's taint. She remembered the words she had memorized, words from an ancient tongue. *Och monde elles brir. Och cor shan arbir. Och aether undes pune. Dekem millia orior sidune.*

A world of noise . . . the woods sharing a single heart . . . the anvil of heaven below . . . a million stars yet to be born.

It was a mantra, a vow, a secret pact to destroy the maston order. A promise to fill the world with noise and chaos. She had never understood that before. A shared purpose and goal of revenge. The anvil of Idumea . . . a punishment as the Myriad Ones were cast out. A million stars yet to be born . . . the Unborn. Maia saw it now, saw that she had used the very words that would summon Ereshkigal to her. The woman in the mist, whom she had believed to be a spirit of the dead, had been the Queen of the Unborn herself. Her trickery and flattery at the lost abbey had completely fooled Maia. And when she had been asked to offer a Gift, she had sworn to give her life.

Maia shuddered at the gall of the truth. The hetaera were deceivers, and she had been deceived. She had been taught to surrender her will to the Medium. But not in an abbey that had fallen. Instead, she had unwittingly given her body for Ereshkigal to inhabit, and having seized it, Ereshkigal had branded her shoulder with the mark. They were bound together, Maia realized. It frightened her to consider what that might mean. As the sheriff's men dragged her from the abbey grounds, she had felt the Myriad Ones swarm to claim her. She had not sensed Ereshkigal there. The Myriad Ones were satisfied inhabiting the flesh of swine or wolves, she knew. But they preferred to take over mortals.

"There is a new threat in the kingdoms," the Aldermaston continued. "When our ancestors took the maston rites, they were instructed about the hetaera as you have learned tonight. When the first abbey was constructed in Assinica, the last Aldermaston had the Gift of Seering, and she added to the rite to help us face the new challenges of the day. She warned of the coming of the Victus."

Maia flinched when the name was said, feeling her stomach tighten like a coil. She leaned forward, eager to learn more about her enemies.

The Aldermaston's face was grave and solemn. "Like the hetaera, they seek to destroy the maston order. The Victus are the religious and political leaders of Naess. They rule through the principle of enmity, which means hatred and anger. Their beliefs are in direct opposition to ours; whereas mastons seek to calm anger and prevent violence, the Victus relish murder, and they renewed the kishion order to fulfill their ends. Such acts are abhorrent to the Medium, and we are commanded to purge the kishion from the realm. When a society or civilization embraces the Victus, corruption is soon to follow, as well as slavery. The Victus allowed the mastons to return and reclaim their lost kingdoms. Through subtlety and deception, they have glutted themselves on our labors and our industry. They have infiltrated all levels of our society, and some Victus have even attempted to pass the maston tests themselves to learn our signs and oaths. You must safeguard the knowledge you have learned tonight. Now is the time for you to enter the Rood Screen and make your oaths."

He paused, his voice heavy with portent. "So much rests on your shoulders, Maia. We will all continue to hold vigil for you. We do not know what will happen when the Apse Veil is restored . . . what we do know is that if it is *not* restored, our brothers and sisters in Assinica will be murdered by the Victus when the armada arrives." He motioned to his wife and her grandmother. "We all sense that the armada has already reached those distant shores." He gestured to her. "Rise."

Maia did and followed them back up the steps and crossed the main hall of the abbey to a secluded section of the floor, where the Rood Screen blocked the way. The workmanship of the wood was impressive and intricately detailed. It was a barrier leading into the chamber where Maia would take her oaths. She swallowed, feeling the momentous nature of the night weigh heavily on her shoulders. She did not fear the maston oaths. Her studies of the tomes had prepared her for this part of the rites. It was the Apse Veil that worried her, yet she knew the Medium discerned her thoughts. She could not doubt. She had to believe in herself. She had to believe that Lia had seen her day, to trust that her experiences as a child and young woman had prepared her for this moment. Sighing, she squeezed and released her grandmother's hand and then entered the Rood Screen.

***

Maia passed the oaths almost ridiculously fast. There was something about her affinity for Leerings, but as soon as she saw them all, carved into the seven pillars, she immediately understood them, their purpose, and the oath required to silence all seven at once. She knew from her reading that learners usually silenced one at a time. Then she bathed her face in the pool, lay on the bier, and dressed in the chaen. Her only moment of concern came when she had to remove her clothes to put on the chaen. The brand on her shoulder and the kystrel's mark on her chestbone felt like ugly stains that did not belong in such a clean place. She did not look at her own skin, dared not, and quickly covered the signs of her past with the chaen. As she slipped the chemise on over it, an instant feeling of safety enveloped her, and when she dressed in the maston robes, it was as if a warm blanket had fallen across her shoulders. She felt clean and resolute, determined never to let the Myriad Ones infest her again. More importantly, she felt the Medium's forgiveness and the approval radiating from the carved columns all around her. Each had a different creature or animal carved into it, the workmanship as exquisite as any she had ever seen.

The chaen would protect her from the Myriad Ones. She bowed her head, feeling so relieved to be wearing it at last. She thought suddenly of Collier and dearly hoped he would make good on his pledge and become a maston one day. Their marriage had not started off in the right way, but she desperately hoped they would at some point be bound by irrevocare sigil. He had seemed so affected by the Medium this night.

Maia sighed and stared at the stones set into the wall. The Medium drew her to one of them, so she approached and took it in her hand. It separated from the wall easily. She stared at the glowing white stone in her palm for a moment, absorbing the details of the intricate design carved into it. Letters appeared on the stone, written in a language she did not know.

Paix.

She stared at it and understood it through the whispers of the Medium. It was a simple word, a deep word, a word that described her deepest wish. Peace. It was a word that meant peace of conscience. Tranquility. Resolve. How strange that it was the one the Medium had chosen for her. She smiled and felt the stone burn her palm. The sensation made her flinch, but she managed to set it back down in the inlet rather than drop it. A pink mark showed on her palm, and she found herself smiling again, even though the hot stone had stung. Then she understood—it was a way of detecting other mastons, a way of knowing who was friend or foe.

Maia clasped her hands in front of her. The ritual was shorter than she had expected it to be. How long had she been in there? It did not feel long, but she would also not be surprised if the sun were just starting to rise. There was no sense of time in the chamber. No windows to show the sunlight or the fog.

Between two of the seven columns hung a veil. The columns next to it exuded power, and the eyes of the Leerings carved into them burned vividly. Maia summoned her courage and approached the Apse Veil. This was the moment for her to complete her special task, which she was unsure how to accomplish.

As she approached, she thought she could see the shadow of someone on the other side. Was it a mirror? Her mouth was dry with her nervousness, and the weariness from her long vigil suddenly weighed down on her. Yet the Medium caused a swelling sense of joy through her, which helped her stay alert.

Maia stood in front of the Apse Veil. She waited.

Nothing happened.

She did not panic. Instead she bowed her head, listening for the sound of the Medium's whisper, waiting to be told what to do. She knew the Apse Veils were portals between worlds and not just between abbeys. Once they were opened, she would be able to pass between Muirwood and Comoros in an instant. It would allow her to visit any of the abbeys already finished in the other kingdoms. What a difference that would make in the political realities of her day, she realized. For that reason alone the Victus would fear the restoration of the Apse Veils.

Instead of hearing a whisper from the Medium, she heard a voice. A woman's voice.

"Welcome. What do you seek?"

The voice sounded strangely familiar. Was it her grandmother speaking? It sounded like Sabine, but it was not her. There was a little formality to the voice.

"To become a maston," Maia answered truthfully.

"What do you desire?"

She knew the answer immediately, and it spilled from her mouth. "I desire Idumea."

"What is your name?" asked the woman. Who was she? Maia had no idea, but the idea gnawed at her. It could not be . . .

"Paix," Maia replied softly, her stomach fluttering, her heart burning with fire. She felt as if something huge and heavy had been dropped, like an enormous stone slab, and the stones at her feet trembled with the reverberation. There was no sound, but she could feel the ripples of the impact. She stared at the Apse Veil, her eyes widening.

The shape behind the shroud was nearly her own height. Maia tried to make out the person's features, but she was unable to distinguish anything beyond the approximate size.

An urge compelled her to reach inside the Apse Veil with her hand. Maia swallowed her doubts, thrust away her worries. She obeyed the impulse and plunged her hand through the gap in the curtain.

She felt a warm hand clasp her own. Maia squeezed and felt as if she should pull. That surprised her. She had thought she was supposed to pass through the Apse Veil herself. But again, although she did not understand why, she obeyed the impulse.

The Apse Veil parted, and a woman emerged wearing hunter leathers. Maia saw the blade belted to her waist, the cloak pinned with a brooch at her throat. And the face . . . it was like looking at her grandmother . . . almost a twin. Except her hair still had some gold in it and was not all gray. A thin tiara of gold was nestled in the curly stands.

Maia stared in disbelief, understanding striking her like a flood.

"Thank you," Lia said, smiling at her warmly. "You are now a maston, Maia."

CHAPTER THIRTY

Covenant Fulfilled

aia's heart leaped with surprise and confusion, and hope flooded her. Lia's manner of dress was different than any she had seen. The stitching on her leathers and bracers was Pry-rian in style, but it did not resemble any of the styles Maia had seen when she lived on the Pry-rian border as a young girl.

Lia reached forward and took Maia's hands, squeezing them with enthusiasm. Her smile was like the sunlight, and it warmed Maia's heart. Then one of her hands grazed up to Maia's hair and smoothed part of it away from her face.

"I have seen you in visions, Maia. But to behold you now . . . such a strange sensation. My father was the ruler of Pry-Ree, and he had the Gift of Seering, looking into the future. He was able to see my future, just as I have been able to see your life. When I left these shores," she continued, staring up at the vaulted ceiling of the chamber, "I saw you coming. Your grandmother and I noticed each other, for her Gift shows the past, while mine focuses more on the future. I am here, Maia, to help you." She clasped her hands again.

The relief Maia felt was intense. "We have not known what to do," she said. "You will help us, truly?"

"Yes. I knew this day would come. Now that you are a maston, you will receive another Gift. You already have it, though you probably do not appreciate what it is, just as I did not appreciate my Gift of Seering before it was revealed to me by Maderos."

"Maderos?" Maia asked in startled surprise. "The wanderer I met in Mon?"

Lia nodded. "He is still engraving the history of my Family. And he will continue to do so until Ereshkigal is bound for a season. That is the destiny of my Family, Maia."

"Is it part of mine?" she wondered.

The smile quirked on Lia's mouth. "I will only tell you what you need to know to move forward. My entire path was not revealed to me after taking the maston test. The Medium will continue to guide you. Now, kneel."

Maia did so, kneeling in front of the woman who should be as old as the trees, but instead looked so young. She was confused by this, wondering how it had happened. Then she remembered hearing that Lia had disappeared on Sabine's mother's nameday ceremony. Lia had left behind her tome and the Cruciger orb. Surely . . .

Lia put one hand on Maia's head and lifted her other arm in the maston sign. Maia quickly closed her eyes, folding her hands in front of her. As she felt the warm touch on her scalp, the power of the Medium built in the room, making the stones tremble. The feeling slit through her like a knife, penetrating her to her core.

"Marciana Soliven," Lia said, "I bestow upon you a Gift. You are strong in the Medium. You have always been strong. It is part of your lineage. You have great faith and a willingness to seek out the Medium's will. With such great power comes the duty to use that power to serve and help others. I bestow upon you the Gift of Invocation. You have already felt these powers stirring inside you. It is the Gift of understanding Leerings, knowing their powers, knowing how to control them, how to make them, and how to *unmake* them. It is a rare Gift to be found for one who is not already an Aldermaston. This Gift is yours and will help you in the purposes the Medium would have you fulfill. By Idumea's hand, make it so."

Upon hearing the benediction, Maia opened her eyes. Lia helped her to her feet, her grip strong and steady.

"How are you here?" Maia whispered, staring at her in awe.

Resting a hand on Maia's shoulder, Lia gestured back to the Apse Veil. "This is the most sacred part of the abbey, Maia. Crossing the Apse Veil requires power with the Medium. In my day, a maston could effortlessly travel between abbeys anywhere in the realms. But as the abbeys were destroyed through rebellion and the hetaera's powers, the Apse Veils ceased to function. Through my Gift of Seering, I knew of the threat to Muirwood and the maston order. I knew about your father and what he would do if unchecked. I departed this afternoon from Assinica. Time has not passed for me as it has for your ancestors. It was my granddaughter's name day and I kissed her little brow and whispered goodbye, promising I would help her great-grandchild. The Apse Veils allow us to travel not just from abbey to abbey, but also within time itself or between worlds. The Covenant of Muirwood must be fulfilled. We have come to help it."

"We?" Maia asked, eyes widening.

Lia gave her that knowing smile again. She turned and walked back to the Apse Veil and thrust her hand through the fold. A shadow appeared on the other side and then a man stepped through, his hair as silver as a wolf's pelt. He was about as tall as

Collier and even wider at the shoulders. Though he was an older man, he was fit and strong and wore a maston sword belted to his waist and the collar of a knight around his neck. He was handsome and stern, but he smiled when he saw Lia.

"We have returned," he murmured softly, his voice deep and solemn, glancing around the chamber and then at Maia. He smiled affectionately at her and stepped forward to pull her into an embrace.

"You are . . . Colvin?" Maia gasped, blinking back tears.

He nodded, squeezing her hard as he stared down at her in awe. She saw a small scar on the corner of his eyebrow, another on his chin. He turned to Lia. "We must bring the others through."

"The mastons from Assinica?" Maia asked, her heart bursting with joy. She wished her grandmother were in the room with them.

Lia shook her head. "No, not yet. We must bring through my guardians, the Evnissyen, and some of my household knights. The people of Assinica, in your time, are peaceful. There has not been war among them for a hundred years. Some have read about it in tomes, but they are not familiar with the hatred of mankind. What you need now, Maia, is help from us, from those who fought to preserve the maston order a century ago." She nodded at Colvin. "Bring them through."

Maia's eyes blinked. "My father," she gasped.

"Is no longer fit to rule Comoros," Lia said gravely. "He brought few soldiers to subdue Muirwood, believing it to be defenseless and meek." Her gaze hardened. "You must summon the abbey's defenses, Maia. You must protect and preserve these hallowed grounds. I will help teach you as we go. Come with me."

Colvin went back to the Apse Veil and reached through to pull another man into the room. He was older as well, but more youthful than Lia and Colvin.

"Ah, Jouvent Evnissyen," Lia said with a smile. "Welcome. Send a group to block the roads leading from the abbey. None of the king's men must escape. Bring everyone to the green with the may-pole when they are captured. Today is Whitsunday!"

***

Fog swirled around the ground, thick and ghostly. Maia stood before the gates of the abbey, facing the village of Muirwood. A crowd had assembled on the other side as well, soldiers as well as most of the villagers, come to witness the confrontation of the High Seer and Aldermaston with the King of Comoros. Collier stood by Maia's side, his expression hard and grim. One hand clenched the pommel of his blade. The other hand grasped hers possessively. They stood in a line with the Aldermaston and his wife and steward, Maia's grandmother, and Lia and Colvin. The Evnissyen slipped in and out of view in the fog as they hurried to fulfill the orders they had been given. Knights of the Order of Winterrowd were clustered nearby, faces grim and fierce, wear-ing chain hauberks and gauntlets, each with a hand resting on the pommel of their knight-maston swords. Jon Tayt stood just behind Sabine, his copper beard wet with dew, his hands clenched around two throwing axes, his gaze full of menace. Dodd Price was beside him, dressed in a hauberk and gripping a battle-axe.

Maia quelled the feeling of nervousness that thrummed through her. She blinked away tears, amazed at the sudden change in events. A raven cawed somewhere in the mist and then a series of roosters crowed. It was dawn, but the sun could not be seen through the dense fog.

There was a commotion in the crowd outside the gates and the jangle of spurs and armor. The crowd parted, giving way to the soldiers. There was her father, wearing a puffed tunic that glittered with gems, furs, and ribbed pleats. A ceremonial sword was belted across his waist, the hilt polished and gleaming. He wore a wide felt hat with several enormous plumed feathers. Ornate necklaces and rings, fashionable boots and cuffs, ruffled shirt. There was a stark contrast between his dress and the simple garb of Lia and her hunters and those within the gates.

Walking next to the king, clinging to his arm with white fingers, was Lady Deorwynn. Her headdress was also ornate to the point of gaudiness, and her gown more extravagant than any Maia had ever seen. The dress was fringed with gold and inlaid with pearls and ivy-patterns stitched in gold thread. The necklace around her throat had rubies the size of cherries, and the girdle was cinched in so tightly Maia did not know how she could breathe in it. Her lips were painted; her cheeks were rouged to provide some color to her pallid skin. Her eyes, despite the smears of color, looked bleached and troubled. In them, Maia saw an odd mixture of pride, defiance, and—strangely—guilt. Murer stood next to her, also dressed in the finery befitting a princess of Comoros. Jolecia was also there. The entire Privy Council was assembled around the king, and though each wore a plumed hat, Maia recognized their faces: the Earl of Forshee, the Earl of Caspur, the Earl of Norris-York, the Earl of Passey, Chancellor Crabwell, Captain Carew and his retinue. Each had tried to outdo the others with an exaggerated demonstration of wealth and power.

As her father approached the gate, the Aldermaston motioned for the gatekeeper to open it. It was unusually quiet considering the size of the assemblage, and the groaning of the iron bars filled the air.

Standing near Lady Deorwynn was Aldermaston Kranmir, his black hat standing out vividly in the fog. His mouth quirked into a frown as he observed those who had assembled to meet them, and a flicker of worry crossed his face.

"Well met, Aldermaston!" the king shouted as his group entered the grounds. His boots squished in the damp ground, and he paused on the threshold. He winced, staring up as if the sun were bothering him, but there was no sunlight to be seen. "I am a little surprised you abdicated willingly, but it was a wise choice. Who are your friends?" he asked, as if suddenly seeing Lia and Colvin and the knights and Evnissyen for the first time. The sight of their grim, defiant expressions caused the king's brow to wrinkle with uncertainty.

"You misunderstand my demonstration of hospitality," Aldermaston Syon said. "I bid you welcome as the ruler of Comoros to the domains of Muirwood as a guest."

"What is this nonsense, Richard?" the Earl of Forshee snarled derisively. "Are you daft?"

The Aldermaston stared at him patiently.

"We discussed this yesterday, what would happen if you defied me," the king said through gritted teeth. "Who are these people?" He glanced at Lia and Colvin suspiciously.

"Allow me to introduce them," Sabine said, stepping forward. "My lord king, the Apse Veil has been opened. These are the first visitors. This is Lia Demont, Princess of Pry-Ree, and her husband, Lord Colvin Price, the *true* Earl of Forshee."

Maia's father snorted in disbelief. "Is it now?" he said, stifling an incredulous chuckle. "Kranmir, you misjudged the High Seer's desperation. Sabine, I truly did not believe you would to stoop to such base trickery. Shall I applaud the performance? Is that what you wish?" His voice was slurred with contempt.

Maia stared at him, implored him with her eyes. He would not look at her. He cast his gaze across the others instead. "If you wish me to shame you in front of the villagers, so be it. I did not wish for this to happen. I hoped you would all be persuaded by reason. The truth is, the maston traditions are a myth. You expect me to *believe* that you have summoned our dead ancestors through the Apse Veil to secure your right to rule in Comoros? What kind of fool do you think I am?"

"A rather conspicuous one," Lia said bluntly. She glanced up at the mist-shrouded sky. "This fog has plagued us for quite long enough. It will cease. *Now.*" She held up her hand in the maston sign, the signal she had given Maia earlier.

Now, Maia, she heard whispered in her mind.

Maia's thoughts reached out to the Leerings that were causing the mist. There were dozens if not hundreds, but now that Lia had touched her with the Gift, she could sense each one of them, understand where they were, how far from each other, and to what purpose they had been carved. With a silent thought of command, she calmed them in unison, and the mists shriveled away into nothingness, dissipated and spent.

The sky was a brilliant blue, and the sun stabbed down at them, having crested the Tor. The air was crisp and cool, and suddenly the birds chirped and trilled and fluttered through the sky. Maia awakened the abbey's defenses, and the eyes on the Leerings in the gate and on the walls suddenly flared to life, exuding a feeling of danger and foreboding.

Behind them, Maia felt the abbey itself, as if it were a caged lion that suddenly roared. She watched as the faces of her father and Lady Deorwynn blanched with dread. The Medium's power brooded, churning with violence and rage. The intruders backed away, shielding their faces from the streams of light shining from the abbey walls, which they had not seen in the fog.

Maia's heart leaped with joy. All the Leerings were acting as one, brought to life by *her* command. The earth shuddered under the strain of so much pent-up power. Maia felt Collier's hand jerk several times in response to the Medium's powerful display. If he had not been convinced before, she knew he would be now.

"You have forsaken your maston oaths," Lia said, marching forward and drawing her gladius. "You have ruled this kingdom with debauchery and evil, and you have slain innocent mastons, whose blood screams out to me for vengeance. I am Lia Demont, and I felled a wicked king on the Medium's command in my past life. It commands me to tell you thus. Seek no more to persecute our people, else you be destroyed yourself. The cost of your wickedness shall fall upon your own head." Maia watched as her father cowered in front of Lia, his eyes wide with absolute terror. The others shrank from her as if she were some avenging spirit. "You betrayed your marriage oaths and forsook your true wife and friend. You have chosen to spend your time in the company of harlots and scheming men. In return, your new consort has forsaken you. She despises you and has taken lovers of her own. As a witness to the truth of what I speak, seek the chambers of Lady Deorwynn's musicians and you will find the evidence written in her own hand. Your chief groomsman is also guilty. Let him dare deny it." Lia turned her gaze to Kranmir. "You, sir, have forsaken your most solemn oaths sworn in Augustin Abbey. I name you Ely Kranmir and strip you of your chaen and stole. You are unworthy before the Medium, and I rebuke you for the murder of innocent men." Moving forward, Lia stood majestically over Maia's cowering father, sword pointed at him. "Cease this evil, or you will be destroyed."

Maia watched her father's terror turn into uncontrollable rage. His eyes burned with spite and hatred. His teeth were bared like an animal's.

"Do not stand there, Carew," he snarled. "Kill them!"

And with that, he shoved Deorwynn away from him and fled.

As mastons, we must always remember why we are here on this earth during the second life. It is not to be endlessly entertained by minstrels and dancing or to be in constant pursuit of base desires. We are here to be tested, to be tried so that we can receive all the Gifts the Medium has in store for us. Some of these Gifts will be discovered in this life; others will come to us beyond the Apse Veil.

—Richard Syon, Aldermaston of Muirwood Abbey

CHAPTER
THIRTY-ONE

The Battle of Muirwood

The air rang with the keening sound of blades drawn from scabbards. The first blows connected, and the sound of swords shattering together rang out from beyond the gates as the king's cohort fled and Lia's knights pursued, battling through the knights who were brave enough to make a stand to protect their king. Maia strained to keep the protections of the abbey in full force, and the Leerings flared with power, emitting a warning to drive away the unworthy. Her father's knights nearly trampled each other in their eagerness to escape, but most only found themselves embroiled in the battle just outside the gates.

Jon Tayt thrust a sword into Maia's hands so she could defend herself and then closed with a knight who charged at her with a naked blade. After blocking the swipe with one axe, the hunter rammed the butt of his other weapon into the man's stomach, doubling him over. Jon Tayt's knee came up next, smashing the man's nose and flipping him backward into the turf.

Maia had not experienced a large battle since her journey through Dahomey and Mon. Surprisingly, she felt a rush of calm despite the utter chaos of the scene around her. The villagers were scattering like leaves, and some members of the king's Privy Council were taking advantage of the confusion to slip away. The looks of terror and fear in the men's faces struck her. Crabwell was trying to mount a horse when one of Lia's Evnissyen yanked him down to the dirt and aimed a gladius at the flesh of his neck. The chancellor quailed in terror and raised his hands in surrender, begging his attacker to take pity. The Evnissyen hauled him up by his collar and dragged him over to the maypole.

"Maia, behind you!"

Maia whirled and saw Captain Carew stealing up on her, sword drawn. She brandished her own sword, bending into a Paeizian stance.

"I am on your side!" Carew insisted, his eyes gleaming with the emotion of the battle. "Come with me to safety." He beckoned to her urgently.

"I do not trust you," Maia responded, and flinched as Carew lunged at her. He deflected her blade and grabbed her arm, pulling her off balance. "Sorry, lass, but I—"

He grunted in pain as a blade slid into the gap between her and his chest. Someone had sliced his breast, ripping open his tunic and sending an angry red line of blood down its ripped remains.

"Let go, or you lose your hand next," Collier warned icily.

Carew did let go, using the hand to stanch the blood from his wound as he spun in another direction, lifting his blade to defend himself. He grimaced with pain and fury.

"I meant not to hurt her," Carew snarled. "Just to bear her to safety."

Collier snorted. "She was already safe," he quipped. "Drop your sword."

"I will not. I am the king's champion," Carew challenged. He went at Collier like a man possessed, his blade flashing in the sunlight. Collier retreated from the ferocity of the attack, whipping his own blade around to block and deflect the whirlwind of blows that came at him. Carew was the king's captain, the most accomplished swordsman in Comoros.

Maia's heart cringed with dread as she saw the look of determination on both men's faces. Neither would yield willingly, she knew.

She watched as Collier continued to give ground. Suddenly he ducked low, twirled, and brought up a dagger with his left hand, jamming it hard into the meat of Carew's leg. The captain howled with pain. As Collier straightened, he kicked Carew in the jaw, knocking him backward in a daze. The dagger protruded from the leg still, and Collier stood over Carew as he scrambled backward in the dirt.

"Is that really the best you could do?" Collier taunted. Carew thrust a fistful of dirt at Collier's face, but Maia's husband nimbly evaded the debris. He dropped low, grabbed the dagger, and dug it in farther before yanking it loose, causing a roar of pain from Carew.

"Drop your blade, or I swear I will take off your hand to get it," Collier threatened.

Carew's face twisted with anguish as he opened his palm, letting the blade go. Collier snatched it up.

Jon Tayt, who stood near Maia in a protective stance, suddenly leaned forward and hurled an axe, which spun end over end and felled a knight charging one of the Evnissyen. The Pry-rian saluted Jon Tayt with his blade, a sign of respect from one hunter to another.

"Watch Maia," Collier called to Jon Tayt. "I will fetch her father." As soon as Jon Tayt nodded, he took off running.

"Do not kill him!" Maia shouted at him. If her father was going to perish, she did not want it to be at her husband's hands. She knew it would not bode well for the beginning of their marriage, even though her father's actions had shown he was not worthy of redemption.

He glanced back at her, gave her a look of annoyance, and vanished into the melee.

The battle continued to rage around Maia as her father's knights closed in combat with Lia's men. One by one, the Evnissyen disarmed their opponents—she noticed they were fighting to wound or maim, not kill. One by one, the knights' weapons were taken away, and those who had been disarmed were being herded toward the village green and the maypole. She saw Aldermaston Kranmir was already there, his face chalky white and horror-stricken. So was Crabwell, his elegant clothes now ridiculously spattered with dirt and grass.

Maia's heart pounded inside her chest as the conflict raged around her. With so much commotion, it was difficult to keep track of the events that were unfolding. Suddenly three knights charged her and Jon Tayt at once. Jon Tayt positioned himself in front of her and howled with fury at the men who surrounded them, using axes in both hands to parry. One of the knights tried to run him through, but Maia deflected the death blow with her sword. Jon Tayt spun low to the ground, using the flat of his axe to break a knee and punch another man's stomach. One of the knights fled. The other two dragged themselves away.

Moans and cries of pain sounded everywhere. Hearing the Earl of Forshee's voice, she glanced over to see he was cursing savagely at Dodd. The two were battling each other, an unseasoned younger man versus a much older and more experienced warrior. Her heart seized with panic.

"Jon, you must help Dodd!" she told him.

"I am not leaving you," he answered hotly. "The boy can handle himself."

"No, he is too young. He—"

"I trained the lad, by Cheshu!" Jon Tayt said with a laugh. "He fights like an Evnissyen. Watch!"

The earl had a huge two-handed sword, and he swung it down at Dodd with savage fury. The younger man sidestepped the earl and then stomped on his foot, crippling him. The next moment he cracked an elbow against the earl's cheek, stunning him momentarily. Spitting out another epithet, the older man swung his blade again, limping noticeably, but Dodd blocked the blow with his battle-axe and jabbed the haft into the earl's throat. Forshee coughed and spluttered, and Dodd wrenched away his weapon and threw him to the ground. The earl tried to crawl away, but Dodd kicked him hard in the ribs and then seized his collar and dragged him toward the maypole.

"Maia! Maia, help me!"

Jon Tayt whirled as Murer rushed up to them, her skirts filthy with dirt, as if she had rolled around and been kicked like a ball. Her tresses were disheveled, some of the pins sticking out awkwardly, and tears ran down her face, trailing makeup and dust. She looked completely unhinged and terrified as she clutched at Maia as if she were her only protection.

"Please! Save me! Someone tried to kill me. Please! I have done nothing! Help me!" She blubbered incoherently, and Maia's heart softened in pity.

"No one will harm you," Maia said soothingly, drawing the girl away from the fighting. "Where is your mother?"

"Over there," bawled Murer, pointing to the maypole. She sobbed bitterly, pressing the back of her hand to her smeared lips. "My Family is done for," she moaned. "How did that woman know such things about Mother? Was it the Medium that told her?"

"They were true?" Maia asked.

Murer nodded miserably, sniveling. "I warned her about taking lovers. I told her it was foolish, but she was angered by Father's dalliances. She wanted him to feel the cut." She broke down sobbing again.

A knight approached them quickly.

"He will kill us!" Murer shrieked in panic. Maia turned and saw the man was a knight of Winterrowd, one of Colvin's men.

"No," Maia said soothingly.

The knight bowed to her. "The fight is nearly done. Some of it is spreading to the streets, but we will have it contained swiftly. Lord Colvin asked me to watch over you as well."

"I have a protector," Maia said, nodding to Jon Tayt. "But can you take this girl to the maypole, please? She is frightened."

"Maia, no! Wait!" Murer begged, gripping Maia's arm. She stared at her imploringly. "You will have everything. I will have nothing. You have already taken the man I love from me. I suppose it is only justice. Please . . . remember me in pity. It was my mother who hated you. I never did. Please do not hate me!"

Maia stared at the girl, her heart brimming with compassion. "I do not hate you, Murer."

"It is wrong to beg for mercy when I showed you none," Murer said with a sniffle. She wiped her dripping nose. "I am *sorry*," she sobbed.

Maia nodded to the knight to take her away and the man obeyed, looking at the weeping Murer as if he had been ordered to fulfill some distasteful but necessary duty.

Jon Tayt frowned at Maia.

"You think I should have been more harsh with her?" Maia asked. The fighting around them had died down, and the prisoners were being escorted to the maypole. The clang of weapons could still be heard in the distance, and there were screams of fright as well.

Jon Tayt pursed his lips. "Ach, I have never seen you be harsh to any creature," he said with a chuckle. "You have my love and my loyalty, Lady Maia," he said, tears gathering in his eyes. "Though I suppose that means I must serve the *Mark* after all. A fiendish trap he laid to snare me. Ah well, that is a fine kettle of fish." He sheathed his axes in his belt and wiped his nose.

"I miss Argus too," Maia said, putting her hand on his meaty shoulder.

"You *had* to mention the hound," he chuckled, a tear trickling from his lashes.

"Remember? You once told me a man should only cry if he has lost his mother or his hound."

He roared with laughter. "Yes, I did say that! Those are the only good reasons to weep, by Cheshu. The death of your mother or the death of your hound. Everything else is a trifle to be endured."

She hugged him fiercely, feeling the tears fall on her own cheeks. There was a time when weeping had brought her shame. Her father had complimented her as a little child for her lack of tears, so she had thought it was her duty to forbear them. Now she saw that tears were a balm. They were a gift. As she had learned in the tome of Ovidius, tears at times have the weight of speech.

Pulling back, Maia saw Captain Carew writhing in pain near the maypole, gripping his bloodied leg.

"There is a time for war," Maia said to Jon Tayt. "And a time for healing."

With the hunter at her side, she went and began binding Carew's wounds.

***

Maia's father had been captured trying to escape Muirwood on horseback. A wall of Evnissyen led by a man named Jouvent had blocked his escape, and as soon as he turned, he found Collier riding hard on his heels. He was brought back to the green on horseback in time to see the rest of his host subdued.

Maia washed her stained hands on a soaked rag as Collier helped her father dismount and brought him to Lia and Colvin at the center of the green.

She handed the rag to one of the nearby villagers and approached to see what would happen. Her father's gaudy hat had been lost during the commotion, and his hair looked salty. He wrung his hands in consternation, as if he could not understand the turn of events that had left him a prisoner in his own kingdom.

"What are you going to do?" he demanded of Lia, his voice betraying a slight quiver of fear. His gaze shifted to Sabine, his lips twisting with suppressed emotion. "You have your victory, Sabine. Will you kill me? Will you murder an anointed king?"

His tone of voice made Maia flinch. He looked frantic, his eyes darting through the crowd for some sign of support. His knights were all disarmed. His Privy Council sported bumps on their heads and bruised, swollen jaws.

"The Medium delivered you into our hands," Sabine said.

"Your cunning, more like," he muttered darkly.

"Can you *really* be such a fool, Brannon?" Collier seethed, shaking his head.

The king shot a venomous look at Collier, his eyes full of fury. "Am I *your* hostage now, Gideon?" He turned back to Sabine and Lia. "Tell me what is to be done with me! I have surrendered. What are the terms you require? A ransom? My head? Tell me!"

His look was so terror-stricken that it moved Maia with pity. He was not used to being helpless. Was his brush with imminent death harrowing him so much?

"I will not decide your fate," Lia said.

"Nor will I," said Sabine. Both of them turned to Maia. "The Princess of Comoros will decide it."

A startled shock went through Maia at the pronouncement. She stared at them both in disbelief. Was the decision really hers to make? Both her elder relatives were much wiser than she was. Her father's eyes widened with surprise, and a smile stretched his mouth.

"Yes!" he breathed excitedly. "Yes, I see the justice in that. She is, after all, my heir. She is of royal blood and of strong lineage."

"I am your heir?" Maia asked doubtfully, gazing at her father.

"Yes, of course, my child! Crabwell? Crabwell! Get over here! You will see, Maia, he has already drawn up the act. I came here with it. I was going to legitimize you this very day, this very Whitsunday. It is all right there. Crabwell, show her!"

The dusty chancellor approached. "The papers are not *with* me, Your Majesty," he said, wringing his hands. "They are in my chambers at the inn. I can have them fetched. But I assure you, Lady Maia, that your father speaks the truth. The Privy Council was all in agreement, my dear. With your . . . marriage to the King of Dahomey, it is only suitable and proper that you should receive your inheritance."

Collier stood by Maia's side, his eyebrows wrinkling with distrust and contempt. He stared at both of the men with deep suspicion.

"And what is that inheritance?" Maia asked.

Crabwell coughed into his fist. "Ahem, yes, of course you would wonder at that. The act names King Gideon as the new Earl of Dieyre, making him a vassal of the Crown of Comoros in his own right and entitled to all the revenues of that earldom. It provides a dowry of a hundred thousand marks payable from the royal coffers to King Gideon, which will assist you in repaying the debt from your ransom, my lord." His obsequious smile was revolting.

"Indeed," Collier said flatly, revealing nothing.

"It could be more," her father said, his eyes boring into Collier's. "You are my son-in-law, so you are entitled to other royal honors and favors." Then he looked at his daughter. "Maia, your banishment has ended. You will have the Hampton estate in Comoros as your own manor . . . it is one of the finest palaces I have. Plus you have possessions in every earldom throughout the realm, including castles. The revenues, Maia, are in excess of fifty thousand marks a year. They are yours this day."

Maia stepped toward him. "What of the abbeys, Father? What of the Act of Submission?"

He stared at her, his eyes glittering. He waited a moment before speaking, as if considering his words carefully. "I . . . of course . . . repudiate it, Maia. It will be burned immediately, and the abbey lands restored. Only the High Seer can name new Aldermastons." He nodded briefly to Sabine. "All shall be as it was, Daughter. I have seen the error of my ways. Help teach me repentance." His lip curled slightly as he said the word. "I do this all in front of witnesses, my Privy Council. You will rule with me, Maia. No act will be passed, no punishment given, without your approval or consent." He stared at her hard. "You will help to make all decisions for the realm. Will you come home with me, child? Will you aid me with your wisdom and goodness? I need you. You are . . . you are . . . so precious to me."

Maia glanced at Lia and saw the look of deep distrust on her face, then turned to look at her grandmother, who was staring at her with sympathy.

"It is *your* decision," Sabine told her softly.

CHAPTER
THIRTY-TWO

Irrevocare Sigil

Maia felt the oppressive weight of the moment. Her father, his councillors and knights, even her own husband—they were all more familiar with the ways of the world than she was. She had the sense that one wrong step could plunge her down a steep ravine. Her father's words still rang in her ears. He had said the very words she most longed to hear, yet a heavy certainty in her gut urged her not to believe him. Actions mattered more than promises. In her studies as a learner at Muirwood, she had discovered many gems of wisdom from the tomes, and one of them flitted into her mind at that moment. *The first duty of a king is to preserve his Crown.*

She was not blind to what her father was doing. He would make any promise that would secure him his freedom. And then he would betray her as he had so many times in the past.

Maia stared at him, feeling her insides twist with sorrow and confusion. She turned to Collier and seized his hand in one of hers, stroking his arm with the other. "When your father was captured," she said softly, and he inclined his head to meet her eyes, "you were held hostage on his behalf. You always resented it. Being held in Naess also caused you pain."

"True, but mine was undeserved," Collier answered, his voice hardening. "He will not keep his word."

Maia nodded to him and then turned back to her father. "A king who will not keep his word is no king at all. By our deeds are we known, but by our words are we trusted." She released Collier's hand and walked up to her father. His eyes widened and his nostrils quivered with anticipation.

"A hostage then?" he said, his voice trembling with suppressed anger.

Maia shook her head. "No, Father. I will not banish you as you did me. You are still my father." She swallowed, believing what she did was right, but not knowing what would happen as an outcome. She stilled her breath and listened for the intervening voice of the Medium to whisper to her if she were making a mistake. Nothing came. She paused a moment longer, just to be sure. There was nothing in response.

"I grant you freedom, immediately and voluntarily, if you covenant before all assembled here that you will never violate the rights of the abbeys again and will return all that you have plundered from them thus far. You will maintain the roads and protect the grounds. This you will do before the High Seer of Pry-Ree and all of these witnesses. I want your sworn oath."

"You will release me if I do?" her father asked skeptically.

"I promise," she answered.

He nodded curtly. "Then I do swear it."

"I release you voluntarily and with no conditions or expectations for myself. You may deal with me as you and the Privy Council deem just and honorable. You have offered me great rewards, but I do not need money or lands or servants to be happy. You may banish me from the realm if you desire. I only request that you honor my marriage to the King of Dahomey as legitimate and grant me leave to depart from and return to Comoros as befits my station as his wife and queen." She stared into her father's astonished face without looking away.

"Done," her father said curtly. "What else do you want?"

"Your leave to remain at Muirwood to celebrate Whitsunday. I would also ask that Jayn Sexton be allowed to stay for Whitsunday, if she wishes, for she studied here and has friends among us." Maia bowed to her father. "Release them," she ordered to the Evnissyen who guarded the prisoners. The hunters sheathed their weapons, and a murmur of relief passed over the crowd.

Her father's eyes burned into hers. "That was . . . generous of you, Maia. I will not forget it." His jaw tensed, and he gave her a hard look. "Will you . . . kiss your father?"

She stared at him, taken aback by the outrageous request, but then she realized he was testing her. He knew she was a hetaera, though he could not say so because of the binding sigil.

Maia shook her head no.

A small smirk came over his lips. Chancellor Crabwell was already at his elbow, his eyes dangerous and furtive. The king turned to his chancellor. "Get to Comoros," he whispered. Then he turned to Maia. "I will also stay and celebrate Whitsunday with my daughter."

***

Collier and Maia walked hand in hand through the rows of purple mint near the abbey laundry. His hand felt so natural in hers now, and she felt herself clinging to him, savoring these moments they spent together. It amazed her how quickly the day had changed from panic and despair to hope. The abbey was thick with people. Healers tended the wounded. The commotion and disorder had been repaired. There were many final preparations still to be made for the festival, and visitors wandered the grounds, leaving little opportunity for privacy. Maia was exhausted from the long vigil and all the subsequent events and found herself walking sleepily, breathing in the calming scents of the purple flowers, listening to the drone of bees, and enjoying the pressure of Collier's shoulder against hers.

"You should know this, I think," Collier said, turning to her. "My spy in your father's court. Simon Fox, I believe you have met him. He is posing as a Dahomeyjan wine merchant. He has been here at Muirwood, but I sent him to spy on Crabwell. I do not trust you returning to Comoros until we learn something of Brannon's plans."

"You do not trust him to keep his word," Maia acknowledged with some pain.

"As much as I trust Jon Tayt not to snore," Collier quipped with a chuckle. "I have no doubt whatsoever that your father will not uphold his oath. What I do not know is how he will choose to punish *you* for shaming him in front of everyone. It was a humiliating defeat, Maia, you must realize that."

"But *I* did not shame him or defeat him," Maia said, shaking her head. "It was the Medium that saved us, not I."

"We are clearly in agreement on that," Collier said, his voice softening. "I have been wrong all these years. I think I even knew I was wrong, deep inside. But I could never admit it. What I have witnessed here at Muirwood, I cannot deny."

Maia nudged him happily. "Which *evidence* finally persuaded you?"

He laughed. "When your grandmother ransomed me, it should have; I will grant you that. I am still reeling from that kindness, honestly. The generosity and goodness of that woman . . ." He shook his head. "I am astonished there are people like her in the world. When a husband takes a wife"—he squeezed her hand affectionately—"he gains not only her great beauty, poise, and desirable qualities, he also inherits relations who may not be so . . . worthy. I never knew much about your mother's Family, for your father was quite conspicuous with his double-dealing and treachery. It was a burden I was willing to bear long ago, back when I was planning to dethrone him." He shook his head wistfully. "He clings to power too tightly. It will slip through his fingers, as today proved. What I had not accounted for were your *mother's* relations. Sabine is worth a thousand kings. I will treasure earning the High Seer's good opinion of me." He looked down at her and smiled tenderly. "You have changed me, Maia. I still feel the knife edge of ambition, but I feel . . . how can I describe it? I feel I am meant to be a sword used by the Medium. Does that make sense?"

Maia stared at him, feeling her heart fill with buttery warmth. "And so . . . you truly intend to become a maston?"

He gave her a small, soft smile and nodded once.

She squeezed his hand and then hugged him fiercely. He put his arms around her and held her, gently stroking her hair. As she squeezed her eyes shut, she felt as if she were living in a dream she might awaken from suddenly.

"We have visitors," he whispered in her ear, and she pulled away, feeling a little shy. She was surprised to find Colvin and Lia approaching them, hand in hand. Colvin was tousling the purple mint as the couple walked, and their faces were so full of contentment and joy that Maia yearned to someday have with Collier what they had built.

Maia bowed to them, but Colvin gestured for her to stop, his expression amused.

"We have been enjoying the grounds as well," Lia said. "They have changed since our day. There is a walled garden over there that was not here before. Your mother's, I understand. What a lovely display of flowers and a precious place of solitude."

"The gardener was kind," Colvin said. "He explained some of the flowers and the history. But I have always enjoyed this particular spot the most." He gave Lia a knowing look and a tender smile.

"May I speak to you?" Maia asked Lia. She glanced at Collier and gestured that it would not be long.

"Can we trust these two not to start a sword fight?" Lia teased. "The Earl of Dieyre and Earl of Forshee were once great rivals, you know."

Collier laughed at that. "I would never presume an *old man* is incapable with a blade," he said saucily to Colvin. "I saw him fight this morning, and I am satisfied his reputation is well deserved."

Colvin smirked at the remark, and the two men began to talk as Lia and Maia wandered a short distance away.

"What is it, Maia?" Lia asked, putting an arm around her as they walked.

"How long will you stay at Muirwood?"

"We go to Pry-Ree on the morrow," Lia said. "I have given your grandmother the rights and authority to open the Apse Veils throughout the kingdoms. I will go to Tintern, for I made a promise there as well. From Muirwood to all the other kingdoms, if you recall from my tome. Then I will write about our role in what happened at Muirwood today and seal that part of the tome with a binding sigil so that no one can speak of it. The memory will fade when there is no one to tell it."

Maia wrinkled her brow. "But why keep it secret? You . . . you saved us!"

Lia shook her head. "*You* saved your people, Maia. Not I. Your faith and strength in the Medium are what allowed me to pass through a century. This is not my time. It is yours."

A heavy sadness began to weigh on Maia. She had hoped against logic that Lia and Colvin would stay. Maybe some of that disappointment shone on her face. Lia smiled sadly at her and hugged her.

"The Apse Veil is open. The dead are returning to Idumea as we speak. I have sensed them all around us today. While everyone here is preparing for the festival, there have been celebrations happening unseen in the other realm." She stroked Maia's arm. "I have sensed your respect and affection for Richard Syon, your Aldermaston, which is how I feel about Gideon Penman, who was the Aldermaston here when I was a child." Her voice became thick with emotion. "I saw him in the abbey, Maia. He is remaining on the grounds until all the dead who were trapped have passed through the Apse Veil. And he will stay behind until the future of the abbey is secure."

Maia started. "What do you mean?"

Lia shook her head. "The danger has not passed. It is only delayed. Sabine must go to Assinica to open the path for the refugees from that land. The armada has already arrived on their shores. They are beseeching the Medium to fulfill the Covenant of Muirwood and deliver them from death. Sabine will arrive, as High Seer over all the lands, to bring them to safety. That will take time, Maia. The Victus will hear rumors of what happened in Muirwood this day, and the armada will return for vengeance." Her gaze was serious and concerned. "Maia, they will launch an invasion of Comoros unlike any seen in any kingdom before. They will seek to make this kingdom void of life. They will use every power, every soldier, every warship they possess to crush the mastons and raze the abbeys." She shook her head, her eyes full of sorrow. "I have seen it."

Maia's heart felt the dread. "A void," she whispered. "What must we do?"

Lia shook her head. "I cannot tell you. The Medium forbids me." She smiled sadly. "No one told me my future before it happened. I had to make my decisions without knowing the full consequences of them. Just as you did today with your father."

"You know what will happen?"

Lia nodded. "Sometimes the Gift of Seering is a curse. I will not be here to face those challenges with you. *You* must learn what to do on your own, just as I did. Trust the Medium, Maia. Whatever happens. Trust the Medium."

The overwhelming feelings made her knees tremble. "I must ask you this, Lia. It may be my last opportunity."

"Very well."

"I visited the Leering in Dahomey. The hetaera Leering that you cursed." She swallowed, summoning her courage to ask the question, fearing what the answer would be. "I did not accept the brand . . . willingly. I abhor the hetaera and what they stand for. Being a maston now, I understand the implications more fully, and I deeply regret what happened. Is there no way—Lia, I killed an Aldermaston with a kiss. I would give *anything* for this stain to be purged from me."

Lia looked at her with deep sadness, and Maia knew the answer before she spoke it. "I cannot." She winced as she said the words. "The Scourge was bound by irrevocare sigil. Even if you were to destroy the Leering, the curse would still exist. Maia, Ereshkigal's thirst for revenge will never be sated. She will always attempt to destroy us. In every world governed by Idumea, there are mastons and there are hetaera. And there are kishion who murder and men like the Victus who plot for power. Even if every last one of these evildoers were destroyed, others would rise up. This is a war that has been fought for millennia throughout the spinning weave of the heavens. And it will continue to be fought for all time." She rested her hand on Maia's shoulder. "If I could remove this from you, I would. Sometimes we suffer because of our own choices. And sometimes we suffer because of the choices of others. But suffering brings wisdom. Do not underestimate the Medium's compassion for what we endure. Believe, Maia. It is *your* faith and strength that will inspire kingdoms yet born."

It was not the answer she wished. But she was not surprised by it. Somehow, she had known she would have to endure the mark for the rest of her life. She knew that someday, if her life was lived in adherence to her maston oaths, she would be given a new body in Idumea, one free of the hetaera's taint.

Glancing over at Colvin and Collier, she marveled at her husband's willingness to endure the restrictions of her curse.

Lia looked over at her husband expectantly. "There are wonderful memories for us to revisit here. If you will excuse us, Colvin and I would like to walk the grounds a little longer." As she walked over to Colvin, Collier bid his farewells to them both and joined Maia.

Maia watched thoughtfully as Lia and Colvin walked off together, heads bent low as they spoke and gazed at the sunlit grounds. The depth of their friendship, their love, and their bond was obvious. It had not always been that way, she realized with a spark of hope. Perhaps she and Collier would one day share an equally strong bond.

"You were gone longer than you suggested," Collier said, folding his arms, also staring after the two as they wandered away.

"I am sorry."

"I am glad. Colvin and I had a good talk."

"About swords?" Maia teased, trying to lighten her own mood from the heavy oppression of her conversation with Lia.

"About stones," Collier replied. "He is a wise man."

"Tell me," Maia said briskly, linking arms with him and starting toward the Cider Orchard. She was hungry for another apple.

"I asked him when he knew the Medium was real. Is it something he learned from reading a tome? An experience that he had? His answer surprised me. It surprised me because I could relate to it."

"Really?"

He nodded. "It was something his father taught him. Imagine a stone in a heath—one side facing the sky and the light, the underside facing the dirt with all its worms and insects. It takes effort to raise the stone enough to topple it over so that the underside faces the sky. It takes effort up to a point, and then the slightest touch will topple it. Does that make sense?"

"Yes, I envision that."

"When Colvin was a child, he was like the stone facing the sky. He grew up believing in the Medium, and he enjoyed the signs and wonders of it. When his mother died giving birth to his sister, it was as if some great force had upended him, and he found himself facedown in the muck, unable to see or experience what he had before. All was darkness, doubt, and despair. It changed so quickly. He could not access the Medium because of his *attitude*. If he had retained that attitude, he would have never felt the Medium again. But by applying himself, by reading the tomes and studying, he began to lift himself up until he reached the tipping point again. And then everything from the past returned to him." He stopped and turned to face her, their arms still linked. "That is how it felt for me, like it all came rushing back to my memory. Things I had forgotten long ago." He looked dazed. "It is all back again in a rush. There are things I did, Maia . . ." He stopped, swallowing. "When I believed the mastons were lying, I did things I now regret. But I no longer feel enmity for the beliefs. I must repair . . . maybe that is not the right word, but I know of no other. I must repair the harm I did. I plan to ask the Aldermaston and Sabine what I can do to correct things. But for the first time in my life, I feel it is possible to hope."

He stared at the afternoon sky, his countenance different than she had ever seen it. He looked more serene and infinitely more handsome to her than when she had first met him.

We must never give up what we most want in life for something we think we want now. All things received begin with a thought. Therefore, we must be cautious what we allow ourselves to think.

—*Richard Syon, Aldermaston of Muirwood Abbey*

CHAPTER THIRTY-THREE

Whitsunday

Suzenne had let Maia wear one of her fancier dresses for the Whitsunday celebration, and they walked arm in arm to the abbey gates leading to the green. The sun was just setting, though the village of Muirwood was aglow, and not just from the hanging lanterns. The abbey itself radiated peaceful, iridescent light from its many Leerings. In the distance, the tower on the Tor could barely be seen above the trees, and the few fleecy clouds did little to mask the striated orange and pink of the sky.

"I am grateful we took a little rest before the celebration," Suzenne said, smiling. "This day has ended so much differently than I feared it might. This morning with the fog and battle, I was dreading the abbey would be overthrown by nightfall."

Music started playing on the green, and a cluster of learners raced past them in their eagerness to join the celebration. A crowd had gathered in the green, and the sight of all the flowing gowns and clean tunics, the smell of sizzling meat and baked treats, and the sound of clapping and viols made Maia smile with relish. This was not her first Whitsunday, but it was her first opportunity to enjoy one since she had come of age. There was a grave conflict looming ahead, but they had won an important battle that day, and it felt proper to celebrate.

Waiting for them just outside the gates, she spied Collier and Dodd. Both were dressed in more formal attire that highlighted their handsome features. Collier was taller and cut a more dark and brooding figure, but his face brightened when he saw her, his mouth forming an admiring smile that made her blush. Dodd greeted Suzenne with an affectionate hug and smashed his mouth against hers in an eager kiss that made Maia wince with residual pain.

Collier bowed ceremoniously and then took her hands in his, drawing her away from the couple. "You look stunning," he murmured to her, dipping his head and grazing his lips across her knuckles. "I was determined to wait outside the gate for you, for I knew if I did not, you would be snatched away by a dozen little first-year learner brats and I would not get the chance to dance with you without threatening bloodshed." He winked and put his arm around her, guiding her at a languid pace toward the maypole. Her heart fluttered with the excitement and simple joy of being able to experience this moment with him.

"You were kind to wait for me," she answered graciously. "Though you had me all to yourself at the Gables in Briec."

He smiled at the shared memory, then reached over and touched her long hair. His eyes were shining, so blue they seemed like the spring sky speckled with sunlight. She felt a familiar longing as she gazed up at him, an ache that lodged inside her breastbone.

"I need to stop looking at you," he admitted, turning away and chuckling to himself. "You distract any sensible thoughts from my brain. It makes me want to kiss you, and I know I should not, especially after what Lia told you." He squeezed her hand. "Thus I must take my enjoyment of you in other ways. Through tender caresses and longing glances." He butted her arm with his. "Ah, look at those two. It is poignant to see."

Maia thought he meant Suzenne and Dodd, but he was nodding toward the maypole dance already under way. The circle was large, for there were many who were anxious to dance the first set, but Maia's gaze cut straight to Lia and Colvin. Hand in hand, they skipped around to the claps of the onlookers and the strain of the minstrels' music. The look on their faces said they could not see anyone but each other. Maia knew much of their story—in particular, how the Medium had kept them apart for the sake of duty and to preserve the lives of their friends and Family. Maia was named after Colvin's sister, and she felt a keen sense of affinity and kinship to them for the many separations they had needed to endure before being together.

Maia and Collier walked together, watching the dance, and passed the booth of treats from Collet's kitchen. She stopped to greet the cook and her two helpers, who were not old enough to participate in the dancing. Aloia and Davi shared an almost mournful expression of longing. When the two girls noticed Maia and Collier, they gawked blatantly.

"Have you noticed the Evnissyen shadowing us?" Collier whispered in Maia's ear as they walked away from the kitchen stand.

She had not, so she circumspectly glanced around. Warriors were indeed wandering through the revelers, including Jon Tayt, who kept a respectful distance away from them. She noticed Jon Tayt speaking to the others and imagined he was revealing to his countrymen and ancestors the possible dangers lurking and where the best food could be found as they shadowed Maia and Collier.

"They are watching carefully for any danger tonight," Maia said. "Look, there is my father."

"I would rather not," he replied curtly. "He is with the Sexton girl." He grunted disparagingly.

Maia's stomach twisted with unease as she took in the sight of them. The poor girl looked uncomfortable on the king's arm, though Maia's father was laughing and joking with several of his courtiers, looking for all the world as if he were celebrating the festival as he had intended, and his plans had not gone awry only a few hours ago.

She sighed. "I wish we could rescue Jayn from him. I have not met her yet. I sense Jayn desperately wishes to talk to Suzenne."

"If my lady wishes it, then I will arrange it. Even though I find it distasteful. Would you like some cider?" he asked, motioning toward a cart.

"Yes, please."

He fetched two cups, paid the man, and gave one to Maia. Made from the famous Muirwood apples, the cider was sweet and full of flavor. The first song came to an end, and the dancers dispersed, many to find new partners. Collier bowed to her gallantly, requested her hand, and then escorted her to the new ring as it assembled. Though she had danced with Collier before, she felt strangely nervous. She felt several eyes seeking her out and noticed Suzenne and Dodd had joined the circle as well. The music began, and suddenly she was flying, experiencing the giddy thrill of the maypole dance with a partner for the first time in her life.

***

The night seemed to pass as a dream. Maia's legs were weary from the constant motion, but although she was tired, she did not want to miss a single moment.

After resting for a spell after a dance, Collier touched her shoulder. "Watch for the opening and be ready," he said, his mouth pressing against the hair by her ear. He tousled some strands, smiling at her, and promptly left her side and walked up to her father, who was reveling nearby. She heard Collier speak to him, asking for an opportunity to address a particular matter with him in private. Her father looked annoyed, but he broke away from his escort and allowed Collier to lead him toward the musicians. That left Jayn Sexton alone, and Maia seized the opportunity to approach the girl. As soon as she saw Maia, Jayn flushed and did a deep curtsy.

"You are Jayn Sexton," Maia said, motioning a hand for the girl to abandon the formality.

"And you are Lady Maia," the girl replied in a meek voice.

"There is someone here who wishes to see you," Maia said. "Will you walk with me?"

Jayn glanced back at the king, her face pinching with worry, but then nodded vigorously. Maia linked arms with her and led her away. She was as quiet as ashes as they walked and kept glancing back at the king, who was engrossed in conversation with Collier.

"I hope you are not afraid of me," Maia said softly. "I bear you no ill will, Jayn."

The girl looked at her in stunned silence. She was a pretty girl, for certain, and the quality of her gown showed her fine youthful figure. She had dark hair, though lighter than Maia's own, paired with dark eyes. "I did not know how you might feel about me," she confessed in a trembling way. "I imagined you might be resentful."

"I am not," Maia said, shaking her head. "There are Suzenne and Dodd. She wanted to see you, but did not think she would get a chance."

Jayn's face brightened visibly when she saw her friend. When Suzenne saw her, she smiled with delight and rushed forward to pull her into a feverish embrace. It made Maia smile to see them so affectionate with each other. The girls started to speak to each other in hushed tones. Maia was about to slip away to give them some privacy, but Suzenne reached out and caught her wrist.

"Jayn, you do not know Maia very well. But let me say that she reminds me so much of you. Your temperaments are very similar. You care for every forgotten creature and are kind to anyone, regardless of their station. Maia, as you know, Jayn was my companion for many years while we were learners." Her expression turned serious. "She is still one of us, a Cipher," she added.

Jayn smiled demurely. "I have sent the Aldermaston's wife messages as I could," she explained. "I brought her news today of your father's reaction to the events thus far. He is furious with Lady Deorwynn. I have never seen him so wroth, and I have often seen him angry." Jayn looked at Maia in desperation. "She is still my lady whom I serve, and I fear for her." She swallowed. "I fear the king may do more than banish her. He sent Crabwell hastily back to Comoros."

"I observed that as well," Maia said, intrigued. "What does he intend?"

Jayn glanced back at Collier and the king, biting her lip. "Crabwell interrogated me about my mistress before we left Comoros. There have been rumors of her infidelity for many weeks now. Lady Deorwynn made sure to keep such activities from my awareness, of course, but her daughters knew of it. I am not often . . . in her company anymore." She looked both guilty and miserable. "But the accusation Lia made against her is true. I have heard both of those men mentioned by Murer and Jolecia, and they would always give each other a knowing look. Only through the Gift of Seering could she have known something like that. The evidence she mentioned must be kept very secret. I am sure Crabwell rides to intercept that evidence before Lady Deorwynn can destroy it. When the king sees proof, he plans to execute her."

Maia stared at her in shock. "Truly? No one has ever executed a woman for adultery."

Jayn shook her head. "Not for adultery. For treason. I have heard him whisper of this to his advisors. He will make a public example of her." Maia felt sick inside at the thought of her father executing his own wife. And of course, the hypocrisy of it galled her.

"He is looking for me," Jayn said, her eyes feverish. "I must go. Be careful, Lady Maia. He is not pleased with you, either. You shamed him this morning. He never forgets a slight. I must go." She reached out and squeezed Suzenne's hand fiercely. Her eyes were smoldering. "I am *still* a maston," she breathed, clutching her friend's hand.

Maia and Suzenne watched her hasten to the king's side. Her expression changed as she approached him, like she was putting on a mask, and she bowed before Maia's father and said something they could not hear. Maia was saddened by what they had learned from Jayn Sexton, but she was so proud of her for holding firm to her maston oaths. The king looked a little peevish, but he took the girl's hand in his, kissed it, and stepped in front of the maypole as the next round of dancers assembled. He raised his hand, and all fell silent.

"We are pleased," he said in a rich, ebullient voice, "that you have enjoyed this Whitsunday festival. It is our solemn honor to preside over this festivity. The tradition of the maypole dance is quite familiar to you all. With us, this evening, we enjoy the companionship of the King of Dahomey. In his honor, I would like to introduce a dance known as the Volta, which is a favorite of his court at Rexenne. It is similar to the galliard, but with a twist. My son, if you would demonstrate the first set, we shall all accompany you in the second."

The ring dancers stepped back, and Collier approached the fluttering maypole. He turned to Maia, bowed gracefully, and extended his hand in invitation. Now she understood. He had arranged this with her father in her absence.

Maia approached him and dropped into a deep curtsy before him. She took Collier's hand, feeling its warmth, and stared into his piercing eyes.

"For Briec," he whispered, winking at her.

The minstrels began the passionate tune of the galliard, only slower, and Maia and Collier danced before the assemblage. Though hundreds of eyes were focused on her, she looked only at Collier, trying to ignore the others' attention. His hand pressed against her hip as their steps built toward the lift and twirl. She swallowed, anticipating it, and then she was flying, pressing against his firm shoulders and looking down at him, the tips of her hair just touching his. There was an audible gasp of delight from those watching them. He twirled her slowly before bringing her back down, and she felt dizzy and alive. The minstrels' flutes cast a haunting spell on her.

Collier took her around the circle again, then lifted her high, bringing her around. She felt her skirts swishing, felt the palpable thrill of the dance invade her heart. When it was time for the third lift, she was patently exhausted and dipped her head down, resting her forehead against his. Their noses just touched. He set her down.

"Are you all right?" he whispered, his eyes staring into hers.

"A little faint," she answered, smiling shyly.

The smile he gave her was a reward in and of itself. Their performance was met with a round of applause, and a circle of dancers who wanted to try the new style favored in Dahomey formed around the maypole. Maia saw Lia and Colvin join the circle. Then Suzenne and Dodd. Then Jayn and her father, which made her wince. The music began once more.

As the next dance began, Maia caught sight of Maeg Baynton, standing alone in the shadows, without a partner. She was wiping her eyes. Maia's heart went out to the girl who had just lost her father.

"What is it?" Collier's question drew her eyes back to his face. "You look pained."

She smiled wistfully. "You always watch my expressions."

"Always," he answered. "Whenever I am near you, I am drawn to your face, to your gestures, to your glances. I can tell how much you truly care about others just by observing you, Maia. You are constantly assessing their needs. Truthfully, I find you remarkable . . . most princesses are fixated primarily on themselves. Why did you wince just now?" he asked her and then lifted her high again and twirled her.

As Maia came down, she glanced back at Maeg. "I saw Maeg Baynton over there, and my heart went out to her."

"Where?"

"By the hanging lantern near the cook's stall."

"Ah, I see her. She was the sheriff's daughter?"

"Yes. His death last night . . . oh, she looks so miserable. I wish I could do something for her."

Collier smirked. "Sending me to dance with her would create the wrong impression. Hopefully you were not thinking that."

Maia shook her head decidedly. "I want you to myself."

"I could almost kiss you for saying that," he said, pleased. "But I will not. I respect you for your compassion, Maia. Truly I do. I have much to learn from you. But you cannot meet the demands of all the people your heart pities. Who was there to ask you to dance when *you* were banished?"

Maia stared at him thoughtfully. "Perhaps that is why I do it," she answered. "Because I know what it feels like to be so alone."

He stopped in the middle of the dance, ignoring everyone else around them, and reached out to take her chin in his hand. "*That* will never happen to you again."

CHAPTER
THIRTY-FOUR

Assinica

The Leerings throughout Muirwood Abbey thrummed with power and radiated cool light. Maia and Lia stood with Sabine, who clung to a carved wooden staff and was garbed for a long journey. A strap and satchel hung behind her cloak, and part of her hair was braided on one side. They were in front of the Rood Screen inside the abbey, and Sabine looked a little nervous about what lay ahead of her. It was time for her to go to Assinica and prepare the mastons there for their return to Comoros.

Sabine looked to Lia. "Will I have trouble understanding them when I reach Assinica?"

Lia smiled knowingly. "You have the Gift of Xenoglossia, Sabine. You will be fine."

Maia gave her grandmother one last hug and felt a few tears go down her cheeks.

"I will return as soon as I can," Sabine whispered into her ear, then pulled back and squeezed her hands. She looked to Lia again. "Will I not see you again?"

"If the Medium wills it. Colvin and I will go to Tintern Abbey next to fulfill a promise there. Sabine, now that you have authority over the Apse Veils, as High Seer, it will be up to you to open the rest of them. This is not our era. We do not belong on the records here and must leave you to your destiny." She looked knowingly at Maia. "Remember everything I have told you."

"I will," Maia promised. The prospect of never seeing Lia again flooded her with tender sadness. Lia's tome had influenced so much of her thinking and maston training. The little girl who had been a wretched in the Aldermaston's kitchen was a legend. But she was still a person, and Maia could feel the intensity of her love for Muirwood.

Sabine adjusted her satchel strap and turned to enter the Rood Screen. Maia watched her disappear behind the wooden latticework.

"Are you and Colvin leaving today?" Maia asked. "Could I persuade you to stay longer?"

Lia shook her head. "We are not taking the Apse Veil into Pry-Ree. We have decided to travel into the Bearden Muir first. There are memories there. Old friends to bid farewell. The mountains of Pry-Ree are special to us." She took Maia's hand and gently squeezed it. Her countenance became serious. "If there is one thing I have learned, Maia, it is the loneliness of leadership. Bear it as graciously as you can. I do have compassion for what you have suffered . . . and for what you will suffer yet."

Maia fidgeted, feeling her stomach wrench with anxiety. "Yet? Can you not prepare me for it?"

Lia shook her head. "The Medium coaxes us along the road we must travel. It does not tell us the destination from the beginning. If we knew the travails we would face on the road, would we have the courage to step forth at all?" Her grip tightened. "Have courage, dear one."

Maia embraced her, relishing the time she had spent in her presence. As they left the abbey together, Maia saw one of Lia's Evnissyen waiting for them. She recalled his name, Jouvent. Lia gave him an enigmatic look. Jouvent nodded subtly and walked away.

***

Maia and Collier walked together in the Queen's Garden, both of them enjoying the smells of the flowers and the blossoming trees. The workers at the abbey were still harvesting the apple crop from the Cider Orchard and the air had a sweet aroma. The learners had left with their Families after the Whitsunday festival, and the village was slowly returning to its normal, languid pace.

"Have you decided where you will take the maston test?" Maia asked him after watching him bend to examine a bee sipping from a bloom.

He glanced back at her, his expression somber. "How did you know what I was thinking about?" He smiled wryly. "I thought Lisyeux, the chief abbey in Dahomey. It would certainly startle and shock my old Aldermaston if I returned to Paeiz to finish what I started there."

"Why not Muirwood?" she pressed.

He shook his head. "It should be in my own kingdom. I have been visiting here for long enough. I need to make preparations to receive you for your coronation. You are already queen in my mind, but not officially. There are rites and customs—" He waved his hand as if that all bored him. "The people need to know you as I do. They are lucky to have you, Maia. As am I."

He moved to a stone bench and sat pondering for a moment before lifting his finger, inviting her to come closer. "There is something else we must discuss. I must break my oath to you."

A prick of apprehension shot down her spine. "What do you mean?" she asked in a small voice. She stood near him but did not sit.

He winced. "This is difficult. I am a man of my word. Yes, a good lie seasons the truth, but it does not change the dish. You see, when I accosted you in Dahomey, I asked what your conditions were for becoming my wife. You wanted me to spare Jon Tayt and even that ugly kishion. I need to educate you further on negotiation tactics, Maia, but we will save that for a later discussion. My terms were rather specific and I regret them now." He looked at her seriously. "My condition was that I would not love you." He shook his head slowly and clucked his tongue. "My dove, I am afraid I have broken that oath. I am sorry."

Maia stared at him in surprise and then felt a playful smile tug at her mouth. "Is that your way of declaring yourself, Feint Collier?"

He tried to keep his expression neutral, but failed miserably. He reached out and took her hips with his hands and pulled her down onto his lap. "If I must say it, then you had best be here where I can see you better."

She sidled even closer to him. "Is this close enough?" Her heart was hammering in her chest, and she felt a flush creep onto her cheeks. She was used to his attraction to her by now, but hearing his tender profession of love felt marvelously heady.

His arms wrapped around her. "I do love you, Maia. My dearest, sweet Maia. I have been tempted all this while to risk fate and kiss you." He shook his head. "I will not, though part of me feels it would be worth dying for. You are my friend, my companion, my queen. I must go to Dahomey, but I will not leave until I am sure you are safe. I do not trust your father. Nor should you."

She smiled and stared into his piercing blue eyes, losing herself in them. "You have my heart as well, Collier. I think you started to steal it when I was a very young lass. I often daydreamed that my parents would fulfill the plight troth."

He hugged her warmly. "Then it was time well spent. Parting from you will be painful. So is not being able to kiss you. But I will endure it for you." He grinned slowly. "You are worth the suffering."

She dipped her forehead until it touched his, closing her eyes. The feel of warmth transferring from his skin to hers made her shiver. The urge to kiss him was so intense it caused pain. But she pulled away and traced a finger over the little scar beneath his eye.

"How did you get this?" she asked, touching it.

He smiled. "I have had it since I was a child," he said. "A story that makes me look quite foolish, actually."

"Then I will enjoy it all the more," she teased. She put her arms around his neck.

"When I was quite small, I climbed up on some wine barrels. It was Whitsunday, I think. Some celebration. As I stood there on the barrel, I felt so tall and proud of myself. And then I had the notion that I could fly. If I just believed enough, I could jump off the barrel and soar back up the stairs and startle everyone, especially my little brother." He smirked and shook his head. Maia smiled at him, imagining what must have happened next.

"I leaped," he said, chagrined. "I leaped as high and hard as I could, and for just a moment . . ." He paused for effect and winked at her. "For just a moment it *felt* like I was flying. I saw the ground rushing at me . . . the cobblestones, really. I hit them hard and knocked myself senseless. There was a broken bit of wood or a small nail on the ground where I fell. It could have taken out my eye, but it only scarred my cheek. When most people ask, I tell them it was a badge of honor given from a Paeizian fencing master. But to you I give the whole truth, unvarnished."

He paused for a moment, chuckling to himself. Then his expression became serious again. "About my *other* oath," he murmured softly. "I said I would let you continue on your mission to Naess that night without first consummating our marriage."

"I do recall you promising that," Maia said, nodding sagely, though it felt like her insides were being burned with a hot brand.

"I regret letting you slip away from me so easily." His whisper purred in her ear. "We are husband and wife, you and I. Would it take much persuasion to start acting like it?"

She looked into the intense blue fire of his eyes. "I might be convinced," she quavered. "If . . ."

The door to the gardens opened, the Leering swinging wide. It was the gardener, Thewliss, with his rickety cart. Maia was surprised she had not heard him approach. It embarrassed her for him to find them in such an intimate position, but Collier did not seem concerned a bit.

"You were saying?" he whispered, grinning at her.

"He is in here," Thewliss said, turning to someone who was following him.

It was Owen Page, and he seemed shocked to find Maia sitting on Collier's lap. The boy had damp hair and was gasping for breath. Maia and Collier both scrambled to their feet, sensing the grave urgency in the air. Owen beckoned to someone behind him and a tall man entered, wearing a merchant's tunic, several bags of coins buckled to his belt, and a rapier.

"My lord," the man said in Dahomeyjan, bowing stiffly. He had a golden goatee and his hair was receding up his scalp. "Fox sent me."

"What is it, Piers?" Collier asked, replying in the same language. Maia was grateful she knew Dahomeyjan as well.

"I did not spare horseflesh to come," he stammered. "Think I killed my mount to get here fast enough. My lord, news from Comoros. There was a quick and shabby trial, and Lady Deorwynn was found guilty of treason."

Maia gasped, and the servant gave her a startled look, as if surprised she understood him.

"Say on," Collier muttered darkly. "She is to become your queen, so you can say what you must in front of both of us. I trust her."

"Very well, my lord," the servant said, then glanced at Owen and Thewliss.

"They do not understand us," Collier said, gesturing with impatience for him to continue.

"Lady Deorwynn is to be executed tomorrow at dawn. The king has divorced her and has announced his impending marriage to Lady Jayn Sexton, his wife's lady-in-waiting."

"No," Maia whispered in dismay. "Not Jayn!"

The servant nodded vigorously. "It is a hard ride from Comoros. I barely just arrived. Simon is going to attend the execution and send word. I think the king is planning to renege on his promise to share his rule with his daughter. No one from the Privy Council spoke in favor of Lady Deorwynn, not even her own uncle, Aldermaston Kranmir."

"Is Kranmir still part of the Privy Council?" Maia asked him forcefully. He nodded yes.

Collier frowned. "This is not just," he said, shaking his head. "I have no compassion for Deorwynn, but it is the height of hypocrisy to execute her for adultery when he himself is guilty of it."

The spy nodded vigorously, stroking his goatee. "Indeed. Though the charge is treason. She and her children have been imprisoned in Pent Tower. Simon wanted you to know in case you were planning to travel through Comoros or Doviur to return to the kingdom. The ship is still waiting for—"

Collier held up his hand sharply, silencing him.

"What ship?" Maia asked.

He shook his head, muttering to himself. He sighed and turned to look at her. "I had a plan to abduct your father here at Muirwood and hold him hostage in Dahomey," he said in a very low voice. "If the abbey fell, I was going to abduct you as well, unless you came willingly. The mist the morning of Whitsunday thwarted my plans and prevented my soldiers on board from coming. Another testament to the Medium's powers, I daresay. I have a ship waiting to take us to Dahomey." He looked at Maia pleadingly. "Come with me."

Maia stared at him in disbelief. "No," she said. "Now is not the time. I must go to Comoros and stop this murder."

"You just heard the man," Collier said, his color rising. "Even if we rode immediately, we could not prevent it. It is midafternoon and there is no way to reach Comoros until after it is done."

"There *is* a way, in fact. I am a maston, and Claredon Abbey is near the keep. I can cross through the Apse Veil. My grandmother is making it possible for other mastons to use them, but I have the power to use them before they are officially opened."

His eyes widened with horror. "That would be utterly foolish!"

Maia bridled with offense, but she knew he was just concerned for her. "I can *not* stand aside and let Deorwynn be murdered. If my father is going to abrogate his oath to listen to my counsel, then he will do it in front of everyone, in front of the people. His Privy Council will not countermand him, but if *I* am there, some of them might have the courage."

He clenched his jaw, his eyes scathing. "He will kill you, Maia."

Maia refused to listen. "I do not believe he will. Not after I spared him here at Muirwood. He is humiliated and ashamed. He is wounded by his wife's betrayal. I will calm him and help him see reason. He may divorce her, if he chooses, but putting her to death is an atrocity."

"What that woman did to *you* was an atrocity! How can you possibly defend her?"

Maia shook her head. "Justice is not justice if it only satisfies our need for revenge. Besides, I spoke with Jayn Sexton at Whitsunday. She is a miserable, trapped creature. If I can manage it, I will help her cross the Apse Veil back here to Muirwood. My father would not go through with his threat if she were missing. I can do this. My heart is burning inside me, telling me that this is the right thing to do."

Collier put his face in his hands, his expression bleak and tormented. "Talk to the Aldermaston first. We must be wise, Maia. I do not trust your father. He will seek your death. *I* cannot cross the Apse Veil with you, and it tortures me to be unable to protect you. You cannot go alone."

Maia reached out and gripped his shoulder. "Then let us seek the Aldermaston's wisdom. We have little time to decide."

Hatred is settled anger.

—Richard Syon, Aldermaston of Muirwood Abbey

CHAPTER
THIRTY-FIVE

Pent Tower

M aia had listened patiently to the counsel of those wiser than her, but she could not escape the pressing sense of urgency she had felt upon hearing the news of Lady Deorwynn's pending execution. Perhaps she was being too hasty in making this decision, but it felt right in her heart, and no opposing whispers from the Medium warned her against it. In the end, the Aldermaston said it would be her decision. She had the power to cross the Apse Veil and try to prevent the murder and save Jayn.

"I feel a sense of danger regardless of the decision," the Aldermaston said, his gaze penetrating hers. "Not a warning to proceed. Also, not a warning against it. Judging from my experience, the Medium is allowing you to make this decision yourself. Whatever the consequences."

"But I do not like her going alone," Collier pressed resolutely. He had already changed into his riding gear, the disguise he used with the identity of Feint Collier. He intended to ride hard for

Comoros, but a horse was not fast enough. He paced the chamber, awaiting the final decision so he could embark quickly, not wanting to spare a moment.

"I will go with her," Suzenne said, her tone serious. "She is my companion and my friend . . . as is Jayn." She looked at Maia. "My heart pities Jayn's situation. I have passed the maston test as well. If you can help me cross the Apse Veil, then I will join you."

Collier stared at her doubtfully, his brow wrinkling. "I was thinking more like a half-dozen Evnissyen."

"They all left the abbey to return to Pry-Ree," Joanna said. "Only Jon Tayt remains, and he is not a maston."

Collier frowned.

"Dodd will come with us," Suzenne reassured Collier. "He has been training with Jon Tayt."

"Not perfect, but better," Collier said, wrinkling his brow. "I would feel calmer if you had someone there who could protect you. But was not Dodd's Family killed recently?"

Maia looked at Suzenne in concern. "I know Dodd is eager to help us, but if he were recognized . . ."

Suzenne looked determined. "He will not let me go alone, and we need a protector. His Family is from the north. The people of Comoros would not recognize him, especially if he is not dressed like a noble. I would feel better if he came with us."

"Then we will do it. We will travel in disguise in case my father's servants are looking for us. The decision may be foolish, but I cannot stand by while my father abrogates his word so quickly. He swore an oath in front of the Privy Council. No act would be passed, no decisions made without my voice. If the situation is hopeless, we will return immediately."

Her husband shook his head. "I can tell you already that it is. But I see you are determined, Maia. I will ride hard and try to join you." Collier faced the others in the chamber. "Simon Fox is my spy at court. He is part of the merchants' guild and transports wine from Dahomey to court. His business is close to the palace." He turned back to Maia. "I am sure you can hire a guide to bring you there. It is on Flax Street. When you arrive, go there first and seek his counsel. He has connections with the court, especially with the chancellor, so he may be able to get you information or have a message delivered for you. That is where I will meet you."

Maia nodded. "Thank you. I will plan to meet you there." She stared hungrily at his face, feeling the sharp pain of separation already.

Collier swept her into his arms, giving her a fierce hug while clenching his teeth. Then he pulled away, caressed her cheek with his thumb, and gazed possessively into her eyes. "I must go now."

Maia touched his arm tenderly and then watched him stride out of the chamber, rushing over to his horse.

Maia's preparations were much simpler. She was not packing for an extended journey. She changed back into her wretched's gown and fetched her cloak to add to the disguise. Suzenne wore one of her plainer gowns, and Dodd put on his hunting tunic and bracers. He strapped an axe across his back and added a few throwing axes in his belt. He was only too eager to accompany them to Comoros in disguise.

***

Maia stood before the billowy Apse Veil, staring at the chamber she had previously entered to pass the maston test. A small pink scar was on her hand, marking the spot where the stone had burned her. It was a little odd being in the room with other people, but her companions had been here before too. They were all ready for whatever challenges lay ahead, their faces solemn.

"Are you certain you wish to come with me?" Maia asked them once more.

Suzenne looked a little nervous. "Of course. I have not been to Comoros very often. All I remember is that it is a big city and the streets are filthy."

"My father and brothers were executed unjustly," Dodd said grimly. "While I do not fancy Lady Deorwynn, I wish someone had possessed the courage to speak up for them. If the king will not submit to reason and justice, we may have to compel him."

Maia looked at him, her brow furrowing. "You do not have any thoughts of revenge, do you?"

He shook his head and took Suzenne's hand, squeezing it. "I have no other motive than to protect you both. I am nervous just standing here. Shall we go?"

Maia nodded and turned to face the Apse Veil, summoning her courage. She stared at the smooth fabric of the Apse Veil, then closed her eyes and focused her thoughts on Claredon Abbey. She had visited that abbey before and knew the look of it from the outside. Holding the thought in her mind, she stepped forward and entered the Apse Veil.

There was a dizzying sensation, a lurching feeling in her stomach as if she were going to stumble. She tried to catch herself, her legs weak and her thoughts disoriented, and found herself staring at the oath chamber of Claredon Abbey. This one was smaller, and the workmanship of the carved Leerings was quite distinct. The feeling in the room was different as well. The abbey felt . . . weak. That was the only way Maia could think to describe it. The Medium was much more subdued here.

Maia turned and waited a moment, then pushed her hand back through the gossamer shroud. She felt Suzenne's warm hand and grabbed it, pulling it to draw her friend through the Apse Veil. Suzenne spilled onto the floor, her face twisted with nausea, shuddering from the experience that had only mildly disturbed Maia.

"That was . . . singular," Suzenne whispered, holding her stomach and gasping. She tried to stand, wobbled, and sat back down. "Give me a moment."

Maia smiled and reached back through the Apse Veil again. Dodd's hand was callused from his months of splitting wood and roaming the Bearden Muir with Jon Tayt. He came through the Veil on faltering legs and promptly joined Suzenne on the ground. She gave them a moment to collect themselves and tried to subdue a smile as they helped each other stand.

"I have often wondered what plummeting off a waterfall feels like," Dodd said, shaking his head and smiling roguishly. "I think I have a comparison now. We just crossed the entire kingdom in a moment." He stared at Maia in awe. "In the past, the mastons did this regularly. Think on it, Maia. Think what it will mean."

Maia nodded. "Think what it will mean among the mastons throughout the realm," she said. "The ability to communicate and send messages so quickly. What a blessing for my grandmother. It will be a dramatic change. This is just the first instance." She gripped Suzenne's arm. "Are you ready to try walking?"

"I feel like a newborn foal," Suzenne said, smiling queasily. "But I am ready. To Flax Street?"

Maia led the way out of the maston chamber, and they quickly departed the abbey. A maston was approaching the pewter doors from the outside. He startled when he saw them.

"Who are you?" he asked. "I do not recall seeing you earlier. No one is supposed to be in the abbey at this hour."

He did not wear the gray cassock of the Aldermaston order, so Maia assumed he was someone who taught at the abbey. He had a large, hooked nose, reddish-brown hair, and a stern expression.

"We hail from another abbey," Maia said, nodding to him. "And only just arrived."

His brow furrowed in confusion, and while he walked past them, he kept glancing back.

"Keep walking," Dodd whispered. "We do not want to attract more notice."

Maia remembered to lift the cowl and cover her hair as they approached the gates. Most abbeys were built on sprawling grounds with woods and gardens and multiple buildings, but Claredon Abbey was situated near the palace and had a tall, spiked wall that kept it out of view for cityfolk. The palace, much higher than even the abbey's double turrets, could be seen looming over the eastern boundary. Maia felt the prickle of apprehension inside her turn into a festering sore. The last time she had entered the palace was at night, guarded by Captain Rawlt and the kishion, before her father sent her on the mission that had branded her a hetaera.

The sky was hazy with soot smoke, and the wind carried foul odors on its breezes. Suzenne mimicked her example by covering her head with a cowl, and Dodd walked in front, leading the way. They reached the gates, which were closed, and the porter rose and stared at them suspiciously.

"Who be ye?" the grizzled man said with a crusty accent. "Did I greet ye earlier?"

Maia stared through the bars of the gate at the busy commotion on the street. Carts splashed through the filth and people walked quickly but carefully to avoid heaping mounds of dung. Flies hurried this way and that. The city reeked, making Maia recollect the fastidiousness of Hautland's capital.

"Open the gate," Dodd said with a tone of command.

The old porter scratched his neck and rose, then trudged to the gate to fit a large iron key into the lock. He twisted it, stopped to scratch his lower back, and pulled on the gate, which squealed. The sound drew the attention of many passersby, but Maia hoped the hood would shield her from notice. Dodd gestured for them to follow and entered the rush.

As soon as Maia left the arch of the gateway, she felt the presence of the Medium gutter out. It was almost like plunging into a brackish pond. There were Myriad Ones everywhere, skulking and sniffing and panting at them as soon as they left the abbey's protection. These were not skulking beings waiting for them . . . they were part of the normal ebb and flow of the city, joining the squalor and reveling in the decay. Maia saw in the faces around her the hard looks of bitterness and disappointment. Of people living in cramped quarters, suffering from want of bread and meat, joy and happiness. Of men and women terrorized by their neighbors and accustomed to having things stolen by thieves. The very air was a sickening miasma, and Maia wondered immediately at the wisdom of her decision. The Myriad Ones who sniffled at them seemed to sense they were mastons and began mewling with savagery.

"What a horrid place," Suzenne whispered, her face white.

Dodd looked more hardened. "Even the Bearden Muir feels less miserable than this."

Maia followed Dodd, feeling completely defenseless. Angry shouts erupted all around, and people jostled them. Even though their clothes were plain, they were not filthy like the inhabitants of Comoros, which made Maia feel even more conspicuous.

Her shoulder began to throb and burn, and she felt something awakening inside her.

Maia gritted her teeth. Of course she felt the hetaera brand in this place. It was aroused by the attractive brew of grief, misery, and greed. She focused her thoughts, remembering their destination. Simon Fox. Flax Street. She saw Dodd stop a man, head bent low to ask him for directions.

She felt an urgent need to return to Muirwood. This city was utter blackness. Had it always been this way? Could she only feel its true character now that she was a maston, or had her father's corrupt ways ruined it? After so many years of banishment from the capital, she was unsure.

When the sheriff's men had forced her to leave Muirwood Abbey, she had been attacked immediately by the Myriad Ones. It felt different here, for she had the chaen to protect her.

The man Dodd had stopped gestured with a greasy finger down the street, pointing toward a tavern sign. Dodd nodded and thanked him.

A hand clamped around Maia's arm, startling her. She turned just as another man grabbed Suzenne.

The man forced her to turn and yanked the cowl back. He was unfamiliar to her, but he seemed to recognize her. "Ah, it is her," he said, his teeth crooked. His breath was awful. "Crabwell thought you might come through Claredon and not the city gates." He leered at her. "Welcome home to Comoros, Lady Maia."

"Unhand her," Dodd warned, gripping one of his throwing axes.

The man looked at him without concern. "You do not think the chancellor left us unprepared?" he mocked. "Gaze up at the roof, boy. See the crossbowmen? You pull your arm back to throw that little hatchet, and you'll be a porcupine."

Maia's insides twisted with terror. "You are the chancellor's men? I insist you bring us to him at once."

He chuckled darkly. "Insists, she does? How polite. I always heard *the king's daughter* was polite."

Maia saw the circle of men ghosting from the crowd to surround them. None of them wore uniforms marking them as the chancellor's men, but there were easily a dozen. Though his grip on her arm pained her, she did not let it show on her face. She gestured with her other hand for Dodd to lower his weapon.

The man smiled and nodded at her with a twisted smile. "Wise too. A good decision, lass. You probably do not recognize me, but I remember you. Name is Trefew. I was one of the ones who threw you out of court last time. When you went to Lady Shilton's manor." He smiled again, his expression full of angles and seams. He stared at her, his eyes smoldering with threats. She remembered him at last—he had been commanded to rip the gown from her if she did not willingly change into a servant's smock. "I have not forgotten you, lass. Now, the chancellor *would* like to see you. But his orders are to bring you immediately to Pent Tower. You are under arrest for treason as well."

"Very well," Maia said, trying to keep her voice from shaking. "Take me, and let these two go."

Trefew pursed his lips and clucked. "Oh-ho now! That lad is a Price. Looks just like his *brothers*. And the flax-haired girl is too pretty to wander the streets alone. No, missy. We will all be going to the tower together."

Keeping his hand locked on her arm, Trefew drew Maia toward the rear of the palace and Pent Tower. For years she had been terrified that her father would one day send her there. Her heart filled with dread as she marched toward that fate.

CHAPTER THIRTY-SIX

Deorwynn's Fall

Lady Deorwynn sat in the dank cell, shivering uncontrollably. Every noise startled her, every groan from her fellow prisoners in the ward made her twitch. She was terrified beyond her wits, and she dreaded the brightening of the dawn sky. It would be the dawn of her execution. Would it be possible, somehow, to suspend the brightening light by staring at it? She blinked feverishly, her stomach twisting with panic. At least her death would be quick. A whimper escaped her lips, and she could not refrain from shuddering.

Her daughters were also in Pent Tower, locked in a cell together. She had heard Jolecia shriek for hours until she fell into a fitful sleep. Murer was calmer. Murer was more like her; she hid a cunning mind behind the flirting smiles. Sometimes Lady Deorwynn regretted how much her daughter had learned from her, especially when she used those very stratagems against her. Lady Deorwynn clamped her hand over her mouth, stifling a tremulous sob. She would not see her children again. Her young boys had been sent to one of her husband's manors under guard. What would happen to them?

The groans outside turned into shouts for mercy and Lady Deorwynn lifted her head. Something had changed in the mood of the corridor. Soon she heard guards approaching, and her pulse quickened with the anticipation of what was to come.

The flirting and affairs had felt so trivial at the time. After all, everyone in court was engaged in it. Her own husband's acts were much more depraved, fawning over girls as young as his own daughter. She had grown to hate him over the years. A sizzle of heat and jealousy spiked through her heart when she thought of Jayn Sexton's demure eyes. Her refusals to give in to his passions only inflamed him more. She trembled with fury and hatred and sickening fear.

The key rattled in the lock and the door opened. She rose quickly, panting, to face her executioners. To her surprise, her uncle entered—Aldermaston Kranmir.

"Am I to be freed?" she gasped with a spasm of desperate hope. She could see from his expression that it was a foolish question.

He looked calm and dreadful, his eyes narrowing coldly. "Did you really believe he would forgive you?" he whispered darkly. He motioned for the guards to leave them alone, and the door was shut and locked.

"Please, Uncle!" she begged. "Why not banishment? I would leave Comoros—"

"You are wasting your precious last breaths with such talk," he said. He shook his head as if she were a simpleton, and it galled her. "Your husband *wants* you dead. He wanted it before you went to Muirwood. You never learned to curb your anger, child. To better control your malice. Even a little brook can wear down stones. I pity you, truly. But you will die this morning."

Lady Deorwynn felt herself nearly faint. She sat on the stone-rimmed pallet covered in moldy straw. She had suffered all night from cold, wishing in vain for a brazier to offer some warmth. The memory of Maia suffering with cold in the attic was like a sword wound in her breast. She grunted with the pain of it.

"Remorse, child?" Kranmir said mockingly. "It ill suits one of your temperament. You made yourself Queen of Comoros. That was quite a triumph. You climbed the steep pole of power, enjoyed a few tottering moments at the apex, and look how fast you fell. Was it worth it?"

She turned the dagger of her gaze to him. "Look what *you* have lost, Uncle," she seethed. "What of your ambition? You lost Muirwood. You will soon lose your own abbey."

Kranmir looked at her placidly, unconcerned. "How much you still have to learn."

"Me? Who helped *you* rise to power, Uncle? Who softened the king's heart toward your counsel and secret advice? I did!"

"And at the same time, you alienated him against his own flesh and blood, his only child. Deorwynn, can you not see the extent of the damage you did yourself by persecuting the princess?"

"She is *not* a princess!" Lady Deorwynn shrieked.

He took a step toward her. "She is. And you were a fool not to see it. Not to understand your enemy better. You made her powerful by treating her with shame and contempt. The people are thundering for her to be named the king's heir again. They are *rioting*. If they knew she was in the city right now, all Sheol would be loosed on us."

Lady Deorwynn gaped at him in astonishment. "What do you mean? How can she be here?"

He shook his head sadly. "The Apse Veil, of course! That foolish girl, after everything you have done to her, came here with the notion of saving you." He snorted with disdain. "Yes, the Apse Veils are open again. I have had word that certain Leerings in Augustin began to shine for the first time last night. I believe what was said. The refugees from Assinica are coming."

"You do not seem very concerned about losing your abbey," she said again.

He chuckled softly. "Still, you do not see the possibilities. I have not lost anything yet. The king needs me. He needs legitimacy. He needs to have power over the maston order, and he uses me to accomplish that. Trust me, Deorwynn, if the people will riot to acclaim Lady Maia, then she is of no further use to the Crown. She will join you in an ossuary in the cemetery. Shortly."

Lady Deorwynn stifled her breath. "He will not kill his own daughter."

Kranmir smirked. "Oh, I think he will. You have never truly understood him, Deorwynn. If you had, you never would have shamed him by taking lovers. What you have neglected to realize is that most men, and *this one* especially, have an infinite capacity to feel sorry for themselves. It is so easy to placate him, it is like feeding scraps to a dog. Touch for a moment on his inner pain, his frustration at being disobeyed, dishonored, or even disheveled, and he laps it up like milk. He was utterly *humiliated* at Muirwood. He also feels himself tottering on the pole of power. He will do anything to remain king. His two greatest risks are you and his daughter. Both will be dealt with. Crabwell is seeing to it right now."

Lady Deorwynn stood and rushed to him. "What about my children?"

A wry smile answered her. Nothing more.

"Tell me!" she begged.

"There are kishion for that sort of thing," he said coldly.

"No!" she groaned, seizing his arms. She trembled violently.

His brow wrinkled. "The king is preparing for the invasion. The armada will come here next. We have gathered a sizable sum in the treasury. Dahomey has been plundered, so we need not fear Gideon. Yes, he will be wroth when he learns his bride was executed. But surely he knows what she *really* is. Even though a binding sigil prevents me from saying it, we all know the truth. The king will have her gown stripped off before her execution to show the kystrel's taint and the brand on her shoulder. In front of the people! Oh yes, their love of Princess Maia will turn to horror when they realize the truth. Did you hear Cruix Abbey was burned? Hmmm? The king would have given her a chance to join forces with him, to become the tool he had intended to make her. A tool to save Comoros from the invaders. A tool to challenge the authority and power of Naess and its dark pools. But we all know she will not submit. The king must destroy Maia instead of letting her destroy him. Any king would do that to preserve his throne."

Lady Deorwynn felt her hopes crumbling to dust. "She is innocent. She is not truly evil."

He snorted. "That did not stop *you* from speaking against Forshee and his sons. Their room was just above yours. Good-bye, child. I will miss you. Until we meet again . . . in Idumea." The smile he gave her was dark and twisted.

She felt like she would start weeping again, but she forced herself to control her emotions. She stared at him coldly.

"I will face my death as strong as any man," she said angrily. "Let the headman's axe fall."

Kranmir shook his head. "A swordsman will do the honors," he replied, tapping at the door. "Either way, it ends this morning. I have already signed the annulment of your marriage, which renders all of your offspring bastards. That is the first step. Maia will follow you to the gallows."

The key turned and the door opened.

"What of the refugees from Assinica?" she demanded. "They are coming, surely."

He looked at her without concern. "Have you ever heard the saying of being tossed from the pan into the coals? Artisans, musicians, sculptors. They will make excellent slaves. Ah, Captain Trefew. Escort Lady Deorwynn to the plinth."

"As you say, High Seer," he replied, grinning at Lady Deorwynn as he spoke. Her eyes widened at the new title. Trefew was a vulgar man. He had been too drunk to board the *Blessing of Burntisland* the night it had set sail for Dahomey. Deorwynn had since suspected that he was too wise, not too drunk. He shackled her wrists proficiently and then took the lead chain and brought her out of the cell.

As she walked, her conscience began to spasm with dread. There was no hope left. No reprieve would come to her, just as there had been no reprieve for the others she had caused to be sent to the block. Her heart thundered in her chest, and she wondered if she would be able to face the headsman with equanimity after all. She wanted to faint, but she steeled herself, determined to see it through.

They passed several cells that were secured with bars rather than doors.

"Mother!" Jolecia screamed, rushing to the bars. "Mother, no!"

Lady Deorwynn glanced at the weeping girl and saw Murer huddled in the shadows at the back of the cell, her face ashen. She nodded to the girls, but could not make her tongue work to say anything.

As they breached the outer doors to the greenyard, she felt the cold morning air penetrate her thin gown. It fluttered her hair, and she shivered.

"A favor, Captain Trefew," she said.

He snorted. "As if you could do *me* any favors now. Though there are some favors I would have liked."

"Please, Captain. You have seen Lady Maia. Tell her I am sorry. Tell her I regret the way I treated her. It is my fault she was poisoned. It is my fault her mother is dead. Tell her this. My dying words. It was *my* doing."

"Look at the window yonder," he said, grinning cruelly, and pointed. "If you shout it, she may even hear you."

Lady Deorwynn stared at the window. It was near enough that she could make out Maia's dark hair. Her heart twisted with regret and pain. She longed to apologize to Maia directly, for her hatred and for the harm she had done. Even Lady Deorwynn's mother, her *ruthless* mother had eventually been softened by Maia. Yet not Deorwynn herself. For some reason, the girl's meekness had only infuriated her more. Eventually, it had driven her to seek Maia's death.

Lady Deorwynn glanced at the small crowd assembled below. She could hear the murmuring of voices, see the sneers of contempt as Trefew hauled her toward the scaffold and the stone plinth that awaited her. There was a hooded headsman standing there, his hands resting on the pommel of a great sword that looked cold in the dawn light. She prayed it was sharp. There was Crabwell, smug as a lap spaniel. Not her husband, of course. Though he had ordered enough murders, he was a coward when it came to seeing blood shed. Many of the earls from the Privy Council were assembled, though. None of them gave her any looks of sympathy. They were reveling in her downfall.

Let them.

She mounted the steps to the scaffold, trying to control her riotous feelings, desperately working to keep her legs from buckling.

The wind caused some of her hair to stray before her eyes, and she lifted the heavy manacles to smooth it back. She stared at the executioner, a man paid for the horrid task of ending a criminal's life.

There was something about his bearing, his size, which was . . .

By the Blood, no!

She saw the scars just under the hood. The icy blue eyes. Part of one ear was missing. He was smiling. He seemed to be enjoying himself as if he were out for a stroll on a riverbank. It was the kishion *she* had hired. He had not received full payment for his services yet. If he killed her, he never would. What was happening? Why would he be there?

The kishion grabbed her arm and forced her to kneel in front of the plinth.

"Farewell, madame," he whispered hoarsely. "I serve another now."

She closed her eyes. The last thing she heard was the sound of his boots as he stepped away from her.

Falling.

EPILOGUE

S abine Demont had visited every kingdom and people, including the benighted realm of Naess. Her journeys on the *Holk* had led to the waterfalls of Avinion, the lush vineyards of Mon, and the snow-capped mountains of Hautland . . . to countless ports and shores where she had eaten dishes of melted cheese, meat of every kind, fruits and vegetables that always surprised and delighted her. She loved people. She loved learning about their habits and traits, not just individually, but collectively. She had seen some customs and traditions throughout the kingdoms that were pleasing and some that were offensive, and had quietly longed for the quiet glades and mountains of Pry-Ree, her homeland, her people.

Standing on a scrub-choked hill overlooking a vast lake, she saw the dazzling realm of Assinica and wept for its simple, elegant beauty and the knowledge that the Victus were about to demolish it.

From the crest of the hill, she could see the armada at anchor.

AUTHOR'S NOTE

There is something magical about a second book, at least for me. I am normally on a fast journey to bring my readers through the roller coaster of events, but I like to slow things down (just a little) in book two and delve more into the relationships between characters. That is why *Blight of Muirwood* is my favorite of the original trilogy and *Ciphers* will likely be my favorite in this one.

When my oldest child finished reading the original Muirwood series (after staying up nearly all night to finish it—as a parent I wasn't happy with her sleepiness the next day, but as an author I was more than flattered!), she told me that Colvin and Lia had never had their maypole dance. She looked me in the eye and said that I *had* to make up for it in the next series. I looked at her, sighed, and then as usually happens, my imagination started to spark with some ideas. One of the guiding principles of the Medium is that it connects things, like a bridge between elements, a conduit between the living and the dead. But it has power over time as well. Astute readers from *Blight* remember that Garen Demont's army evaded destruction from the Earl of Caspur by entering an abbey on one day and showing up in time to save

Muirwood on another day. The jump was only a few days. But bridging centuries isn't any more difficult. I have to admit that I enjoyed bringing Lia and Colvin back for a cameo as well. That was fun to write.

I will also admit that I loved bringing much of the action back to Lia's childhood abbey. Muirwood itself is a character in the story with its own personality. There are certain places I know that feel like the abbey grounds to me.

I titled this book *Ciphers* because the word has many definitions. In modern times, it means a code to scramble letters to help conceal a message's true meaning. Another definition is "one that has no weight, worth, or influence." In Maia's day, women were like ciphers. They were not permitted to read for fear of them becoming hetaera. To challenge this notion, and to help further the Covenant of Muirwood, the Aldermastons of Muirwood trained girls in secret. Even their title misconstrued their true purpose and identity. As a medieval history major in college, I discovered evidence of female spies at work in the political kingdoms. More on this in my *next* trilogy!

As Maia has proved, even someone completely shunned and forsaken is never powerless. It begins with a thought.

ACKNOWLEDGMENTS

Many thanks to all the staff at 47North for bringing this book out on the heels of *Banished*. I love how Amazon Publishing partners with its authors to bend the rules and try new things. I would especially like to thank my wife, Gina, for her insights into Maia and Collier and their tangled relationship, which really added to the story. I'd also like to express appreciation to my small cohort of readers for their continued feedback, input, and encouragement: Gina, Emily, Karen, Robin, Shannon, and Rachelle. Once again, I would like to thank the fabulous Angela Polidoro, whose input and enthusiasm improved the book and made it better. Her ability to catch little mistakes spread hundreds of pages apart and fix them is truly astonishing. My apologies for killing Argus. I liked him too.

ABOUT THE AUTHOR

Photograph © Kim Bills

Jeff Wheeler took an early retirement from his career at Intel in 2014 to become a full-time author. He is, most importantly, a husband and father, and a devout member of his church. He is occasionally spotted roaming hills with oak trees and granite boulders in California or in any number of the state's majestic redwood groves.

Visit the author's website: www.jeff-wheeler.com.